THE MAGIC COTTAGE

THE MAGIC COTTAGE

JAMES HERBERT

NEW ENGLISH LIBRARY

First published in Great Britain in 1986 by
Hodder & Stoughton Ltd.

New English Library paperback edition 1987

NEL Books are published by
New English Library,
Mill Road, Dunton Green,
Sevenoaks, Kent.
Editorial office: 47 Bedford Square, London WC1B 3DP
Typeset by Rowlands Phototypesetting Ltd,
Bury St Edmunds, Suffolk

Printed in Great Britain by
Richard Clay (The Chaucer Press) Ltd,
Bungay, Suffolk

British Library C.I.P.

Herbert, James
 The magic cottage.
 I. Title
 823'.914[F]   PR6058.E62

ISBN 0-450-40937-6

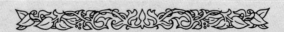

CONTENTS

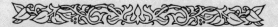

DESIRABLE PROPERTY. Cottage, secluded position adjoining woodland, needs renovation, but excel. potential. 2 beds, recep, kitchen, bathroom, $\frac{1}{2}$ acre garden, offers invited. Cantrip 612.

MAGIC

Do you believe in Magic?

I mean, real Magic, capital M. Not rabbits out of hats, disappearing sequined ladies, or silver spheres that dance in the air. The real stuff, not tricks, illusions. I mean spells, enchantments – witchery, even. Damaged limbs that heal overnight, animals that trust in humans, paintings that come alive. Shadowy figures that aren't really there. More, there's more, but it's too soon to tell.

Maybe – probably – you don't believe. Maybe you half believe. Or maybe you want to believe.

A kind of magic I once knew, long before we took the cottage, came from powder or pills shared with friends; but that was just delusion. And a waste. I learned of real Magic when we came to 'Gramarye'.

That was Good Magic.

Yet everything has its opposite, and I found that there, too.

If you like, and if you're willing to suspend belief for a while – as I eventually had to – I'll tell you about it.

LOOKING

Midge saw the ad first. She'd been scouring the classified columns of the *Sunday Times* for weeks, circling the more interesting properties with a red felt-tip, her enthusiasm for leaving the dirty city a little greater than mine. Every week she'd been presenting me with a whole number of red circles to peruse, and we'd go through each one, discussing their merits and drawbacks, following up those that survived. So far none had come up to expectation.

On that particular Sunday there was only one circle to look at. A cottage. Adjoining woodland, secluded position. Needed some restoration.

So what's so special? I thought.

'Hey, Midge!' She was in the kitchen of the apartment we rented near London's Baron's Court – a large place with high ceilings and high rent, and a complex of rooms that allowed for Midge's painting and my music, with never the twain unnecessarily meeting. But we wanted something of our own. Something 'rustic' was in our minds although, like I say, Midge was keener than me.

She appeared in the doorway, dark haired and pixie eyed, five-foot-one of pure small-featured lusciousness (to me anyway, and I'm not unchoosy).

I tapped the newspaper. 'Only one?'

Midge tossed the dishcloth back towards the sink – we'd just finished a late (very late) breakfast – and padded barefoot towards the sofa I loafed upon. She knelt, chastely drawing her summer-thin dressing gown over her knees. When she spoke she looked directly at the ad, and not at me.

'It's the only interesting one.'

That puzzled me. 'It doesn't actually say much. A dilapidated cottage is all it tells me. And where the hell is Cantrip?'

'I looked it up. It's near Bunbury.'

I couldn't help grinning. 'Oh yeah?'

'That's in Hampshire.'

'At least that's in its favour – I was getting worried about some of the remote places you were taking an interest in.'

'A remote part of Hampshire.'

A groan from me. 'Is that possible?'

'Any idea of how big the New Forest is?'

'Bigger than Hyde Park?'

'Somewhat. A huge-what.'

'And Cantrip is in the heart of the forest.'

'Not quite, but you're getting warm.' Then she smiled, her eyes even more pixieish. 'Don't worry, you'll be able to get back to London for sessions easily enough. You can pick up motorways practically all the way.'

I ought to tell you now I'm a session musician, one of that quiet breed that earns a generous living behind the scenes of the upfront pop-world, working in recording studios and occasionally backing touring artistes – usually those whose bands aren't allowed over from the States. My instrument's the guitar, my music – well, you name it: rock, pop, soul (I've even dubbed punk), a little jazz and, when I can, some light classical. Maybe more about all that later.

'You still haven't explained why this one,' I persisted.

She was quiet for a moment, just studying the page as though looking for the answer herself. Then she turned to me. 'It feels right,' she said.

Yep. *It feels right.* That's all.

I sighed, knowing Midge always had great intuition, but not quite prepared to accept it this time. 'Midge . . .' I warned.

'Mike . . .' she said, just as gravely.

'Come on, be serious. I'm not trekking down to Hampshire just on a whim.'

The imp took my hand and kissed the knuckles. 'I like forests,' she had the nerve to say. 'And the price is right.'

'There's no price mentioned.'

'Offers invited. It'll be right, you'll see.'

Mildly exasperated, but not annoyed, I replied, 'The place is probably really run-down.'

'All the cheaper.'

'Think of the work!'

'We'll send the builders in first.'

'You're a bit ahead of yourself, kiddo.'

The merest shadow of uncertainty flickered across her face – or perhaps it was a sudden anxiety; I can read all sorts of things into that expression, knowing what I do now.

'I can't explain, Mike. Let me ring tomorrow, find out more. It could be totally wrong.'

Her last sentence was hardly convincing, but I let things go at that. It was peculiar, but I was beginning to have a good feeling about the cottage myself.

GRAMARYE

Y ou've seen the film, you've read the book. You know
the one – there've been so many: The young couple
find the home of their dreams, the wife's ecstatic, the
husband's happy but more controlled; they move in, the kids
(usually one of each) tear around the empty rooms. But *we*
know there's something sinister about the place, because
we've read the blurb and paid our money. Slowly, THINGS
start to happen. There's something nasty in the locked room
at the top of the old creaky stairs; or something lurks in the
cellar below, which is possibly itself the Gateway to Hell. You
know the story. At first, Dad's oblivious to his family going
nuts around him – *he* doesn't believe in the supernatural, or
things that go *splodge* in the night; to him, there really is No
Such Thing as a Vampire. Until something happens to him,
that is. Then all hell breaks loose. You know it like you wrote
the story yourself.

Well, this is similar. But different. You'll see.

We drove down to Cantrip the following Tuesday (our
work-style allows such freedom), Midge having rung
the number in the ad the day before and finding it belonged
to an estate agent. He'd told her a little more about the
cottage, not much, but enough to increase her enthusiasm.
At present it was unoccupied, the owner having died some

months earlier; it had taken this long to have the deceased's affairs sorted out before the property could be put on the market. Midge was keen-edged throughout the journey and kept telling me she didn't expect too much, the place would no doubt be a huge disappointment, but it did *sound* interesting from the agent's description, it could just turn out to be ideal . . .

The journey took a couple of hours or so, maybe closer to three by the time we'd taken a few wrong turns looking for the village of Cantrip. Still, the scenery, once we reached the New Forest with its wood- and heathland, was worth the long drive in itself. We even came upon herds of ponies and, although we didn't actually catch sight of any deer, there were plenty of signs telling us they were about (and for a city-bred boy, that's almost as good as the real thing). The weather was May-fine, the air crisp and bright. We'd kept the windows of the hatchback down once we were off the last motorway, and despite her barely-hidden apprehension, Midge had joined me in choruses of Blue Suedes and Mean Womans and the like (I was going through my old rock period that morning, my musical mood varying from day to day). The fresh air was making me hoarse before we saw the village ahead.

I have to admit, Cantrip was a bit of a letdown. We'd expected thatched roofs, old inns, and a village green with its own rusty-handled pump – National Trust stuff: what we got was a fairly uninteresting high street whose houses and shops must have been built around the late twenties or early thirties. No, it wasn't quite that bad on closer inspection – there really were some ancient properties of crumbling character among the less-old structures – but the overall impression was pretty drab. I could feel Midge's heart sink.

We crossed the bump of a small bridge and drove into the high street, keeping our eyes peeled for the estate agent's and our disappointment to ourselves. We found his office jammed between a post office-cum-grocer's and a butcher's shop, the frontage so small we'd gone past before Midge tapped me smartly on the shoulder and indicated.

'There!' she cried, as though she'd discovered the Missing Link.

A cyclist wobbled by, scowling because of the car's sudden halt. I shrugged a friendly apology and pointed at Midge so that she could take the blame, but didn't catch his grumbling response. Probably just as well: he looked a mean local.

After reversing into a space, Midge and I left the car and strolled to the agent's office, Midge suddenly nervous as a kitten. Now this was something new to me. We'd been together a long time and I was used to her occasional skittishness, especially when she'd accepted a new commission (I should have mentioned that Midge is an illustrator, and a damned good one, specialising in children's books: you'll see her work on the shelves alongside Shirley Hughes and Maurice Sendak, although you'd know her as Margaret Gudgeon), but nervous of a brick-broker? I quickly realised it wasn't the agent but the prospect of viewing the cottage that had unsettled her. Hell, the mood had been building from Sunday through to now, and I couldn't understand why.

I pulled her to a stop before pushing open the door and Midge looked at me distractedly, her attention more involved in what lay beyond the glass.

'Take it easy,' I told her softly. 'There'll be plenty more for sale and we may hate this one anyway.'

She took a quick breath, squeezed my hand and went in ahead of me.

Inside, the office was less cramped than it should have been, because although narrow, the single room stretched back a fair way. Pictures and details of properties covered the length of one wall like badly pasted wallpaper. An ample-sized secretary thrashed an Adler just inside the doorway, while further down a man in a neat grey suit and thick black-rimmed glasses, seated behind an untidy desk, looked up.

I peered over Midge's shoulder and said, 'Mr Bickleshift?' (Yeah, I promise you.)

He appeared not to mind his own name, because he smiled broadly. No, not really; I think he just liked the look of Midge.

'Yes indeed,' he said, rising and waving us forward.

I nodded at the secretary, who had stopped clattering to give us the once-over as we passed, and I might just as well have greeted a sullen whale for all the expression she showed.

'You'll be Mr and Mrs Gudgeon,' Bickleshift surmised, reaching across his desk to shake Midge's hand then mine. He designated two chairs angled towards him on our side.

'No. She's Gudgeon, I'm Stringer.' We both sat and the agent glanced from face to face before following suit.

'Then it's only you, Miss Gudgeon, who is looking for a property.' I'm not sure, but he may have said Ms just to show he was part of the new order.

'We both are,' Midge replied. 'And it's the cottage advertised in the last *Sunday Times* that we want to see. I told you on the phone.'

'Of course. Flora Chaldean's roundhouse.'

We both raised our eyebrows and Bickleshift smiled.

'You'll understand when you see the place,' he said.

'And Flora Chaldean – she's the woman who owned the cottage?' asked Midge.

'That's correct. Rather an, er, eccentric old lady. Well-known hereabouts, something of a local character, you might even say. Well-known, but not much known about her. Kept very much to herself.'

'You told me she'd died . . .' said Midge.

'Yes, some months ago. Her only surviving relative was a niece living in Canada. They'd never met apparently, but Mrs Chaldean's solicitor eventually traced the niece and advised her of her inheritance as next-of-kin. I imagine there was a small amount of money left also, but I doubt it amounted to much: I understand Flora Chaldean led a very frugal existence. The niece instructed the solicitor to sell up and send on the proceeds.'

'She didn't want to see the place herself?' I asked.

Bickleshift shook his head. 'No interest at all. However, Flora Chaldean was sufficiently concerned about the fate of her cottage to have a certain proviso inserted into the Will regarding its sale.'

Midge looked anxious all over again. 'What kind of proviso?'

The agent's smile widened to a grin. 'I don't think it's anything for you to worry about.' His hands came up and flattened themselves on the desktop so that for a moment, with elbows bent sideways, he resembled a bespectacled grasshopper. 'Now,' he said breezily, 'I suggest you take a look at the cottage, then we'll discuss the details if you find you're interested.'

'We are already,' Midge responded and my foot flicked at hers: no need to appear *too* keen before bargaining started.

Bickleshift reached into a drawer and brought out a set of keys, three in all, old and long, attached to a ring and labelled. 'The cottage is empty, of course, so feel free to have a good look round. I won't accompany you unless you specifically want me to; I always feel clients prefer to inspect on their own and discuss things freely between themselves.'

It was Midge who reached for the keys and she grasped them so reverently you might have thought they were the Keys to the Kingdom.

'Fine,' I said to Bickleshift. 'So how do we get there?'

He drew us a quick map which was simple enough provided (as he stressed) we didn't miss the small turn-offs. Then we were on our way.

'Okay,' I said as I steered through a winding lane, a leafy canopy overhead subduing the light and cooling the air. 'I still don't get it.'

Midge looked at me curiously, but she knew – oh, she knew – what I meant.

'You act like you're already in love with the place.' I tapped the wheel with the back of my hand. 'C'mon, open up, Midge. What's got into you?'

Her fingertips sank into the hair at the back of my neck and she lightly stroked; yet her voice was a little distant. 'Just a feeling, Mike. No, more of a conviction that it's going to be all right for . . . for us.'

The slight pause didn't go unnoticed by me. 'Then how come I don't feel the same?'

She was back with me, eyes shining with humour. 'Oh, probably because anywhere that isn't within walking distance of a pub, a Big Mac, and a three-in-one cinema isn't civilised to you.'

I was hurt. 'You know I want to get out as much as you.'

She gave a short laugh. 'Perhaps not *quite* as much, but all right, I admit your values have changed recently. I'm not sure our complaining neighbours haven't had something to do with that, though.'

'Yeah, I'll agree I need somewhere to play when I want and as loud as I want, but that's not all of it. And anyway, I didn't appreciate *their* noise too well, either.'

'Nor me. Or the traffic, or the dust –'

'– or the hustle –'

'– and the bustle –'

'– Let's get away from it alllll –' we harmonised, putting our heads together.

When she'd stopped giggling, Midge said, 'It's true, though. Sometimes I think the whole city's going to collapse in on itself.'

'You could be right.' I was busy looking for a turning on the left, one of those that Bickleshift had warned us not to miss.

'I know it's weird,' she went on, lifting from her lap the particulars leaflet the agent had given us, 'but when I looked through the paper on Sunday, this place seemed to fly out at me. I couldn't concentrate on any others, my eyes kept coming back to this one. It was as if everything else was out of focus.'

I moaned, long and low. 'Midge, Midge, I hope you're not going to be disillusioned.'

She didn't reply, just looked straight ahead. And suddenly I wanted to turn the car around and go back the way we'd come, and keep on going, right back to the smoky old city. A shiver of premonition? Yeah, I think it was. But such things were uncommon to me then, and I thought the feeling was only cold feet at the prospect of moving out. Maybe she'd been right: I wasn't ready yet for the little house on the prairie.

Of course I kept going. What kind of fool would I have looked if I'd U-turned? What good reason could I have given?

I loved Midge enough to make changes in myself and I knew that what was good for her would eventually become good for me. She had values and motives that I admired and loved her for, and I'm not too proud to say that I felt a need to acquire some of those ideals for myself. I'd had too many good times and not enough *right* times. She made *right* times.

The turn I was keeping an eye out for soon materialised and the agent had been correct – it was easy to miss. I slowed the car, almost coming to a stop to take the sharp corner. Our Volkswagen Passat used up most of the road as it gathered speed, and we were still in a wooded area, trees brimming the lane right up to the edge. The roadway dipped and curved too, and Midge loved every yard we covered, her eyes alight, while I concentrated on taking the bends, occasionally stealing glances at her happy face.

'Shouldn't we have reached the cottage by now?' I was beginning to wonder if I hadn't taken the wrong turn.

Midge consulted the sketched map. 'Shouldn't be far –'

I'd slammed on the brakes, an arm automatically stretching across Midge's chest to hold her back even though she was belted in. She rocked with the car and turned to me in surprise.

'Will you look at the nerve of that guy.' I indicated the road ahead with a nod.

The squirrel was sitting upright slap-bang in the middle of the road, nibbling an acorn or something between its paws, pale tan-to-white tail fluffed up behind. The little devil didn't appear to be oblivious of us – it kept darting its tufty head in our direction – but we didn't seem to bother it any.

'Oh, Mike, he's gorgeous!' Midge was leaning forward as far as her seat belt would allow, her nose only inches away from the windscreen. 'He's a red. I heard they were coming back to this part of the country. Oh, he's lovely!'

'Sure, but he's – it's – taking up the road.' I was about to thump the horn, but Midge must have read my mind.

'Let him stay there for a moment,' she urged, 'he'll move on soon enough.'

I sighed, although I quite enjoyed the sight of the furry little brute munching its lunch.

Midge clicked free of her seat belt and peered out of the side window, smiling all the while. That was just too much for our friend: he dropped the acorn and scampered off.

I couldn't help but laugh. 'Terrific. It didn't turn a hair at this great, noisy, metal monster, but your grinning face sent it into shock.'

Then I had to eat my words. The squirrel streaked back, retrieved its lunch, looked our way for a second, and hopped up to the Passat on Midge's side.

'Hello,' Midge said nicely.

I couldn't see, but it might have smiled back. I leaned over and just caught sight of the stirring of undergrowth as the squirrel departed once more. I expected Midge to give me one of her smug smirks, but there was only immense and innocent pleasure on her happy face. I pecked her cheek, amused, and shifted the automatic gear-stick into D. 'Onwards,' I said.

Midge settled back and scanned our surroundings as we sped by.

We soon came clear of the trees, rough grass verges on either side of the lane opening up into stretches of heavy green bracken and yellow gorse, pushing back the thick woodland as if to say enough is enough. The sun was high now, at its zenith, and the sky around it was bleached a pale blue. We'd chosen a perfect day for a trip into the country and my enthusiasm was picking up once more, despite the disappointment of Cantrip itself.

Midge clutched at my arm. 'I think I see it,' she said with restrained excitement.

I squinted but didn't catch anything.

'It's gone,' said Midge. 'I thought I saw a splash of white ahead, but now the trees are in the way.'

The car was rounding a long sweeping bend and the woodland was coming back at the road with a vengeance. In places, leafy low-hanging branches brushed against the windows.

'This forest could do with a trim,' I grumbled and then we saw the cottage, set back from the road, a low, weathered fence, with many of its uprights reclining at angles or fallen out completely, bordering the front garden. The small gate was closed and a sign, peeling and weary-looking, was battened across the struts. In beautiful but faded script, the sign said:

Gramarye

THE COTTAGE

So there it was before us. And on initial observation the cottage *was* enchanting.

I'd pulled the car over onto the grass in front of the crumbling fence and now we both sat staring at Gramarye, Flora Chaldean's roundhouse, Midge, it seemed, as if in awe, and me – well, let's say pleasantly surprised. I'm not sure what I had expected, but this wasn't quite it.

The building really was round, although the main section facing us was conventionally straight, only one end curving away (we were to understand the structure a little later), and it was on three levels if the attic was included, so maybe 'cottage' was the wrong description. Yet it did look like a cottage, because it was set into a grassy bank which somehow reduced its size. The bank swept around from the sides, moss-covered stone steps eating into the left-hand slope, levelling down to the front garden. There were trees on the rise, some with branches scraping against the white brickwork, and beyond was further woodland (wouldn't you know?). The windows at the front were small and multi-paned, adding even more charm to the general setting, and the roof was of discoloured red tiles.

Okay, that was our first glimpse, and the overall impression was more than pleasing.

'Mike, it's wonderful,' Midge said in a kind of hushed breath, her gaze roaming over the wild colours rampaging through the garden area, flowers that had got used to having their own way.

'Pretty,' I had to admit. 'Let's take a closer look before –' Midge was already out of the car.

She ran round to my side and stood facing the cottage, the brightness in her eyes increased. No disappointment, no disillusionment, there. She bit nervously into her lower lip, but all the while her small smile remained. I joined her and slipped an arm around her slim waist, studying her expression at first, and smiling myself. Then I turned to take in Gramarye more fully.

A tiny shock of recognition touched me, but the sensation was fleeting, too nebulous to be understood. Had I been there before? No, never in a thousand years. I couldn't remember having even visited this part of the country at any time. Yet there was something familiar about . . . I shrugged off the feeling, putting it down to some form of déjà vu, perhaps a peculiar but mild backlash of anticipation.

There was no need to ask Midge her impression so far: it was all there shining in her eyes. She left me and slowly walked towards the gate; I had to call out to remind her of my existence. She turned and my mind freeze-framed.

The shot's with me now, always will be, clear and sharp, and almost mystical: Midge, small and slender, dark hair falling without curls close around her neck, her lips slightly parted, and in those sweet blue-grey eyes that tilted a little at the corners, a gleam of wonder and joy, an expression that disturbed me yet made me happy for her at the same time; and she wore jeans, a loose short-sleeved blouse tucked into them, sandals on her small feet; and behind her loomed – no, not loomed, because the whole scene, with Midge in the foreground, blended so well, was so complete – *stood* Gramarye, its white walls now visibly crumbled and stained, windows lifeless yet somehow observing, the grounds sun-dazzled with colours, while beyond and around was the all-encompassing forest. You might say it was a storybook scene, and certainly one to be impressed on the mind.

Then she'd turned back, breaking the spell, and was leaning over the gate's catch. The entrance squealed open and Midge stepped inside as I moved to join her. I reached to take her arm but she was gone again, tripping down the overgrown path like an eager child, making for the cottage door.

I followed at a more leisurely pace, noticing that on closer inspection the late-May flowers were not quite as bright as they had appeared from the distance. They had, in fact, that end-of-summer look, when most flora is past its prime and wearying into decline, their petals curled and dry. Not to put too fine a point on it, they looked pretty sick. Weeds flourished everywhere, healthy enough specimens these. The path was made of flat broken stones, and long grass pushed through the cracks, almost smothering the hard surfaces in parts.

I found Midge peering through a grimy curtainless window, one hand forming a shadowed tunnel between forehead and glass. Grubby though the panes may have been, they were of good old-fashioned thickness – I could see smooth ripples near the base where the glass had relaxed before hardening. Unfortunately, the frames were rotting and flaky.

'Not exactly House-and-Gardens, is it?' I ventured, leaning forward to peer in with Midge.

'It's empty,' she said.

'What did you expect?'

'I thought there might still be furniture inside.'

'Probably auctioned off soon after the Will was settled. We'll have a better idea of how the place could look without the old lady's clutter.'

Midge gave me a reproving glance as she straightened. 'Let's see around the outside before we go in.'

'Uh huh.' I was still gazing through the window, wiping at the glass with my fingers for a better view. All I could make out was a big black range set into a chimney breast. 'It'll be great cooking on that.'

'The range? It'll be fun.' There was no dampening her enthusiasm.

'More like a forge,' I added. 'I suppose we could have both – an electric cooker as well as that monster. Still, no shortage of wood to fuel the thing.'

Midge pulled at my arm. 'Could be very *avant-garde* in

a "back-to-our-roots" sort of way. Come on, let's take a look around the back.'

I pushed away from the window and she stabbed at my face with her lips, then was off again. I trailed behind, examining the front door as I went. The wood looked sturdy enough, although there were one or two thin cracks running the length of its lower panels. Above, set in the surround, were two narrow windows no more than four inches deep, and a pull-bell hung to one side of the door, mounted against the brickwork. The entrance was sheltered by an open-sided storm porch, which looked thoroughly useless to me. A coach lamp hung on the opposite side to the bell, its interior smeared with cobwebs. I tugged at the bell's handle as I passed and its chime was dull and disinterested, but the *clunk* gave Midge cause to look back. I hunched over and did Quasimodo for her, mad-eyed and tongue filling one cheek.

'Mind the wind doesn't change,' she called as she mounted the steps running around the building's curve.

I lumbered after her, catching up on the fourth moss-layered step. Arm in arm we rounded the curve and began to appreciate better the cottage's structure. The main portion certainly was circular, with the kitchen area (where the range was located) and the rooms above branching off as an extension. All very small scale, you understand. The shape certainly gave Gramarye character, and undoubtedly added an odd charm. Unfortunately, its general condition was as poor as the unhealthy flowers in the garden.

The brickwork, originally washed white but now greying and considerably stained, was crumbling in parts, the pointing virtually absent in several sections. Tiles littered the ground beneath our feet, so I imagined the roof to be pitted with holes. The steps had led us to another door, once painted a dismal olive green and now blistered and peeling, revealing rotted wood beneath. The door faced south and the woods that were no more than a hundred or so yards away across an expanse of tall grass and bramble, a few individual trees dotted here and there like members of a cautious advance party; a clearer area, obviously trampled down over the years, spread out ten or twelve yards from the building, with smaller trees – plum and

27

crab-apple I thought, though I was no expert at the time –
standing fruitless (and somewhat dejected, I also thought)
closer to the cottage. On this side, because Gramarye was built
into the embankment (or rise) the cottage appeared to have only
two storeys, and was as round as an oasthouse. The apparent
'ground'-floor windows were arched at the top and Midge had
already left me to press her nose against one.

'Mike, come and look,' she called, 'it's fabulous inside.'

I joined her and was as impressed as she – although
'fabulous' was stretching it a bit – for the curved walls accom-
modated three longish windows which must have enabled the
room to capture the sun's rays throughout the day. Opposite,
and through an open doorway, I could make out a hallway
with stairs leading up and down; presumably another door led
off into the squared section of the building from the hall.
Sunlight fairly glowed from the walls, no shadowed corners
to be found, even the dirt on the windows unable to suppress
the radiance from outside. It looked warm and happy in there,
despite the bareness. And oh yeah, it looked *inviting*.

'Let's sit for a moment.' I'd noticed a weather-beaten
bench tucked in the corner where the straight wall of the cottage
peeled away from the circle; the wooden seat looked as if it had
either taken root or had grown from the very earth itself.

'I want to go inside,' Midge replied impatiently.

'Sure, in a minute. Let's just take stock of what we've
got so far.'

She was reluctant, but moved with me to the bench,
where we sat and gazed out at the nearby woods. They
seemed thick and impenetrable, but at that time not the least
bit sinister.

'It's wonderful,' Midge sighed needlessly. 'So much better than I expected.'

'Oh really? Between you and me, I thought you expected
quite a lot.'

A frown marked her face, but didn't make her any less
pretty. 'I – I just knew instinctively it was going to be right.'

I held up a hand. 'Wait. We haven't been in there yet.'

'We don't need to.'

'Oh yes we do. Let's not get carried away here. The ad

said in need of renovation, right? That might just be enough to push it over our price. The outside alone's gonna need a lot of repair, and God knows what the inside's like.'

'We can take that into account when we make our offer.'

'I think that's already been done by the agent. He told you over the phone the kind of price they're looking for, but unless we go under that we could have trouble finding the cash to make the place liveable.'

I was saying all the wrong things to Midge, but I had to make her face up to the reality of the situation. She studied the ground as though an answer might lie in the soil. When she looked up again I could see stubbornness had set in – no, not exactly stubbornness, Midge wasn't that kind of person; let's call it a quiet determination. She was generally pretty soft, pliable even (a facet that often annoyed me when her agent pressured her into accepting commissions she didn't really want either because of timing or subject-matter), but underneath that lay a resoluteness which surfaced only when she knew she was absolutely right about something, or needed that particular trait to carry her through a difficult time. I suspected, in fact, that her quiet determination had been *born* out of bad passages in her life, and believe me, Midge had had some.

My arm went around her shoulders and I hugged her to me. 'Just don't want you to build your hopes too high, Pixie,' I said softly, using the nickname saved for tender moments. 'So far, I like the place myself, even though the location scares me a little.'

'It'll be good for your work, Mike,' she replied, and there was an endearing earnestness in her voice. 'It's what you need, away from all those distractions, those . . .'

She had paused and I said the word for her. 'Friends.'

'So-called "friends". And Gramarye will be so right for me, too. I just know I can work here.'

'You don't figure we'll get lonely?'

She shook her head emphatically. 'No chance. Not together, Mike, you know that. And have you already forgotten all those times we've talked of being away from everybody, somewhere out of reach, with no agents or musicians dropping in or sacking down for the night? Being lonely would be bliss.

Anyway, I bet there's a lively community hereabouts. We'll soon make new friends, friends of a different kind though, and ones we can keep at a safe distance.'

'They might be too different for our liking.'

'We're in Hampshire, not Outer Mongolia. A couple of hours away from the city. They speak the same language here.'

'Maybe not quite the same.'

Midge rolled her eyes heavenwards. 'You city slickers are full of it. You'll learn soon enough.'

'All right, but don't forget that today the sun is shining, the sky is blue –'

'There's not a cloud to spoil the view,' she rhymed.

'But when it *is* raining, when winter comes and it's freezing, or when we're cut off completely because of snow –'

'Mmm,' she murmured, snuggling up, 'that'll be lovely. We probably won't be able to leave the cottage for weeks and we'll have to have a roaring fire going to keep ourselves warm, or cuddle under bedclothes for days on end. Just imagine the things we can get up to to keep ourselves amused.'

Midge had a knack of hitting below the belt, my weakest point. 'Be sensible,' I complained.

'I am. I'll make things so cosy you'll become a hermit.'

'That's what I'm afraid of.'

'And I'll have to force you out into the harsh cold wind to bring back bread for the table.'

'You're not helping.'

She became serious again, but still smiled when she said, 'Feel this place, Mike. Close your eyes and really *feel* it. Gramarye is so good and so perfect for us.'

I didn't actually close my eyes, but a peculiar sense of well-being definitely rose inside, an intoxication that was very mild yet filling. No, not the kind that comes from a good toke, but something else, something more real, somehow more permanent. Say it was the warmth of the sun's rays, the very pleasantness of the day itself and my surroundings. Call it, even, the strength of Midge's own conviction flowing into me, a sensing natural enough to true lovers. At one time I'd have concluded it was only those influences. Not now, though. Oh no, not now that I know so much more.

'Let's look inside,' I said to avoid the final commitment, and Midge's smile only became more knowing. She stood and drew out the three labelled keys from her jeans' pocket. Dutifully she handed them to me, a gesture that seemed to say, 'Okay, fate is in your own hands and inside is where you'll find it.'

I took them and moved towards the back door with Midge close on my heels. Stopping before the marked and tired-looking old door, I held up the long keys and pondered on which one to try first. Two were cut the same, so I decided they would probably be for the front door. I pushed the odd one home and it fitted easily. But it wouldn't turn.

Neither would the next key. Nor the next, the second's twin.

I groaned. 'Looks like Bickleshift gave us the wrong set.'

'Let's try the front,' Midge suggested.

'Okay, but one of these has to be for this door if they're the right keys.'

We descended the curving steps carefully because of the moss and were soon under the open porch. I chose number one and inserted it into the lock to find it still wouldn't turn. Growing more frustrated I tried two and three again with no luck. The door wouldn't budge, even when I twisted the handle and used shoulder pressure. The wood creaked, but didn't move a fraction.

'Let me,' said Midge, pushing between me and the door.

'It's no good. The lock's either rusted solid, or Bickleshift made a mistake with the keys.' I examined the label and GRAMARYE was clearly typed.

She took them from me without a word and held one of the 'twins' up to her face for a second before decisively pushing it home into the lock. Her wrist twisted and I thought I saw her give a little gasp, almost as if the key had turned of its own accord. I may have been mistaken.

The door opened easily and smoothly, without even the hint of a horror-movie creak; the air that rushed out was musty and damp, and seemed glad to be free.

THE ROUND ROOM

I was ready to go straight on in, puzzled though I was that Midge had succeeded where I had failed; Midge, however, hesitated. Again I'm not sure – quite a few things are still not entirely sharp in my memory – but there seemed to be some kind of trepidation in her manner now. Enough, at least, to dismiss any mock-gloating on her part. Perhaps I'm not sure because the sudden change in mood was just as quickly gone; I know she had disappeared inside before I could voice my concern.

Shrugging to myself, I ventured in after her and the instant coolness was an unwelcome contrast to the warmth outside. We found ourselves in a smallish room, no more than ten by twelve I guessed (the house particulars had been left back in the car), with an open door ahead and stairs beyond leading up to the next level. We could see the kitchen area through an opening to our right. The floor here and in the room next-door was quarry-tiled and I noticed an unnatural darkness to the surface. Crouching, I touched the stone.

'Feels damp,' I said and searched the skirting. Sure enough, a dark waterline stained the opposite wall just a couple of inches above the floor. 'The far wall there must cut into the embankment and when it rains water seeps down through the soil and into the brickwork.'

Midge didn't appear that interested, which irritated me

a little; I knew that kind of dampness could be serious and I was thinking in money terms. She'd already gone through into the kitchen. With an exasperated shake of my head, I rose and went after her. 'Midge, you've gotta take note of these things,' I whined. 'They're gonna decide whether or not we buy this place.'

'Sorry, Mike.' Pretending contriteness, she slid up to me and momentarily rested her head against my chest. Then she was over by the huge black cooking range we had seen through the window and stooping to open oven doors, squawking with delight when she peered into them, then rising to exclaim more loudly when she laid eyes on the skillet hooks on the side of the recess above the range, filled with long-handled saucepans and a rather large frying pan. On the floor just in front of the range stood an iron kettle on a trivet, adding an extra charm.

'It's like something out of an old fairy-tale,' Midge called back to me.

'You mean where the witch boils frogs and babies' legs on her stove to make her spells?' I asked as I joined her. I saw there were pots, also of black metal, inside the largest of the ovens.

'Nothing so nasty,' Midge admonished. She leaned into the recess and squinted up into the chimney. I hastily pulled her back when I noticed the dangerous flaw in the massive stone lintel above the range. She looked at me in surprise until I pointed out the crack.

'That looks ready to collapse,' I warned and she had sense enough to back away.

'I doubt it runs all the way through.'

'Maybe not, but why take the chance? That's another item that would have to be taken care of.'

Midge frowned, not liking the list I was already compiling.

'Ten-to-one the chimney's blocked by now, and nobody's going to clear it until that stone's been made safe.' There was no fun in mentioning these things, but I felt that someone had to be realistic.

'Perhaps the damp and this are the worst faults,' Midge remarked hopefully.

I shrugged. We'd only seen the ground floor so far.

One of those deep earthenware sinks stood under the window we'd peeked through earlier, the kind you could bath a Shetland pony in, and I wandered over to it and turned on the hot and cold taps. Both ran brown after several clunks from the pipes and sudden spats from the taps themselves. I let them run for a minute or so and the colour hardly changed at all.

'Tank's probably rusted through,' I commented. 'Or maybe that's how they drink it around here.' I was beginning to feel gloomy.

Meanwhile, Midge was opening cupboards and drawers; the wooden units looking pretty early fare but none the less not in bad shape. I investigated another door, expecting to find a larder or broom-cupboard, but instead discovering a toilet with a high-mounted chain flush.

'Least we don't have to use a shed in the garden.' I pulled the rusty chain and the system groaned loudly, the bowl flooding instantly with the not-unexpected brown water which seemed to take an unreasonably long time to gurgle away, burping and hiccuping as it went. 'I think the leaflet said cesspit drainage,' I said as I closed the door again. 'I wonder when it was last emptied.' I was wondering if it had ever been emptied.

Midge was standing in the middle of the kitchen and I could tell that nothing I'd said so far had deterred her.

'Can we go upstairs now?' she asked.

'I can't wait,' I answered.

'Keep an open mind, Mike.'

'Will you do the same?'

There was no annoyance in our words; we trusted in one another too much for that kind of pettiness. I suppose you could say we were tinged with apprehension, both of us fearing that either one would be disappointed. I knew Midge really wanted me to want this place and I would have done almost anything to please her, but we were not just talking about a financial wrench here, but a social one too. If it was going to work, it had to be *right*.

We mounted the stairs to the next level holding hands, Midge leading as if drawing me up with her.

The stairway doubled round into a mini-hallway, the outside door I had first tried to our right and the doorway leading into the round room to our left. Sunshine hit us like a softly exploding shell and for an incredible instant I felt as though I were floating. So strong was the sensation that I became giddy, and only Midge clutching my hand and pulling firmly saved me from toppling back down the stairway. I blinked rapidly, blinded by the sudden dazzle, and Midge's sweet image swept in and out before me as though I were in a dreamy, slow faint. I remember concern in her light eyes, yet warmth also, a confidence that encompassed and reassured me. My vision cleared and I was vaguely aware that although no more than a second or two had passed, a vast expanse of time had swayed before me.

I found myself in the round room, although I couldn't remember having entered. The sun blazed outside and the landscape through the large windows looked microcosmically clear, as though every leaf could be seen singly, every grass blade viewed as a separate entity. The sky around was of the cleanest, purest blue I had ever witnessed. Mistakenly, I thought I understood that abrupt and unnatural lucidity. I'd heard that the effects of certain drugs could spring back at you when you least expected it, even years after their original use, and I got no pleasure from that notion, only a withering sense of shame. I assumed that the sudden change from cool shade into dazzling light had triggered off lingering chemicals in my mind – strobe lighting can sometimes do the same thing – taking me on a short and confusing trip. That's what I thought then, and I'm still not discounting that possibility.

My eyes quickly refocused (perhaps it would be more accurate to say *de*focused) back to normality, everything losing that peculiar linear depth. Midge had both hands around my face and was studying me with that same warm concern of a moment ago.

'Are you okay?' she asked, her hands soft against my cheeks.

'Uh, yeah, I think so. Yeah, I'm fine.' And I was, for the mood, the unexpected shift in perception, had vanished, leaving hardly any after-effects other than the memory. 'Felt faint for a minute there; must have been the change in altitude,' I joked.

'You sure you're all right?'

'Yeah, I promise, I'm okay.'

I looked around, seeing the room itself now, not the landscape outside. 'This is something else,' I remarked after a low, appreciative whistle.

'Isn't it beautiful, Mike?' Midge's smile threatened to split her face in two, so broad and beaming was it. She skipped away from me and did a quick tour (circular, of course), ending up at a quaint fireplace with a rough brick surround. She leaned an elbow on the narrow mantelpiece and grinned at me, her eyes sparkling with merriment.

'Puts a different complexion on things, doesn't it?' she said.

It did. It certainly did. There was a glow to this room that I realised was due to the sun's unhindered rays reflecting off the round walls; yet contained therein was something more, a liveliness, a vitality, something intangible but nevertheless very real. *You have to be open to it, though*, a tiny voice at the back of my mind whispered. *You have to want to feel it.* Cynic at times I may be, but I had finer feelings too and the atmosphere of the room itself (coupled, I'm sure, with Midge's enthusiasm) was somehow unleashing these feelings. God, yes, I *did* want to feel it, I *did* want this place. Despite that, the other side of me asked whether it would be the same in winter when the rain clouds hid the sun. Would this energy inside be lost? Would the *magic* – there, the word had sprung into my mind for the first time, although I hadn't realised its significance – be gone? But at the moment, I didn't care. The present, and the yearning so suddenly induced, was all that mattered.

I walked over to Midge and held her so tight she gasped. 'Y'know, it's beginning to work on me,' I told her without really comprehending.

The rest of the cottage was somewhat of an anticlimax. We found a long jagged crack that ran from floor to ceiling in the more conventional room next-door, and mould on the walls in the one next-door to that. The tiny bathroom was at best functional, with dark stains discolouring the bath itself. The staircase led up to what were no more than attic rooms, oddly shaped because they were built into the roof, with small windows providing inadequate daylight. The ceilings were squared off, though, and a trapdoor led into the loft area. I'd have needed a chair or a stepladder to climb up and take a look, so I didn't bother, but I imagined there were quite a few gaps open to the skies judging by the amount of tiles lying scattered on the ground outside. We poked around on levels two and three, finding rotting windowframes, warped cupboard doors that wouldn't close, more damp and more cracks in the walls, though the latter were less serious than the floor-to-ceiling one. Even the stairs protested against our weight and one board bent so badly I quickly hopped off, fearing it would collapse. Naturally, there was a fine layer of dust everywhere.

I don't know why, but we deliberately avoided entering the round room again – possibly we subconsciously felt its effect was too much to take twice in one day, or maybe we just wanted to remain more objective after having inspected the rest of the cottage. I had no trouble in turning the key when I locked the front door behind us, and we walked back down the path more slowly than we had walked up it.

Beyond the gate, Midge and I turned and leaned against the bonnet of the Passat, my arm around her shoulders, both of us lost in our own thoughts for a while. The ragged state of the garden and the generally poor condition of the cottage itself seemed to be impressing themselves on me in a strong way, and when I looked at Midge I was sure I detected the merest flicker of doubt in her eyes, too.

I was disturbed by the waxing and waning of my own enthusiasm and had sought reassurance from her. Her own uncertainty was the last thing I'd expected.

Glancing at my wristwatch, I said, 'Let's discuss things over a beer and a sandwich.'

Her eyes never left Gramarye as she climbed into the car, and she craned her neck to watch through the rear window while I drove away. I didn't turn the car around but headed in the same direction as when we'd been searching for the cottage, remembering that we hadn't passed a pub during the journey from Cantrip. A good ten minutes later I found what I was looking for and the sight cheered me considerably. Stout oak timbers and gleaming white paint-work; even a shaggy thatched roof. Rough wooden tables and bench seats in the front garden with no bright brand-name umbrellas to spoil the rural charm. The Forest Inn was my kind of watering hole.

The interior wasn't a disappointment either: low beams, horsebrasses and thick leather belts mounted on the walls, huge inglenook fireplace big enough to roast a pig in, and the cigarette machine discreetly tucked away in a darkened corner. No juke-box, no Space Invaders. Not even a micro-wave oven on the bar, although a chalked menu advertising hot snacks was set in the wall to one side. The inn was nicely crowded without being full and I ordered a pint of bitter for myself and an orange juice for Midge from a thickset barman with mauve-veined cheeks and long thin strands of hair flat-tened sideways over an otherwise bald scalp. He had the bearing and authority of a landlord.

'Passing through?' he enquired without any curiosity at all as he filled the glass jug.

I'd been studying the food list and replied abstractedly, 'Sort of.' Then, realising he might venture some information about the locale, if not the cottage itself, I added: 'We've been looking at a place for sale not far from here.'

He raised his eyebrows. 'Old Flora Chaldean's place, is it?' There was the faintest burr in his accent.

I nodded. 'Yeah, Gramarye.'

He chuckled before turning to reach for a small bottle of orange, and Midge and I exchanged surprised glances.

'Nice little place,' I prompted as he poured the orange juice, 'the cottage.'

He looked up, first at me, then at Midge, still pouring and still grinning, but all he told us was the price of the drinks.

Now Midge is usually quite reserved, not to say shy at times, not to say *timid*, so I was somewhat shocked when she said clearly and coldly: 'Is there something funny in that?'

The barman reappraised her and I could see that, like

many others before him, he was not totally unmoved by her appealing good looks. For myself, a slab of concrete had gone to rest somewhere in the lower regions of my gut: like I said, he was thickset, and perhaps I should have mentioned that his bare forearms, now resting on the bar top, appeared solid enough to grind wheat by themselves. I swallowed beer as he leaned forward.

'Sorry about that, Miss,' he apologised. 'Didn't mean to be rude.' And then he strolled to the other end of the bar to serve another customer.

Just watch it next time, I said to his back and silently to myself, of course. 'The idea, Midge,' I said patiently, 'is to get on with the natives. We didn't even order any food.'

'I'm not so hungry any more. Can we sit outside?'

Only a few tables were occupied in the garden area and we sat at one that was some distance away from those. I placed our drinks on the rough-hewn surface, then slid onto a bench on the opposite side to Midge (we always enjoyed eye contact). I could tell she was still miffed at the barman, so I squeezed her hand and grinned.

'It's just the locals' way of keeping visitors in their place, letting on they know a bit more than we do,' I said.

'What? Oh, him. No, he doesn't bother me. Flora Chaldean was probably the token eccentric hereabouts, someone they could all have a chuckle over because she was different from them. She was probably just a lonely old woman with no family, who kept very much to herself. No, I was thinking of Gramarye itself.' She sipped her orange juice.

'You're not so keen now?'

She looked startled. 'Oh, I'm more than keen. It's just that there seem to be conflicting elements in the cottage.'

My turn to be startled. 'What the hell are you talking about?'

'The peculiar emptiness of the place . . .'

'It's been unoccupied for a long time.'

'Yes, but didn't you notice? There were no spiders or their webs, no insects of any kind in there. No signs of mice even. There weren't any birds nesting in the eaves of the roof, and the cottage is surrounded by woodland. Gramarye is just an empty shell.'

I hadn't noticed, but she was right. It should have been a haven for creepy-crawlies and nesting birds.

'Yet,' she continued, 'the round room was so vibrant. You felt it; something happened to you in there.'

'Sure, I felt dizzy for a moment, that was all. Probably hunger.' I looked longingly back towards the inn.

'No more than that?'

I didn't want to get into this. 'Like what? If you must know, I think the sun hit me hard when I came up those stairs. The glare disrupted signals going to my brain.'

She studied me for a second or two, then said, 'Okay.' Simple as that. No arguments, no further discussion. She'd either accepted what I'd told her, or accepted that I didn't want to delve further. That's what made Midge easy to live with.

I drained half of the bitter and Midge watched me. Tilted eyes, dark-haired, and delicate little pointed chin. Yeah, that's why sometimes I called her Pixie.

'So where do we go from here?' I asked, wiping the back of my hand across my lips. 'You know I'm worried about how much it's gonna cost to put the place right.'

'But you like the cottage, don't you?' She leaned across the table and her words were almost a conspiratorial whisper. And she was fixing me with that smile again. 'Don't you think the location is ideal? Imagine the work we'll do there. My paintings, your music. Mike, you'll do so much, I just know it. And maybe you'll finally get around to writing those children's stories for me to illustrate. We'll make a wonderful team!'

I mulled it over. Sometimes Midge escaped into a world of her own, on a plane far removed from choking cities and avaricious mortals, and she had the ability to draw others into it, too – that is, if she *wanted* them along. I had to remain the pragmatist most of the time, although it never ceased to amaze me how down-to-earth practical she could become when the occasion truly demanded.

'Look, I'll tell you what we'll do,' I said. 'We'll go back to the agent and lay our cards on the table. We'll point out all

40

the faults, major and minor, and put in a lower bid to cover our costs. If Bickleshift goes for it, all well and good; if not – well, we'll have to face up to the facts of life.'

She could hardly argue with that, but I couldn't help disliking myself for putting anxiety behind her eyes.

So that was what we did. We finished our drinks and drove back to Cantrip, me with a grumbling stomach and Midge in a moody silence. When we passed Gramarye, her eyes locked onto the cottage and once more she craned her neck until it was out of sight.

It was well after lunchtime when we reached the village and we found Bickleshift wondering how to occupy the rest of his day. I explained our position, telling him we loved the cottage, were extremely keen to buy, but that there were certain nasty faults that needed attention, and these would burn a sizable hole in our finances. How about knocking off at least four thousand from the bidding price?

He sympathised. He understood perfectly. But he said No.

The ad had mentioned that Gramarye would require some renovation, and quite possibly the costs would be high. But he did not have the authority to accept our lower offer, nor, he had to admit, the professional inclination to do so. It *was* a 'desirable property' in an extremely 'desirable' part of the world, after all.

I could feel Midge's spirits slump, and mine also took a nose-dive. Although I had mixed feelings about the place, learning we couldn't afford it anyway left me more frustrated than I thought possible. I tried three thousand.

Bickleshift sat firm, explaining that the executors of Flora Chaldean's Will had set a minimum price, apart from which we were only the first in a line of others wishing to view the property. He was very friendly when he told us this, but estate agents aren't renowned for having generous natures.

Our problem was that not only would we have to live in Gramarye, but we'd have to work there too, so conditions had to be reasonable for both of us. Also, I'd wanted to build some kind of mini recording studio for myself; nothing fancy, you understand, but the bare essentials would require a certain amount of ready cash. It was no good, useless to try and kid ourselves. Nice idea, but impractical. Bye-bye our cosy love-nest in the country.

We left with lead-weight hearts and Bickleshift's promise to be in touch if there were any further developments. Midge was silent all the way back to Big Met., and I could say nothing to console her.

That night she wept in her sleep.

THREE SCORES

There's an old Chinese proverb I've just invented that goes: *'When luck is on your side, numbers don't come into it.'*

The doorbell woke us around 8.30 next morning. That kind of hour is rarely even mentionable to me, so it was Midge who had to crawl out of bed to answer it. With one open eye, I noticed her face was still puffy and her eyelids red-rimmed from salty tears as she pulled on her nightshirt and left the bedroom. I groaned and pushed my head further into the pillow when she opened the front door of our apartment and I heard a familiar growly 'Good morning'. Val Harradine, her agent, had heralded in the dawn.

Their voices wandered off into the kitchen, Midge's barely audible and Big Val's grinding on like an asthmatic cement mixer. Actually, Val was okay, although a bit dykey of the *bullish* kind; what irritated me was the way she sometimes tried to force work onto Midge that Midge didn't want. When I learned of her mission that morning, I could have kissed her big head, moustache and all.

Midge came flying back into the bedroom and leapt onto the bed, her milky thighs straddling my tummy and her hands shaking my shoulder. I yelped and tried to shift her weight.

'You'll never guess!' she cried, pinning me there and laughing.

'C'mon, Midge, it's too early,' I protested.

'Valerie tried to reach me all day yesterday –'

'That's wonderful news. Will you get off me?'

'She couldn't, because we were out, weren't we? She couldn't phone last night because she was out herself.'

'This is fascin—'

'Listen! She had a meeting with the art buyer at Gross and Newby yesterday morning.'

'That's the agency you don't like.'

'I love 'em. They've got a huge presentation to make next week and the account's art director wants to use my style of illustration for posters. They want *three*, Mike, and they're willing to pay a heavy price.'

Now unlike book and magazine publishers, advertising agencies are astonishingly high payers where artwork is concerned – usually client's money, you see – so £-signs flashed through my head and cleared the last dregs of sleep.

'Five hundred a-piece,' said a gruff voice. I looked over to see Big Val's broad visage peering round the door, not a pleasant sight on an empty – if Midge-burdened – stomach. However, it wasn't unwelcome on that particular morning, and I did my best to be nice.

'Less your twenty per cent,' I said.

'Naturally,' she replied without a smile.

I blew her a kiss anyway – it wouldn't have been decent in my naked state to make it physical. My hands rested on Midge's thighs and I asked suspiciously, 'When are they going to need 'em?'

'Monday,' she told me.

'Aah, Midge, you're gonna knock yourself out.'

'It'll be okay, I'll work through the weekend. If the campaign goes through, the agency will double-up on the price.'

'Three thousand?'

'Less my twenty per cent,' put in Big Val.

'Naturally,' I said.

The idea of Midge producing three such illustrations

44

worried me: she never skimped or cheated on her work, and she had a particularly fine-detail style. Even with the restrictive time limit I knew she would put everything she had into those paintings.

'Do you realise what it means, Mike?' Her eyes were wide and shining. 'We'll be able to afford the cottage, we'll be able to meet their price.'

'Not quite.' I reminded her of the figures involved. 'We'll still be a thousand short, even if you do eventually get the full amount for the posters.' If I imagined that would cast a cloud, I was wrong: my words didn't seem to have any effect on her at all.

'I just know everything's going to be all right. I knew the minute I woke up this morning.'

'We really have to get moving, Margaret,' interrupted Twenty Per Cent. 'I promised I'd get you to the agency for a briefing as soon after nine as possible. I'm going down to find a cab and I'll give you five minutes to join me.'

Within seven minutes, Midge was gone, leaving me with the wet imprint of a kiss on my cheek and a semi-troubled mind. I was both pleased and concerned at the same time. The money just might allow us to compromise on the amount of work to be carried out on Gramarye. Maybe. Anyway, I promised Midge before she left to give Bickleshift a call and propose a revised offer to him. Things turned out the other way round, though.

I'd shaved and showered and was spooning my way through my Alpen, nose into *Rolling Stone*, when the phone rang. Bickleshift was on the other end of the line.

'Mr Stringer?'

'Yeah.' I sipped the coffee I'd carried through into the hall with me and winced when I burnt my lips.

'Bickleshift here.'

I became instantly alert. 'Oh, hi there.'

'I said I'd call if there were any new developments concerning Gramarye. You know, I did understand your plight yesterday and I took the liberty of getting in touch with the late Flora Chaldean's executors after you left.'

I didn't say anything about the queue of prospective

45

buyers he'd mentioned. 'Really? That was kind of you.'

'Yes. You see, I don't quite know how to put this, but the sale of Gramarye is unlike any other I've undertaken.'

'I don't understand.'

'Well, apart from the purchase price, there are certain other aspects regarding the sale. I've been asked by the solicitor in charge of the estate, a Mr Ogborn, of Ogborn, Puckridge and Quenby, to keep him advised of the, er, type of purchaser interested in the cottage. It seems Flora Chaldean was rather fussy as to who should take over if her niece put the place on the market.'

'I see.' No, I didn't see, but what else could I say?

'Mr Ogborn wondered if it would be possible for you and your – sorry, Ms Gudgeon, to pop along to his offices in Bunbury some time tomorrow, or even today.'

'Uh, that might be difficult. I don't think Midge can make it – she's pretty tied up for the next few days.' I didn't like the idea of being vetted, either.

'Ah.' There was a short silence at the other end. 'Well, it is rather important apparently that your good lady goes along too. Mr Ogborn is most anxious to see both of you.'

I get my own kind of intuitions now and again and something told me that Midge was the important part of the partnership. 'She isn't here at the moment, so I can't give you a definite answer. I suppose we *might* both be able to make it down there.' Poor Midge was really going to be under pressure workwise.

'That would be excellent. Now let me give you the telephone number of Ogborn, Puckridge and Quenby, then you can make your own arrangements regarding an appointment. With regard to your earlier offer for the property, I think you'll find Mr Ogborn very amenable, although he might not come down to quite the figure you suggested. I wish you luck, anyway.'

I took the number and we exchanged goodbyes. I suppose I was a bit numbed when I returned to the kitchen, because I sat there for some time staring into the bowl of muesli, wondering what the hell was going on. And the morning was still not finished with surprises.

46

The next call came about an hour later. Midge hadn't come back yet and I was pondering on whether or not to ring the agency to get a message to her. Between ponderings, and now in jeans and grey sweater, I had been sitting at the kitchen table working out figures on a sheet of paper, while propped up against a milk bottle before me was a list of Gramarye faults that *had* to be fixed (like that floor-to-ceiling crack in the bedroom). I walked out to the phone again, tucking the pencil behind an ear, still mumbling numbers to myself.

'Mike? It's Bob.'

Bob's a tour manager (for rock groups and the like) friend of mine and we go way back. We used to be quite a team where play was concerned, but I was the one who got *the* girl. Fortunately there isn't a jealous bone in Bob's body.

'Hey, Bob, what're you up to?'

'Never mind. You busy next week?'

'I could fit something in.'

'I mean *all* next week. The Everlys are back in town.'

'Another Reunion?'

'Never fails. Albert's getting another backing group together and he wants to know if you're free.'

'Are you kidding?'

'Do I ever?'

'Yeah, you do. I can break off all my other engagements.'

'You familiar with their routine?'

'They're a bit pre my generation, but I know most of the stuff, and Albert'll put me right on anything I don't.'

'Terrific. It's a grand in the bread-bin, by the way.'

Score Three.

After arranging details and promising to meet Bob for a 'definitely the last one' (muso-speak for a drink-up) in the nearest future, I hung up and wandered back into the kitchen, shaking my head at this funny day. Now I was left with no excuse at all for *not* buying the cottage, and I wasn't quite sure of my feelings about that. Nevertheless I grinned in anticipation of the look on Midge's face when I told her the news.

OGBORN

We made an early start for Bunbury the following day. Midge's reaction had surprised me when she'd returned from the agency and I told her of the two phone calls; surprised me because she'd only smiled as though the turn of events had not been altogether unexpected. She'd put her arms around my neck, kissed my nose, and said enigmatically: 'It was meant to be.'

Working from the art director's rough scamps (the client was an up-market chain of children's fashion stores, catering for tots and teens and everything that went on in between), she'd sketched out all three of her poster illustrations by late that night; I'd phoned the solicitor, Ogborn, earlier on in the afternoon, and arranged to be in his office by 10.30 the following morning. He said he looked forward to meeting us both.

The journey meant that most of the day would be lost as far as Midge's project was concerned, but she was quite prepared to work night *and* day for the rest of the week and weekend to have the illustrations ready for the following Monday. The agency needed them by that time so that they could be copied photographically, with copy-lines added, for presentation to their client later on in the week. Like a lot of artistic things, the pictures could either go beautifully right first off, or disastrously wrong: for Midge's sake, I prayed this time it would be the former.

Bunbury turned out to be one of those thriving market towns, with a lot more charm than the village of Cantrip: narrow streets, timbered houses and inns, overhanging gables and bow-windowed shops; just off the busy market square was a modern shopping mall, but even this managed to blend unobtrusively with the older buildings around it. There was a healthy bustle to the place that revived us after our early-morning rise and long journey. We found the offices of Ogborn, Puckridge and Quenby situated in a secluded, cobble-stoned cul-de-sac, the terraced buildings of ageing red brick with shoulder-height railings guarding the basement areas and a flight of steps leading up to each front door. The interior of O, P and Q was somewhat austere in comparison; functional without frills, dignified yet characterless. There were not many frills about Mr Ogborn either, although he certainly had olde-worlde dignity and a character that was not so far removed from Dickens. Putting an age on him wasn't easy, but anywhere between sixty and eighty would have been close.

He was quiet-mannered, yet crisp, his back a little crooked, his frame thin. Gold-rimmed spectacles rested on an unashamedly prominent nose, and his eyes, with their long, almost hooding lids, were of the palest grey I'd ever seen. But they were not unkind eyes.

He offered me a long, bony hand and when I shook it I was surprised by the firmness of its grip. He held Midge's a shade longer than necessary, I thought, and scrutinised her with an interest he hadn't shown me. Maybe you're never too old. We had been shown into his office by a secretary whose age could not have been too far off his own, and treated him with a quiet reverence that might be due to a cardinal or television newscaster, and as she left, softly closing the door behind her, Ogborn offered two chairs opposite his leather-topped desk. Midge and I sat.

'It was extremely good of you both to come all this way,' he began in a voice that was as dry and brittle as were probably his old bones. 'Mr Bickleshift informed me of your

49

interest in Gramarye and I thought it might be appropriate for us to meet. I take it you are genuinely interested in the property?'

Midge's response was very swift. 'We'd love to buy the cottage.'

I shifted in my seat and nodded when the solicitor eyed me.

'But the financial requirements appear to be some problem to you.'

This time I was swifter than Midge. 'The place is going to need quite a bit of renovation. There's a great, gaping crack –'

'Yes, I understand that the cottage has deteriorated considerably over recent months,' he interrupted. 'As executor of Flora Chaldean's estate I have the authority to consider any reasonable bid, and it's my opinion that the sooner Gramarye is occupied, the better for its general condition.'

'Well, it'll take a tidy sum to prevent further deterioration, Mr Ogborn,' I pointed out to him.

'Quite so. Money and good will.'

Good will?

He smiled at my mute surprise. 'It's my belief that homes live and breathe through the people who reside in them, Mr Stringer.'

I wasn't going to argue the point, not when negotiations were still at a 'delicate' stage. Midge, however, appeared eager to agree.

'That's what Gramarye needs so much right now, Mr Ogborn – life inside its walls.'

I didn't detect any embarrassment whatsoever in the solicitor's steady gaze, but I quickly added, 'All unoccupied houses become like mausoleums eventually, don't they? Stale and decrepit. Just a good airing does them a lot of good. Y'know, sometimes –'

'May I ask you a personal question, Miss Gudgeon?' Ogborn said.

'Please do,' Midge replied.

'I wondered if you had a career, a profession of some kind.'

'I'm an illustrator.'

'Ah.' That appeared to please him.

'I illustrate children's books mostly.'

'I see.' He studied her for several seconds and I began to get a little vexed at his attention.

'I'm a musician,' I told him.

'I see.' His smile seemed thinner somehow.

'Could you tell us something about Flora Chaldean?' Midge asked. 'She must have lived at Gramarye for a good many years.'

'Indeed she did,' replied Ogborn, straightening in his chair as much as the curvature in his spine would allow. 'I understand she was an orphan taken in by the owners of the cottage, who were childless themselves, some time before the First World War, and raised as their own daughter. There was no official record of adoption, and nobody appears to have known her exact age when she died. I don't believe that years had very much significance to Flora herself.'

'Was she ever married?' enquired Midge.

'For a short time only. Her husband was killed in the last war after, I think, barely two or three years of marriage. The niece who inherited the estate was his, you see, and proved the devil of a job to trace, I might add. She herself is in her sixties, and has no interest in Gramarye whatsoever, and hardly any in her late aunt-in-law. Quite understandable under the circumstances.'

'How did Mrs Chaldean manage to support herself?'

If Ogborn found Midge's question impertinent, he didn't show it. 'Oh, her adoptive parents left her a small inheritance and I believe she also collected the usual meagre war-widow's pension. Generally, I'm led to believe she used the barter system with locals, which is much favoured in the more remote parts of the country.'

'The barter system?' I didn't know what all this had to do with buying a house, but I was willing to play along.

'Flora Chaldean had the reputation hereabouts of being something of a healer. Nothing spectacular, you understand, but she made up medicinal potions for ailing locals, those with heavy colds, sore throats, that sort of thing, and in exchange they supplied her with the odd chicken or rabbit or vegetables or whatever. Small things, nothing grand, nothing for the Inland Revenue to be concerned about. She concocted her potions from old, perhaps ancient, remedies, the kind passed down the years through word of mouth. It seems she also had a wonderful way with sick or injured animals.' Ogborn looked down at his hands folded on the desk and added, as if to himself, 'Quite remarkable.'

I almost smiled, thinking of witches' brews and spells, and boiling babies' legs. If I could have without being noticed, I'd have nudged Midge. Instead I stole a quick glance at her and found she was still absorbed in what Ogborn had been saying.

Clearing my throat, I said to the solicitor, 'About the price . . .?'

His manner instantly became more crisp. 'Yes, of course. I know you're rather concerned over the cost. I'm prepared to accept that conditions in the property have become far worse during the winter months since the previous owner's demise, so perhaps the original valuation was too high, although I'm bound to say that house prices these days do not generally devalue.'

'Mr Ogborn, the price isn't –' Midge began to say, before I cut in.

'I thought maybe we could meet halfway.'

'You mentioned a reduction of three thousand to Mr Bickleshift . . .'

'Uh, four thousand, actually.' I ignored the sharp glance from Midge. Ogborn consulted a note pad on the desk.

'Oh, I see. I understood the figure to be three,' he said.

'Well, yes, it was mentioned, but the more we can save on the price, the more we can spend on the cottage's renovation.'

'Another couple came to see me yesterday, and they, too, were very interested . . .'

'But I guess we could scrape up that extra thousand from somewhere.'

'I do have an obligation to my late client's surviving relative to obtain the best price possible. However, I also have an obligation towards the wishes expressed by Flora Chaldean in her Will. That is, to find a suitable person, or persons, to continue the occupation of Gramarye.'

I didn't quite like the sound of that, and liked even less the feeling that I was not necessarily included in that particular grouping. Again he was looking directly at Midge.

'What would you say,' Ogborn went on, 'if I allowed you a £1500 reduction?'

'We'd say yes, Mr Ogborn,' Midge said promptly.

'We'd say yes,' I agreed more slowly.

'Then your offer is accepted,' Ogborn said.

I breathed out a secret sigh and Midge, less introvertly, bounced in her seat. 'That's wonderful!' she enthused and, unabashed, leaned over and kissed my cheek.

'A deposit will be required, naturally,' Ogborn told us, 'and perhaps your own solicitor could contact me as soon as possible. I trust you are purchasing in your joint names?'

We nodded jointly at his raised eyebrows. I had a silly grin on my face and it was because of Midge's exuberance. Not only that: I also felt good about the deal myself. Suddenly I was a man with conviction. Yes, I was going to *enjoy* living in the country. Nobody said it had to be completely back-to-nature. And Gramarye was going to be our first proper home together.

But still that niggly tormentor enjoyed itself at the back of my mind.

'Um, I'm just a bit puzzled,' I said to Ogborn. 'Mr Bickleshift implied that a number of people were interested in the cottage.'

'There have been six positive enquiries since the advertisement was placed and, as I've already informed you, I, myself, met with another young couple only yesterday.'

I felt awkward, but I couldn't let it go. 'So why us? Don't get me wrong – we want to buy, the deal is as good as sealed so far as we're concerned – but I can't help wondering if the other offers were lower than ours.'

He seemed genuinely amused. 'On the contrary, Mr Stringer. Those who were interested were willing to pay the full price.'

Curiouser and curiouser.

He went on: 'But as I've already explained, Flora Chaldean was insistent that Gramarye be passed on to someone suitable. Several of those other prospective buyers were merely property speculators, the kind who would renovate and modernise, to sell again immediately at some exorbitant price, while others would only use the cottage as a weekend retreat. That was far from what my late client had in mind for Gramarye.' He paused. 'And then there were those who had altogether different purposes for the place.'

The last sentence had been said very quietly, almost to himself.

'Sorry?' I said.

He rested back in his chair. 'Not important, Mr Stringer, not important. Now, I know you have a long journey ahead of you, so I shan't detain you any further. I'll make Bickleshift aware of our agreement and perhaps you could let me have that deposit within the next day or two – naturally my own offices will handle the conveyancing of the property.'

'Mike . . .' prompted Midge.

'I can let you have a cheque right away.' I was already reaching into my inside pocket.

'Splendid. I'll make out a receipt for you and then the matter will be safely in hand. The agent tells me you haven't the problem of selling a house yourself, so that's a complication out of the way.'

'That's right, we're renting at the moment. How did Bickleshift know that?'

'I told him when I rang on Monday,' came the answer from Midge. 'I thought having no chain of contracts would be in our favour.'

She really had been so sure of the place.

We concluded our business with the solicitor, shook hands with him and left. Midge was surprisingly subdued once we were outside, although I could tell she was deliriously happy, and I guessed it was due to the tension of the past couple of days draining from her. That being so, we still wanted to celebrate right there and then, but unfortunately her work commitment wouldn't allow: she had to get back and start on those illustrations. Also, I had to get together with Albert Lee and work on arrangements for next week's lightning tour. It was going to be a heavy schedule, and I looked forward to it; long time since I'd been on the road, and I'd already half forgotten the hardships involved.

We drove from Bunbury and jabbered all the way to the city, amazed at our good fortune and busily making plans. Midge and I had a lot of sweat ahead of us, but we knew it was going to be worth it. Oh yeah, we knew.

MOVING

The five or six weeks that followed were just a dreamy kind of blur, events moved so fast. The Everlys tour was a sell-out and I enjoyed every minute – tearing around the countryside for six concerts in various towns didn't faze me one bit. I was on a high which had nothing to do with illegal substances. Before I went on the road I had the chance of seeing the results of Midge's painstaking nights-and-days' toil, and I have to say it, despite my natural bias, they were BRILLIANT. The campaign was aimed specifically at toddlers and the art director had envisioned fairy-tale settings – white castles, dark forests, prancing elves, the usual ingredients – with our little modern-day tykes superimposed photographically among them. Clever photography would ensure (hopefully) that they blended in well. I forget how the copy-line went, but it was pretty crass, I know that. And yet I could imagine the posters working: they presented the sort of nostalgic images mothers would love, and the clothes themselves were cutesy-stylish enough for those same mothers not to feel they were regressing their infants. I couldn't make up my mind whether the message was blatant or subtle, but if they were successful I was sure a lot of credit would be due to Midge's artwork.

Because of her moderate fame and my ability to keep in

regular employment musically speaking, obtaining a mortgage was no great problem, even though we wanted it in joint names and we were only cohabiting. Probably the fact that either one of us could have coped easily with the repayments on our own had a lot to do with the Building Society manager's favourable attitude. Not that we were seeking that much; we'd been tucking away savings into that very Society for such an event ever since we'd been together, and the amount had risen to a tidy heap.

We managed to get down to the cottage only a couple of times over the next few weeks, and on both days the weather was overcast so the effect was not quite the same as before. Sunshine can produce all kinds of warmth, not just physical. I was even more pleased, though, for on both occasions the place looked better to me.

I arranged for a firm of local builders to invade as soon as final contracts were exchanged, providing them with a list of faults that required urgent attention, and another list of lesser defects that would also need treatment afterwards. Painting and decorating we could manage ourselves, but anything that smacked of technical skill had to be tackled by them. We agreed a date for the workmen to start, and on that very morning came the odd phone call.

Midge was out in the rain on a shopping expedition and I was re-stringing my Martin, feeling slightly ashamed that I'd allowed the instrument to die on me, when O'Malley, the foreman, came on the line. He wanted to know if I'd made a mistake with my faults list. There was water in the kitchen to be sure, and the inside wall that backed onto the embankment would need complete damp-coursing, but he couldn't for the life of him locate any dampness in the walls upstairs at all (no, he didn't add another 'at all' – he wasn't *quite* that kind of Irishman). And what did I mean by the crack in the lintel over the range? The stone looked perfectly okay to him. The floor-to-ceiling split in the bedroom wasn't as bad as I'd indicated, either; it could easily be repaired. There were one or two rotted windowframes that would need replacing, but for the life of him he couldn't locate the dangerous stairboard. The roof certainly needed fixing, unless I liked sleeping under the stars, but the water tank wasn't too badly rusted; however, he advised replacing that to save problems later.

I don't know if I was more taken aback at finding such an honest builder, or at apparently having exaggerated Gramarye's failings. Whichever, it was good news, if puzzling. I instructed O'Malley to carry on with whatever he felt was necessary, and returned to stringing the guitar, mystified yet chuffed at the same time.

I told Midge the news when she returned from her shopping trip, drenched from the rain, hair matted flat around her face. She stood there, dripping on the carpet, her expression one of bewilderment. We had written the list together from notes we'd made on one of our trips to the cottage, so there was no question of overactive imagination on my part. I remember remarking at the time that the defects were not as bad as I'd first thought, but they were still *there*, and very apparent. We discussed the mystery throughout the day and into the evening, but still hadn't reached any satisfactory conclusion by bedtime. We fell asleep still wondering.

Too busy to consider it much over the next few days: I was tied up with recording sessions, mainly for advertising jingles – very lucrative – and Midge had embarked on a series of illustrations for a new book – something of a departure for her this time because it was for farmhouse recipes. We also had to organise our future lives: sending out change-of-address cards, arranging for electricity and the phone to be switched back on at the cottage, the cesspit to be cleared, signing cheques for this, that, and God knows what else, buying odd bits of furniture we'd need, having a brand new electric cooker installed . . . the list went on.

Bob managed to find me, at a low cost, an unemployed Ford Cargo Box 3-tonner, usually used for transporting musical equipment to and from gigs, plus a couple of humpers to go with it (humpers are the trolls who manhandle massive amplifiers, etc. from show to show), so a professional removal company wasn't necessary.

Moving Day was set and Midge and I declined any further engagements or commissions for a whole month. We figured it would take all of that time at least to get straight, and although we weren't exactly flush with cash after all the outgoings we certainly had enough to carry us through – the gods had been very kind. Midge's posters had been accepted by the kiddies'-wear people, by the way, and under Big Val's financial terms of 2¼ per cent interest for non-payment two weeks after delivery date (you had to be good to get away with this) the fee was already in the bank. My session work was paid on a three-hourly basis and gratefully received at the end of each day's or half-day's work.

It was a fine morning for a change on Moving Day and we stood in our now empty apartment, the van loaded and waiting downstairs. We were suddenly wistful: we'd had good times in this place, even though we'd yearned for something more, something that would be our own. And love had deepened here.

We hugged each other and took one long, last, look around. Then we left.

With the humpers following close behind in the van, we drove down to Hampshire, the New Forest, and Gramarye.

IN

By six o'clock that evening the humpers, with tenners in their pockets and tired grins on their faces, were gone, leaving Midge and me alone in Gramarye.

Standing at the door, we watched the empty 3-tonner disappear around the curve in the road, and even then we lingered awhile, drawing in the slowly cooling air. I let my gaze wander over the grassy stretches and woodland opposite the cottage, wondering if the road ever became really busy, and if the quietness of it all might eventually send me slightly crazy. From Baron's Court to the wilderness in one bold leap. Daunting.

But I felt good, oh so *good*. Exhausted too, but pleasantly so; I didn't resent my aching muscles at all. I pulled Midge close and she slipped an arm around my waist, resting her head against my shoulder.

'I'm so happy, Mike,' she said softly. 'I can't tell you how much. Gramarye means so much to me.'

I smiled and kissed her forehead. 'Me too, Pixie. Me too. I think we made the right decision. Look, even the flowers out there have revived themselves to make us welcome.'

'It must be all the rain we've been having lately. The colours are so beautiful.'

'No need to look far for your inspiration around here.'

'I've got all I need right beside me.'

'Yuk.'

'I know, but it feels good to tell you.' Her pale eyes shone up at me. 'Things are going to work, aren't they, Mike?'

'No question. Things are gonna be terrific. God, I feel a song coming on!'

'Spare me that!'

'I can't help myself!'

I opened my mouth wide, but she dug me in the ribs. 'You'll frighten the animals.'

'Oh yeah. Forgot. Jeez, I could sleep for a week.'

'Can I get you a beer?'

'You mean Igor and Mongo didn't finish 'em off?'

'I kept them too busy shifting furniture. One half-hour for beer and sandwiches was all any of you were allowed.'

'I remember. You know what I'd really like?'

'You said you were tired.'

'Not that. Well, not right at this moment. No, I'd like some tea.'

'Can this be the same hellraiser I shared a flat with in London? Must be the pure country air. Not even coffee?'

'No. I'm in the mood for tea.'

'Simply because you're near me.'

'Funny but when you're –' I began to sing. Then, 'Just put the kettle on.'

She skipped inside, chuckling to herself.

I strolled to the front gate and heard a car approaching. It soon appeared round the bend and I watched it pass by, thinking entertainment sure was spare in this neck of the woods. The Citroën's occupants gawked back at me and I gave them a friendly wave. One of the two passengers, a girl in the back seat, smiled and then the car was gone, leaving only a faint smell of engine fumes in the air.

The show over, I sauntered back down the path, taking in the chocolate-box view of the cottage with its brooding woodland behind, the wild array of flowers enlivening the foreground. I experienced a deep flush of contentment. This new life might take some getting used to and there was still a lot of hard graft ahead to make the place comfortable, but the good vibes were already weaving their spell, calming and delighting me at the same time, alerting my senses to everything that was around. I was acutely aware of Midge's presence within those irregular-shaped walls, as if she had instantly become a part of Gramarye's personality, a little of its essence. She belonged in such a setting.

I stopped dead. Hold on here, I admonished myself. Let's not get carried away. I wouldn't like to upset you, Mrs Chaldean, but we're talking about bricks and mortar with a pleasant view, not a goddamn shrine. Shaking my head at my own cogitations, I walked on.

I came to a halt once more when I noticed the chaffinch on the doorstep. The bird's back was to me as it peered into the gloom inside with jerky stretching movements, occasionally cocking its head to one side as if listening for something. I waited, not wishing to scare it off; this was my first close encounter of the feathered kind.

Midge appeared inside the doorway and she was moving smoothly forward, cooing a gentle welcome. She knelt as she drew close and I was surprised that the chaffinch didn't hop back or fly away. It watched with bold interest.

Midge had breadcrumbs in her outstretched hand and she offered them to the bird, who eyed them with suspicion. I remained frozen, enjoying the scene. Midge placed the crumbs on the floor just inside the doorway, only inches away from the bird. The chaffinch cocked its head again and watched her, ignoring the food. Then it hopped to the very edge of the step and I felt sure it would venture inside. Not so, though; it skipped back again, gave one loud chirp that could have been a 'good-bye' and off it flew.

We both laughed as the bird swooped and glided around the garden before disappearing into the nearby woods, and I think that little episode made Midge's day.

'That's it,' I said good-humouredly as I went into the cottage. 'Now they know we're here they'll be expecting a house-warming party.'

'We'd make them welcome,' replied Midge, her face flushed with joy.

Still grinning, I crossed the room and squatted down by

the wall, running my fingers across the surface there, feeling for any dampness.

'Looks like O'Malley and his crew did a good job,' I remarked. 'Did you get a chance to take a look at that crack in the wall upstairs?'

Midge was busy opening a cardboard box containing easy-fix food. 'Yes,' she answered, delving in. 'You wouldn't know it'd been there. The whole room's been painted over so there are no marks at all. You hungry yet?'

'Something light'll do.'

'Something light is all you'll get. I'll pop into the village tomorrow and stock up, but for now, pizza, burgers, or soup?'

'Uh, soup. Let's give it an hour or so, though, to get straight.'

'Okay.' She brought over the mug of tea she'd already made. 'Water's running clear, by the way.'

'Yeah, I already checked.' I stood and took the mug from her. 'Seems like we're set, doesn't it?' I guess by now my grin had turned a little sloppy. My free hand curled around the back of her neck.

Her eyes began to glisten with moisture and there was no need for her to reply, no need at all.

Later we relaxed on the old, rooted bench at the back of the cottage, watching the sun sink lower into the darkening wood-land and dunking the last of our bread into mugfuls of hot soup. The evening was still warm and we were bathed in a soft glow, the white walls of Gramarye hued a pale pink. O'Malley's men had worked expertly on those walls, scraping them clean and repairing, then giving them a couple of coats of cement-based masonry paint. We could hear the chatter of birds getting ready for bed, and occasionally the muted sound of a passing car drifted round the corner of the cottage from the road.

Most of the essential stuff had been unpacked: my music gear, still in cases or under covers, was in one of the attic rooms I intended to use for writing and taping; Midge's art equipment and drawing board was in the round room, which would obviously be our living room, but in which she had decided she would also like to work. It was a sensible arrangement and one we were used to, her particular occupation being so unobtrusive anyway. I'd fixed up our bed next door to the freshly painted room, neither of us wanting to breathe in fumes while we slept; because the latter was slightly bigger, we'd move the bed in there when the smell of paint had faded. Framed paintings leaned in stacks against the walls, and ornaments stood in various groups around the place like friends sticking together in a strange environment; but chairs and tables and lamps and things were more or less positioned – refining could be done over the next few days. Big Val had rung earlier to make sure we'd settled in okay; fortunately she was never one to waste time on idle chit-chat, and the line was awful anyway, so Midge wasn't on the phone for long. We'd decided to quit as soon as the sun was halfway down its lazy glide.

'Tastes good,' I said, smacking my lips appreciatively.

'You're sure you don't need something more?'

'This is fine. Too tired to be hungry.'

'Mm, me too. Doesn't the forest look tantalising with the sun turning its roof reddy-brown, while underneath it's so dark and mysterious.'

'Looks kinda creepy to me.' I finished the last of the soup and put the empty mug down beside me, picking up a can of beer as I straightened again.

'And already there's a mist rising.'

'Must be pretty water-logged out there in the open with all the rain.' I pulled the tab and drank from the can. 'D'you think it gets really cold here at night?'

'Maybe a bit more than city boys are used to, but I don't think you'll need your thermals for a while yet.'

'Bet it gets dark too. No street lamps.'

Midge stretched out her slim legs, her shoulders snuggling down against the back of the bench. 'You'll get used to it, Mike.' She sighed long and deep, a comfortable sigh, and said, 'It's good to be back.'

'Still a country girl at heart, eh?'

'I suppose I must be. Nine years in the city can't completely eradicate an upbringing, nor would I want it to.' The change in mood was swift – often the case with Midge. She lowered her eyes. 'I wish they could have seen Gramarye, Mike; I know they would have loved it here.'

Putting down the can, I took her hand in both of mine and held on to it.

She said quietly, 'I think they had hopes of me eventually marrying a nice country vet, or a parson.' She smiled, but it was an expression of sadness. 'Dad would have loved that. Imagine the long evenings they'd have spent talking shop.'

'He wouldn't have found much in common with me.'

'Oh, Mike, I didn't mean it like that. Dad would have loved you. You're both very alike in many ways.'

'I'd have liked him, Midge. From all you've told me, I think I'd have loved him too.'

'Mother would have thought you a rascal. That's how she'd have put it – a *rascal*. And she'd have enjoyed that.'

The first tear emerged to dampen her cheek. 'It was so cruel, Mike, so horribly cruel.'

My arm went around her shoulders and I moved my head close to hers. 'You've got to try and forget that part of it. They'd have wanted you to remember the good things.'

'It's impossible to forget what happened to them.'

'Then accept. Accept the cruelty of that along with all the good times. And think of how proud they would have been of you now.'

'That's what hurts. They can't know, they can never know about my work, about you . . . about – about this place. It would have meant so much to them. And to me, it would have meant so much to have them proud of me.'

There wasn't a lot I could say, so I just held her close and let her weep, hoping as I had many times before that the tears were part of her letting go, each measure of outward grief part of the healing process. How much hurt was still locked deep inside, I had no way of knowing, but I could be patient; she was worth that.

'I'm sorry, Mike,' she said after a while. 'I didn't mean to spoil everything.'

I kissed away tears. 'You haven't. Here and now, with

me, is a good time for you to cry. I only wish there was more I could do to ease it for you.'

'You've always helped, you've always understood. I know it's foolish of me to be still grieving after all these years . . .'

'There's no special time limit for such things, Midge, there's no clock you can suddenly switch off. It has to run down on its own.' I lifted her chin with my finger. 'Just remember what the doctor told you: don't let that sorrow taint everything else. You've a right to be happy, and that's what your parents would have wanted.'

'Am I that bad?'

'No, not at all. Though it's when you're at your most contented that memories seem to edge their way in.'

'That's when I miss them so.'

I felt inadequate, as I suppose we all do at such times, and all I could offer was the comfort of my arms and the depth of my own feelings for her. Her weeping had stopped, the darkness in her spirit relenting enough to allow other emotions to seep through.

Her kiss was tender and my senses sank into hers. I was used to the sensuous intensity of our intimacy, especially after tears had been shed, but now I was almost overwhelmed. When we finally broke away from each other, I literally felt dizzy and had to draw in breath like a swimmer emerging from a long dive. Midge, too, was a little shaky.

'This country air has a weird effect,' I quipped and was unable to control a mild tremor in my voice.

'I think . . . I think we should go in,' she said, her face bathed in a warm glow from the setting sun. Although there wasn't a hint of lasciviousness in her tone, we both recognised our mutual need.

I stood, bringing her up with me. 'Been a busy day,' I murmured.

'Been a long day,' she responded.

'Need our rest.'

Midge only nodded. Taking my hand, she led me towards the door, but we stopped in surprise when we saw into one of the windows of the cottage. I heard Midge gasp and her hand tightened in mine.

The round room looked as if it were ablaze, so vividly did the sun's dying rays reflect from the curved walls.

Yet there was nothing frightening about the phenomenon, for the radiance was peaceful, strangely calming in its effulgence, with no fierceness to it at all. We watched, and even our shadows were suffused into a soft hue against the redness.

I turned to Midge and for one crazy moment I thought I saw tiny fires playing in her eyes, but when she blinked they were gone, and only reflected warmth shone from her. She looked serene standing there, her lips curved in a small, knowing smile, her hair coloured a rich auburn by the sun behind, and for some reason I felt a tiny stab of . . . I don't know – unease, nervousness? I couldn't define the sensation.

This time, it was I who led her away. We went inside and I locked and bolted the doors. We were more drowsy than either of us had realised, the tiredness falling rapidly like a warm smothering blanket, making our movements slow, almost sluggish. We undressed, leaving our clothes where they fell, and climbed wearily into bed.

We slept, but I've no idea for how long. When we woke, it was together, as one, as if we'd sensed each other's rousing, and there was total darkness around us; again, there was no fear in this black void. Midge reached out for me and I moved to her.

Then we drifted back into a deep encompassing sleep.

NOISES

The sounds of tapping woke me, sharp noises in various rhythms, breaking into my dreamless sleep. My eyes opened with none of their usual reluctance and I twisted my head towards Midge to find her wide awake and smiling happily. She was peering over me at the window beyond, the source of the tapping.

Turning my head the other way to follow her gaze, I spotted the culprits. Three or four birds were perched on the window ledge and they were pecking at the glass as though indignant that we were still in bed.

'Oh Christ,' I moaned. 'Did you put in an alarm call?'

'No, they took it on themselves to get us up.'

'What time is it?'

'Just after six-thirty.'

'I don't believe it. You think they're a permanent feature?'

'Likely as not. It's lovely, isn't it?'

I pulled the pillow over my head, although in truth I was wide awake. 'Quiet would be lovelier.'

'All part of country living, Michael. It certainly beats the sound of rush-hour traffic and pneumatic drills.'

'Only just.'

She whipped back the covers and crawled across me to reach the window. I rolled over into the warm space she had left behind.

'Say hello from me,' I told her, pulling the sheets up around my chin.

She stooped close to the window and I relished the sight of her naked little rear. Although there wasn't an ounce of unnecessary flesh on Midge's body, there were delicately sensuous curves there that never failed to delight and absorb me. I wanted her back in bed.

She cooed at the birds and began a conversation with them. Even when she tapped the glass on this side, they didn't fly away. Instead they cocked their heads and chirped all the more loudly, while others fluttered above them, their wings brushing against the panes.

'I think they're demanding breakfast,' Midge called back to me. 'I bet Mrs Chaldean fed them all the time.'

'Well, tell 'em Gramarye is under new management. No freebies any more.'

I'd closed my eyes for a few moments in case sleep wanted to snuggle back in, and the next thing I knew, Midge's weight was sprawled across me.

'You pretend you're so mean,' she said, tweaking my exposed nose painfully, 'but underneath that rough, grizzled exterior lies a heart of pure . . .' another tweak '. . . granite.'

I twisted onto my back and she straddled me, her eyes gleaming with mischievous pleasure. It was hard to protest with the pink tips of two small but beautiful breasts hovering only inches away from my lips.

'You're embarrassing the wildlife,' I told her.

She ducked her head to kiss me, her tongue a soft-stabbing probe, her mouth moist and sweet. My hands broke cover and reached out to grasp her hips.

The vixen was only toying with me, though. 'We've got a lot to do,' she whispered in my ear, not forgetting to dampen that orifice with her wayward tongue, just to ensure all my senses were fully alert. 'I'll go down and start the breakfast while you shave and generally make yourself civilised.'

'Hey, it's early,' I whispered back, not wishing to make the birds blush. 'And anyway, we've got a whole month to get ourselves organised. This is our very first morning and it

69

should be celebrated.' By now my tongue was doing its own persuading.

False coyness wasn't part of Midge's nature: what she enjoyed, she embraced. She embraced me.

Lifting the sheets, I pulled her in and her body, cold from the early-morning air, was delicious against mine. Now Midge and I had always been compatible in the fullest meaning of the word – our bodies, not just our personae, seemed to have been made for each other (and I mean that literally) – and our love-making had always been *beyond* this side of heaven; but the mutual ecstasy we experienced that first morning in our new home was far greater than anything that had gone before. Don't ask me why, just call it magic. Yeah, just call it Magic.

Later, dressed in old sweater, faded jeans and sneakers (my usual uniform), I followed Midge down and found her in her dressing gown crouched on the kitchen doorstep, feeding the multitude. The birds – wrens, blue and great tits, wagtails, chaffinch, a real multi-racial gathering it seemed – showed hardly any caution, a few of them actually pecking food from her hand, while others advanced within touching distance. I noted that size had nothing to do with boldness.

Midge was gently encouraging them with words I couldn't hear, and I chuckled when a wren perched on her wrist and dipped into the palm of her hand with its tiny pointed beak. I waited until the last slice of bread had been broken up and the pieces devoured before I stepped from the stairs into the room. An invigorating freshness breezed into the kitchen from the open front door and, although it was still early morning, there was no intrusive chill.

'Heeey, what's this?' I pointed to the table where the breakfast setting included a bottle of champagne and a glass jug of orange juice.

Midge looked over her shoulder and smiled up at me. 'Another part of our celebration. I smuggled the bottle inside a packing case yesterday.' She stood, brushing crumbs from her hands. The birds outside continued their chatter, perhaps demanding a second course. I went to Midge and squeezed her so hard she gasped.

'You're something else,' I said, and my voice was husky-soft.

'The birds have eaten your breakfast,' she responded.

My grip on her loosened. 'Tell me that ain't so.'

She nodded gravely, but didn't stop smiling. 'I was going to give you Buck's Fizz and toast, but what was left of the bread from yesterday went to our feathered friends. There were so many of them I got carried away. Sorry.'

'You're sorry.'

'I'll get to the shops as soon as they're open, I promise.'

'The cupboard's really bare?'

'There's a few stale biscuits left . . .'

'Wonderful.' My voice was flat, but I was only posing and she knew it.

She stood on tip-toe to kiss me. 'You open the bubbly and I'll get the biscuits.'

'You sure your pals don't want the champagne too? Maybe they could bath in it.'

My nose took a tweaking again and she scurried away to the adjoining room where the biscuits were presumably mouldering.

As it turned out, breakfast was terrific. Even Midge, who normally would never touch the grape, had some champagne with her orange juice, and we toasted each other's health and happiness and sexual prowess, and we munched on the biscuits (which were not too bad, incidentally) in between. Our third or fourth salutation was to Gramarye and our mugs clunked together – as yet we hadn't unpacked the glasses – in a most satisfactory way. Those of the birds who were still interested watched from the open doorway, no doubt wondering what we were cackling over.

After 'breakfast' it was all business. Midge bathed and dressed while I washed the mugs and re-corked what was left of the champagne (bad form, I know, but I wasn't going to waste it). I took another look at the lintel over the old cooking range while I was in that part of the kitchen, still puzzled by the fact that the hairline crack had apparently sealed itself.

Funny how memory can accommodate the mind when things are illogical; I suppose it's a reflexive instinct because we need some kind of mental order to prevent ourselves from going crazy. I began to reason that what we'd actually seen was a shrivelled cobweb matted against the side of the dark stone, and it had only *looked* like a crack to us in what was, after all, an area of dim light.

Partially satisfied with my theory, I started unpacking what was left inside the cardboard boxes and was pleased when I came across the transistor radio. I switched it on and jumped when the static roared out at me. Quickly turning down the volume, I tried tuning in to a clear station and when I hit music I extended then swivelled the aerial. The reception was still crackly. Thinking the batteries might be running down, I reached back inside the box and found the mains lead, which I attached to the radio and plugged into a wall socket. The heavy static persisted.

Muttering to myself, I switched off the set, turning as footsteps sounded on the stairs.

'Problems?' asked Midge as she entered the room.

'We must be in a bad reception area,' I told her, 'although I'm surprised it's this bad. We may need an outside aerial, maybe on the roof.'

She didn't seem concerned. 'All right, I'm just off,' she said. 'Anything you need from the village?'

'Uh, I'll probably remember when you get back. Watch yourself with the locals, 'specially those with bug-eyes and high foreheads.'

She gave me a reproving glare, then blew a kiss and was gone. I sauntered to the door and watched her hurry down the path, stooping to sniff at flowers here and there as she went. She waved back at me from the gate, then climbed into the car and started the engine. Pulling hard left to swing the Passat off the grass verge, Midge gave me a final wave goodbye. The car disappeared around the bend and I was alone in the cottage.

I loitered in the doorway for a short while, enjoying the bright freshness of the day, a little light-headed from the champagne and orange juice.

So far, so good, I told myself.

The rest of the morning was spent unpacking, moving furniture, reassembling units, fitting plugs, looking for items that had gone astray – the usual run of things when you move house and begin to wonder if your life will ever be organised again. Fortunately, having lived in an apartment for so long, albeit a large one, we didn't have that much furniture to bring with us; even so, what we had was easily adequate for Gramarye.

Eventually I found myself upstairs in one of the attic rooms which, I have to admit, was the place I'd been itching to get to all morning. That's where my musical equipment had been put, you see, and was the intended location for my own simple recording studio. I squatted on one of my amps and considered the problems.

Noise was one. I don't mean noise going out – who the hell could it bother? – but the sounds coming *in* might prove a nuisance. I didn't want every tape I made during the day to have a bird chorus. Fibreglass panels alternated with equal amounts of battening for bounce-back should overcome that particular problem, and two layers of plasterboard would also be needed for the ceiling. The room's two small windows would either have to be double-glazed or blocked in.

I mentally positioned a mixing desk, mastering machine and patch bay, forgetting for the moment the high cost of such equipment, content to enjoy the dream. Racks would be awkward because of the sloping roof, but the nineteen-inch assembling units could be spread outwards instead of up if necessary.

What pleased me was that the atmosphere in the attic room felt so good. Certainly there was a mustiness about the place, but that could soon be cleared by leaving the windows open for a few days and installing heating for the colder times. I wondered what the acoustics were like and immediately reached for the pride of my guitars, a Martin 28.

When I took the instrument from its case I was surprised to find it needed hardly any re-tuning after the move down. I chorded an E and the sound was rich and beautifully full, mellow but with that touch of hardness which could be softened or exaggerated depending on how the strings were struck. I did a few progressions, a few intricate runs, a few licks; I tried subtle augmentives and melancholy diminisheds and minor 7ths, loving the sounds, touching bass notes, taking lightning fingers up to the highest frets, filling the room and my ears and my mind with music, relishing one of those rare and exhilarating occasions when I felt total master of the axe.

Only the noises from the loft brought my playing to an abrupt halt and my head back to the attic.

I stared upwards and I'm sure my mouth was agape.

No sounds now. Had I imagined them? I scanned the ceiling, my search coming to rest on the small square hatch that led into the loft. Rising slowly and wishing I hadn't watched so many horror movies in my misspent youth, I stepped forward so that I was directly below the hatch. My head tilted back and I examined the trapdoor that was only a couple of feet or so above.

My heart boogied when the sounds came again. I shuffled backwards, almost knocking over the Martin balanced against an amplifier. I grabbed the neck to save the guitar from toppling and its strings vibrated metallically. My grip tightened across them to kill the noise.

I had no such control over the other noises, though. They came again, a kind of scratching scurrying. Maybe not quite that, but it was difficult to define.

Ahh come on! I said to myself, going into one of my self-conversation modes, a way of goading myself on when I was uneasy about a situation. *You're acting like a maiden aunt! The first time you're on your own in your new home and a couple of unexpected noises make you piss-scared. So there are mice up there. What can they do? Nibble you to death? It's an old house and bound to have lots of little creatures skulking around. Hell, this is the countryside and full of non-rent-paying lodgers! Birds, mice, spiders –*

But the cottage was empty before.

No, you just didn't find anything on that particular day. Now get up there and take a look.

Dragging over the room's one and only chair, I placed it beneath the hatch. The noises had died off, but that was no encouragement.

I didn't know why I felt so nervous – something to do with 'fear of the unknown', I imagined – but my knees were less than firm when I climbed up onto that chair.

Now my face was only a few inches away from the trapdoor and I listened intently. Nothing there. Huh! No manacled, grey-haired, claw-fingernailed, dressed-in-tatters loony whom old Ma Chaldean had kept locked away for the past half-century because he, she – *IT!* – was the unfortunate product of family inbreeding. Oh no. No clinking of chains up there, no demented howls, just . . .

. . . Oh Christ, just that scurrying scratching sound. There it goes again, on the other side of the wood.

I stretched up a hand that wasn't very steady. The fingers flattened against the surface. I pushed.

The trapdoor resisted for about half a second, then lifted. Only an inch, that's all I opened it. Blackness inside hung on to its secret. I slowly began to straighten my arm and the gap widened like a dark and toothless mouth . . .

'Mike!'

I nearly toppled from the chair as the trapdoor banged shut (I thought I heard more scurrying noises up there). I hesitated, hand poised to try again, but Midge's voice called from the stairs once more.

'Mike, I'm back! Where are you? Come on, I've got something hot – well, it was hot – for your lunch! I raced back from the village so it wouldn't get too cold! Mike, can you hear me?'

'Yup!' I called down.

I glanced back at the closed hatch and shrugged. I was in no hurry to find out what was up there. Probably only mice in the rafters. Plenty of time to look later. Besides, I'd had hardly any breakfast and I was famished.

That was my excuse, anyway.

I jumped off the chair and went down to lunch.

THE GREY HOUSE

The 'hot' pasties Midge had bought in the village may have been lukewarm by the time we got to eat them, but they were delicious and filling. I wolfed down two to her one, and reached into the bag of apples she'd also brought home.

'I'll cook a proper meal tonight,' she said.

'This is great,' I told her between bites. 'How was Cantrip?'

'Okay. The people in the shops were very friendly once they discovered where I lived.'

'You told them?'

'They asked me in the greengrocer's and the baker's if I were just passing through. I thought they were a bit reserved until I let them know I was going to be a regular customer. Even then they looked suspicious until I told them we'd moved into Gramarye. They really opened up after that.'

'They say anything about old Ma Chaldean?'

'Mike, don't call her that.'

I looked towards the ceiling. 'No offence, Flora. Just my way.'

'They didn't talk much about her, but I gathered she was something of a local legend; someone who kept very much to herself, though.'

'That's not surprising living all the way out here.'

'It's not so far from town.'

'It might have been for an old lady. Y'know, we never did find out what she died of.'

'Old age, I'd imagine,' Midge replied, and there was an element of regret in her voice. 'I hope she didn't suffer alone out here.'

'I doubt it. She'd have called a neighbour or friends on the phone, I'm sure. The social services hereabouts probably kept a close eye on her as well. All the same, life must have been sad for her, living on her own, with no relatives, not seeing many people.'

Midge twisted in her chair so that she could see out of the open kitchen window. 'I don't think so. I don't think she was ever really lonely in Gramarye.' Her eyes were not focused on the view outside, but on somewhere distant, not on this planet.

'You're getting weird, Midge,' I warned.

She laughed, instantly back in this time and space. 'Weird, am I? Who used to lie down on railway tracks and make me swear undying love? Who eats hardboiled eggs with the shell still on? Who came home on New Year's dawn wearing a policeman's helmet and no trousers? Who –'

I held up a hand. 'The egg was for a bet. Anyway, that was in my youth.'

'The helmet escapade was two years ago.'

'See how I've aged? Come on, we've got work to do.' My policy is to change the subject when on shaky ground. I rose from the table, the chair scraping against the floor tiles. Midge reached out and touched my arm.

'You've worked hard all morning, so why don't we take a break? There's no great urgency to get everything finished at once.'

'There's a lot of scrubbing, painting . . .'

'We haven't explored yet. Let's go for a walk, get some fresh air, find out just where we're living.'

'I don't know . . .' I said as if pondering.

'You're such a fakeout, d'you know that? You can't wait to get out of all those chores.'

I grinned. 'You're right. They'll still be here tomorrow. Shall we drive somewhere?'

'No.' She disdainfully drew out the word. 'I want to look at our surroundings. I want to go into the forest.'

'That place? You mean it's real? I thought it was just a set.'

'Titter, titter,' she said, shaking her head.

Outside, warm air wafted over me as if I'd opened an oven door and I could feel its goodness seeping through to my bones. A bee droned by and hovered over flowers, spoilt for choice. A fluttering above our heads caused me to turn and look up; I saw there were birds nesting in the eaves of the roof.

'So that was it,' I said aloud.

Midge regarded me curiously. 'That was what?' She followed my gaze.

'I thought we had mice in the loft. I was just getting ready to take a look earlier when you called me. It must have been birds mooching around up there.'

'Inside?'

'I'm not sure. They could have got through the eaves. I'll check it out later.'

'My man,' she sighed, and dodged my pinching fingers.

We climbed the embankment on the straight side of the cottage rather than take the steps round the curve, me pulling Midge up behind, grasping a tree branch that leaned over from the top of the incline for support. We crossed the stretch of grass, scrub and single trees and, hand in hand, like babes, we went into the woods.

That wasn't quite as easy as it sounds, because first we had to find a way through the tangle of bracken and blackberry bushes which formed a dense barrier along the forest's edge. There were several openings, but not all were obvious at first glance and some only led into a second line of defence. Still, we eventually found a way in and it wasn't long before the cottage behind us was lost from view and the air had become gloomy damp. Our feet sank into what felt like a springy deep-pile carpet and Midge informed me that the topsoil was formed by dead leaves, plants and decomposing animals. The last part made me feel uncomfortable and it didn't help when she further informed me that what we walked on was filled with living organisms that broke down and rotted the above-mentioned. That was how the forest thrived rather than becoming cluttered up with litter year after year – nothing was wasted, every dead thing, plant or animal, contributed to the life of something else. Interesting, I told her, and so it was.

Enjoying herself, she pointed out trees and things, not in an attempt to broaden this city slicker's education, but to get me interested and *involved* in my new environment. Oak, ash, sycamore, maple – I began to appreciate the different shapes and characteristics (not that I was quite as dumb as I pretended). She explained that there were several layers to a forest. Subsoil, topsoil, and the field layer, which included herbaceous and woody plants, tree saplings, bracken and stuff. Then there was the shrub layer which contained the flowering shrubs such as hawthorn, dogwood, elder, etc. These were topped by the forest roof, or canopy as she called it; up there was where most of the big boys nested, predators like the tawny owl and the sparrow-hawk, along with others such as the carrion crow, magpie and that bunch.

I mention all this not as a nature lesson, but as an indication of how keen Midge was to indoctrinate – no, wrong word: *instruct* is better – me in the ways of the countryside. She dearly wanted me to become part of it, as was she, knowing in her Midge-wise way that I'd need substitute interests now that I was away from the hustle of our other life-style.

And I played along with her, not just to please, but because I genuinely wanted to embrace this different kind of world. You could say I'd become a little disillusioned with the last one, although again that wouldn't be entirely accurate; I think I was just looking for something more, maybe something better than I'd known so far. That's probably true of most of us, I suppose, but not many get the opportunity to change. Maybe if I'd known what I was going to find I wouldn't have been so eager.

We stopped by a fallen tree, much of the insides rotted

away to a brown clumpy powder, dark green moss creeping up what was left of the bark. Ferns did their best to camouflage the trunk further, but the tree's deadness hung around the quiet glade like a ghost over a grave. Bright red patches caught my eye and I moved forward for a closer inspection.

Squatting down, I said over my shoulder to Midge, 'Take a look at these, then tell me there's no such thing as pixies and elves.'

'I never said there weren't.' She knelt close to me. 'Oh. I should leave those alone if I were you, Mike.'

I prodded the toadstools with a finger. The cluster could have come from a child's storybook, something from one of Midge's paintings, so fairy-tale did they appear with their light stalks and scarlet roofs dotted with white patches.

'Poisonous?' I asked, fascinated.

'They'll give you a very nasty tummy for a few days. They're fly agaric mushrooms, and most definitely not for eating.'

'They look pretty enough. You think there are any elves at home?' I tapped on a roof.

'Elves don't come out when there are humans around. Let's leave them in peace or they may get cross.'

Hands against knees, I pushed myself up. 'Right. I don't want any hex put on me.' I looked at her seriously and said, 'I wonder if there's –'

'No, Mike, you'll only find those kind of "magic" mushrooms in some parts of Wales as far as I know. I very much doubt if they grow in Hampshire.'

I could tell she wasn't pleased with my curiosity and I drew her close. 'Hey, you know I wouldn't touch anything like that.'

She relaxed into me. 'The thought frightens me, Mike. If anything happened to you like before . . .'

The words were left suspended, but Midge was referring to my bad old days and ways when I toked a little, snorted some – nothing heavy, no needles, just pass-around stuff that was hard to avoid, moving in my particular circle of musician friends. One night at a party someone had slipped me some bad coke. I'd turned blue, they told me later, and was out of

80

it for three days. Midge had never left my side all the time I was just hanging on, my breathing a touch-and-go thing, and she nursed me through the aftermath, never once scolding, always caring, treating me like a sick baby. I was lucky to pull through with no brain damage and no police prosecution – I guess they thought I'd had enough punishment, and anyway, it wasn't me who was in possession. As far as drugs were concerned, that was it for me. No more, never again. They hadn't been exactly a habit before, and I'd never been on the really hard stuff, so leaving them alone wasn't difficult. But maybe now you'll understand why I was so shaken when I'd mildly freaked out in Gramarye's round room on that first day. Some mistakes in life are hard to escape from.

I cuddled Midge and stroked her hair, the quietness of the forest itself producing its own calming effect.

'You still trust me, Midge?'

Her reply came unreservedly. 'Of course I do. I don't want to be that scared for anyone ever again, that's all.'

She looked so small and forlorn I couldn't help but smile. 'I'd cut off a leg rather than cause you worry,' I said.

She sniffed, but the traces of a smile appeared at the corners of her mouth. 'Where would I keep a spare leg?'

'You'd find leg-room somewhere.'

She groaned so loud a bird fluttered from a nearby bush. 'That's awful.' She picked up broken leaves and threw them at me. 'That's really *awful*!'

Ducking and brushing the debris from my hair, I ran from her. She followed with more woodland dust in both hands, but sprawled over a hidden branch, hitting the deck in a shower of crumbly leaves.

She swore and I waggled a finger at her. 'Now, now, what would all the little kiddie fans think if they heard that kind of talk? Did Enid Blyton ever use language like that? Did Christopher Robin ever speak that way to Winnie-the-Pooh?'

I ducked again as the branch she'd tripped on came sailing by my head.

'Tut-tut,' I said. 'Does your publisher know about this vicious streak?'

'I'll get you, Stringer. You just wait, I'll get you.' She

then went on to describe what she intended to do to certain delicate parts of my anatomy once she laid hands on them.

I kept out of reach. 'I can't believe I'm hearing this. Did Gretel ever do such things to Hansel? Was Jill ever like this to Jack? Did the princess ever threaten the handsome newt with such sadism?'

'Frog.'

'What?'

'It was a frog, not a newt.'

'Whatever turns you on, babe.'

She was on her feet and coming at me, so I ran, chuckling at the outraged shrieks from behind. The odd missile bounced off my back as we raced through the trees, but I easily outdistanced her.

We'd come quite a ways through the forest already, following what seemed to be some kind of vague path with several even more vague tributaries branching off, and before I knew it, like stepping across the threshold between night and day, I was out in the open.

Sunlight dazzled me for a moment, but after a few rapid blinks and raising a hand to shield my eyes I found myself looking across a broad sloping meadow. At the bottom, and backdropped by continuing woodland, stood a large grey house – well, a mansion really.

The buildings had two principal storeys with dormer windows set in a hipped roof above, chimney stacks ranged across the top like up-ended boxes. There must have been eight or nine long windows extending along the ground floor and as many smaller windows above those. I could make out a wide flight of steps leading up to a fairly big entrance; there was no porch, but square columns and a cornice projected from the walls to frame the door. The meadow ran directly down to a rectangular turning area, with no lawns to separate them, and the driveway angled around the quoined corner of the house, presumably to a public road through the forest.

The place was certainly isolated and the greyness of the walls gave it a dark broodiness, despite the sunlight. Although the setting was beautiful, I couldn't help but feel there was something very uninviting about the house.

Soft footsteps creeping up from behind and then pincer arms moving around my waist, clawed hands reaching for those delicate parts which I'd run so hard to protect. I grabbed Midge's wrists before she could inflict any damage and she let out a yell of frustration. Turning and crushing her to me so that she was powerless, I bit into her small nose.

She jerked her head away, laughing and breathless at the same time, her wriggling to break free eventually subsiding when she realised the struggle was useless.

'Bully,' she said sulkily, but loving every minute of it.

'Gonna behave?'

'Hummph.'

'What was that? I didn't quite hear.'

'Rat.'

'Agreed. But you haven't answered my question.'

I felt her head nodding against my chest. 'Does that mean yes?'

A muffled grumble and more movement.

'Okay.' I let go, still wary.

She stepped away and kicked my shin.

'You bloody cow!' I yelped, hopping and rubbing my injured leg.

'My dad taught me how to deal with creeps like you before I was out of pig-tails,' she taunted, dancing out of reach.

I sprawled, aiming for her ankles, just managing to grasp one and bringing her down on top of me. We rolled a short way down the sloping meadow, Midge giggling and cursing, beating at me with clenched fists, while I tried to hold on to her, enjoying the feel of our bodies tight against each other's.

We came to a panting stop, me on my back, Midge resting half over me. Her eyes were wide when she saw the house.

'What a strange place,' she said, the words uneven because of her breathlessness.

She sat up and I rested on one elbow to stare with her across the meadow. 'Looks grim, doesn't it,' I remarked.

A breeze swept up the gradual incline, ruffling the grass;

it touched us briefly and sped by. I shivered, although I was warm.

'I wonder who lives there,' said Midge.

'Someone with more money than we'll ever see, and someone who obviously likes privacy. Even the entrance is facing away from the road.'

'It looks . . . it looks empty.'

'Maybe the owners are away, or maybe it's one of those old family estates that nobody can afford to run any more. The past few decades have been tough on quite a few lords of the manor, I hear.'

'No, I didn't mean that kind of empty.' She frowned, trying to put the feeling into words. 'It looks bleak,' she said finally. 'Such a beautiful location, and yet the house seems . . . miserable.' She looked down at me. 'It feels unfriendly.'

'Oh, I wouldn't go that far. Though, of course, there is the possibility that we're trespassing on private land. Somebody around here might get hostile if they see us.'

She was immediately scrambling to her feet.

'Take it easy,' I said, remaining where I was. 'I was only kidding. We haven't seen any private-property signs.'

She turned her head as if looking for approaching game-keepers with loaded shotguns. 'I don't like it here. I feel as though we're being watched.'

I rose, brushing bits of grass off my jeans. 'You're incredible. Nothing could be more peaceful and you've turned to jelly.'

'I just feel uncomfortable. Let's go, can we, Mike?'

Now I regarded her with some concern; there was an anxiety in her tone that the situation hardly called for. 'Okay, Midge,' I said, taking her hand, 'we're on our way.'

We walked back to the trees and I took one last peek at the grey house before entering the shadowy preserve. From that distance, Bleak House looked innocent enough.

We found the injured thrush some time later when we were almost through the woods, returning along the same path as our outward journey (at least Midge assured me it was the same path). She led the way unerringly while I followed behind, fingers tucked into the pockets of my jeans, occasionally whistling the dwarfs' Hi-ho song.

Midge gave me a start when she suddenly stopped dead and pushed out an arm against my chest. I froze, lips still shaped in a whistle.

'What's wrong?' I whispered, but she only waved her hand at me, then crouched low on the path. I heard a frantic scuffling movement and I dropped down myself.

Midge cleared foliage beside the path and a tiny, sharp *cheep* warned her off. The bird peered up at us with black startled eyes and twisted its head around in frightened jerks.

'Oh, poor little guy,' Midge cried sympathetically. 'Look, Mike, he's got a broken wing.'

I shuffled closer on my haunches and the distressed bird flapped at the earth with its good wing, desperate to get away. Midge put out a gentle hand and its struggles immediately calmed, although it still eyed me with some alarm. She cooed softly and to my amazement the bird let her finger stroke its spotted chest.

'He's a mistle thrush,' Midge quietly told me. 'He must have flown into a tree or become tangled in bushes. It doesn't look like he's been attacked by any other animal – there're no signs of blood or wounds anywhere.'

I studied the grey-brown bird for a moment, noticing how Midge's stroking was having an almost hypnotic effect on it; the dark eyes were becoming lidded as though the thrush were nodding off to sleep. 'What are we going to do with it?' I whispered.

'We can't leave him here. He'd never last the night with all the predators in the forest.'

'We can't take it home.'

'Why not? We could keep him safe and warm for tonight, then tomorrow I'll take him into Cantrip or Bunbury, wherever there's a vet.'

'Midge, the bird's wing is too badly broken – you can see how badly twisted it is. Even if the shock doesn't kill it, that wing's never gonna mend.'

'You'd be surprised how tough these little guys are; he can be taken care of, you'll see.' She cupped her hands around the thrush's sides and slowly lifted, the bird protesting only mildly. Midge cradled it against her chest and I think the thrush appreciated the comfort, because the shutters closed down completely and it seemed to fall asleep. She gazed down at the small feathery body snuggled against her with such tenderness that I felt something inside me melting. Soft as I was on her, there was always that capacity for extra lump-in-the-throat softness. Call me a sentimental fool.

We both stood and I put one hand over her shoulder as she led the way back along the path, her movement even more graceful so that the injured thrush would be disturbed as little as possible.

Soon I glimpsed a tiny flash of white ahead, and knew we were approaching the forest edge and Gramarye.

But I also glimpsed something else. At least, I thought I did, because when I tried to focus it was gone.

I thought I'd caught sight of a figure standing some distance away among the trees. Midge's attention was still on the bird cushioned in her hands, so I knew she wouldn't have noticed anything. I squinted my eyes again to sharpen my vision, wondering if I'd merely noticed a shadowy bush shifted by a breeze, and scanned that section of woods. Nope, nobody there.

Yet I found it difficult to shake off the impression of someone standing among the trees. A figure dressed in black, perfectly still and watching. Watching us.

A VISITOR

We relaxed in the round room that evening, Midge lying on the carpet, her head propped up by cushions, me on the sofa with a guitar – a concert Spanish – tucked into my lap, wine bottle and glass on an occasional table by my side. The hurt thrush was downstairs in the kitchen, resting in a cardboard box lined with soft material, and looking pretty snug if a little mournful. Midge had coaxed a small amount of milk-dipped bread into its beak, and had laid out the broken wing as carefully and as comfortably as she could. Now it was up to the bird itself to pull through.

The sun was almost lost behind the trees and the room was bathed in that rich warm light as before, but this time more mellow, somehow deeply soothing. I touched the soft strings of the guitar, and the notes resonated against the curved walls, filling the room with lovely sounds. Midge didn't just look impressed as I moved into a piece I'd had difficulty with for some time, Paganini's Grand Sonata in A (oh yeah, I'm not *only* a rock-'n'-roller) – she looked positively entranced. As I was too, with my own music. No part was hesitated over, nowhere did my fingers stumble. I was overjoyed with my own dexterity, my hands confident and strong, the intricacy and the length of the composition never daunting (it always had been in the past). I made mistakes, of course, but they were lost in the flow of bright music, and when I'd finished, I think even old Segovia himself might have given me the nod. As it was, the wonder on Midge's face was enough.

She crawled over and rested an arm across my knees. 'That was . . .' she gave a quick shake of her head '. . . *brilliant.*'

I held up my hands, palms facing me, and looked at them as though they belonged to someone else. 'Yeah,' I agreed breathlessly. 'I was good, wasn't I? Jesus, I was incredible.'

'More,' she urged. 'Play some more.'

But I laid the guitar down. 'I don't think so, Midge. It's odd, but I don't think I've got any more left in me tonight. Or maybe I don't want to spoil anything – quit while I'm ahead, right?' That was partly the truth – I didn't want to fail with something else – yet there was another reason: I was exhausted. Whatever it had taken to play like that had also drained me of energy, physically and mentally. I slumped back into the sofa, eyes closed and smiling. Oh, that had felt *good!* Midge snuck up beside me and rested her head against my chest.

'There's magic in Gramarye, Mike, and it's working on us both.'

She'd said the words very quietly and I wasn't sure I'd heard them correctly. I reached for the glass of wine and sipped, content to just sit there, with Midge close and the world – if there really was a world out there – peaceful and still.

By this time, of course, I'd dismissed the lurking figure in the woods as imaginary, my own rationality dulling the memory: why should anyone hide once I'd spotted them, and how could they have disappeared so quickly anyway?

Besides, another event had distracted my mind shortly after, when we reached the cottage itself: the kitchen window had been left open and we discovered Gramarye had a visitor.

The red squirrel was perched on the table finishing off pastie crumbs left on our plates from lunchtime. I'd swung the door open so that Midge could enter carrying the injured thrush, and the squirrel's head had snapped up, then looked in our direction. It saw her first and if animals can smile, this one certainly did. There was no fear in this little beggar at all and it didn't appear to be in any hurry to leave. Our intruder resumed nibbling the crumbs.

Only when I approached the table did the squirrel become skittish. It took one look at me and jumped onto the nearby dresser, causing the hanging cups and mugs to rattle against each other. I held up a hand in a gesture of peace, but the universal sign meant nothing to the departing animal. It skipped onto the windowsill and with a last cheeky look here, there and everywhere, leapt out into the garden and was gone.

Midge and I laughed delightedly and she said, 'D'you suppose all the red squirrels in this part of the world are that bold?'

I remembered the one we'd come across in the road on our first visit to the cottage. 'Could be,' I replied, 'unless that's the same guy as before.'

Her mouth dropped open as if she were really considering the possibility, then she said, 'We're lucky to see any at all. They were almost wiped out by an epidemic some years ago and I know not many survived in this area. The greys rather took over their territories.'

'We'd better make sure the windows are closed next time we go out, otherwise we might come back one day and find we've been invaded.'

'Now that would be nice.'

'Not if it were by rats or mice.'

'Trust you to look on the dark side.'

For a moment I was serious, although I meant no jibe. 'One of us has to keep their feet on the ground.'

She regarded me quizzically, then became aware that she still cradled the injured thrush in her hands.

I found a cardboard box and lined it with an old sweater of mine and a scarf of Midge's; she laid the bird inside and placed the box in a corner by the dresser. After that, she attempted feeding the thrush, giving up after a while to try again later, this time with a degree of success. What was left of the afternoon – which wasn't much – was spent sorting out clothes and ornaments, finding a more permanent home for tools, equipment and various household items, hanging pictures, sweeping and cleaning, and generally bringing things together a bit more. O'Malley and his men had done a fine job on the cottage, fixing, painting, and pulling the building into shape. Even the cupboard doors everywhere fitted snugly and I assumed they had been planed down before being repainted. Some of the floorboards still creaked here and there, but there was no sagging and I could find no serious cracks in the wood.

After dinner, a stroganoff which Midge had prepared with much care and devotion because it was to be our first 'proper' dinner at Gramarye, we adjourned upstairs to the round room. I tried the TV but the picture was annoyingly snowy and as neither of us was really interested anyway, I soon switched off. I resolved to do something about the aerials for the set and the radio next day. We relaxed to some vintage Schmilson for a while and I was relieved that at least the stereo wasn't dogged by interference. We both felt at peace that evening, no sad memories marring the contentment for Midge and no reservations about the move nagging at me. When the album was finished, she asked me to play for her, something I often did during the evenings she had to work at her drawing board or those times we merely felt in the mood. I went to fetch the guitar while Midge opened a bottle of wine for me.

Now I was slumped back in the sofa, fingertips of both hands still tingling from their contact with the guitar strings, Midge's head resting against my chest, and it wasn't long before our mutual warmth turned into mutual desire.

Unlike that morning's gloriously frenzied love-making, this time it was languid and exquisite, every movement and every moment savoured and lingered over, all fervency contained yet still indulged in to the full. As the sensuality built in our bodies, so the room seemed to spin and weave around us, the last fading rays of the sun becoming a spectrum of colours, although always influenced by the sanguine flush that stained the walls.

The love act between us slowly became something more. It became a great expansion of emotion that went far beyond our physical bodies, that did not so much explode within our spirits, as erupt in a leisurely-spreading shower of energies. Imagine a slow-motion film of glass shattering into thousands – *millions* – of fragments, every single part caught by the light, each tiny piece reflecting its own entity, its own being: that might represent a physical equivalent to the sensory response aroused in us, although the comparison is far from accurate, because such a brittle splintering is the very antithesis of the soft starbursts we both experienced. We joined together, fusing not just with each other but with the air around us, with the walls, with every living organism contained therein. In some way we had reached another level, one that perhaps we all glimpse from time to time, but are always on the periphery of, always just at the edge, knowing dimly of its existence, but never able to perceive it clearly, our minds always defeated by their own limiting truth.

Heavy stuff, right? But in my own inept way I'm trying to give you a glimmer of what happened to us that evening in Gramarye. And maybe put it into some kind of perspective for myself.

There was more. We sensed the aura of Gramarye, a spirit that had nothing to do with Flora Chaldean or all those others who had occupied the cottage before her, but was the *essence* of that place itself. Its *own* nature, if you like. In the structure, the grounds, the atmosphere around, there was immense goodness, an outflowing of earth purity.

And as every positive has its negative, there was also a dark, lurking badness. But that was on the fringes, a shadow that could not be defined, a power that was dormant, having little strength. Yet it existed.

We experienced these things, but they were not sharp in our minds, and the perception was soon gone, fading swiftly with the subsiding of our physical pleasure, the sensations, the essential primal urge, which had led us to that recognition carrying the awareness away from us in its own ebbing. Only now, after so much has happened, can what occurred to us that evening be remembered and partially explained. Even so, everything is just *my* interpretation, and long after the event at that.

I was the first to speak – Midge was still too bewildered or exhausted, or both. 'Did you lace the stroganoff with something?' It was meant as a joke, a glib aside while I got my head together, but she wasn't laughing. 'Midge, you okay?'

She looked my way, but didn't quite see me; sleepy wonderment was still glowing in her eyes.

'Midge?'

She drew in a long, deep breath, her shoulders and chest rising, then let the air go just as slowly. Finally she said, 'What happened?' The question was to herself as much as to me.

I smiled lazily. 'We made love.' The phenomenon was already leaving me, material reality asserting its steadying influence the way it does when waking from a dream.

Midge ran both hands over her eyes and when she looked up again it was as if she'd wiped away the wonderment. Then she yawned and my own jaw was quickly infected, because I yawned too. I helped her with her clothes – she was fumbling at buttons like a weary child, her mind distracted, co-ordination all but gone.

'I don't understand,' she mumbled. 'I can't think straight, Mike . . .'

My movements were slow too, and more awkward than I cared for, but I was filled with warmth, my senses now pleasurably dulled. And I couldn't stop smiling. 'I think we've just passed through some kind of ecstasy barrier, Midge. I think the earth really did move for us. Jesus, I never imagined such a thing was possible.' (See how the human brain works, how it tries to rationalise the irrational for its own sanity? I was putting it down to *romance*, for Chrissake!)

Midge wasn't that easily persuaded, though. 'No, Mike, it was something more . . .'

I stopped her with a kiss. 'We're both tired, Pixie. Like you said, the country air does something to you. Why don't you get yourself into bed while I lock up?'

'I need a bath . . .'

'No you don't.'

'Brush my teeth . . .'

'That'll take you half a minute. I'll join you before your head hits the pillow.'

'All right. Mike. Mike . . .?'

'Yeah?'

'You love me, don't you?'

'You know it.'

I lifted her to her feet and she swayed against me.

'God,' she murmured. 'I didn't realise how tired I was. I feel as if I'm drunk.'

'How could you know? Come on, I'll take you through.'

I did more than that: I picked Midge up and carried her into the bedroom, her slight weight no burden at all. Lowering her onto the bed, I remained leaning over her.

'Think you can manage the rest by yourself while I see to the doors and windows?'

She nodded, then teased, 'Still nervous of the country-side, Mike?'

'It's all them wolves and bears out there.'

'And the wood demons. Don't forget the wood demons.' Her words were almost slurred as sleep stole in.

'I wish you hadn't mentioned the wood demons.' I bent lower to kiss her forehead, then straightened. Midge's eyes had already closed when I looked down on her.

Quietly leaving the bedroom, I went out to the small hallway over the stairs and bolted the door there, then descended to the kitchen. Ridiculously, I had made myself jittery with talk of wolves and bears, not that I imagined for one moment that there were any such animals out there, but because now that the sun had sunk completely and it was pitch black outside, I had begun to appreciate how isolated the cottage was. Talk of wood demons hadn't helped either.

I bolted the downstairs door, then went to the open window, sticking my head out to feel a cool breeze against my skin. I could hardly see a thing, only the vague shapes of the nearest trees. Clouds must have hurriedly covered the stars as they'd switched on after sunset, and there was no moon to outline even the rolling edges of those clouds.

Even more uneasy, I ducked my head back inside, closing the window and setting the catch after me. I stood watching my own ghost reflection in the glass for a little while, then shivered.

'Dumb bastard,' I called myself and went back upstairs whistling a less than happy tune.

I woke suddenly, as I had the night before. Only this time I was immediately alert and apprehensive. I could hear Midge breathing evenly beside me, still lost in sleep.

My whole body was tensed as I lay there wondering what had roused me, only the luminous digits of the alarm clock and dim outlines of furniture giving relief to the oppressive darkness.

I thought of nudging Midge awake, but that would have been unkind as well as cowardly. When I'd returned to the bedroom earlier that night her clothes were in a heap on the floor and she was beneath the blankets, sound asleep. There was no smell of toothpaste when I kissed her lips. The move and the frantic weeks leading up to it had caught up with a vengeance, I remember thinking.

Noises. From above. And familiar.

I nudged Midge, but she didn't stir.

I looked up at the dark mass that was the ceiling. Someone was creeping around up there!

Still craning my neck back, I raised myself onto my elbows, unsure if the room was cold or the goose-bumps on my skin were caused by something else. The sounds were muffled and I realised they were not coming from the room directly above, but were from the loft. My sigh of relief was cut off halfway. Surely birds would not be moving about in the middle of the night? Then what the hell was up there? My pernicious mind immediately suggested rats and I sank back into the bed, pulling the covers up to my chest. Maybe mice? I wished I could convince myself, but mice would never make that much noise.

Forget about the hero who leaves his bed in the dead of night to investigate mysterious noises, that guy who mounts the creaky stairs up to the attic, flashlight or candle lighting the way and, if he's a movie star, creepy music keeping him company. He's a figment of some idiot's imagination: I'm me, and I was born with a modicum of sense.

There was no way I was going to leave that cosy bed to look in the loft. No way. It could wait until tomorrow.

The strange thing is that I didn't stay awake for much longer. I listened for a while, my heart jolting with every fresh sound – and I'd become aware of plenty of other creaks and groans around that place, although I told myself these were merely the settling of old timbers after a warm day – but soon tiredness overcame even fear.

I sank away, fingers crossed so the boogeyman wouldn't get me.

RETURN VISIT

'Mike, come on, wake up!'

I'm not sure how uncivil my response was, but it didn't stop the hand tugging at my shoulder. I opened my eyes and daylight trampled in.

'Mike, I want you to see,' Midge persisted.

Her face was close to mine and looking considerably brighter than it had the night before. In fact, Midge fairly bristled with life and her touch must have sent volts shooting into me because I came alive in a rush. This was the second morning I'd awoken feeling vital and refreshed and, as already stated, this wasn't my usual condition at all. I was becoming a born-again early riser.

I pulled her down on top of me and she laughingly resisted.

'No, I want you to come down and see!' She pulled away and grabbed my robe draped over a chair, tossing it at me and sweeping back the bedcovers.

I swung my legs over the edge and slid my arms through the sleeves of the robe. 'You mind telling me what all the excitement's about?' I groused, but faking it.

'You'll see.'

She was laughing and tugging at me, drawing me from the bed and towards the door. The white nightshirt she wore (one of my old collarless shirts with the sleeves rolled up) flapped loosely around her bare legs. a pleasing sight first thing in the morning.

'Nice day again,' I observed as we passed by the window. Our friendly neighbourhood birds were making their presence known.

'Every day is nice here.'

I saw no gain in pointing out that we'd only been resident for two days, and allowed myself to be hauled to the stairs.

'Oh, Gudgeon, this'd better be good.' The stair carpet we'd had laid before moving in was soft and springy beneath my bare feet, but the wood underneath was good and firm. O'Malley had missed nothing.

We reached the kitchen/dining area and Midge stood aside, waving me through. Hands in my robe pockets, I stood there expectantly. The room looked exactly the same to me.

I turned to say something to Midge when a fluttering of wings made me jump. The bird flew across the room and landed on top of the dresser. It chirped a greeting or a warning, I'm not sure which.

'How did that get in here?' I'd already noted the window was still closed.

'He's the mistle thrush, stupid. He's the one who had the broken wing yesterday!'

I gaped at her, then at the bird, which was jauntily hopping along the dresser top. It launched itself into the air again to find another perch over the window.

'That isn't possible, Midge. It can't be the same.'

Midge laughed, pleased by my incredulity. 'Check the box. You won't find the thrush in there.'

'But it isn't possible,' I repeated, actually going over to the cardboard box, which was still tucked away in a corner. The mistle thrush over the window begged to differ by flying onto the table where there was a pile of breadcrumbs, presumably put there earlier by Midge. The bird pecked at them, its appetite as healthy as its wing.

'Midge,' I warned. 'Are you having a sly joke with me? Is this one of your friends from outside?'

97

'I promise you, Mike, he's the same bird. Isn't it fantastic!'

'I don't believe it.' I was shaking my head, watching the thrush and still suspecting I was being fooled. 'There's no way, Midge – *no way* – that its wing could have mended overnight. As a matter of fact, the break was so bad I thought the bird would be dead this morning.'

'You were wrong.' Midge moved towards the table and our robust friend stopped pecking to watch her. She picked up a crumb and held it towards the bird who, to my amazement, beaked it from her fingers, showing no fear whatsoever.

One bird looks much the same as another if they're of a breed, so I couldn't tell if this really was our patient or not. But the question still begged, of course: If this was a different thrush where was the injured one? It was then I noticed one wing was ragged, feathers missing, and something went cold inside me. Now I was convinced. This was the original thrush all right, but its remarkable recovery made no sense. Surely we couldn't have been that wrong about its condition yesterday?

I suppose this was the point where my underlying uneasiness over several aspects of Gramarye began to move onto a more conscious level. Nothing definite, just a vague sense of disquiet over a culmination of things, none of which I could pinpoint precisely to say: 'Hey, this is totally bizarre.' If any of these had been bad, or at least were completely inexplicable, then I'd have been a mite anxious. You see, it was just possible that the bird's wing had been locked into a grotesque position the day before and had worked itself free overnight (again the old brain reasoning where there wasn't much reason). And the rest – well, what was the rest? Good music, glorious lovemaking (true recollection of the previous night's experience had already dimmed), a crack in the stone lintel that hadn't been a crack at all. Certainly there were good vibes from the place, particularly from the round room, but what did that mean in itself? We were in love and this was our first proper home. The curved walls of the round room caught the sun's rays so that a serene warmth literally *exuded* from them. There really was no more than that. And yet. And yet . . .

The mistle thrush was now perched on Midge's hand and trilling happily. Doubts were eased aside as Midge's joy touched me. Her eyes were vibrant with contained excitement as she spoke soothingly to the small creature, who answered her in kind. She slowly raised her hand so that the thrush was level with her face, then blew a soft breath towards it, ruffling feathers only slightly, causing the bird to blink.

I watched entranced as Midge smoothly walked to the door, her bare feet silent on the quarry tiles. She turned her head towards me and whispered, 'Mike . . .'

Equally cautious, I went to the door and drew back the bolts, making as little noise as possible. The bird seemed oblivious to me. Twisting the key in the lock, I quietly pulled open the door and Midge moved forward to stand on the step.

Lifting her hand high, she said, 'Off you go. Find your family and say hello from me.'

The thrush appeared reluctant to leave, but Midge dipped her hand so that the bird's wings fluttered and it was airborne. It soared high above the garden, calling fiercely and swooping down over Midge's head. The thrush skimmed across the flower beds, then rose once more into the air heading back into the woods from where it had been rescued.

Midge clapped her hands in delight and I stood next to her on the step, an arm around her shoulders, wearing a grin and cheering the bird on. When it was gone I hugged Midge and mussed her hair.

'Did you really do that?' I asked.

'It was his idea to climb onto my hand.'

'I meant its wing . . .'

She shook her head, eyes still full of shining. 'He did that all by himself. It was his own magic.'

The word 'magic' again, the second time she'd unselfconsciously used it since we'd moved in. I opened my mouth to speak when the doorstep was abruptly besieged by other birds, all noisily demanding breakfast. We ducked inside, away from the squawking, Midge making for the wrapped loaf on the table and taking out a handful of slices.

'Okay, you guys,' she called, returning to the doorway, 'there's plenty for all, so little ones first.'

They refused to form a queue, but not even the smallest sparrow was intimidated by any of the big chiefs: they rushed together in a mad mêlée of feathers and screeching, the nimblest fleeing the throng with prizes in beaks.

I left Midge to the feeding of the multitude and went upstairs to shave, my thoughts dogged by the thrush's 'miraculous' recovery. The wing *had* to have unlocked itself, there really was no other explanation. I was back downstairs again within ten minutes, and muesli and toast with strong coffee was there on the table waiting for me, a single rose, freshly picked from the garden, in a tiny china vase brightening the breakfast setting. Brightening the room considerably more was Midge's beaming face.

There were still one or two birds loitering around the doorstep as if daring one another to venture in, but the majority had disbanded to fly off and do whatever it is birds do all day.

As I buttered toast, I said, 'I still can't figure it out. That bird looked pretty sick to me yesterday.'

Midge sipped coffee before replying. 'What does it matter? His wing healed, that's the main thing, so why worry over how?'

And she meant it. In fact, I got the impression that she didn't want the cure questioned, that she had no wish to delve any further. I shrugged, prepared to let it go, having semi-accepted my own 'unlocked bones' theory anyway. Flimsy, but it would suffice.

'Plans for today?' Midge enquired, the subject already dismissed from her mind. She looked small and childlike in my oversized converted shirt.

'Uh, some investigations first,' I told her, and she raised her eyebrows. 'I heard noises coming from the loft last night.'

'You thought there were birds nesting in the eaves.'

'Yeah, that was yesterday afternoon. This was something moving around in the middle of the night when all good little birds are sound asleep.'

She was slightly alarmed. 'D'you have any idea what it could be?'

'Not really, but I'm sure as hell gonna find out this

morning, in daylight. I don't want to lie in the dark with my imagination running loose again.'

'You should have woken me.'

'I didn't like to disturb you.' I munched toast.

Midge came around to my side of the table and pushed herself onto my lap, making me scrape back the chair to accommodate her. She pecked my forehead.

'Want me to come up to the loft with you?' she asked, and I didn't miss the trace of mockery in her tone.

'And have you get hysterical if we find mice?' I shook my head and added stout-heartedly, 'I'll go it alone, thank you.' Things never seemed quite so threatening in daylight.

'You know mice don't frighten me. Still, there's a lot of scrubbing and cleaning to be done, so the sooner I make a start the better. I think O'Malley's men created more mess than they shifted.'

'Aah, they were pretty good, considering. They certainly put the cottage back in shape, even though we've got a fair amount of painting and decorating to do ourselves. Less than I imagined on our first recce, though. Any ideas on how you'd like the round room done? That's the important one.'

She frowned. 'I like it exactly as it is. I don't think we should change anything.'

'Up to you. It's in good condition, I'll admit that. Maybe Flora had the room redecorated just before she, uh, she passed on.'

'We'll need curtains, perhaps white or beige – all the colour we need comes from the sun. Have you noticed how the walls change throughout the day?'

'Yeah, from bright white-yellow in the morning to fiery gold at sunset. Then that warm red just after the sun's gone. They've got a life of their own, like that big rock in Australia that's always changing colour.'

'Ayers Rock. They say it has mystical qualities . . .'

'Who say?'

'The aborigines.'

'The aborigines have seen the round room?'

My nose took its usual tweaking (I swear it was a different shape before I met Midge).

'What do I have to do to get a serious conversation out of you nowadays?' she said, pouting.

'Talk about me?' I suggested, gingerly remoulding my released nose.

'Boring,' she droned.

My hand was up inside the nightshirt and fingers poised around the side of her lower ribs before she had a chance to move. 'Boring?' I asked.

'No, Mike! You know I can't stand that!'

I nodded and squeezed, sudden and hard, rigid fingers finding those ticklish zones between ribs. With a shriek she leapt two or three inches off my lap, but my other hand held her down again.

'Boring?' I repeated with a pleasant smile.

'Mike, please, you know –'

My fingers twitched spasmodically, showing no mercy, and she jumped again to land squirming in my lap, hiccuping with her own laughter as I kept probing.

'Mike, noooo!'

'Did you say boring?'

'No, no! Interesting! No – exciting! Yes, exciting! The most . . . Mike! . . . ex – exciting . . . no, fascinating . . . person . . . I've . . . stop it, Mike, please no more . . .'

I could barely hold her there, slight though she was, and I was laughing almost as much as her. Her legs flailed the air and soon she was slipping from my lap, nightshirt rising as she sank.

She screamed when her naked bottom touched the quarry tiles. 'It's cold! Oh you bast . . .' The rest was unintelligible amidst the laughter.

I buried my face in her hair, hands sliding down her body to clasp together beneath her breasts. The memory of last night's lovemaking was not too far from my thoughts as I nuzzled her ear. My teeth gently nipped at her neck.

'Well hello again,' she said brightly.

It wasn't the response I'd expected. I looked up and saw she had been greeting another caller at the door. Our friendly neighbourhood squirrel was grinning at our fun from the open doorway.

'Come on in,' I invited the animal, noticing Midge modestly pulling the nightshirt down over her thighs. 'This is Open House, no tickets for admission.'

The squirrel looked uncertain.

'Hush, Mike,' warned Midge, 'you'll frighten him. Come on, little 'un, pay no mind to this big old ugly brute behind me. Snarl and he'll hide under the table.'

It hopped inside. Another hop and it was only a couple of feet away from Midge's wriggling toes. I think my eyebrows must have touched my hairline in surprise. Midge giggled as the squirrel chattered.

'Yes, I know he looks like a big bad bear with toothache, but he's very nice once you get to know him,' she told the noisy mite.

It looked at me and then at her, and then at me again. I gave it my best smile and the squirrel's tail swished in annoyance.

'Hey, I live here, y'know,' I said, then wondered what the hell I was doing. Talking to a squirrel? The boys in the bands had said I'd flip outside my natural environment. The animal jerked its tufty head in funny little ducking movements, narrow shoulders hunching up, and to me it looked like it was chortling.

'This guy's got no respect,' I complained to Midge.

'He's the same squirrel who came visiting yesterday,' she said thoughtfully.

'Didn't that one look more Jewish?'

She banged my sneaker with the heel of her fist, hurting my toes.

'Come on, Midge, how can you tell? They all look alike. And how d'you know it's a he, anyway?'

'I just know. He's got a personality all his own.'

She put her hands on my knees and levered herself up from the floor. 'Let's find something for you to eat, eh?' she said to the squirrel, who appeared pleased with the idea; without further bidding, it leapt onto the table and chattered all the more. Midge broke off some of my toast and offered the piece to our intruder. Showing no timidity whatsoever, it skipped forward and grasped the toast in its tiny paws, licking at the butter first, not even backing away once it had started nibbling.

'I don't believe this,' I said as I rested an elbow on the edge of the table, palm supporting my chin.

'Neither do I. Red squirrels are rarely this tame, unlike the grey.'

'Red . . . ? Midge, *no* outdoor animal is tame. I mean, maybe in zoos and things, but not out here in the wild.'

'Could be that they got used to Flora. I bet she'd been feeding generation after generation of animals hereabouts. Look how the birds were at the window on our first morning here. It's almost as if this place is a natural habitat for them, part of their own forest.'

'The local fast-food counter, you mean. I can understand how it's popular. The problem is, how long before they start messing up our cosy country retreat? They could do some damage.'

'Oh, Mike, the birds, the squirrels, and any other animal that cares to wander through, are as much a part of Gramarye as are we. Don't forget, they were here before us.' She lowered herself, bending her knees and balancing on the balls of her feet, hands resting on my knees. 'We've got to adapt to them, Mike, don't you see? Feed them and help them survive. Treat them as friends.'

'I draw the line at snakes and lizards.'

She smiled. 'I'll allow you to close the door on rats as well.'

That reminded me I had some investigating to do. I leaned forward and kissed her lips, conscious of the squirrel gnawing toast while observing us.

'Voyeur,' I called it when Midge and I parted. 'Okay, Pixie, all creatures great and small are welcome here, so long as they're not *too* great and not small enough to bore holes in woodwork. Deal?'

'I don't know what you're expecting – so far we've only had a bird and a squirrel inside the house – but okay, it's a deal. Elephants and woodworm are out.'

We shook hands on it and I winked at the squirrel. 'All right, Rumbo, you're in. But don't get me jealous or mad.'

Midge laughed. 'Why Rumbo?'

'I don't know. He just looks like a Rumbo, doesn't he? More like a Rumbo than a Rambo, anyway.'

The squirrel jerked its head convulsively, tiny shoulders juddering, its chattering like laughter. Which Midge found hysterically funny.

'I think he agrees,' she said between giggles.

'Yeah, a real clown,' I said drily. I stood slowly, careful not to startle our chuckling guest. 'This man's got work to do.'

'So's this woman.'

'You think he'll mind eating alone?' Now he had a name, Rumbo was no longer an 'it' to me.

'I suggested we make friends with the animals, not pander to them. He can make his own conversation.'

So we left him there feeding quite happily, Midge departing for the sink next door and me, after taking a flashlight from a downstairs cupboard, for the loft. I felt cheered as I climbed the stairs, glad to be alive and glad to be in love, musing over how real love has constant moments of absolute freshness, as if you've only just fallen, the realisation always exciting, always absorbing. We'd got to know each other – I mean, really *know* – Midge and I, but we'd never got too used to one another, had never become complacent. Don't get me wrong – our relationship hasn't always been as rosy as the picture I'm painting here; in fact, there have been some very stormy patches, times when we've come close to break-up. Fortunately, we've always managed to see sense at the same time and come to terms with the other's faults (or point of view, as Midge would have it). No false modesty here: we both have our own special talents in music and art, and have you ever known any talented person *not* to possess a streak of temperament? Goes with the territory, as they say. I'm not talking about arrogance or ego, but the single-minded drive within to get things *right* (to their way of thinking, of course) and the frustrations that quickly develop when those things aren't so. They're the times when the nearest person to you takes the brunt and has to learn to duck and weave, or just talk plain sense. We'd learned with each other over the years. We'd also learned not to take our respective selves too seriously, a bonus if you're aware of that before you're too old for it to matter.

Resisting the temptation to pick up a guitar, knowing the morning would be gone if I did, I approached the chair left standing directly beneath the loft hatch the day before. The flashlight worked fine, the chair was steady, the hatch cover was waiting: time to make my move.

So why was I hesitating?

Maybe I should have brought the stepladder up with me; climbing into the loft would have been much easier. No, the ceiling wasn't high; the chair would do.

There were no noises up there now so perhaps the problem had gone away. Still no reason not to take a look-see.

I was being sissy and I knew it. Yet something was telling me I really didn't want to look into that loft. Could be that there's a tiny compartment in everyone's mind where the future exists here and now, where archives of events yet to come are kept, where the record keeper (who is, after all, oneself) occasionally slips a hint beneath the sealed door. Could be. Such things are a mystery to me as I'm sure they are to you; all I know is that the urge to back away, to retreat down the stairs and invent some excuses for not going into the loft, was immense.

Come on, Stringer, I scolded myself, get up there and rout some rats, unless you want to face derision and disgrace. Still I hesitated, eyes locked on the hatchway: derision and disgrace weren't *so* bad.

Common sense prevailed, the pragmatist in me won the day; I stepped onto the chair and switched on the flashlight. With one hand I pushed up the hatch – only a couple of inches, though. No menacing eyes peered down at me through the gap, nothing shifted, nothing 'snuffled liquidly'. All was still and quiet. Feeling a fraction bolder, I widened the opening and shone the light through, standing on tip-toe to try and peek over the edge. I couldn't quite make it, but I was sure there was a small amount of daylight coming from low down. I switched off the flashlight to check and then was certain that daylight was coming through the eaves around the roof.

There was the answer: birds had squeezed in and had made a nice protective aviary out of the rooftop. Maybe last night they'd decided to throw a party to celebrate. I switched on the light again and swung the hatch back as far as it would go, my hand sliding towards the base the wider it opened. Finally, the hatch overbalanced and fell backwards, only a little way, though, something behind catching it with a bump.

Putting the flashlight over the lip, I grabbed the sides and pulled myself up; what I lacked in athletic style I made up for in curses as I hauled myself into the loft, white sneakers kicking empty space below like demented doves. Resting on the edge, feet dangling, I caught my breath and immediately regretted the inhalation. The air up there was foul, a kind of acidy stench wrinkling my nose.

'Jesus,' I said aloud and I thought I heard a movement not too far away.

The light was pointing to one side, but I could still make out the dim shapes of rafters and crossbeams. There were no holes in the roof itself, the builders obviously having done their job well. But I could just see something else on the crossbeams, dark objects, unclear in the gloom. They seemed to be hanging from the timbers and with a shudder I noticed there were more – *many more* – on the sloping rafters.

I knew what they were but I reached for the flashlight anyway and shone the beam upwards. I felt a trembly revulsion when I saw what seemed like hundreds of dark little furry bodies hanging upside down like withered fruit on branches, all crammed into the loft space and filling it with their stench.

Even as I watched, a wing twitched, stretched outwards in a quivering movement, then tucked back into the dark body.

'Oh God,' I murmured, frozen there. In the still silence, I imagined I could hear their tiny heartbeats, pulsating as one, a regular rhythm that unified the creatures, gave them mass.

I was shivering when I quietly lowered myself from the loft, afraid that the slightest sound would send the bats into a mad frenzy of shrieks and fluttering wings.

WATCHER

In the bathroom, I doused my face with water, washing away the perspiration that had broken through. Then I vigorously scrubbed my hands as though they'd become contaminated by those things in the loft. I felt sick, but the nausea remained glutinously locked inside my chest.

Bats! Ugly, sinister, wizened monsters. And from what I'd seen, a plague of them! And O'Malley must have known they were there: why the hell hadn't he said something? I now regretted not having accepted sound advice to send in a surveyor to look over the cottage, thinking one fee less would add financially to the repairs we could carry out; at least a surveyor would have discovered their presence and informed us. I dreaded telling Midge, not wanting to spoil this idyll of hers; but she would have to know, there was no way of keeping the fact from her.

Creepy little bastards! There had to be exterminators in the area, or perhaps even the local council handled such things. Were bats a health hazard? They were a mental hazard, that's for sure.

I wiped my face and hands dry, head buzzing with flesh-crawling thoughts. I suppose I may have been over-reacting, but the unpleasant feeling I'd had before opening the loft, together with the shock of being confronted by all those black hanging bodies, was having a strong effect. I wondered how long Gramarye had been the creatures' domicile; had they arrived after Flora Chaldean's demise, or had they taken up residence while she was still around? The latter was hard to imagine, but then again, we knew she'd been something of an eccentric, so maybe Flora had made them welcome. Well, the new management reserved the right not to accept certain parties, and elephants, woodworm and bats were definitely *out*.

I walked through into the adjoining bedroom and went to the window with the intention of throwing it open and gasping in deep lungfuls of fresh, un-musty air; I checked my breath when I saw a group of figures by the garden gate.

Midge, now dressed, and on this side of the gate, had her back to me and was in conversation with three other people, two men and a girl. They were casually clothed – open-necked shirts, slacks, the girl in a longish, patterned skirt and blouse. She had long blonde hair and even from that distance looked vaguely familiar to me. A Citroën was parked half-on the grass verge behind them (by then we had found a clear patch to the side of the garden big enough to accommodate our Passat). Their voices drifted up to me over the garden, but I couldn't make out what they were saying. Feeling particularly receptive to human company at that point in time, I left the bedroom and went downstairs. If this group were local, they might even know how to handle our bat problem.

The strong pure scent of flowers cleared my head of stale fumes as I strode down the path. The three strangers looked past Midge as I approached, Midge herself turning to greet me when I drew near.

'Mike, we've got our first visitors,' she said, obviously enjoying the contact.

'First *human* visitors,' I corrected, smiling at their brief puzzlement. I managed to push thoughts of tiny winged creatures aside for the moment.

'Mike's referring to certain animals who've dropped by since we moved in,' Midge explained, and smiles broke out all round.

'I'm afraid you'll soon learn it's we human folk who are

109

the interlopers in this neck of the woods.' The speaker was as blond as the girl, although his hair was a mite shorter, almost military length, in fact. He was about my size – five ten – and his eyes were Newmanish blue. He reminded me of a time-capsuled '60's Californian surfer, and his American accent enhanced the image, although I sensed an intensity about him that belied his laid-back manner. He was grinning and even his teeth were pure Hollywood.

'Hi,' he said, extending a hand over the low gate. 'I'm Hub Kinsella and . . .' he waved his free hand towards his companions '. . . this is Gillie Slade and Neil Joby.'

I shook hands with all three as Midge introduced me. Each one looked to be in their early or mid twenties.

'We saw you when we passed by the other day,' the girl said, hardly any pressure at all in her handshake.

'Oh yeah, I thought I'd seen you before,' I replied. 'You waved at me from the car, right?'

She nodded. 'You waved first.'

We laughed, the way uncertain strangers do at the slightest hint of humour. She was English enough and quite pretty in a wan sort of way. She wore no make-up and freckles sprinkled the tops of her cheeks and her nose; there was a nervous skittishness about her that was either appealing or annoying, I couldn't be sure which.

The second man, Joby, was short and thin, and close up I noticed he was dressed less informally than the others, inasmuch as he wore a tie with his shortsleeved shirt, his trousers were sharply creased, and his shoes were brightly polished. His hairless arms projected from their sleeves like white bendy sticks and his grip was a little too tight, as if the firmness was assumed rather than natural. There was the faintest Midlands nasalisation to his voice when he greeted me with, 'Hope you like your new home.'

'Yeah, we do,' I said, 'but it'll take a while to settle in.'

'Are you both from London?' Kinsella asked, his tone politely interested rather than inquisitive.

'How could you tell?'

He smiled disarmingly. 'You have that look about you.'

'Ducks out of water?'

'Oh no, I didn't mean to imply that. I just felt this was kinda new to you.'

'Not quite for Midge – she was raised in the country. Me, I'm a novice.'

'You'll soon come to love it out here,' put in the girl, Gillie. 'I did.'

Midge tucked her arm into mine and leaned against me. 'You know the big house we came across on our walk yesterday, Mike?'

'Blea – the grey house?'

She nodded. 'That's where Hub, Gillie and Neil come from.'

'Really? You live there? All three of you?'

'More than three of us, Mike,' said Kinsella.

'What is it? A hotel, a health farm of some kind?'

'Neither of those. Why don't you drop by some time when you're settled and we'll show you around?'

'Yes, please do,' said Gillie, surprising us both by reaching out with both hands to touch our arms. 'The house is beautiful inside and we'd make you so welcome. Please say you'll come and visit.'

I was slightly taken aback with her enthusiasm, but Midge seemed pleased with the idea. 'That would be nice,' she told the girl. 'We were intrigued by the place yesterday, weren't we, Mike?'

'Yeah, intrigued.' I felt warning pressure from Midge's hand on my arm. 'Meanwhile we've got a small problem that needs attending to. I thought maybe you'd have some ideas as you live in these parts.'

Their expressions couldn't have conveyed more eagerness to help. Midge was curious.

'Bats have taken over the penthouse suite,' I explained, pointing back towards the cottage with a thumb. Turning to Midge, I said, 'That was what the noises were last night. They're up in the loft now, sleeping off the party.'

'Bats?' she said.

'Bats,' I replied.

'Oh, they're no great problem, Mike,' the American assured me. 'They really won't do any harm.'

111

'Maybe not, but they make me feel uncomfortable. I'd hate to wake up one night and find them toasting each other's health with our blood.'

They chuckled at that, although Gillie looked slightly queasy.

'No fear of that,' said Joby, folding insect arms across his chest. 'They mostly hunt around dusk and dawn. I can't imagine you'll find many vampire bats in Hampshire, anyway. If you leave them in peace they won't disturb you.'

'They're already disturbing me.'

'Oh, come on Mike,' said Midge. 'They're only like hamsters with wings.'

Her reaction – or lack of reaction – took me by surprise. I knew she adored animals, but *all* animals?

'Unfortunately, there's not much you can do about them by law,' Joby went on. 'They're a protected species, you see. Most of them have been wiped out in this country, mainly by pesticides and ignorance – people deliberately destroying them. Conservationists stepped in just in time to beg the government to act.'

'You're saying we can't touch those things?' I asked incredulously.

He bowed his head gravely. 'Mammals, actually. They're either the pipistrelle or the long-eared bat, depending on size – pipistrelle is the smallest.'

'I didn't take too close a look.'

'The pipistrelle favours woodlands, but is quite used to residential areas, and the long-eared bat likes to sleep in caves or cellars or lofts.'

'That sounds like our boy, then.'

'I promise you, you're in no danger from them. Insects and moths are what they like to eat, so they may even be doing you a favour.'

I was doubtful, but he seemed to know what he was talking about. Slowly shaking my head, I said, 'So it looks like we're stuck with them.'

The guy called Kinsella spoke in a conspiratorial voice: 'Look, Mike, if it really gets to be a bad problem, maybe we can help you smoke 'em out or somethin'. No one else need know.'

'Yeah, well, we'll see how it goes.'

He flashed those pearlies again. 'You know where to find us if you need any help at all, but we'd like to see you at any time.'

'Shall I fetch the gift, Hub?' The girl was looking up at him like a puppy-dog looks at its master.

'Oh, sure, almost forgot.'

Gillie ducked into the open window of the car and drew out a square red biscuit tin. She held it over the gate towards Midge.

'One of our sisters is a fantastic cook, so when we realised you'd moved into Gramarye we asked her to make you a welcoming cake,' Gillie told us. 'Nothing very grand, but I think you'll enjoy it.'

'Our small way of welcoming you to the neighbourhood,' said Kinsella, holding his arms away from his sides as though he could hug us.

'What a lovely thought,' Midge enthused, accepting the gift and beaming all over her pretty face. 'Perhaps we can invite you over once we're straight – we'd love that, wouldn't we, Mike?'

Kinsella cut in before I could respond. 'You can be sure we'll be saying hello from time to time. Once we've made friends we don't like to lose 'em.'

He said that with all geniality, so I wondered why it made me feel uneasy.

'Meanwhile,' he went on, 'we'll let you get on – I'm sure there's a lot to put right in the cottage. The previous owner was a little old to maintain the place properly, I guess.'

'You knew Flora Chaldean?' asked Midge.

'Oh, most people around here knew of her,' said Gillie.

'But no one got to *know* her,' said Kinsella. 'We spoke to her a coupla times, is all. Now you just remember what I told you: any help you need, you only have to call.'

'We'll remember, er, Hub,' I said. Then, 'Is that a nickname?'

'Short for Hubris. My folks had a sense of humour.'

Not much of one, I thought. 'Well, good meeting you and thanks for that info on bats. Doesn't help any, but at least I know where we stand.'

We shook hands rather formally, then the group climbed into their car, Kinsella taking the wheel. They waved from the windows as the Citroën pulled away, and we returned the waves, watching them until they had disappeared from view.

'Weren't they incredibly nice?' Midge exclaimed, holding up the cake box for me to see.

'I suppose so. A mite *too* friendly, maybe.'

'Oh, Mike, you're such an old cynic sometimes. They were only being neighbourly. I wish a few more people had their outlook.'

'Yeah, but what are they, Midge? How come a mixed bunch like that is living together in a manor house? Did you notice Gillie referred to our cake-maker as sister?'

'What difference? They probably belong to some religious organisation. What does it matter as long as they're nice people?'

I shrugged. 'Yeah, you're right. I felt a bit crowded, that's all, like they were too keen to get to know us.'

'How many times do I have to tell you: things are different in the countryside, people are friendlier. You mustn't be so suspicious.'

'Sorry, Midge, didn't mean to be. Finding those bats upset my peace of mind.'

Her tone softened. 'I can understand that. But it's true, you know, bats really are harmless.'

'So long as *they* know that.'

The slightest of breezes rustled the nearby trees and stirred the flowers. Midge tucked the cake tin under one arm and linked her other through mine. We strolled back to the cottage, the sun warm on our faces.

'Let's take a look at those monsters you're so afraid of,' she said coaxingly.

'You want to go up there?'

She became indignant. 'Of course. I can't wait to see them.'

'You're full of surprises.'

'I study wildlife, remember? I paint animals for stories. I *enjoy* watching them. Besides, these little devils may give me an idea for a future book, one I could write myself. Better yet, one you could write for me. It's about time you put that particular talent to good use.'

'A horror story for tiny tots? You may have something there.'

'No, nothing like that. There isn't anything nasty about bats anyway.'

'You wait 'til you see 'em.'

She left the cake on the kitchen table and we went upstairs, me leading the way and muttering under my breath about the dire consequences of socialising with Dracula's kinsmen, while Midge prodded my buttocks and gave me fair warning to quit my craven rambling.

In the attic room, my future music studio, I picked up the flashlight still lying on the chair and tapped it against the palm of my hand, confronting Midge with a sober expression.

'You really want to go through with this . . .' I asked darkly, '. . . despite knowing what happened to Pandora?'

'Get outa here,' she replied, poking my chest with rigid fingers and putting one foot on the chair.

'All right, all right. I'm serious now, Midge: I honestly don't feel like going up there again.'

'You don't have to – just help me up. I won't tell all our friends.' She struck a pose, one fist clenched against her hip, foot still on the chair. Her grin was grim. And, of course, challenging.

Groaning miserably, I pulled her away and climbed onto the chair myself. I'd closed the hatch when I'd scrambled down earlier, perhaps imagining the bats might follow me, and I said, 'I'll open up, then lift you through, unless you want to go get the stepladder.'

'You'll do.' She folded her arms and waited.

'Yes'm.' I pushed at the hatch and it sucked open once more. 'Nothing to get excited about, guys,' I quietly called through. 'Only the landlord come to check the air conditioning.' Although not as nervous as before, now that I knew something about our somnolent guests, my attempt at light-hearted banter was somewhat forced.

The hatch slammed back against an upright timber as

115

before and I ducked low at the sudden bang. I caught Midge hiding a smile behind her hand.

'Don't say I didn't warn you,' I said grumpily, stepping down and handing her the flashlight. I made a stirrup of my hands. 'Catch the side of the opening with one hand and put the light inside, then I'll lift you through.'

'My hero,' she said, resting a foot in my hands.

I straightened and she rose easily, switching on the flashlight and placing it through the opening in almost one graceful movement, her weight no problem. Midge sat as I had, her legs dangling in space.

I scrambled up after her, using the chair and trying to make it look easy now I had an audience; she quickly moved aside to allow me room.

Once inside, I whispered, 'See what I mean?' The familiar smell wrinkled my nose again.

She was swinging the beam around the loft and I shuddered inwardly when I saw the black hanging shapes.

'Oh, Mike, there aren't that many,' she said scornfully.

I blinked as I followed the roving light. There really didn't seem to be as many bats as before. 'I, uh . . . I'm sure there were more than this.'

'I think you were so alarmed you imagined more. Even so, there must be at least thirty or forty scattered around up here.'

'But they were crammed together last time. A lot of them must have taken flight.'

'In broad daylight? No, the light beam must have cast their shadows so it looked like there were more.' She patted my thigh reassuringly. 'When you're basically chicken, things have a way of becoming exaggerated.' She pointed the light up under her chin, making an evil relief of her grinning face.

'Oh that's funny, that's really funny. Just gimme the light, will you?'

I snatched the flashlight from her and crawled further into the loft, keeping to the joists, reluctant to have a knee go through the ceiling below. I shone the beam into the further recesses, although I couldn't see behind the water tank; nevertheless, nothing was skulking anywhere else. Midge joined me, walking rather than crawling, making me feel even more foolish.

I stood, grabbing at a crossbeam for balance, careful not to brush against a sleeping bat. I expected to find Midge smiling mockingly at me, but she was far too intent studying one of the dangling bodies nearby.

She reached out and gently tugged at a folded wing.

'Hey,' I hissed, 'what're you doing?'

'Shine the light over here, Mike, I'd like to get a good look at this chap.'

'Midge, it might be dangerous. Christ, it might have rabies!'

'Stop being such a wimp. There's no rabies in this country. Remember what I said about hamsters with wings? Just keep thinking of them that way. Now come on, bring the light over.'

Spunky brat, I thought grudgingly, doing as I was told and treading warily on the joists. 'Don't blame me if you get bitten,' I warned peevishly.

The bat twitched and tried to retract its extended wing; Midge held the wing firm. The brute's ugly mouth opened in annoyance, revealing tiny Lugosi teeth, although it appeared not to wake. All the same, I kept my distance, stretching my arm to provide Midge with the light she wanted.

'See the fingers?' Her voice at least was hushed. 'See how long the last three are? The wing is just skin between them. Look, it goes right down to the bat's foot and tail.'

'That's really interesting. You think we could let him doze in peace?'

'And look at his furry little body. He's a cute little feller.'

'Cute! He's as ugly as sin!' I instantly regretted raising my voice as the fine membranes over the bat's tiny eyes quivered open for a second.

'He's offended,' observed Midge.

'He'll have to live with it. Look at that horrible squashed-up nose and pointy ears.' I made a disgusted noise.

'That's his radar around the nose.'

'It doesn't help cosmetically. Can we go down now,

Midge? We may have to cohabit with these hanging prunes, but we don't have to fraternise with them.'

She let the wing fold back inwards, then squeezed the flesh above my hip. 'I didn't know you were so allergic.'

'To be honest, neither did I. I've just got a funny feeling about them – can't help it.'

'At least you know there aren't as many as you first thought.'

'I could've sworn . . . No matter, the shock must have made me see double.'

'Or treble. Let's get down to where the air's sweeter.'

We held hands crossing the joists and I stood with legs across the hatchway to lower Midge onto the chair below. With one last look around, I dropped the flashlight into her waiting hands and eased myself through, balancing on the chair to catch the side of the hatch and close it after me. This time the wood was lowered into place with less panic.

I hopped to the floor and slapped dust off my hands, glad to be out of the gloom. By then, Midge had gone over to one of the small windows in the attic and was trying to open it.

'I thought I'd let some air circulate up here,' she said over her shoulder, 'but this window's stuck.'

I joined her. 'Might be paint on the outside. The builders should have left the windows open 'til they were dry. Here, let me have a go.'

Before I could give the sash on one half of the double-window a good thump, Midge held my arm.

'Do the bats really bother you, Mike? You know, we can always do as Hub suggested and find a way of getting rid of them without anyone knowing.'

I gazed at her steadily. 'You wouldn't like that very much, would you?'

'I don't like the idea of them spoiling Gramarye for you. It's more important to me that you're happy here, so if it's a choice between that and the bats staying, then they're the losers.'

We touched foreheads briefly. 'You're probably right,' I said, 'they'll be no trouble at all.' I turned back to the window.

'But any midnight bat orgies and they're out – the sound of all those frenzied wings would drive me crazy.'

I banged a palm against the sash, then tried again, biting my lip at the smarting of my hand. On the third try, the window juddered open an inch, and it was easy to push it wide after that. The half next to it was equally difficult, but again on the third thump it budged open. As I widened the gap, slipping the casement stay onto its catch, I glanced over at the woodland opposite, drawing in a deep breath of sun-warmed air as I did so. I stiffened before exhaling.

Was that a figure standing in the shade just beyond the first line of trees? Somebody watching us again?

'Midge,' I said, the sound strained because I still held a lungful of air. I let the breath go as she moved closer. 'Midge, somebody's over there watching the house.'

I didn't look at her, but I knew she was peering into the forest.

'Where, Mike? I don't see anyone.'

I took my eyes off the still figure for a moment and put an arm around Midge's shoulders, pulling her even closer.

'Over there,' I whispered unnecessarily and pointing. 'Just inside the trees. A dark figure looking directly across at the cottage.'

But when I returned my own gaze, the figure had disappeared.

'Still don't see it, Mike,' said Midge, and I turned to her speechlessly, then quickly looked back at the trees. Definitely nobody there.

I began to wonder if the country air was so fresh it caused hallucinations.

PROGRESS

The next couple of weeks flew by, keeping both of us busy and me free of any more 'hallucinations'. We spent the days (and often the nights) stripping old wallpaper and replacing it with new, and painting the walls and woodwork that we hadn't paid the builders to do. One or two evenings had turned chilly and we soon discovered all sorts of sneaky draughts creeping in to make us shiver; I did my best to locate their source and seal them. We washed, scrubbed, polished and cleaned. I fixed the front-door bell so that it clanged rather than clunked.

We had the chimneys swept in anticipation of cosy winters around the fireside, and we had the cesspit cleared (the smell when they syphoned into their huge tanker was awful and we were warned to keep every door and window shut while the operation was in progress). A plumber came in to do various jobs, including plumbing in the washing machine and getting the hot water to run hot rather than lukewarm (that required a new and bigger immersion heater in a cupboard upstairs, which cut heavily into our budget). The water ran clear thanks to the tank O'Malley had installed in the loft, and even the poor TV and radio reception somehow managed to shape up and clear itself after the first week. The television picture still wasn't brilliant, but then we were in a remote area.

I set up my music studio, still dreaming of the expensive equipment I'd be able to have some time in the future (not too distant, I hoped), while Midge prepared her own self-contained art studio beneath one of the large windows in the round room. I could tell she was itching to get back to painting – pictures, I mean, not walls – just as I yearned to get back to some serious music. Occupied though I was with manual labour, my head was swimming with ideas for songs, stories and the glimmerings of a full-scale rock musical. All ideas were tentative, but they're usually the most exciting kind; I wondered if they would look so good on paper or sound so terrific on tape. Despite that creative urge on both our parts, we resisted the temptation and persevered with the task in hand – that of preparing Gramarye for a comfortable and productive future.

We did our best with the garden – or should I say Midge did, particularly where the flowerbeds were concerned – but strangely enough it seemed to be thriving on its own. Even the rabbits – and it was like Watership Down territory hereabouts – thoughtfully left our flowers alone. We cleared the flowerbeds, but were relieved to find that many of the weeds had disappeared of their own volition, obviously daunted by the flowers' rude health and giving up the struggle to overthrow (I was naïve enough garden-wise to believe this possible and Midge, who knew better, made no comment). I bought one of those hover-mowers from the hardware store in the village for the grass verge beyond the fence and the area around the back of the cottage, and quite enjoyed working in the sun, stripped to the waist, tanning my back. I fixed the fence, replacing missing or damaged struts, nailing others upright, cheerfully painting over rotting wood with plentiful layers of white.

We made several trips into Bunbury, buying a few pieces of second-hand furniture and the odd knick-knack or two.

Rumbo became a regular visitor and I often asked him why he didn't move in permanently. He was a great one for conversation and although we sometimes felt he understood us, his toothful chatter didn't mean a lot to Midge and me. We assumed, however, that somewhere in the woods was a

Mrs Rumbo, and maybe little Rumbos too, a family he was happy to go home to after each day's adventure. He enjoyed games, did Rumbo, chasing after rolling tennis balls, pouncing onto our shoulders when we least expected it, furiously nibbling books or magazines to pieces while we pursued him around the cottage in an hysterical form of household paper-chase. There was something of the dog in that squirrel, a kind of dopey intelligence mixed with hints of craftiness that we found both amusing and often exasperating. He was good company.

Plenty of phone calls came in from friends and business associates, many of the latter ringing up with tempting offers of work – all of which we resisted. We'd decided upon a full month free of any professional engagement or commission and we meant to stick to it. At first the line was annoyingly crackly, as if the wires had gone rusty from lack of use, but the more calls we received the more distinct the voices became.

Our bird friend, whose wing we thought had been broken, came back (feathers on that particular wing were still missing, so we felt sure it was the same mistle thrush) and he had no reservations about flying straight into the kitchen to perch on the table or back of a chair. Others soon followed his example, their wariness becoming merely alertness, and that eventually turning into trust. Birds and the squirrel weren't the only visitors either: mice, bees, a fox, came by; even a stoat looked in one day. We got used to the odd spider or snail inside the cottage, and these were carefully taken outside on newspaper and set down in the flowerbeds.

Our three new friends from the grey house kept to their word by calling in on us from time to time, usually bearing a small gift of some kind – food, a bottle of home-made wine, an inexpensive ornament; nothing fancy, just goodwill things. We were always too busy to chat with them for long, and they never imposed themselves upon us, never outstayed their welcome. They were pleasant and informative about the area, useful with certain tips on countryside living. They were okay.

After a few nights the noises from the loft ceased to

bother me; in fact it was fascinating at dusk to sit outside on the bench and see the bats skittering from the eaves towards the nearby forest, a sight that became less eerie the more we watched. As we'd been advised earlier, they were quite harmless; they were unsociable creatures (thank goodness) who kept very much to themselves.

We ploughed on with the work, determined not to relax until we'd accomplished enough to be able to take things easy. There were only a few overcast days, the rest being brilliantly sunny, the air clear and revitalising first thing in the morning, comfortably sluggish in the afternoon.

We made progress. Life was good.

ROUGH STUFF

I'd gone to the hardware store in the village to buy nails, special oil mix for the mower, electrical plugs, yet more white paint – general bits and pieces – parking the Passat in the small but adequate carpark at the back of the high street. A few faces had become familiar to me because of my frequent sorties into Cantrip over the past couple of weeks, and one or two of the villagers even nodded hello as I walked around to the shops. I suppose that, as in all small communities, word had soon got around that Midge and I were the new occupants of Gramarye; I'd certainly become used to the occasional odd stare, so it was nice to be acknowledged now.

It was mid-morning and the store wasn't very busy. Taking a metal basket from the stack by the door, I strolled down the short aisles between shelving, reaching for the items I needed as I passed and naturally dropping in other articles that I *thought* might come in handy at some later date (funny how they rarely do).

I was examining various 'super' glues wrapped in plastic cocoons and suspended from metal prongs like chrysalids, wondering if the pupae would soon crawl out and take wing, when the gruffness of someone's voice broke through the daydream.

The cash counter was behind the shelf where I stood and I sauntered round, curious but ready to pay my bill anyway. The gruff voice belonged to the shopkeeper, a burly man called Hoggs, someone I'd always found very genial (I'd become a regular customer for my not-too-ambitious DIY enterprises), so it came as a surprise to find him in this brusque mood.

A girl stood at the counter with her back to me, her hair in braids and wearing a loose shirt and long patterned skirt. The thongs of her sandals curled above her ankles, tying just beneath the hem of the skirt. A metal basket was on the counter before her and the shopkeeper was grumpily delving into this and totting up the price of each item on the cash register. The girl herself was holding aloft two items – I couldn't make out what was inside – and I think she must have been asking which one was best for the particular job she had in mind. His reply had been something like, 'You'll have to find that out for yourself, won't you?' and I suppose I was mildly shocked, having found him so affable before.

To her credit, the girl merely handed him one of the tins and returned the other to a nearby shelf.

Hoggs caught my eye, then quickly looked heavenwards to show me his vexation. As the girl came back I saw she was pale, almost sallow-skinned, with a blankness of expression that either masterfully disguised her chagrin, or was a true reflection of what lay beyond. She dipped into a canvas shoulder bag and drew out a purse, while the shopkeeper removed the remaining goods from her wire basket, *clonking* them onto the counter with obvious ill-humour.

I felt sorry for the girl when she meekly handed over money after he had all but barked the amount at her. Her purchases were transferred to a plastic carrier-bag and she hurried from the store, barely glancing at me as she sped by.

Planting my own metal basket on the wooden counter I regarded mine host with some trepidation.

'Morning, Mr Stringer,' he greeted me, and I was heartened by the resumed friendly tone.

I jerked my head towards the now closed door. 'Problem with paying her bills?'

'Eh? Oh no, nothing like that,' he assured me, a trace of irritation still in his voice. 'She's one of that mob, that's all.'

'Oh yeah? What mob is that?'

He stopped removing items from my basket to give me a puzzled look. His face was wide and toned a ruddy pink, as though he hadn't had enough time outside to catch the summer's sun properly. 'No, of course you probly wouldn't know 'bout them yet, would you?' He shook his head and a firm finger stabbed at a key on the old-fashioned cash register. 'She's from the Temple, one of them . . .' the *cling* of the till again '. . . Synergists.' Hoggs looked up again. 'Bloody silly name that.'

I nodded a considered agreement. 'What does it mean exactly?'

'Mean? Means they're a bunch of crackpots, that's what it means.' He leaned forward conspiratorially. 'We don't like 'em, Mr Stringer, not their sort. Bringin' their funny ways and ideas down here. We don't want 'em.'

'They belong to a religious cult of some kind?' I was already beginning to make the connection: the girl would have fitted in well with Hub, Gillie and Neil.

'Somethin' like that, don't know what, though. We just don't want their sort clutterin' up our village, beggin' for money.'

'They beg?'

'Well, almost. Sell things, you know, things that people don't really want. Weave baskets and mats and such. Then they try to convert our youngsters, drag 'em off to their Temple so-called. Somethin' not right about that bunch, I'll tell you that for nothin'.'

'And they all live out at that manor house I've seen tucked away in the forest?'

'Croughton Hall it used to be called, not no more though. They've turned it into some sort of church now, their bloody Synergist Temple.'

I groped for my wallet. 'I guess they're harmless enough.'

The way Hoggs looked through me made me feel like the world's biggest buffoon. He told me how much I owed, took the money, then turned away. 'I'll find you a box for all

126

that stuff,' he said, walking to the end of the counter and reaching beneath it.

With my goods loaded, I bade him a simpleton's farewell and left the store, the cardboard box tucked awkwardly under one arm.

So my slight unease with our three newfound friends hadn't been totally unjustified. Even so, they appeared innocent enough and possibly it was only the poor image the media gave such cults that made me wary. The girl in the hardware store had certainly been innocuous, even though she'd had good cause to retaliate against Hoggs' blunt rudeness. I suppose it took many years for outsiders to be accepted in such a quiet and reasonably remote village as Cantrip, so an organisation that appeared to be steeped in an obscure religion was bound to have problems. What the hell was a Synergist anyway? There were plenty of other strange religions floating around, but this was a new one on me. Was it genuine or lunatic? Or genuinely lunatic? Kinsella and his companions seemed sane enough, and hardly religious zealots (although their forceful sincerity was a little off-putting).

Well, Midge and I were no longer that young and impressionable, so what did it matter if they chose to drop by from time to time? Didn't matter at all.

I'd rounded the corner of the narrow turning that led into the carpark, heading for the Passat which was tucked away at the far end, when I caught sight of the girl again. She was standing by the now familiar Citroën, and she wasn't alone. The hatchback of the car was open and she and Gillie Slade were loading up. Both were stony-faced as three youths paid them unwanted attention.

As I drew near, I saw that the boys – I guessed their ages at no more than fifteen or sixteen – were what could best be described as watered-down punks: spiked hair, torn and bleach-stained jeans, lace-up boots. Even in the hot weather, one wore a studded leather jacket, while his two friends had on ripped and can-sprayed T-shirts. Life down on the farm has changed, I told myself.

Leather-jacket was dancing around the girl I'd seen in the shop, tugging at her braids and chortling at his companions in the gormless way of his type. One of the others was snatching at the basket that Gillie was trying to put inside the car, while punk 3 was standing around picking his nose.

Now me, I'll run a mile from trouble any day, and ladies in distress cut no ice. I wondered if they would be too preoccupied to notice me. Had I forgotten to buy anything from the shops, giving me an excuse to turn back? Even for me, that was a little too cowardly. I walked on, pretending I hadn't noticed anything.

Punk 2 spoilt things by tipping the contents of Gillie's basket onto the ground and lunging for something lying there that took his fancy. Gillie pushed him away and he retaliated by shoving her back much harder, so that she sprawled on the deck. Her face had turned red and she was close to tears. Unfortunately, she saw me at that moment and relief and pleading stayed those tears.

I groaned inwardly. Caught. No way out. Shit! I strolled over, all nonchalance and quivery knees. Keeping my voice low in the best Eastwood tradition, I said, 'You okay, Gillie?'

The punks looked my way, the idiot grin still on Leather-jacket's acned face. Oh God, I thought, this is a scene from a bad teen movie.

Gillie was picking herself up, the other girl watching me with interest.

'Yes, I'm all right, Mike,' Gillie replied, and stooped again to retrieve the items she'd lost from her basket. Punk 2 kicked one of them away from her fingers, shrieking with glee at the fun of it all.

I walked up to him, glad he was shorter than me. 'I think you'd better get lost,' I told him. 'About now, would do.'

His cocky grin lost some of its substance and he glanced around at his companions for support. Leather-jacket sidled closer, and No 3 maintained his interest in the contents of his nose.

'What you fuckin' gonna do about it?' Leather-jacket enquired, breathing heavily on my neck (this one was taller).

'You don't want to find out,' I replied, annoyed that my voice had cracked slightly mid-sentence.

On close inspection I saw they really were only kids, not

bona-fide toughies in the ghetto sense; they were acting the role, but I wasn't sure they'd convinced themselves. That encouraged me.

All the same, there *were* three of them and I was in deep. It was Leather-jacket's turn to speak and he seemed to be having trouble forming a sentence (or maybe even a thought). I saved him the trouble. 'Either you leave these people alone, or I'm gonna flatten you.' I did my best to look mean.

It frightened me, but seemed to have the reverse effect on him: he grabbed my shirt and tried to head-butt me. I ducked reflexively and his mouth and chin came in sharp contact with the top of my head. His surprised howl of pain cheered me considerably, although an area of my skull had gone instantly numb. When I straightened, he was holding both his hands up to his mouth, blood already seeping through his fingers, a one-note moan accompanying the blood.

'There's more where that came from,' I warned, feeling chuffed and refraining from rubbing my scalp.

His pal, No 2, may have been smart enough to realise Leather-jacket's injury had been more by accident than design; he charged me, bellowing a battle hymn that sounded something like, 'Youuucuuuuhhhhnn . . .'

When pain might be involved, I can be pretty nimble: I stepped away from his outstretched arms and his stomach ran into my clenched fist. It was hardly a punch – his own momentum had provided most of the force – but he creased up, sucking air. I threw him across the bonnet of the nearest car and I think the metal surface, obviously having been boiling nicely under the sun for quite some time, must have scalded his cheek because he yelped and leapt up again. I was close behind him, though, and pushed his head back down, using my weight to hold him there and letting him sizzle.

No 3 had finally stopped picking his nose and gone on to scratching his armpit, a bewildered expression striving to give his features some form of intelligence. Leather-jacket was still making muffled noises, his bloodied fingers like a red bandana over his chin.

I was slightly out of breath, but summoned up enough control to smile laconically. 'Don't say I didn't warn you,' I said, almost enjoying the moment and lowering my voice another octave.

To my horror, the other two began to close in, the injured one gurgling curses now, the body I held pinned against the car bonnet kicking out behind, trying to rise.

'Boys, boys, what *is* going on here?'

It was a new voice and belonged to a smallish head jutting through the open window of a car that had just cruised to a halt. I could have kissed that little head, which I noticed was mounted on a white, circular ring. The vicar, or priest, looked shocked, as though he'd just run into the overspill from Gomorrah.

'Miles Carver, is that you?' He was looking directly at Leather-jacket.

Miles? I smiled, beginning to enjoy myself again.

'What on earth are you up to, boy?' The cleric switched off the engine and stepped from the car, looking aghast at all of us. He was a short man with one of those youthful, unlined faces that put him in the sixteen-going-on-fifty age bracket; an indication that it was towards the latter end of the scale was his plastered-down hair, all neat rows as parallel as weavers' warp strands, pink scalp gleaming between the lines. He wore a tweed jacket over his black shirt and white collar, and his fawn trousers bunched around his ankles as though they were his big brother's hand-me-downs.

'Would somebody mind telling me what this is all about?' he demanded.

Miles mumbled something that none of us understood. Punk 2 had ceased wriggling under my grasp, although he strained to keep his face off the hot metal, and No 3's hands had now sunk deep into his pockets in a conscious effort to keep them away from his nose and armpit.

It was Gillie who spoke up: 'The boys were trying to steal from us when Mr Stringer here came along and stopped them.'

I glanced at her in surprise. 'Steal' was a bit strong.

'My goodness,' the vicar exclaimed. 'Is this true, Miles?' He ignored the incoherent protest, probably well-used to such denials. 'Will you never learn? It was only my personal intervention that prevented you from being put on probation last time, and now I find you've let me down again. I'm afraid I'll have to have another word with your father.'

Miles blanched visibly.

'No real harm done,' I volunteered. 'Things got outa hand, that's all.'

The vicar turned his attention on me, sizing me up somewhat coldly I felt. 'I should think it would be all right to let go of that boy now,' he said, pointing at my charge.

'Sure.' I released my grip and the boy sprang away from the car bonnet as if ejected. He regarded me morosely, rubbing at the back of his neck.

'Thomas Bradley, you too.' The vicar shook his head in sad resignation.

Punk 3 hung his head in suitable shame – the vicar was probably on speaking terms with this one's father, too.

'I can only ask you to forgive these lads,' the cleric begged the girls and myself. 'They left school last term and with employment in this area so hard to find . . .' He left the excuse hanging in the air for us to deduce the reason for their misbehaviour. Try as I might, I couldn't find the answer, but I let it go, glad anyway that I'd come through unscathed and looking pretty good at that.

'The boys are extremely sorry that they bothered you ladies . . .' (they didn't look that apologetic to me) '. . . and I'm sure this sort of thing will never happen again.' The vicar gave each second-rate punk a baleful glare, then told them to be on their way, and 'sharply' too. They lumbered off, Miles (Miles? Oh really?) leaving a blood-spot trail behind. I was amused that a little guy like the vicar could have such a subduing effect on them and, not for the first time, realised that village life was a lot different from the city's.

Gillie and her friend picked up their pieces and put them in the back of the car, and I noticed the cleric was watching them with barely concealed disdain.

'Thanks for helping out,' I said to him. 'I was beginning to lose my temper.'

He faced me and his hostility was evident in both voice and expression. 'Yes, well, such incidents are unfortunate.

However, I do wish you people . . .' For the second time he left a sentence hanging in the air.

Her task completed, Gillie came over to me while her friend closed the hatchback. 'Oh, Mike, how can we thank you? Sandy and I were so frightened.'

'They were only kids,' I said modestly.

'Thugs,' she corrected and I shrugged noncommittally. The other girl, Sandy, joined us and I could tell she was still shaky. 'You're Mike?' she said. 'The others have told me about you and Midge. I hope you've managed to settle in at Gramarye.'

The vicar appeared to do a sudden re-appraisal of me. 'You're the couple who've moved into Flora Chaldean's cottage?'

'One half of the couple,' I admitted.

He immediately stepped forward, his hand outstretched. 'Then please let me welcome you to the parish and ask your forgiveness for not having popped out to see you and your good lady by now. I'd heard you'd arrived, of course, but my pastoral duties have kept me rather busy of late. I had intended . . .'

I shook his hand, already becoming used to his unfinished sentences and his entreaties to forgive. 'That's okay, we've been a bit busy ourselves. I'm Mike Stringer.'

'Peter Sixsmythe.' He pumped my hand. 'The Reverend Sixsmythe.'

'We have to get back, Mike,' Gillie interrupted. 'It was so good of you to help us – I hope you'll allow us to repay the debt.'

'No problem,' I said, now feeling a trifle embarrassed (smug, none the less). 'And nothing to repay. I'm just glad I happened along. See you soon, eh?'

'You will, most definitely.'

I hadn't meant it as an invitation. To my surprise, both girls took turns to lean forward and kiss my cheek before climbing into their car. The vicar and I stood aside as Gillie reversed the Citroën from the parking space, and she waved from the window as they left the carpark.

'Mr Stringer,' said the Rev. Sixsmythe, his schoolboyish

face grave, 'are you, er, well acquainted with those people?'

I frowned. 'Not really. Gillie and a couple of her friends have dropped by the cottage from time to time. They're very neighbourly.'

'Yes. Yes.' The words were drawn out as though he were considering the implications. 'Look, would you mind if I came over to see you tomorrow. I know I should have done so before, but as I explained . . .'

I hesitated. Religion wasn't one of my strongest points – not organised religion, at any rate – and I couldn't see myself turning up for Sunday Service on a regular basis; Midge, maybe, but definitely not me. Not that I'm a non-believer – far from it – but such beliefs are a personal and very private thing to me, and sharing only makes me feel uncomfortable. Churches make me fidgety. Still, what could I say to this anxious cleric?

'Sure, that'll be fine. I'll tell Midge you're coming.'

'Midge is your good lady?'

'My girlfriend.'

'Ah.' That was a small 'ah', no 'living in sin' judgement involved. 'I shall look forward to seeing you both. Will some time during the morning be all right?'

I nodded assent.

'Jolly good. And I do hope the little incident today hasn't left you with a bad impression of our village, Mr Stringer. Such upsets are very rare here, I can assure you.' He opened his car door, but didn't climb in immediately; instead he asked me a question. 'Did you know that these new friends of yours belong to a sect called the Synergist Temple?'

'I found out today.'

'I see. They hadn't mentioned it before?'

'No. As a matter of fact, it was Mr Hoggs in the hardware store who told me.'

'I wonder if they have said anything to you about Gramarye itself? Anything at all?'

Weird question, I thought. 'Uh-huh. They're interested generally in how we're getting on there, but nothing more. What makes you ask?'

He checked his watch. 'I'm rather late for an appointment

right now, so I must park my car and get along. Perhaps we might discuss this further tomorrow.' He ducked inside the car, then his head came back through the open window again. 'A word of caution in the meanwhile: be very careful of these people, Mr Stringer. Yes, be very careful.'

I left him reversing into the parking space vacated by Gillie's Citroën and walked on to my own car, not sure of how seriously I should be taking him. Perhaps he just didn't like maverick religions. Or maybe there really was something sinister about these people.

One way or another, I was sure we would soon find out. I had a feeling in my bones.

SYNERGISTS

Kinsella arrived later that evening, alone apart from two bottles of home-made wine.

I was sitting on the doorstep, tossing bread crusts to Rumbo, who was storing them nearby on one side of the path, nimbly catching each piece and dashing back with it, kicking up a storm to warn off the late-shift birds. Midge was inside, clearing up the dinner things.

'You'll need a suitcase to carry that lot home,' I advised Rumbo and he chattered back at me to get on with the game. I'd always thought that squirrels only ate nuts and acorns and berries, so it came as a surprise that the rascal would chomp anything offered to him.

This time Kinsella arrived in a different vehicle, a red Escort, and I looked on curiously when the car drew up outside the gate. When I realised who it was something inside me sagged: the vicar's cautionary words had obviously reinforced my own reservations about this blond bomber and his companions.

He waved to me from the other side of the gate and, for some reason, he stayed there as if waiting for an invitation to enter. It occurred to me that neither he nor his friends had ever set foot on Gramarye property, our conversations always conducted over the fence. Sheer politeness, I told myself, plain old-fashioned good manners on their part. Heaving myself up, I sauntered down the path towards him, Rumbo showing his irritation that the game had been interrupted by clenching his tiny fists and squawking fiercely. I dropped the last crusts onto his pile as I passed, and this soothed him somewhat, although I could still hear him grumbling behind me as he tidied up his hoard.

'Hi there, Mike,' Kinsella called as I approached, the wine cradled in one arm as he raised the other. He was grinning broadly, all sun-tan and white teeth. 'I've brought a little somethin' to show our appreciation for what you did today.'

'Oh, you mean the trouble in the village?' I said humbly and feigning surprise. 'They were only kids out for a bit of hooliganism.'

'Not quite kids, as I heard it. Gillie told me you gave 'em hell. She and Sandy send their love and thanks once again, and I bring you wine.'

'That isn't necessary, you know.'

'Sure it is. Look, why don't we open a bottle of this stuff right now? I promise you, it tastes real good.'

He stood there holding the wine bottles by the necks over the gate and it would have been churlish of me not to have invited him in. I swung open the gate and waved him through. 'Sounds like a great idea,' I said.

I expected him to sweep right past, full of bonhomie and sunshine health; but he didn't – he stood on the threshold like a nervous bride. I stared and it was only when he became aware of me once again that the old swagger returned.

'Uh, sorry,' he said quickly. 'I suddenly wondered if I were imposing. You might be very busy just now.'

'Not this time of day. To tell you the truth, I could use a drink.'

He stepped inside and I thought – I *only* thought – I saw him shiver.

'Boy, you've worked hard on the patch,' he remarked as I led the way.

'Midge has done most of it. She's amazed me the way she's coped with all these different flowers. I think moving down here has revived all her horticultural instincts.'

Rumbo, who no doubt had been pondering on how to get his groceries back to the nest, jerked his head around at our approach and his small sharp teeth bared in alarm. I was amused to discover he was so shy of strangers when he shot off like a rocket, streaking up the embankment at the side of the cottage to disappear into foliage.

'Cute pet,' said Kinsella, chuckling aloud.

'Not so much a pet, more of a regular house-caller. He's usually more friendly.'

We reached the front door and I went straight in while Kinsella lingered on the doorstep, evidently to admire the garden further. 'Fantastic colours,' I heard him say. 'Incredible.'

'Midge?' I called out. 'We've got a guest.'

She emerged from the next room, wiping her hands on a dishcloth and with an expectant smile on her face. I pointed and she peered around the door.

'Hub, what a nice surprise!'

''Lo, Midge. I've brought this hero of yours a token of gratitude.'

'Hero? Oh, you mean his knight-to-the-rescue act this morning.'

(Not being the strong silent type, I'd thought the incident worth mentioning. However, I hadn't said anything about the Rev. Sixsmythe's words on the Synergists; I'd leave that to him tomorrow when he could also explain himself to me a bit more.)

'He certainly saved our sisters from some serious hassle. They came back kinda shaky but full of praise for Mike.'

'Hey, don't stand outside,' I said, feeling my face going red, 'come on in.'

He accepted the invitation and it seemed to me he was as hesitant as before. Maybe tentative is a better word, because he stepped inside like a diver walking underwater, his movement slow and deliberate. As dusk was settling it was more gloomy inside the kitchen than usual and he had trouble adjusting his eyes to the change in light, blinking them rapidly as he peered around.

'We thought we'd open a bottle now,' I told Midge and the idea apparently pleased her.

'I'll fetch some glasses,' she said, going to the dresser. First she pulled open a drawer and tossed me the corkscrew, then she crouched at a cupboard door and brought out two glasses.

'Aren't you going to join us, Midge?' asked Kinsella, rubbing at one of his bare arms as if he felt cold.

'Never touch the stuff. Tell you what, I'll join you with a Coke.'

All three of us sat around the kitchen table and I poured wine for the American and myself, while Midge drank straight from the Coke bottle.

'We're very grateful, Mike,' said Kinsella, raising his glass.

'Aah, you know the type – all piss and wind. They saw a coupla girls on their own and thought they'd have some fun. They wouldn't have bothered if you'd have been with Gillie and Sandy.'

'I don't know about that. Seems we're not too popular around this place.'

'Is that right?' I said, as if it came as a surprise.

He nodded grimly. 'They imagine we're a bunch of religious freaks or somethin'. You know what it's like in these tiny backwater communities, suspicious of all outsiders, especially when they're involved in somethin' the locals don't understand.'

'The Synergist Temple? I've got to admit, I don't understand that either. What is it, some kind of new religion?'

He grinned, and Midge raised her eyebrows.

'Synergist?' she asked.

'Someone in the village has already told you about us,' said Kinsella.

'Yeah, the owner of the hardware store.'

'Then you already know they don't like us.'

I felt as if I'd been found out in a lie, but Kinsella was smiling across the table at me.

'Synergist?' Midge repeated, noisily tapping the Coke bottle on the wood surface for attention.

Kinsella turned to her. 'That's the name for our Order.'

'Strange name. I don't think I've ever heard of it before. What does it mean exactly?'

Kinsella sat forward in his chair. 'Firstly, we're not a crackpot religion, not like many that are around today, so please don't associate us with any of those. We're not a charity, nor are we a religious sect in the strictest sense.' He was still smiling, but now looking reassuringly from face to face. 'So, let me explain about Synergism. Fundamentally, it's the belief that the human will and the Divine Spirit are the two agents that can co-operate in regeneration.'

That statement took time to sink in with Midge and me. We stared back blankly and his smile broadened to a grin. Despite his relaxed manner, though, I detected a serious intent in his eyes.

'Just as various chemicals act upon each other,' he went on, 'so we believe that the thought processes of the human mind – which are, y'know, only a complicated series of chemical reactions – can combine with the Divine Spirit, our collective souls, if you like, to produce a unique power.'

I kicked Midge's foot under the table, but she ignored me.

'What kind of power are you talking about?' she asked Kinsella.

'Oh, it's diverse. The power to cure, to influence, the power to create . . . it can be manifested in so many ways.'

'You mentioned regeneration . . .'

'Regeneration is a word we use to cover all aspects of our doctrine. It means the regeneration of our own spirits, and that of . . .' He broke off there, now his smile apologetic. 'You're probably thinking this all sounds crazy, right?'

I had to agree, although I kept quiet.

'But look, all religious devotees pray to their particular deity, whether Christian, Moslem, Jewish – the list is endless. Most times they pray for Divine Intervention, for certain things to happen, or maybe *not* to happen. They could be praying for themselves, their loved ones, or even the world in general. The point is, they're trying to direct the natural course of events, their own particular god the intermediary or catalyst, or specifically the creator of those events. Our doctrine isn't so different from theirs.'

He sat back in his chair, waiting for us to absorb the revelation.

'But there is a difference,' I prompted.

'Only inasmuch as we, with the help of our founder and guide, are learning to combine and direct our energies in a more physical sense and, of course, acting in conjunction with the Divine Spirit.'

'I'm sorry,' I said, 'but I'm still not quite with you. This, uh, "Divine Spirit", is what?'

'You, me, our thoughts.' He waved his arms expansively. 'The very air around us. And the earth itself, the very power it generates.' His voice had become hushed and I found even I was holding my breath. His enthusiasm had somehow charged the atmosphere.

Nobody seemed to want to break the silence between us for a while and I noticed it was becoming quite dark in the kitchen. The evening had taken on a chill, too.

Midge picked up the Coke bottle to drink from it, her eyes never leaving Kinsella. 'Are there . . . are there many of you at the grey house?' she asked before touching the bottle to her lips.

'Between forty and fifty, I guess. We call the place our sanctuary, by the way; it's our retreat as well as our temple. And we're growing in numbers all the time.' He leaned his elbows on the table, his head jutting forward. 'You know, you two should come over and see us, I really think you'd find it an interesting experience.'

I spoke up before Midge could say anything. 'We're still pretty busy around the place . . .'

He laughed and reached forward to pat my arm. 'Don't get nervous, Mike, we won't try to convert you. No, that's not the way we operate at all.'

I remembered Hoggs' words in the village that morning indicating otherwise.

'You'd meet some very interesting people,' Kinsella continued heartily, 'and from many different parts of the world. You'd maybe get the chance to meet Mycroft, too.'

Some of my wine spilt as I picked up the glass. 'Mycroft?'

'Uh-huh. Eldrich P. Mycroft, our founder, and a *very*

unique man.' Kinsella had hardly touched his wine, but now he took a large swallow. 'This is good stuff, huh? We make a little money from selling this juice. Never ask for donations, y'see, we always sell our home-made goods.'

'Does that bring in enough to keep the organisation running?' asked Midge.

'The Temple, Midge, we call it the Temple. The answer to your question is no, not really. We do have private funds, though. It's turned a little cold, don't you think?' This time he rubbed briskly at both upper arms. Oddly, there was perspiration on his brow. 'Yeah, it's turned cold.' He drank wine again, his eyes roving around the room.

'Perhaps I should close the door,' suggested Midge, already beginning to rise.

'No, it's okay,' he quickly said, looking over at the open doorway. 'Uh, it's nice to take in all those wonderful scents from the garden. The flowers out there are a real joy, Midge. Yeah, Mike, you were great helping out the girls like that today. Everything okay in the cottage? No big problems yet? Apart from the bats. You still worried over those bats, Mike?'

Midge and I exchanged glances. Was this guy getting drunk on one glass of wine?

'They haven't bothered us yet,' I replied. I tasted my drink again and it didn't seem that powerful to me.

'You can always count on us to help in any way, you know that.' His fingers twisted his glass around on the table top. 'Gets dark early in this neck of the woods,' he said, then laughed, the sound sharp against the stillness of the evening.

'Feels like a storm's brewing,' I remarked.

'A storm? Yeah, that's it, there's a storm coming.' Kinsella was still wearing that inane smile, but somehow he looked uncomfortable – almost trapped. He was beginning to make me jumpy.

I think Midge was trying to calm him when she enquired, 'Are all the people at the Temple around your age, Hub?'

'Oh no. No, we're all age groups. As a matter of fact, even one or two of our fosterlings are in their sixties. That's what we call the followers, y'know – Fosterlings.'

Jesus, I thought. 'Is that what you are?'

'No, Mike, I'm a first officer.'

'Sounds big stuff.'

'Well, it's a high number in the Temple, carries a lotta weight. Hope it's not going to be a bad storm out there. Can you feel the thunder in the air?'

I could. It was almost tangible. I felt that if I snapped my fingers, they'd spark.

Kinsella gulped down the last of his wine and I raised the bottle towards him. He waved it away. 'I really oughta be going, it's getting late.'

'One for the road?' I said.

'Thanks anyway, but I should make a start before the storm breaks, huh?'

He stood, his chair scraping noisily against the floor tiles. Midge and I rose with him, but he was by the door before we were properly on our feet.

'You remember what I told you.' The left side of his smile had developed a twitch. 'Call in on us any time, we'll give you a big welcome.'

He was edging out of the door even as we approached.

'You stay put,' he said hastily. 'Don't come out to the gate, you might get wet when the rain comes.'

Although it was quite dark by now, I could see his skin was damp with perspiration; yet he shuddered as though a cold draught had tickled his spine.

Then he was gone, hurrying down the path as if he had an urgent appointment elsewhere. Midge and I looked at each other in astonishment.

'Do you think he's all right?' said Midge, genuinely concerned.

'Your guess is as good as mine. Maybe it was something we said.'

She shivered, victim of the same draught no doubt. 'Weird, Mike. *Weird.* You'd better go after him, make sure he's okay to drive.'

I saluted and went outside in time to see our swift-departing guest climbing into the Escort, leaving the garden gate open behind.

'Hey, Hub!' I called, but he couldn't have heard me; the

car must have left deep ruts in the grass verge, so quickly did it speed away. I strolled to the gate, and by the time I got there the Escort had disappeared from view. 'Have a nice day,' I said to the empty road.

Closing the gate, I turned back towards Gramarye and now I noticed that any storm clouds had moved on. But then I stopped. There were dark clouds on the horizon, obscuring the last rays of the fading sun, their tops tinged red, but the sky above was relatively free of any heavy clouds. A breeze rumpled the flowerbeds and colours softened by twilight bobbed in smooth rhythm. A small black shape flittered from the roof of the cottage, a bat on its evening's forage, and I stood in the garden, metaphorically scratching my head, wondering why we had all thought a storm was looming.

And then that cold draught touched me.

I shivered and my shoulders hunched. Something beyond the garden drew my eyes towards it. Nothing that moved. Nothing that made any sound. Just the figure again, now standing before the edge of the forest, the face no more than a dim blur.

But I knew it was watching me. And I knew it was waiting.

The figure moved forward, just one step. And I fled inside the cottage.

SIXSMYTHE

You may have guessed by now that I'm not one of the world's greatest heroes, and you'd be right. But I do have my moments; it so happens that the evening of Kinsella's visit was not one of them.

I didn't mention what I'd seen to Midge, not wanting to alarm her unduly and feeling slightly ashamed that I hadn't gone over to investigate anyway. Once inside the cottage, I'd run upstairs and peered out of a window in the round room; although the light was murky, I could see the figure had gone. It certainly hadn't had time to cross the clearing to the cottage, so it could only have moved back inside the cover of the trees. When Midge had asked me what I was looking for, I told her I thought I'd spotted one of the famous New Forest deer, which was a mistake because she became excited and I had to dissuade her from going outside to look for it. Too dark, I'd told her, and the animal was probably well inside the forest by now.

She'd reluctantly agreed and wistfully watched the clearing until night fell completely (I watched her, but apprehensively).

I was very much on edge when we turned in later, even though I'd done my best to rationalise matters throughout the rest of the evening. The scuffle earlier in the day, the peculiar

144

change in Kinsella while we drank wine, the expected storm that hadn't materialised: I reasoned that all these things had strung me out, making me a little overwrought. I never doubted I'd seen someone watching from the woods, but the preceding events had made me nervous, and that nervousness had become exaggerated on seeing the mystery watcher once again. You might have felt the same under the circumstances.

I slept badly, waking often to listen to night noises, imagining prowlers trying the windows downstairs, testing the doors. Creaks were footsteps, and soft taps were finger-nails on glass.

It was a relief when morning finally broke.

I'd just finished cutting the grass at the back of the house and was cleaning mulch from the mower blades when the Rev. Sixsmythe arrived. Midge, in shorts and T-shirt, had been busy in the front garden when the vicar had called hello over the fence. She'd been caught unawares (I'd neglected to inform her of his proposed visit), but naturally had welcomed him graciously. She brought him around the side of the cottage to where I was working, pulling a face at me that he was unable to see.

'Good morning, Mr Stringer,' he said cheerily, striding forward to pump my hand. Today he wore a brown trilby, which only served to make him look like a kid dressed in Dad's clothes because it was a size too big for him. 'Good to see you hard at work. Mowing twice a week, I hope?'

'Three times. The grass is over-healthy here.'

He looked around appraisingly. 'Ah yes, you'll find plant and animal life extremely abundant in this area. I believe Flora Chaldean had quite a job keeping it all under control. I haven't come at a bad time, have I? We did agree yesterday.'

'No, I was about to grab a break,' I replied.

'Me, too,' said Midge. 'Would you like some tea, coffee? Or lemonade?'

'A lemonade would be super, Mrs – ah, Miss . . .'

'Gudgeon,' she finished for him.

'Gudgeon,' he repeated. 'Now that name rings a bell . . .'

'Margaret Gudgeon,' I told him. 'Children's books?'

'Why of course, yes indeed!' He positively bristled with the thrill of it. 'Let me welcome you to our parish, Miss Gudgeon. My goodness, I'm very familiar with your work having three young sprogs of my own. My eldest daughter is only just going on to other things, but she still keeps her collection of your books. How marvellous that you should choose to make your home here. And, of course, in this particular cottage! You are aware, I take it, of Gramarye's meaning?'

'Yes,' she said. 'It means Magic.'

I looked at her in surprise. She'd never told me that.

'How appropriate,' Sixsmythe prattled. 'How very appropriate. Isn't Magic what many of your stories are about?'

'I only illustrate the books.'

'Yes, but the pictures *are* the stories, aren't they? The words are really there to serve your pictures, Miss Gudgeon. Now, may I call you Margaret? And it's Mike, isn't it? Surnames are so formal, and we're all friends here.'

I wondered if I should call him Pete.

'Lemonade for you, Mike?' Midge was smiling at me and she also passed on a secret look that said, *who is this guy?*

'Terrific.' I grinned back.

We'd bought a small garden table and a couple of cheap chairs from the village and arranged them around the old bench; I waved a hand towards them and the vicar sat in one, taking off his hat and placing it on the table top. I sat opposite him on the bench. From that position I could see the forest behind him and, not for the first time that morning, I scanned its fringes, searching for you-know-what.

'I must apologise for what happened in the village yesterday,' said Sixsmythe, wiping his brow with a red handkerchief. 'I suppose there has to be an unruly element in any community, and unfortunately you bumped into the worst of ours. They're not bad lads really, just at odds with themselves and at loose ends with the world itself.'

'I'd almost forgotten about it,' I lied (funny how you tend to lie more to men of the cloth, assuming a kind of false piety). 'No real harm done anyway.'

'Good of you to take it that way. We're usually a peaceful community, Mike, and perhaps we have too gentle a lifestyle in some respects for this day and age. However, it suits most people hereabouts and I can't imagine any drastic changes taking place over the next decade or so. Unless they decide to build a motorway through our part of the forest, that is, but I don't think it's very likely.'

He gave a short laugh, but I had the uncomfortable feeling he was watching me closely. I fervently hoped he was not going to suffer from the same hysteria as our friend Kinsella had yesterday.

We discussed the weather, the countryside, and briefly touched on the state of the nation, and I had the impression that he was awaiting Midge's return before going on to more personal topics.

Return she did, and not before time (I'm not very good at small talk), carrying a tray of glasses and iced lemonade. I took pleasure in the distraction of her slim legs, now lightly tanned and, as ever, velvety smooth from top to toe. I caught Sixsmythe having a sneaky look too, but then he was only flesh and blood despite the sweat-smudged white collar.

Midge sat next to me on the bench and poured lemonade from the jug. It was another glorious day – that summer had to hold some kind of record for continuous sunshine – and the very pleasantness of my surroundings allayed my nervousness from the night before. Almost. There was still that niggling unease at the back of my brain, a disquiet that couldn't be sensibly clarified. I sipped lemonade and tried to keep my attention on the cleric, and not on the woods behind him.

'So, Margaret,' said Sixsmythe, having swallowed half his drink in one go, 'are you working on a new book at the moment?'

'Oh no. Mike and I decided we wouldn't take on any more work for at least a month, not until we'd made ourselves comfortable in Gramarye. You could call it an adjustment period, too.'

'Very wise. And what is your line of business, Mike? Are you an artist also?' He was genuinely interested, his clear, schoolboy's eyes eager bright.

'I play guitar, write songs when I can.'

He seemed disappointed. 'I see. You don't work regularly then?'

Midge and I laughed.

'Yes, he does,' said Midge, still amused but indignant too. 'Mike plays at recording sessions mostly, although occasionally he goes on the road.'

'On the road?'

'I back other performers,' I told him. 'You know, as part of a touring band.'

'Ah.'

'And when he's not doing that, he works *very* hard at song writing. In fact, Mike's got the basis for a musical –'

'Midge . . .' I warned good-naturedly.

'Sorry.' She squeezed my leg, then said to Sixsmythe, 'We have an agreement that we never talk about ideas for future projects in company. Mike and I feel it takes out some of the energy for the work itself.'

'Yes, I think I understand that. I suppose pre-explanation can take the edge off creativity.'

'You got it,' I said. 'Too many good ideas, particularly in my business, get talked to death before they even get off the ground.'

'My word, but what an exciting time you both must have.'

We chuckled again at that.

'When a new book is published, or work's going really well – that's when things get exciting,' said Midge. 'Otherwise, it's usually self-disciplined hard slog.'

'Nevertheless, you must meet some very interesting people,' he insisted. 'I do hope you won't get bored too easily with us simple folk.'

'Believe me, half the reason Mike and I moved here was to get away from certain so-called "interesting" people. We find country life quite refreshing.'

'Yes, I was being somewhat harsh on myself and my parishioners. You'll find that many of us are not quite as dull as you might at first think.' He nodded to himself, then gazed up reflectively at the cottage walls. 'Yes indeed,' he mused, 'there are quite a few interesting characters in these parts. I think you'd have found Flora Chaldean fascinating, for instance. A most extraordinary individual.'

Midge rested her elbows on the table, clasping her hands before her. 'Did you know her well?' she asked.

'Flora? No, I'm afraid nobody knew her well. Very much of a recluse, you see. But the villagers and many of the local people came here to see her in time of trouble.' He smiled almost wistfully. 'In fact, many of those I failed to help would visit her, and perhaps she was of greater comfort to them than I. Oh, they never let me know of their visits, kept them very much a secret. But I knew. I knew their old country ways.'

I shifted on the bench, and I could tell Midge was intrigued.

'What sort of help did Mrs Chaldean give them?' I asked. 'Was she just one of those who people like to tell their troubles to?'

'More than that. Yes, much more, I believe.' He suddenly frowned. 'She was a great healer. A healer of the spirit as well as the flesh, apparently. Sadly, I'm hopeless at the latter, and only sometimes good at the former. It seems that Flora had a gift that was centuries-old.'

Birds fluttered close, landing near our feet. If Sixsmythe hadn't been there they would have been on the table itself, chirping for food.

'Her solicitor did mention that she was a healer of sorts,' said Midge. 'Are you telling us now that she was a faith healer?'

'Not exactly. Oh, I'm sure that much of her effectiveness was due to people's utter belief in her powers to cure, but that wouldn't have explained everything. She made up potions of the kind you might find in books on ancient remedies, those that are passed down from generation to generation, but she also had the ability to cure without any such medicines, by talking, or laying on of hands. Not that she would oblige just anybody! Goodness no! There were some she would not let inside her garden gate!' He shook his head, grinning like a ventriloquist's dummy. 'And then, of course, she had a wonderful way with animals. Could cure them of ailments almost overnight, I'm told.'

Midge stole a quick glance at me.

'You'd quite often find a sick cow or pony tethered outside here for a day or so, who were inevitably in fine fettle by the time the owners arrived to take them home again. Dogs, cats – quite a menagerie on occasions! Now you can't tell me that animals had faith in her powers, so it's hard to fathom how they became well again. Yes, yes, a wonderful gift had Flora. Pity that I only got to know her towards the end of her life. May I have another glass of lemonade, Margaret? It's rather cooling on a day like this.'

She poured and was obviously engrossed with the cleric's account of Gramarye's previous owner. 'I'm surprised her fame wasn't more widespread from what you've told us.'

'Heavens, no! All kept very secret in these parts, you know. Yes, very hush-hush. Flora would bind those who came with their problems to secrecy before she would even attempt a cure. However, as with all such delightful mysteries, there were always whispers, a confidence here, a hint there. I think the locals felt that to admit these things openly would somehow break the old lady's spell.'

'That's an odd word for a vicar to use,' I remarked.

He looked reasonably abashed. 'Yes, I admit "spell" has certain mumbo-jumbo connotations, but I'm merely recounting what went on in the minds of the local folk. I think it's quite charming, don't you?'

'Uh . . . yeah, I suppose so. I'm just surprised to hear a vicar talk in those terms.'

He laughed aloud at that. 'Quite so! I can understand your surprise. But spells, incantations and yes, Magic itself, have a lot to do with my particular trade, wouldn't you agree? When we clergy preach the almighty power of the Lord's divine goodness, we are, after all, speaking of Magic.'

'I . . . hadn't thought of it like that,' I admitted.

'Of course not. And I'm teasing you a little. Remarkable though Flora Chaldean was, I'm afraid that such sorcery went out of fashion a few hundred years or so ago. The microchip is the new Magic, isn't it?' He gulped down more lemonade, obviously very thirsty. (I learned from Midge later that Sixsmythe had cycled from the village in the belief that the exercise on such a fine day would do him the world of good. Although the over-sized trilby had kept his neat-lined hair in place, it hadn't done much for his body temperature.)

'Mike,' he said, placing his glass back on the table and regarding me with a beagle-eyed expression. 'These Synergist people – you told me yesterday they'd visited you here a number of times.'

Wondering what was coming, I nodded a 'yes'.

'They also used to visit Flora Chaldean.'

I had no particular comment on that; it seemed reasonable enough.

'The point is, they were very unwelcome. Flora hated this pseudo-religious group with all her heart. So much so, in fact, that she even complained to the village constable, but there was very little he could do to stop them coming here.' He gestured at the landscape behind him. 'These woods are common land and so are the paths around the cottage: they had the legal right to pass by or linger at any time they chose to do so.'

'Wait a minute. Are you saying they harassed the old lady?'

'From what I've been led to believe, yes, most definitely.'

'But why should they do that?' cut in Midge. 'The three we've met couldn't be more friendly, or more harmless. Why on earth should they try to upset Flora?'

He raised his hands slightly, then let them fall onto the table. 'Who can say? Flora was a very private person, despite – or perhaps more correctly, because of – the discreet services she provided to those in need. She was certainly eccentric, not to say a trifle cranky on occasions, so she might have taken a particularly strident dislike to them for any number of personal reasons.'

'I got the impression yesterday that not many of the locals *do* care for them, so she wasn't alone in that respect,' I said. 'I still can't understand why they're so unpopular, though. What have they done to pis– to cause such resentment?'

'They're strange people, and they live in a strange way.'

I sighed. 'That's hardly reason –'

'They're a suspect organisation, Mike, not unlike a few

151

others I could mention that are around nowadays. They came here five years ago, led by a man named Mycroft. There were only a few of them at first, and they moved into Croughton Hall, keeping very much to themselves. Others followed, though, people from different parts of the world, assembling on the Croughton estate as if it were some focal point for their religion. And it wasn't long after that they set out to recruit more followers, many from around here, locals, mainly youngsters, enticing them away from their families, brainwashing them to accept their ways, Mycroft's teachings, so that they never wanted to leave, no amount of persuasion from their families or loved ones drawing them back into the real world again.'

'Surely the authorities would have stepped in if it's as bad as you say.' Midge's eyes were sharp with concern.

'Since there were no minors involved, and no laws have ever been broken, they deemed they were in no position even to investigate. Odd cults and religions are hardly rare these days, after all. The Synergists aren't even registered as a charity, so even their financial status cannot be questioned as long as their records are carefully maintained and presented.'

'Isn't there some law against secret societies?' I asked.

'The Synergist Temple is hardly that. They keep very much to themselves, but I wouldn't describe them as a secret society.'

'Have you ever met this man Mycroft?' Midge watched the vicar over the top of her glass while she drank.

'No, never, even though I've called at the house more than once. I suppose I should refer to the place as their temple, but it's awfully difficult for me to regard it as such. No, our Mr Mycroft always appears to be either indisposed or away on business at the time of my visits. As a matter of fact, I don't believe anyone hereabouts has ever set eyes on the man.'

'You haven't explained why they should be interested in Flora Chaldean,' I said. 'She was a bit ancient to become one of their fosterlings, wasn't she?'

Sixsmythe raised his eyebrows. 'You know how they refer to their followers?'

'One of the three who've been visiting us regularly dropped by yesterday evening to thank me for helping out the girls in the village. He told us something about the Synergists.'

'I see.'

I grinned. 'Don't worry, he wasn't trying to convert us. We were interested, so we asked. And he gave us answers.'

Sixsmythe was quiet for a moment or two. Then he said, 'I firmly believe that you both should take the utmost caution where these people are concerned. Yes, I'm well aware that they appear to be extremely affable, even rather innocent, yet I can't help but feel there's something more to them than they would care to admit.'

'That sounds very sinister.'

'Perhaps so.'

'Oh come on, you'll have to give us something more than that,' Midge scoffed mildly.

'I'm afraid I can't. Call it a gut-feeling, one that's shared by many of my parishioners. If it was anything more, any evident acts of misconduct on the Synergists' part, then our local council might have been able to exercise its authority and have done something about their presence in the district. As it is, they keep to themselves and, so far, haven't committed any public offence.'

'Then why all the fuss?' Midge was quite irritated by now. 'Just because they don't conform to the natural pattern of life around here, it's no reason to shun them.'

'Dear girl, if only it were that simple. As I said, call it gut-feeling, intuition – whatever you like, but the locals are wary of them and, as a man of God, so am I. There's an air of secrecy about them that we find extremely disturbing.'

Midge giggled and Sixsmythe frowned.

'I didn't intend to amuse you,' he said, somewhat crossly I thought. 'We may lead rather sheltered lives in this part of the country, but I can assure you we are not all superstitious country bumpkins. I've proffered my advice, and there's little more that I can do.' He reached for his hat and made ready to leave. 'In my view, this Synergist sect is not to be trusted; however, I leave you to make up your own mind about that.'

I was taken aback by his touchiness. 'Hey, look, we're

not mocking you and we really do appreciate your coming out all this way to tell us about them. We hardly know these people, but they seem neighbourly enough, so it's difficult for us to blindly accept what you're saying. You've gotta own up, you haven't offered any firm evidence.'

His miffed expression softened, but he stood anyway. 'Yes, I do understand how it must look to you,' he said. 'I imagine I sound extremely foolish, yet all I ask is that you take heed of my words. And if you should have any concerns whatsoever – anything at all – promise me you'll phone me at the vicarage. Can we agree at least on that?'

'Sure,' I replied, rising with him.

Midge was less obliging, and I could see why: the first arrow had been fired at her Shangri-La; she didn't really want to know about bad neighbours, especially when she had already taken a shine to them. Nevertheless, she politely got to her feet and we accompanied the vicar back to his bicycle. Sixsmythe was well aware of her mood and probably felt a tiny bit contrite, because he did his best to direct the conversation onto other, more pleasant matters – Gramarye's beautiful situation, the wonderful garden, the loveliness of the forest itself (even lovelier, according to him, in the autumn months when the trees held a vast canopy of countless shades of russet golds), and whether or not he could welcome us to next Sunday's services at the church (I knew that would come up). Synergists didn't get a mention.

I opened the gate for him and he went through, slid clips around his trouser ankles, then pulled his bicycle upright from the fence where it had reclined as if exhausted by the journey.

'Mr Sixsmythe?' said Midge as he swung a leg over the machine.

He twisted around to look enquiringly at her.

'Can you tell me something?'

'Of course, providing I know the answer.'

'Well, we . . . I . . . I wondered how Flora Chaldean died.'

He became momentarily flustered. 'Oh, dear girl, I hope I haven't given you cause for too much concern by overstating my case. Please forgive me if I've alarmed you to that extent.'

'No, honestly, you haven't. I've been wondering for a while now.'

'Flora was a very old lady, Margaret. Nobody is quite sure of exactly how many years she had lived, but it's reasonable to assume she had reached her eighties – possibly her late eighties.' He smiled kindly at Midge. 'I suppose you could say Flora died of old age itself. Her heart grew weary and she passed away in her beloved Gramarye. Unfortunately, because she was a recluse, nobody knew until weeks later, although there were those who claimed they had passed by the cottage and had caught sight of her in the garden only a few days before her body was found. But then, people are often confused about specific times, particular dates; it's very difficult to be absolutely certain about such things.'

'Why should there be any confusion?' asked Midge.

'Ah,' the vicar replied, as though her question were pertinent. 'It so happened that I was the one who discovered her body. I used to call in now and again to see how she was, just part of what I consider to be my regular duties, even though I can't remember Flora ever attending my church. I make a point of always visiting the elderly of the parish when I have time, particularly during the winter months.'

He adjusted the trilby, pulling the hat firmly down over his head so that the breeze would not sweep it away when he started cycling. The brim bent the top of his ears. 'I saw her through the kitchen window, sitting at the table, cup and saucer before her as though she had only just brewed herself a fresh pot of tea. It was an overcast day and the kitchen was very gloomy, so that I was unable to see clearly; I remember thinking how grimy the windows were, because that hindered my view also. When I tapped on the glass and got no response, well, that was when I became anxious. I'd already tried the door and found it locked, which was odd, because I had never known Flora to lock either doors or windows before. Most peculiar, I thought, and immediately drove to the nearest public phone box and called out Constable Farnes from the village.'

He shook his head sadly, as if the memory was still all too clear inside his head. 'I waited for him at the cottage, meanwhile discovering that the door around the back was also locked, as were the windows. When Farnes arrived he broke a pane in the kitchen window and undid the latch; then he climbed in.'

Midge moved closer to me. A car sped by, a wooden dog nodding its head at us from the rear window as if it already knew what was coming next.

'He was quite pallid when he opened the door and beckoned me inside. Because of the expression on his face, and the odious smell that came from the kitchen, I entered with some trepidation.'

Sixsmythe was looking back at the cottage, not at us. 'As I told you, Flora Chaldean was at the table as though she had only just sat down to drink tea. But the cup was filled with a liquid green mould. And Flora's body was so corrupted and crawling with maggots that it was obvious that she had been dead for several weeks.'

My stomach turned over like a sluggish spin-dryer and I thought Midge's tan had become a shade lighter. She reached for me and I held on to her.

Sixsmythe appeared oblivious, his attentions concentrated on the puzzle that he, himself, had posed. 'So the passers-by couldn't possibly have seen her in the garden just days before. The coroner later confirmed what we already knew: the deteriorated condition of Flora's body indicated that she had died at least two or three weeks before, alone and, for all that time until my arrival, unnoticed. Rather sad, wouldn't you say? Yes, rather sad.'

With that, he pushed his bicycle from the grass verge and pedalled off down the road, waving goodbye over his shoulder at Midge and me without once looking back.

Which was just as well: the angry expression on my face might have unbalanced him and caused a nasty accident.

As you'd imagine, the rest of the day was somewhat spoilt. The kitchen of Gramarye lost a lot of its rustic charm with the idea of poor old Flora's rotting corpse sitting there at the table drinking mouldering tea fixed in our minds, and Midge lapsed into a miserable silence right through until the evening. She sat on her own in the round room for a long time, and I let her be.

I felt uneasy, not to say queasy, myself and could cheerfully have throttled the vicar for his insensitivity (more than once I wondered if his graphic bluntness hadn't been deliberate, perhaps a petty retribution for our mild scoffing at his warning – but then, men of the cloth are not the vengeful type, are they? Well, are they?).

Still, the day wasn't all bad. Later on in the afternoon Bob called with some terrific news. Phil Collins liked one of the songs I'd co-written with Bob, wanted to record the number for an album some time during the following week, and would I care to sit in on the session? Would I? Bob took my garbled rambling into the receiver as a firm 'yes'.

Midge was naturally delighted for me when I broke the news – our self-imposed period of not accepting any professional undertakings would be almost over by next week, and recording with a mega-star wasn't a bad way to get rolling again, especially when one of my own songs was involved. She did her best to throw off her gloom, although she was still a little subdued, and spent the rest of the afternoon and evening enthusing with me. Early that night we enthused our way up to the bedroom and the excitement didn't end there. Let's say it was nicely rounded off.

Eventual sleep was marred for me by a dream of taking tea with the maggoty Flora Chaldean downstairs in the kitchen, tiny wriggling white things dropping from her leprous hand into the brew as she stirred it before passing me the cup.

Thank God I awoke before I drank, for the last nightmare image was of a decomposed, almost fleshless, finger floating on top of the green furry liquid.

MYCROFT

The following Sunday we drove out to the Forest Inn for a snack lunch and a well-earned drink. What with the forthcoming recording session, set for the following Wednesday, and most of the tasks around the cottage now completed, we were in the mood for celebration.

I drank two pints of bitter with my lunch while Midge stuck to her customary orange juice; maybe it was because I was out of practice, but I felt fairly light-headed after I drained the last of the second pint, and more than ready for another. Midge had had enough of the pub, though, and in a way I couldn't blame her: after the tranquillity of Gramarye, the crowd and the noise – this place was obviously a popular Sunday watering-hole for both tourists and locals alike – was a little hard to take. The bustle and smoky atmosphere were in direct contrast to the peaceful and unpolluted existence we had quickly become used to (although I have to admit I quite enjoyed the change). Without *too* much protest from me, we left and walked arm in arm towards the Passat.

It was Midge's suggestion that we take a drive and explore some. We hadn't had much opportunity before, apart from walks into the woodland surrounding Gramarye and shopping trips into Cantrip and Bunbury, so it wasn't a bad idea providing we kept away from the main roads which would be busy with day-trippers. I reversed the car from the parking space and headed away from the inn, breaking into loud song as we hit the road.

We soon turned off onto a quiet lane that snaked into a dense part of the forest, the twists and turns demanding all my concentration. The upper branches of trees formed a leafy tunnel, providing a pleasant relief from the hot sun. To be honest, I think we both had an idea where this road might lead, even though neither of us voiced an opinion: we were curious about the Synergists, our interest kindled by Sixsmythe's warning rather than cooled. Not that we wanted anything to do with them – in fact, it had been a relief that neither Kinsella nor the others had visited us since the blond bomber's departure the previous week. We only wanted to take a closer look at the grey house, the Temple itself. Nothing earnest, no deep motivation – only a destination for an afternoon drive. We'd discussed the Synergists, sure enough, and had easily come to the conclusion that they were no threat to mature and sensible people like us. Possibly Sixsmythe's stupid disclosure of Flora Chaldean's macabre death scenario hadn't exactly endeared him to us, so his views were not taken too seriously. Midge had been pensive for days afterwards, but had eventually shed dark thoughts and relaxed in Gramarye's warm ambience once more. I'm sure the constant attention of birds and various animals around the place helped in this respect, bristling life banishing shadowy spectres. The cottage would never be *quite* the same, but our peace of mind had been only slightly dented, not permanently damaged.

As you've already gathered, it had been an exceptionally glorious summer, and a small price had to be paid. The debt collector was about to rap on the windscreen as we sped down that secluded lane.

The Passat had spent weeks out under the boiling sun, used regularly and, to my discredit, rarely checked over. When I saw steam rising over the bonnet I tried to remember when I had last topped up the radiator. The temperature gauge was way up in the danger zone and a red light glared disgustedly at me.

'Shit!' I growled as clouds rose up in front.

Midge, who had never been machine-minded, said, 'What's wrong with it, Mike?'

I could glare just as hard as that bloody red light, and Midge turned her head to the front once again.

'Sorry I asked,' she said.

I brought the car to a halt and sat there, letting the engine and myself steam for a while.

'Can you fix it?' Midge ventured after a while, watching the billowing clouds as though they were part of the afternoon's entertainment.

Forcing myself to relax, I replied, 'Only by spitting in the radiator.' I studied the clouds too, but with less awe than Midge.

'Don't you think you should try and do something?'

I sighed. 'Yeah, you're right. Maybe only the fan belt's gone. You wearing tights today?'

She gave me a quick flash and dashed my hopes. Groaning, I pushed open the door. 'Pull that thing up, will you, Midge?' I pointed at a lever on the passenger side. She did so and the bonnet sprang open an inch.

I got out of the car and walked around to the front, muttering to myself as I slid my fingers through the gap and released the bonnet catch. Pushing the lid all the way up and turning my face away from the tumbling steam, I secured the bonnet with the retaining rod, then peered into the dragon's mouth. The fan belt was in good shape.

Maybe the demon drink had been enough to dull my senses, or I could have just had a mental relapse for a moment or two, because then I did something stupid, something that all motorists are warned against by those who know better: I took out my handkerchief, bunched it up over the radiator cap, and twisted.

The idea was to release the pressure, but of course once the cap was loosened, boiling water exploded upwards like a thermal geyser. My left hand instinctively shot up to protect my eyes as I staggered backwards and I howled – no, I *screamed* – when my skin was scalded by the fiery jet.

I fell, clutching at my arm and writhing with pain in the

roadway. I was dimly aware of Midge kneeling beside me, trying to hold me still so that she could examine the burns. Some of my face and neck had been scalded, but the all-consuming pain was in my left hand and lower arm. My short-sleeved denim shirt was wet, but had at least provided a thin barrier against the boiling water for my chest.

I managed to sit, Midge supporting me with an arm around my back; my vision was too blurred with pain-squeezed tears for me to see the damage to my hand, but the agony was more than I'd ever felt in my life before.

Suddenly Midge was on her feet waving her arms frantically in the air. I was conscious of a red car drawing up, two figures getting out and hurrying over to me, one of them vaguely familiar. They knelt in the road and the man – the other was a young girl – gently pulled at my injured arm.

'Oh dear, oh dear,' I heard him mutter. Then he reached behind me and hauled me to my feet. 'You'd better come along with us so we can quickly attend to that.'

I looked down at my injured limb, blinking away the dampness from my eyes, and saw that the skin was already beginning to bubble. Gritting my teeth, I allowed them to lead me to their car.

If anything, Midge was more distressed than me so, now I was over the initial shock, I did my best to grin reassuringly at her. It must have come out as an agonised grimace, because her mouth went down at the corners like a small child's and she fought back tears.

I was guided into the back seat of the couple's car, clutching my arm before me as if it were a freshly boiled lobster, and when the girl climbed into the driver's seat I recognised the braided hair, then the face as she turned anxiously towards me: it was Sandy, the girl I had rescued from the village punks the week before.

She said, 'Mike, we're going to take you back with us to treat those burns. The Temple is less than a minute away.'

'He needs a hospital,' insisted Midge, next to me in the car.

The man had just opened the front passenger door and was leaning in. He was middle-aged, balding and very thin, his cheeks so sunken that the bones above cast shadows. 'The nearest hospital is many miles away and he needs something done about the pain immediately. You can take him on to hospital afterwards – if you think that's necessary.' He sat and didn't speak again throughout the brief journey.

Sandy executed a hasty five-point turn in the narrow road and headed back in the direction from which they'd come. As Midge dabbed at the cooled dampness on my face with a tiny handkerchief, I realised I was in the same red Escort that Kinsella had arrived at the cottage in several evenings ago. She left my hand and lower arm alone, the skin there mottled a fierce scarlet and the flesh already beginning to swell.

The car stopped and Sandy jumped out. We were before tall wrought-iron gates set between staunch, grey pillars, a high wall of old brick continuing on either side. Beyond the gate we could see the huge house, the one we'd only seen from the back on our walk through the forest – *Bleak House*, as I'd mentally dubbed it. The girl swung open the gates while her older companion watched impassively through the window. Sandy hurriedly returned, her expression as anxious as Midge's, and set the Escort in motion again.

Although very much preoccupied with my own dis-comfort, I took note of the house as it loomed larger. It seemed strange that the place should be set back-to-front, the rear at the end of the long drive and facing towards the gates; even so, Croughton Hall *aka* The Synergist Temple was still coldly impressive from whatever view.

We passed around the side of the building, drawing up in the rectangular turning area. From there, the meadow stretched upwards towards the woodland. By now I was begin-ning to tremble some, delayed shock I supposed. The man in front got out and opened my door; gingerly protecting my arm, I struggled from the car and looked up at the house. Don't ask me why, but even then when I could barely think of anything other than the intense burning pain, I was reluctant to go inside. Midge, however, appeared to have no such qualms.

'Come on, Mike, the sooner we immerse your arm in water, the better for you,' she said, tugging firmly at my elbow. Sandy positioned herself on my other side, while the bony man

162

led the way up the wide stairway to the entrance. Before we'd even reached the top step, one side of the big double-door opened and Kinsella was there frowning down at us.

'Mike, what the hell's happened to you?' he called out.

'A disagreement with a car radiator,' I quipped, not really feeling that humorous. In fact, I thought I was going to throw up at any moment.

His face blanched when he caught sight of my clawed hand. 'Oh God, you'd better get him in here fast.' He threw open the other side of the door to allow us all through.

By now I was really shaking, try as I might to control it. Midge clung to me as if afraid I would collapse.

We were in a large hallway, a broad staircase opposite leading up to a gallery. The pain was growing worse, so I wasn't taking too much notice of my surroundings, but still I was aware of the sudden dim coolness inside the house.

'Can we get him into the kitchen or bathroom and put his arm in cold water?' I heard Midge implore.

'We can do much more than that,' Kinsella replied. He turned to the girl and said in a voice that was barely audible, 'Tell Mycroft who's here and exactly what's happened. Hurry.'

Sandy hurried.

He spoke to the Bone-Man next and only later did I wonder at Kinsella's authority. 'Let the others know,' was all he said, and the older man immediately scurried off.

'Okay, Mike, let's try and get you comfortable.' The American opened a door off the hallway and ushered us through.

We found ourselves inside a large drawing room – or it may have been a library, so crammed with books were the walls. The heavy mustiness of the atmosphere which, even in my condition, was distinct and somehow unpleasant, suggested that most of the volumes were old editions. Not that I was in the mood for browsing.

Kinsella seated me at a large oval table, its surface highly polished. Angled shafts of sunlight struck into the room in clear, delineated rays, like searchlights, and he went to each tall window to draw the curtains, leaving them open barely a fraction, so that light was no more than narrow beams. The door we'd entered by had been left ajar and I could see and hear movement outside as though people were gathering. I was damp with perspiration, feverish almost, and I really wanted to scream out at the pain's growing intensity. It was as if nerves numbed by shock (or heat) were now awakening and absorbing the hurt more fully.

'We must *do* something!' Midge urged as I sucked in air between tight lips to stifle my own moans.

'Be patient a moment longer,' Kinsella replied calmly, which was easy for *him* to say. He sat beside me at the table and laid out my arm on the glossy surface, careful to guide me by the elbow only. Midge stood over me, hands on my shoulders.

'The car radiator burst, huh?' said Kinsella.

'No,' I answered between clenched teeth. 'I was stupid enough to unscrew the cap.'

'You were lucky your arm took the full blast. If your face had . . .'

'Yeah, I know. I was stupid and lucky at the same time.'

He was examining the blotchy scald marks on my face when the door opened all the way. A man stepped in and Kinsella said, 'Mycroft.'

I'm not sure what I'd expected, but the very name, coupled with the vicar's sinister warnings about the Synergists, had conjured up visions of someone tall and powerful, with leathery, wrinkled skin and piercing pale eyes that could shrivel another's soul at will. A cross between Vincent Price and George C. Scott, maybe, or even Basil Rathbone's older brother. This guy was medium height and paunchy, skin smoothly unblemished; almost, but not quite, characterless. He wore grey slacks and a maroon cardigan over a bright white shirt, a beige tie formalising what otherwise might have been a relaxed effect (these observations were assembled as a whole afterwards, you understand, when my suffering had eased – at the time, his appearance wasn't my prime concern). I suppose his eyes could have been described as penetrating, but there was a gentleness to them also. Sorry I can't make the man sound more insidious (sorry because of *later* events), but that's how he appeared then. He could have been anybody's favourite uncle.

Kinsella stood as Mycroft approached, standing aside and pulling back his chair so that the white-haired man could move in closer to me. Mycroft leaned forward, one hand resting on the table top, and I caught a faint whiff of spicy breath. He looked first at my face, then down at my injured hand and arm.

'You must be in great pain,' he surmised (quite unnecessarily, I thought). His voice was mild and oddly dry, and the American accent was more New England than further south. There was also a great deal of concern in his tone, almost as if he shared my pain.

'If you want the truth, it's not getting any better,' I confessed, growing a little weary of all this inspection and no action. The raw flesh of my arm was beginning to puff alarmingly.

He looked directly into my eyes once more, then at Midge. 'We'll waste no more time,' he said, more to her than me. He waved a hand and the door opened wide: in came Sandy, our friend Gillie with her; between them they carried a clear, rectangular bowl containing a greenish liquid. They placed it on the table before Mycroft and myself.

'Call them in,' Mycroft said to Kinsella, who promptly went to the door and gave the order. I looked around, becoming quite nervous; Gillie smiled reassuringly at me, but didn't speak. I noticed Midge was also worried.

People began filing into the room, all silent and all watching me. Neil Joby was among them but, although he stared straight at me, he gave no acknowledgement.

I started to rise. 'Hey, wait a minute . . .'

Mycroft placed a firm but not forceful hand on my shoulder. 'Please sit down and don't be afraid. Your pain will be gone in a few moments.'

'No, I don't think so,' I began to say, and it was Midge who intervened.

'Mike, wait.'

I stared at her. She gave a brief shake of her head.

'I want you to trust me, Mike.' Mycroft's voice had altered subtly: it was both soothing and commanding – and very hard to resist. I sat down again and he drew up a chair

165

so that he could be close. 'I want you to trust us all,' he said, pushing up his sleeves to the elbow. I wiped perspiration from my eyes, agog at what was going on and uncertain of how far I was prepared to let it go.

Mycroft smiled at me as though aware that I thought him crazy and he was quite prepared to enjoy the joke with me. His smile was knowing and encouraging at the same time. He then did something I hadn't expected: he put his own hands into the liquid.

The people around the room – they were of all ages and of more than one nationality – joined hands and closed their eyes. Mycroft, too, had closed his eyes, his lips moving slightly as though intoning a silent prayer. I thought the mob might start chanting 'Ommmm' at any moment.

I suppose I must have looked desperate, because Midge held on to me as if to prevent my escape.

'Midge . . .?'

There was a peaceful kind of excitement in her eyes, an inner shining that hinted she was beginning to believe in these nuts.

I felt my burnt arm being lifted, and turned back to Mycroft, ready to pull away. His smile discouraged any such reaction and I allowed him to bring down my arm into the greenish liquid.

I got ready to scream, yet not once did I attempt to draw back – I was already learning that this mild-looking man had a hidden persuasiveness. He immersed my hand, then the rest of my arm up to the elbow, and although I couldn't feel the fluid I knew it had more substance than plain water. It looked oily smooth.

Immediately the terrible burning pain ceased, soothed by the cool liquid; I felt as though my arm had been frozen in ice.

Mycroft's fingers lightly stroked the skin, his eyes closed once more, lips moving only slightly. The relief was so immense that I nearly whooped with joy; instead I breathed a huge sigh. I was conscious, too, of the pressure from Midge's fingers on my shoulders and when I turned my head to look up at her, her eyes were also closed, her brow wrinkled in concentration.

'Midge,' I said, 'the pain's gone.'

She opened her eyes, looked at me, looked at my immersed arm. Her relief seemed as great as mine when she hugged my neck.

Mycroft still held me there, continuing to gently stroke my flesh; his fingertips somehow left a tingling trail in their wake. Glancing around the room, I saw that the others still had their eyes closed, one or two of the women swaying on their feet as though about to swoon; their hands were clenched tight in each other's and I had the impression of energy flowing through every individual, passing on to the next, then the next, going full circuit.

Insane, I voiced, strictly to myself. But I couldn't deny I was no longer hurting. *Yeah, and what happens when the hand comes out of water? The liquid's obviously a pain-freezer, so how's the arm gonna feel without it?* I was soon to find out.

Mycroft opened his eyes and lifted the limb clear. He held it there while liquid drained off, then turned to me and I was unsure if there wasn't just a trace of mockery in his smile.

The swelling of my flesh had definitely subsided, although my fingers remained puffy; that awful glowing redness was still there, but no more blisters were forming. Best of all, I could feel no pain, only a numbed stiffness.

'I don't believe it,' I said incredulously.

'There's no need to,' he replied. 'Accept, that's all you have to do.'

Mycroft rose and the people began to open their eyes, some of them being held steady by those beside them. They released each other's hands to break into applause and I wondered if Mycroft was going to take a bow. Instead, he held up a hand and the clapping stopped.

'We must only be thankful that our young friend no longer suffers,' he told them. 'You've witnessed our mutual strength, now reflect upon that for a while on your own.' He was so casual, so matter-of-fact, his voice even and friendly; no tub-thumping or showing off as you might expect from some quasi-religious leader who'd just pulled off a pretty good stunt.

His followers left the room, most of them smiling happily, the rest deep in thought. They were a mixed bag all right, of various ages and nationalities as I've said, but also of different types, from the slightly freakish (wild hair, wild eyes) to the mundanely straight (smartish clothes, bland faces).

Gillie came forward and carefully wrapped a linen towel around my arm, allowing the excess moisture to be absorbed before removing it again. Then it was Sandy's turn: she'd produced bandage and gauze from somewhere and proceeded to dress my arm, ever so gently laying the gauze over the burns first before applying the bandage.

'We oughta let a hospital handle this end of things,' I suggested uncertainly.

Kinsella was grinning all over his all-American face. 'No need for that, Mike. You're gonna be fine, you'll see.'

'The dressing is perfectly sterile,' reassured Mycroft, 'and you'd find a nurse would do no more than this.'

'They might give me a shot or pills or something.'

'Unnecessary, but of course you must do as you see fit. I suggest you rest today and see a doctor tomorrow if you're still uneasy. There won't be any more pain.'

I found the last bit ridiculous – Christ, I'd been really *scalded* – but I didn't want to appear tetchy, not after what he'd done. 'Yeah, well, let's see what tomorrow brings.'

I was able to smile.

Mycroft, apparently, had already lost interest in me, and was studying Midge with that minimal smile (I was sure it was slightly mocking) on his face once more.

'And you are obviously Midge,' he said.

His gaze was a bit too penetrating for my liking, oddly bringing to mind Ogborn the lawyer's barely disguised interest in her all those weeks ago. I'd never looked kindly on dirty old men.

'I don't know how we can ever thank you enough,' she replied, and I could tell the tension was only slowly draining from her. Despite the room's dimness, I could also see that she was very tired.

'Thanks are neither sought nor required. I've heard much about you and you'll forgive me if I say I'm glad that you finally had cause, unfortunate though the circumstances were, to visit our Temple.'

Gillie and Sandy had gone to the windows and were drawing back the curtains. The light broadened and brought some cheer back into the room.

'Hub has invited us on several occasions,' said Midge, 'but with so much work in the cottage . . .' She flapped her hands at our standing excuse.

'Ah yes, Gramarye.' The name pleased him, his smile becoming warmer.

'You know our place?' I asked.

He didn't even look my way. 'It's been described to me. Tell me, young lady, are you very happy there?'

If Midge was surprised by the question, she didn't show it. 'Yes, very. We both are. It's a wonderful home.'

'In what sense is it wonderful?'

Now she was taken aback. 'It . . . it's so peaceful, so serene. And yet full of life. Lots of animals are attracted to it, and there's so much . . .' She floundered, unable to find the right words.

Mycroft found one for her. 'Vitality.' It wasn't even a question.

'Yes,' Midge agreed eagerly. 'Yes, that's it exactly.'

Mycroft seemed satisfied. He dried his own hands, then pulled down his sleeves. 'I would dearly love to speak to you again,' he said finally.

Midge just nodded, then turned to me. 'How are you feeling, Mike?'

'Me? Good. But I'll never play the piano again –' I broke off and groaned. I'd realised the consequences of my accident. 'The recording session on Wednesday – there's no way I'll be able to play.'

'Oh, Mike, I'd forgotten.' Midge bit into her lower lip and knelt beside me, her arm hugging my waist to comfort. I was too angry at myself to be comforted, though.

'I'm not sure I understand,' said Mycroft. 'Is there some kind of professional engagement you think you'll have to miss?'

'I'm a musician,' I explained. 'There was an important session set for later this week, but it looks as if I'm out of it.' I stared at my bandaged hand and felt like banging it against the table. I didn't, of course.

Mycroft sat facing me again and put his hand on my shoulder. 'Go home and stay there for the next day or so. Don't go out anywhere, just stay inside.' He leaned forward confidentially and said, 'Your hand will be completely healed by Wednesday.'

Grateful though I was, I had to restrain myself from shouting at him. 'Right,' I said evenly. 'I'll go home. I'll stay indoors. Thanks a lot.' I stood. 'We'd better be on our way, Midge.' My eyes told her: No more talk, no more thank-yous; let's just get out of here.

She understood perfectly.

But it was Mycroft who left the room before us. 'I'll say goodbye to you now,' he said, his voice revealing no resentment of my sudden brusque manner. 'Please don't forget my invitation.'

'I won't,' replied Midge – he'd been speaking to her, not me. She held out a hand as if to shake his, but he appeared not to notice; he turned briskly and walked from the room. I say 'appeared' not to, because I'm sure his eyes flickered downwards at Midge's hand for a second and he involuntarily drew backwards, the slight movement transformed into a complete turn as if his mind were already on other matters. I could have been wrong, but in the light of later events I think not.

'You've still gotta problem, Mike.' Kinsella was grinning at me, fingers slid into the pockets of his tight Wranglers.

We looked quizzically at him.

'A dried-out radiator,' he reminded us.

I nearly hit my forehead with my bad hand.

He chuckled. 'S'okay, I'll organise a can of water and drive you back to your wheels. Let's hope the engine's not messed up.'

'Yeah, let's hope.'

We left the house and I was glad to be outside, happy to feel the sun on my face again. Weird, but the only soreness I now felt was, in fact, on my face and neck where droplets of scalding water had managed to hit me. Even so, that pain was mild compared to what I'd experienced earlier. Parts of my chest may have felt a bit tender, but the coarse material of my shirt had prevented any real damage. My bandaged lower arm and hand was still tingling, but the feeling wasn't unpleasant.

'Incredible stuff,' I remarked to Kinsella as the three of us walked towards the red Escort.

'Huh?' he said, squinting against the sun.

'That green liquid you used on my arm.'

'Oh, that was nothing special. A cleanser, that's all, laced with antiseptic.'

'But it stopped the pain.'

'Mycroft stopped the pain, my friend.'

'That isn't possible.'

'Yup, we both know it.'

'Then why –?'

He flashed those sickeningly perfect teeth. 'Mycroft's a wonderful man.'

He seemed to think that was explanation enough.

We reached the car and Kinsella opened the rear door for us. Midge climbed in first and I followed, careful not to bump my hand against anything. He took the driver's seat and we waited for someone to arrive with the can of water.

Midge leaned forward in her seat. 'Are you feeling better yourself, Hub?' she asked.

He turned to her in surprise. 'How d'you mean?'

'You left rather hurriedly the other evening. We thought you'd been taken ill.'

He shifted uncomfortably in his seat and pointed towards one corner of the house. 'Here comes Neil with that water.' He cleared his throat, then said, 'I guess I did feel unwell that time. Sorry, it was kinda rude of me to rush away like that. Something I had for lunch didn't agree with me, y'know?'

The passenger door opened and Neil Joby got in, placing the plastic water-can down by his feet.

'Okay, wagons roll,' said Kinsella, switching on the engine. 'You folk'll be home in no time.'

We drove around the house and both Midge and I turned as we gathered speed on the long driveway. The grey house – the Synergist Temple – was much larger than we had imagined when we had first caught sight of it from the forest edge.

To me, at least, it now seemed far more ominous. Yet Midge was looking back with a trace of a smile tilting her lips.

My second thought when I woke next day was of my hand: would it be a huge swollen mess pushing out at the bandages?

The previous night we'd decided we would go over to the hospital in Bunbury first thing in the morning and get the burns treated by experts, despite Mycroft's crazy assurance that it wouldn't be necessary. I'd fully expected to spend the night in constant pain but, in fact, I'd slept like a baby, dreaming of Gramarye itself and all kinds of pleasant things – growing flowers, animal friends, sunshine and brilliant skies. I hadn't felt even a twinge.

My inclination had been to ring Bob the moment we got back to the cottage and break the bad news, but Midge had talked me out of it. Wait and see, she'd said. Wait and see.

Midge had gentled me through the rest of the evening, had even kissed each exposed and sore-looking finger to make them better; I'd revelled in the attention, although dreading the time when the powerful pain-killer that had obviously been mixed into that green stuff (I didn't give any credence to Kinsella's assertion that it was only an antiseptic) would begin to wear off. Mercifully, it hadn't.

Midge was still asleep next to me, looking ten years old, which made my first thoughts well-nigh criminal; I soon remembered my prime concern. My left arm was tucked beneath the sheet and I was almost afraid to peep. There was a slight discomfort down there – the bandages felt tight – but no throbbing pain. Maybe sleep was still drugging my brain; I clenched my teeth, waiting for the hurt to hit. It didn't, and I summoned up the courage to look.

Lifting the sheet, I slowly brought my injured hand up to my face. If anything, the bandages had loosened during the night, the discomfort due to the sticky tape holding them in place rather than pressure from swollen flesh. The exposed fingers were only a little reddish. I flexed them and they were hardly stiff. I waggled my wrist and my hand moved loosely, the bandages the only restraint. I waved my arm in the air and it was fantastic and it was mobile and it was painless and it was unbelievable!

'Midge!'

She woke with a start, jumping up and crouching in the bed, eyes wide with alarm.

'Midge! My arm! It doesn't hurt at all!'

She looked from my face to my arm and she squealed. Her hands came together and she only just stopped from clutching my raised hand.

'Mike, are you sure?'

'Am I sure? Jesus, Midge, I should know if it hurts or not. Look, I can even wave the fingers.' I waved the fingers.

'I knew, Mike, I just knew! I was sure you'd be all right.'

'So you believed in that Mycroft stuff?'

'No, I felt sure when we got back here. I can't explain . . .'

She didn't even try. She hugged me, and we both toppled back against the pillows.

'Hey, hey, take it easy!' I cried, holding the bandaged hand aloft. 'Let's not ruin a good thing with too much excitement.'

She smothered my face in kisses. 'I knew, I knew,' she told me again.

I pulled her away by dragging at the back of her nightshirt with my good hand.

'Why don't we check it out properly before we get carried

173

away, huh? You know, what's happening here isn't really possible. You saw for yourself that jet of scalding water hit me.'

'You're right,' she said mock-severely. 'This isn't happening, the Magic didn't work at all.'

She was joking, she hadn't meant that last remark. At least, the conscious part of her hadn't.

I held up my arm between us. 'Okay, Pixie, I want you to take off the bandages ever so slowly, and if it starts to hurt I'll let you know with a scream. Maybe then we'll come back to the real world.'

She carefully peeled off the tape and began unwinding the dressing, the gauze beneath coming free as she progressed. It took less than fifteen seconds for my lower arm and hand to be completely exposed.

'Sheeeee . . .' It was no more than an escaping breath from me.

The flesh was tender-looking and blotchy-red, but there were no blisters, no stripped skin, no scald marks. It was the most beautiful arm in the world.

MOTION PICTURE

I didn't get back to Gramarye until late Thursday afternoon. The recording session had been fantastic – Collins had to be one of the most professional musician/singers in the business, and one of the easiest to get along with (so long as *you* were doing your job right) and he made Bob's and my song sound a hundred times better than it really was. I'd stayed on through the day (Wednesday), invited to work on another couple of tracks for the album, and had loved every relaxed, jokey moment. I hadn't realised how much I'd been missing the scene until then, and it was great to catch up on all the news with Bob and one or two of the other musos afterwards in the nearest bar.

I began by going steady with the booze, but I was on a high and easily led. Relieved, too, that my hand hadn't let me down (I'd spent the previous two days with my guitars, working out the slight stiffness left in my fingers – which could have been due to the long lay-off anyway). The buzz I felt took over all sensibilities and I was soon knocking them back like a man out on parole.

Bob didn't believe in the seriousness of my accident at all, insisting that I must have moved back faster than I'd thought, getting scalded a bit but not badly, and making my usual namby-pamby fuss. Sure, my hand and arm were more pinkish than normal, and there were a few nasty splodges on my face, but the damage could only have been superficial. I told him about the Synergists and Mycroft's trick with the coloured liquid. Fucking crazy, was Bob's comment.

He suggested I stay the night at his place and I had to admit the thought of driving all the way back to Hampshire, loaded as I was, didn't appeal. I found a phone and rang Midge.

She agreed it would be senseless to drive that far so late and told me to stay with Bob and enjoy myself. Watch yourself, though, she warned, and I knew exactly what she meant: Bob could be a great junkhead at times.

After getting excited over my day, Midge informed me she'd spent her time painting, enjoying the solitary confinement, but naturally missing me a lot. How much? How high the mountains, how deep the sea . . .?

I told her she'd pay for her mockery when I got home, and then we both got mawkishly serious, telling each other we really hated not being together, even for a day, that being apart didn't feel natural, that love was a hurting thing – you know the stuff. Cliché endearments, maybe, but we meant them. There were watery blobs in my eyes when I returned to Bob and the others.

Still, I managed to have a good time. We went for a meal from there and ended up back at Bob's place, a Victorian terraced house in Fulham, about one in the morning. By then, we were feeling no pain. His latest lady (Bob had been married twice and was now legally separated from the second wife) was in bed and she flatly refused (a bit disgruntledly, I felt) to join our party. We played hard rock on the stereo until thumps on the wall indicated that the neighbours weren't in a partying mood either. Our pals left shortly after, and Bob and I carried on with reminiscences of great old times together – gigs, scrapes, practical jokes and women just about covered the field – breaking open fresh cans of beer and suffering bouts of girlish giggling. It was a good night, a night for talking, and I was glad my friend needed no other stimulants than the beer we were drinking and our own conversation. I've no idea what time we both finally crashed out.

I awoke around noon, stretched out on a sofa, shoes

removed and a dressing gown tossed over me. Bob had (surprisingly) been up before ten and had gone off to 'put a deal together', as he would say; his girlfriend, Kiwi (I still don't know to this day what her real name was, or why she was called Kiwi), informed me of this as she handed me a huge Peter Rabbit mug of strong black coffee. I sat there like a zombie, drinking coffee and nursing my head, and after a while (when she started up the hoover within three feet of me, in fact) I guessed it was time to leave.

Kiwi was pleased enough to switch off her turbopower machine for a moment when I told her I'd be on my way, and she smiled prettily. 'Look forward to Saturday,' she said. 'Saturday?' I asked. 'Bob told me before he left that you'd asked us down to dinner,' she trilled. 'Oh yeah,' I said, remembering vaguely. 'Yeah, see you then,' I added. 'Look forward to it,' she repeated. The resumed hoovering quickly sent me on my way.

I stopped on the way back to Hampshire for a light snack and a hair-of-the-dog, also taking the opportunity to ring Midge to inform her of the hero's return. There was no reply from Gramarye, so I assumed she'd gone for a walk although for once the weather wasn't terrific – not raining, but overcast. She couldn't have gone shopping, because I had the car.

I was soon on my way again and the throbbing in my head eventually started to ebb. By the time I reached the Hampshire border I was feeling pretty good again, although looking forward to an hour or so in my own bed to clear away the last dregs of the hangover.

And you know, the closer I drew to home the happier I became: I'd cut loose for a while and had a great time, enjoyed fast company and working again with professionals; but that one day and night had been enough – at least enough to last me quite some time. Great feeling, that. And new to me.

At last I reached Cantrip and drove through the high street, catching sight of the Rev. Sixsmythe on his bike ahead. Still angry at him for upsetting Midge (not to mention me) with his gruesome recount of Ma Chaldean's death, I was tempted to thump my horn as I drew level to make him wobble, but I resisted.

Out of the village, then into the lanes, the forest closing in on either side. Light raindrops speckled the Passat's windscreen.

A few turns and God bless her, there she was, a splash of white in the distance. I was grinning all over my face when I pulled onto the grassy verge at the side of Gramarye's garden. Now I did toot the horn, just to let Midge know I was back. Opening the hatchback, I hauled out my two guitar cases and rested them on the ground while I closed up again. Guitars in either hand, I stepped over the fence rather than walk around to the gate, and trudged through the flowerbeds to the path, expecting to see Midge's happy pixie face peering from the doorway at any moment. I was disappointed, though. Midge either hadn't heard my arrival, or she hadn't yet returned from her walk. But surely she couldn't have been out all this time, particularly as the weather wasn't up to much? Perhaps she was asleep, or in the bath: either one would suit my purposes admirably.

I glanced at the upstairs windows, and they were dark and lifeless.

A small scratching noise, and my attention went back to the front door. There was Rumbo, gnawing at the paintwork. He turned and his expression seemed to say, 'So where the hell have you been?'

I chuckled and he joined in. Bob had scoffed when I'd told him about the cottage in our boozy state – about the animals and birds who came every day, the wild growth of beautiful flowers, the atmosphere itself – demanding to know what kind of 'weed' was I growing down here and could he order a case-load? I hadn't risen to the bait, because even *I* felt much of what I said was exaggeration now that I was back in this real world of cynics and grafters. But you had to be in Gramarye to know; logic took over once outside.

'Come on, Rumbo, let a man get inside his own home,' I said to the squirrel, gently easing him aside with one foot. He found my shoelace tasty.

I reached for my key, but decided to test the door first. As I'd half expected, Midge hadn't locked up after her despite

178

my warnings. We were no longer in the big bad city, she always rebuked me.

I pushed open the door and Rumbo scampered in before me. It was very gloomy inside and I had a nasty vision of a rotting corpse sitting at the kitchen table swinging around to greet me with a lipless grin. Oh Stringer, you've gotta forget the vicar's little tale!

'Midge! You around?' I dumped the guitar cases on the floor and went to the foot of the stairs. 'Midge? The hunk's home!'

She was definitely out. The place was so quiet it was loud.

Disappointed, I went through to the adjoining room and filled the kettle. Rumbo had preceded me and was darting backwards and forwards along the top of the old iron range.

'Don't go up that chimney,' I advised him. 'You'll come down so black your own family wouldn't recognise you. And I hear you red squirrels have had enough trouble from the greys – so imagine what would happen if a *black* squirrel showed up in the neighbourhood.'

Rumbo looked up into what must have been to him the equivalent of a lift-shaft, and accepted my advice (maybe he knew something about racialism), hopping off the range, then over to the fridge-freezer, leaping onto its top. From there, he gnashed his tiny teeth at me.

'Okay, feller, I know what you're after.' Reaching up to a shelf behind me, I took down the biscuit jar and unscrewed the lid. 'One for you, one for me.' I tossed over a digestive which he deftly caught in his paws and immediately munched into. Mine was gone in two bites, but his took considerably longer; he daintily gnawed around the edge, turning the shrinking biscuit in his paws and occasionally glancing my way, presumably to check if any more were in the offing. He was a fascinating little tyke all right, lovably cheeky (we'd once found him snugly asleep in our bed, burrowed down beneath the sheets) although sometimes irascible (he'd thrown bacon rind down at my head one morning from the top of the dresser after I'd scolded him for running across the kitchen table and knocking over the sugar bowl). A month or so ago I would never have believed an animal could be so tame – at least, not a wild squirrel – or so smart (he always knew when breakfast or lunch was about to be served, rarely failing to make an appearance at those times – he enjoyed our scraps more than regular squirrel food, I think).

Steam billowed from the kettle and I spooned instant coffee into a cup, adding one sugar, and milk this time. Pouring the boiling water made me nervous and, not for the first time since Sunday, perplexed. You were lucky, is all, I told myself, lucky your arm got dipped in the Synergists' own special brand of Fairy Liquid so soon after the accident. They could market the formula for a million. No, several millions. But they'd have to cut out the holding-hands-voodoo bit if they wanted to be taken seriously. Antiseptic only – huh! Who did Kinsella think he was kidding?

I sipped coffee, burning my lips. Maybe they already did market the green curative, only in discreet quantities – under the counter, as it were. That would explain how they could afford such a large estate as Croughton Hall. Their secretiveness didn't make much sense, but then if they were some kind of nutty religious sect, it didn't need to. Interesting, though.

I left the kitchen, taking the cup of coffee with me, Rumbo racing ahead up the stairs, the last of the biscuit hastily devoured. The whole place was unusually dull and grey, the sun's absence making quite a contrasting impression on the atmosphere of the place. Long, rainy winter days were obviously going to prove a trial for both of us. Still, weren't they always, wherever you lived? I went straight from the hall into the bedroom – did I mention we'd moved into the bigger room by now, the one that had had the crack in the wall repaired and painted over? – just in case Midge had fallen asleep in there. I ordered Rumbo off the empty-of-Midge bed where he was having a fine time tangled up in the top sheet, and went through to the round room. Even in here, with the three large windows, it was gloomy. The smell of paint hung in the air and, because it was a familiar scent and one I associated with my live-in-partner, it wasn't unpleasant. Her drawing board was sloped at an acute angle, and I remembered she had told me she'd spent yesterday painting. Now, every new illustration from Midge was a delight to me (not to mention to all her fans, young and old) and I lost no time in getting across the room to see.

One thing I did before peeking, though, was to lay down my coffee on the small table beside the swivel-board where she kept her paints, brushes, and bits and pieces. Our rule was that I never went near her artwork – nor was anyone else allowed to – with dangerous substances in my hand. I made the mistake once, when we were only just getting to know one another, of opening a can of beer while admiring her work at close range; you can guess where the spray went. Midge had taken it well, but I resolved 'never again'.

Only when the cup was safely out of my hands did I turn and look. And was instantly lost in pure, worshipful awe of her talent.

The painting, in her favourite medium of designer's gouache, was of Gramarye itself.

She had obviously worked from the grass verge outside the garden gate, using her small easel to support the artboard, because the cottage was viewed from there, the garden, with its wild patterns of colours, in the foreground. The forest behind provided a strangely brooding backdrop, albeit insignificant against the exuberance of Gramarye itself, the walls brilliantly white, yet detailed, marked where the real walls were marked, worn where the real brickwork was worn. The colours may have been exaggerated – no roof could ever be quite that shade of rusty red, the grass and nearest trees could never be that vividly green – yet they conveyed the true vibrancy of our home and its surroundings, the invigorating quality we had both felt when we first moved in, but which only Midge, with her unique and skilful, child's-view artistry could express. You know, my knees actually went weak as I took it all in.

But that was nothing compared with what was to come.

Outside, the sun broke through the clouds, washing the room with a sudden brilliant warmth, striking those lucid colours before me so that they dazzled and surged, yes, *surged*, with sparkling energy, the brightness striking into me, deep into me, and reproducing – not just duplicating – the image inside my head, as if it had solidified in there, was as real as the original.

Remember that first day Midge and I had come to look at the cottage, when I thought I'd gone into some kind of delayed drug excursion? Well, this was it again. Either I started swaying or the artboard started moving, because the picture kept dancing in and out of focus.

The sun behind me blazed on my shoulders and the top of my head felt so hot I wondered if it were on fire. I could feel myself going, my knees sagging, the picture captured inside my head swelling, becoming too immense to contain, threatening to expand through my brain and push against the inner walls of my skull. The pressure was almost unbearable.

In some kind of fantastic and frightening way, I became part of Midge's picture, living and breathing in it just as surely as if I were outside standing before the garden gate; only whether I was truly inside the picture or the picture was inside me, I had no way of knowing. The smell of fresh paint was slight, but the smell of flowers, of grass, of fence, of road – of sky! – was intoxicating. I was hallucinating and I was totally aware that I was doing so. But nothing, no effort of will could bring me back. I'm sure I cried out, because I was scared, Jesus, I was so scared!

Everything was a chromatic replica, an illustration, but it was all real – the sky was real, the forest was real, and Gramarye, stylised, the colours too fresh, too synthetically manufactured – too bloody fairy-story! – was real. And the clouds moved, and there were birds lazily arcing in the sky. It was alive and it existed. But it was only paint! Moving, *breathing*, paint! And I was part of it!

And there was the path, the flowers on either side dipping with the easy breeze. And of course the path led up to the cottage door. Which was open. And the cool darkness inside was inviting me in, an alluring emptiness, but an emptiness that really wasn't empty, because although I couldn't see into the darkness there was something, there was *someone*, there. Someone sitting at the kitchen table. Someone who was really a some*thing*. And that something was beginning to move, beginning to rise from the table on which stood a cup filled with mouldering tea, undrunk and festering with all kinds of minute, crawling life.

And the someone who was now only something was a darker shadow moving among other shadows, shuffling rather than walking, coming to the open door, coming to greet me, coming to encourage me forward, raising a hand – I could see that hand rising, see the fingers that were no more than bones with thin lumps of rotted flesh still clinging.

And that something was nearly at the door, almost in the light. But it lingered there, because light revealed too much, light was unnatural for a thing such as this. I could see what was left of the finger curling inwards, gesturing, beckoning me, telling me to come closer, wanting me.

And I found myself opening the gate, setting foot on the path, walking forward, confused and wondering why I didn't resist, the flowers beginning to wilt now, starting to crumble, the petals' edges turning brown, dying, and the door was open to me, a darkness waiting and something waiting in the darkness.

And daylight was fading – the cottage walls were grey, the windows black, and the roof had become muddy dark, and there were black pits where tiles had fallen through, and as the light dimmed, the sun swallowed whole by painted ebony storm clouds, creatures fluttered out from those pits, wheeling in the heavy, murky air, screeching their welcome, circling above the cottage, occasionally diving erratically, but never approaching me, content to wait until I was inside. Only then would they return . . .

I was near the doorway, and I was trying to hold myself back, my footsteps weighty, cumbrous, my shoulders almost leaning backwards. But still I continued that sluggish journey, impelled by what I *knew* was just inside that door, watching me and waiting patiently.

And my foot was on the step. And she was coming forward. And even in the gloom I could see she was almost faceless. And when both her rotted hands reached for me I opened my mouth in a silent scream . . .

. . . And a voice called me back . . .

183

First her voice, and then her, Midge, standing in the
upstairs hallway, the door behind open wide, the greens
outside muted by drizzling rain.

She was watching me as though I were an intruder, a
sneak-thief inside her beloved cottage; and in truth, that was
how I felt.

The illustrated scene that had been more in my mind
than on that artboard was wrenched from me as if into a
vortex, the root of which was the painting itself. Visions of
reaching bones left me, in part dissolving but mostly
swallowed, sucked away. I staggered back, suddenly released
from the spiralling images like a jettisoned first-stage from a
rocket, and my shoulder hit the windowframe behind. The
brief pain jolted my senses even more and my eyes rapidly
focused.

Midge's painting was there before me, a bright, daylight
landscape, correct in essence to the original, yet idealised in
its presentation. A pretty cottage in a pretty setting. But I
had glimpsed something dark.

'Mike? Mike, what's wrong?'

I turned to her, and I still leaned weakly against the
windowframe. I was too confused to speak.

Midge strode into the room and her hair and face were

184

wet with rain, the anorak she wore shiny with moisture. She came to me and I all but collapsed into her arms.

'You look dreadful,' she said. 'You're so pale. And your eyes . . . oh God, your eyes!'

'Let me . . . let me sit down.'

I hardly understood my own words they were so garbled, but she could see for herself that I was barely able to stand. She helped me to the sofa and lowered me onto it. Gratefully, I sank back against the cushions.

I stared over at the drawing board, the picture taped to its surface no longer visible from that angle, while Midge stroked my cheek with a damp and cold hand. She left me, but quickly returned with a small tumbler of liquid.

'Brandy,' she said, holding the glass towards my lips.

I took it from her, barely able to lift the glass. The brandy tasted awful, but the warming shock was good.

'Oh, Midge, you've no idea . . .'

'Your eyes are so bloodshot, Mike. How much did you drink last night?'

'The picture . . .'

'You may not have liked it, but isn't this an over-reaction?'

'No, Midge, no joking . . .' I drank more brandy.

She steadied my hand as the glass trembled against my mouth. 'Tell me what's wrong,' she said, her voice hushed.

'Jesus, it's this place, Midge. There's something going on here that we don't understand.'

'Oh now, Mike, how can you say that?' she chided. 'It's perfect here, and you know it.'

'The picture moved. I looked at it, and the picture bloody moved!'

Reasonably enough, she looked at me as though I were crazy.

'It's true, Midge! It came . . . it came alive! I saw things happening there, I could smell the flowers, I could *feel* the breeze. And there was someone inside the cottage, and I'm sure I know who it was –'

I expected bewilderment, incomprehension. I expected concern, maybe even alarm for my state of mind. What I didn't expect was her fury.

'Just what the hell did you and Bob get up to last night? You promised me, Mike, you promised yourself! No more of that stuff! No more junk!' Tears came with her anger.

'No, nothing like that, Midge! I promise you, we drank, that was all. You know I wouldn't –'

'Liar!'

I almost dropped the glass. She had shrieked the accusation and her eyes were blazing through a moist, glittering screen.

'We only drank –'

'They warned you, the doctors warned you last time! They told you how lucky you'd been to survive! God Almighty, Mike, couldn't you learn from that? The whole point of us coming here was to move away from that crowd, that scene. One night on your own . . .'

'It wasn't like that. What's got into you?'

'Into me? You're the one who's freaking-out, who's seeing perfectly ordinary pictures move! What did you take last night? Coke again? Smack? Don't you remember how I hated seeing you on even the soft stuff years ago? Doesn't it mean anything to you?'

Right then, of course, I didn't realise that her vehemence was more of a defence against something she didn't want to acknowledge herself, rather than anger directed at me. It was only later that I found out Midge had begun to understand a lot sooner than me, but she hadn't wanted the unreality questioned, hadn't wanted logic to destroy what was growing inside her and re-awakening inside Gramarye. For that moment, though, neither of us understood anything that was going on.

'Midge, you can ask Bob. I've invited him down this weekend –'

'Oh, terrific! He's just the person I want to see here!'

'You're being unreasonable. Why don't you hear me out first?'

'Listen to you describe your hallucinations? You think I'd enjoy that?'

'The animals here, the bird with the broken wing, the

186

way those flowers we thought were dying in the garden picked up – none of it's natural.'

'How would you know? What do you know about anything that's beyond city walls, anything that's beyond the gutter?'

I stared at her aghast and she avoided my eyes.

Midge was kneeling before me and her chest was rising in exaggerated movement as though her anger could barely be contained. She gained control, then said in a low, almost resentful voice, 'I didn't mean that. I'm sorry –'

She broke off and pushed herself away, her tears finally breaking through to join with the rain-dampness already on her cheeks. She ran from me, slamming the bedroom door behind her. I could hear her muffled sobs.

I sat there stunned. Confused, too. Totally. What the hell had happened? To me. To her. *What the hell had happened?*

I slugged back the rest of the brandy, nearly choking on its raw heat, then put the glass on the floor. I wiped my eyes and cheeks with my hands and wasn't sure which was damper, face or palms. Beginning to rise, knowing I couldn't let matters rest there, couldn't leave Midge in such mistaken misery, I was stopped by a remote scrabbling sound. It came from behind the sofa.

I stood, afraid because I was still disorientated and vulnerable; there wasn't much more I could take that afternoon. The noise persisted. Stepping to the end of the sofa, I peered into the shadowy abyss between the back of the chair and the curved wall. And was relieved to discover what was hidden down there.

I pulled the sofa away from the wall, exposing the tiny, shivering figure of Rumbo, his tail fluffed up, his paws digging at the carpet in nervous agitation.

With a quick, startled look at me, he shot from his hiding place, across the room and out through the door that was still open, quickly vanishing into the foliage beyond.

I wondered why I had the feeling a sinking ship had just been deserted.

O n second thoughts, I decided not to go in to Midge straight away: she would be easier to deal with when her anger had cooled. Besides, there was something of a storm going on inside my own head which another brandy might help ease. Picking up the glass again, I went downstairs to the kitchen. All our liquor (of which there wasn't much) was stored away in the bottom of the larder (as good a drinks cabinet as any), but the brandy bottle was still on the table where Midge had left it.

I scraped the chair against the tiles and was already reaching for the bottle before I sat. The brandy really didn't help much, but at least I had something to do while my nerves settled.

You may consider I'd been a bit slow in realising things weren't quite normal down here in the country, but none of what I've previously mentioned seemed so unnatural – apart from this last incident – at the time. Unusual, yeah, but not spectacular. It's worth repeating: the mind has a way of naturalising the unnatural. Even the moving painting could be explained away as an hallucination (and at the time I was convinced that had to be the case, although not because of drugs indulged in the night before, as Midge had suggested). There was an abundance of nature here, is all. And the atmosphere of the place created its own magic, keened our senses so that Midge's artistic skill was heightened, my musicianship enhanced. I believe certain environments can bring out the best or worst in someone, and Gramarye had done just that with me and Midge. Maybe the dull weather of late had changed the mood, and now something bad had surfaced from inside us; I hadn't often seen Midge act like this, that's for sure.

I sipped and brooded down there in the kitchen (where Flora Chaldean had withered away), and I hoped I hadn't scared off poor Rumbo for good. God knows how I'd appeared to him, tripping-out in front of the picture, and no wonder he'd dug in behind the sofa. The look he'd given me before bolting past my legs was as though I were about to introduce him to squirrel pie – from the inside looking out.

The glass was soon empty and I resisted pouring another. I was still bewildered by my freak-out and still upset by Midge's remarks, but sulking down there in the gloom wasn't going to help matters. Time to talk to her, time to be friends again. I climbed the stairs, closing the hallway door to stop rain drizzling in. The doormat there was wretched and soggy and I knew just how it felt.

Midge's anorak was lying in a heap on the bedroom floor and she was lying in a heap on the bed, legs curled up, shoulders hunched over, foetal and looking very lonely. The dampness in the air had made the room smell musty. I stood in the doorway, almost hesitant to go in further; I felt guilty and didn't know why.

'Midge . . .?' I ventured.

No response at first. Then she rested on one elbow so she could look across at me. Her hand stretched out towards me and I hurried over to lie beside her. My arms went around her waist and back and I hugged her close; she lay against me, trembling and sniffling.

My cheek nuzzled against her forehead and the scent of rain and fresh air was still in her hair. 'Midge, I want you to believe me – I stuck strictly to booze yesterday. I admit I had a lot, but I didn't touch anything else, no pills, no drugs – nothing like that.'

189

She stiffened against me, the trembling abated for a moment. Then I felt her body slump.

'So what happened in there, Mike?' she whispered. 'Why did you look that way, why did you say my painting came alive?'

'I wish I understood, myself,' I sighed. 'It seemed so real to me, as if I were inside the picture itself, walking up the path, smelling the flowers, feeling everything around me.' I had to smile. 'Remember that old film where Gene Kelly danced with the cartoon mouse? Well it was almost like that, as if real life and animation had come together, but with no black lines around the painted parts. So much more real, nothing to do with fantasy. And scary. Jesus, I've never been so frightened.' I pulled back my head to look at her face and her eyes were mournfully wide. 'You've gotta believe me, Midge,' I all but pleaded.

'I guess I do,' she responded, and a familiar softness returned to her expression. 'They said there might be long-lasting after-effects, that nobody knew precisely how long certain drug traces might remain in the system. But all these years . . .?'

'Doesn't seem possible, does it? That has to be the answer, though. Unless I'm going crazy.'

'You mean you used to be sane?' Feeble, and spoken in a doleful voice, but at least it was a stab at humour. My fingers tucked into her hair at the back of her head.

'You must have a check-up, Mike. It could be dangerous for you.'

'No real harm done, just a fright for both of us.'

'More than that. What if it happens again only with worse consequences?'

I didn't enquire what *they* might be. 'I'm tired, I've been up most of the night talking old times and drinking with Bob. *And* we'd worked hard at the session yesterday. Maybe I'm more exhausted than I realised. The combination of weariness and alcohol may have sparked off something that's still sneaking around inside me.' I wanted to say: *But it could be the cottage itself, Midge. Maybe there's something going on here that's way beyond our comprehension, something that creates illusions (hadn't I seen a hundred bats at least inside the loft when there weren't half as many? Didn't I keep seeing someone watching us from the edge of the woods? Hadn't I been absorbed into a painting so that I'd become a part of it, a human element walking in living paint?), some kind of Magic that cures sick animals, and even people if the stories about Flora Chaldean were to be believed (and what about my own arm? Had the Synergists healed the burns, or had Gramarye worked its powers during the night while I slept? Their green liquid might have stopped the pain, but had it really soothed away the burns?)* That's what I wanted to say, but it sounded ridiculous enough in my own mind. Midge would have thought I'd really flipped, and my fear was that she'd be right. So I kept quiet when I should have brought everything out into the open there and then. At least that way Midge might have been given cause to acknowledge some of her own feelings concerning Gramarye, intuitions that she was unable to accept consciously. It wasn't to be, though, not just then.

'Promise me you'll go back to the hospital, Mike, the one they took you to before. They know your history, so they can give you the appropriate tests and find out if you really are clear.'

'You're talking as if I used to be a regular junkhead, Midge. You know I was never that way.'

'You indulged.'

'Occasionally, and only soft stuff, for Chrissake. And never since *that* time.'

'All right, Mike. Please don't get angry, I don't want to fight any more.'

'Me neither. But don't let things grow out of proportion: doping was never a habit with me. Yeah, I know – they nearly all claim that, but you know it's true in my case. I've seen too many good lives wasted for me to get hooked.'

Her fingers dug into my back, but her kiss was soft. 'Forgive me for getting mad earlier?'

'I can't blame you – God knows how it must have looked.' I returned her kiss, glad the wall was down (partially down, anyway: I was still holding back on vague and sinister notions and, although I wasn't aware of it at the time, so was she). To change the subject, lest I got in too deep, I said, 'I tried

191

to call you on my way back this morning and got no reply. Have you been out most of the day?'

'I went for a long walk.'

'In the rain?'

'A little rain doesn't bother me. I felt the need to be in the open, among the trees, to feel grass beneath my feet. I'd worked on the painting all day yesterday and some of this morning and I needed to clear my head.'

'So you went into the forest?'

'Yes. Believe it or not, I managed to lose my direction and found myself looking down on Croughton Hall again.' Her voice had become low once more, as though not keen to continue that particular line of conversation.

Naturally I persisted. 'You mean the Synergist Temple – it isn't called Croughton Hall any more. What did you do? Did you go down there?'

'I thought I'd just say hello – you know how kind they were to us at the weekend. I thought they'd like to know how your arm was, too.'

'Oh yeah? Who did you see? Kinsella, Gillie?'

'I saw Mycroft.'

'Considering he's supposed to be a mystery man, he's been pretty much in evidence as far as you're concerned.'

'I've only met him twice now, Mike.'

'Twice more than the local vicar.'

'Who wouldn't want to avoid *him*?'

'I don't suppose our Reverend realised he was upsetting you – upsetting us *both* – with his gruesome little story. He probably imagined it would make Gramarye more interesting to us, y'know, add more character.'

'It did that all right, unpleasantly so. I've begun to get nervous when I go down to the kitchen in the morning, wondering what I'll find sitting there at the table.'

I didn't mention I'd had the same trepidations. 'Put it out of your mind. You don't believe in spooks anyway.'

'Not that kind. I don't believe death is the end of everything, though – there has to be something more that gives meaning to all this. We can't exist and then not-exist, otherwise all we do or try to do would be so pointless.'

'Well, that's something we'll never know until they close the lid on us, will we? I've gotta admit, I'm not that curious right now.'

'Mycroft told me we can know. Or at least, we can glean some idea of our state after death.'

'Ahhh, Midge, you're not falling for all that shit, are you? "*Is there anybody there, Uncle George, can you hear me, is there anyone around the table who had a grey-haired grandma who passed over recently, say within the last twenty years or so?*" You've gotta be kidding.'

'No, not that kind of nonsense, I don't go along with any form of footlights spiritualism. It's no better than certain religions which only make a mockery of people's beliefs.' She paused, as though unsure whether or not to go on. Then she said, 'Mycroft teaches that when the will is truly attuned to the Divine Spirit, then the mind can achieve a higher perceptual condition than ever before experienced. He believes that our own spiritual force can be united with the perpetual essence of those who once lived.'

A small, weary groan from me halted her for a moment.

'No, Mike, not by the simplistic and phony methods used by so-called mediums and their like, but in a truer sense, solely through awareness. Perhaps in a form that's outwardly less substantial than voices or movement of objects, or even visions, but all the more pure and undistorted because of that. No chicanery, no illusions; just a mutual contact between psychical energies, with Mycroft as guide and, if you like, interpreter. Words can't explain it properly – certainly mine can't; you just have to believe.'

'I bet you do. I'll bet his whole cult is based on that kind of blind faith. How can you seriously consider what he's been telling you?'

'I never said I did.' The tightness was back in her voice. 'But his ideologies and concepts are interesting to hear, and if you're open-minded enough they make a lot of sense. You have to listen for yourself, though, Mike – listen to him, not me. You'd soon realise he's a remarkable man.'

'No, thanks, I think I'll remain my ignorant, unimpressed self.'

'I should have known that's all I could expect from you. Always the cynic, for ever wrapped up in your own non-beliefs. You have to step outside that jokey little world of yours sometimes, Mike, you have to *try* and reach for something more.'

'Jesus, he's really got to you.'

Midge turned away from me, a wild, disgusted movement, and I immediately regretted my scorn, justified though I thought it was. I laid a hand on her shoulder and felt a sob jerk through her.

'Midge, I'm sorry, I didn't mean to upset you like this. Guess our bio-rhythms are out of sync today, huh?' Quit the gags, I warned myself, and closed the gap between us so that we spooned together, my front against her back, as snug as yin and yang. I wished our attitudes towards each other at that moment could be as comfortable. 'I should know by now that you're always willing to listen to fresh ideas and philosophies without necessarily accepting them. That's always been one of your virtues, the ability to absorb new thoughts and consider them.' I expected to hear 'brown-nose' from her, a usual reaction to nice comments from me, but she really was too upset. 'Maybe I've got Mycroft and his groupies all wrong. I'm sure he's completely sincere in his beliefs, but you can't really expect an old die-hard cynic like me to swallow them, can you?'

Snuffles from Midge.

'Let's talk about it,' I went on. 'You can tell me more, and then maybe I can throw in some other points of view. It's always worked that way for us in the past, hasn't it?'

She spoke, but she didn't turn around. 'Mycroft says he can help me reach my parents.'

I was too stunned to say anything right away, and probably that was just as well. Eventually, I did say, 'Oh, babe . . .' and immediately felt her go rigid.

But I was firm, and pulled her round to face me. This was something we really did have to discuss.

It was dark when I woke up later, although a bright moon somewhere from view did its best to compensate; light from the window made a monochrome quilt of the bedsheet. I turned to Midge and her breathing had the evenness of deep sleep.

I'd made an effort to keep cool earlier, holding back on a lot of things I'd like to have said about Mycroft and his crazy notions. I know I took the coward's way, but I was anxious to repair the silly rift that had developed; trouble was, Midge took my lack of argument as condonation and became more enthused with the idea of reaching her parents through this self-deluded Synergist. I tried to pull on the reins gently, but she'd soon become carried away, filled with the idea of actually 'talking' to her folks again, almost as if she could in some weird fashion lay their spirits to rest. Their deaths hadn't been easy, you see, no slipping smoothly away into eternal sleep, and she had the unhappy thought that somehow the traumatic circumstances in which they'd died wouldn't allow them peace in the after-life (whatever *that* was).

I shivered and pulled up the sheet around my neck; the day's rain had left the night chilly. And there was a definite damp mustiness to the bedroom now, much stronger than it had been earlier on. The digital clock on the small, round table beside the bed told me it was 22.26 and it took me more seconds to work out that it was twenty-six minutes past ten. We'd slept through the afternoon and evening.

As I lay there, a shadow flitted past the window, a bat or an owl on its nocturnal jaunt. The flapping of wings sounded hollow in the windless air.

My throat was still hangover dry and I was tempted to rouse Midge so that we could go down to the kitchen together, have coffee or hot milk, a sandwich maybe, and talk some more. I felt our afternoon's conversation might be advanced a little, hopefully with me infusing a modicum of logic into the situation. There was a need to tread warily, though, because I'd never known her quite so gullible about anything like this before, but I was sure patient reasoning would sooner or later win through.

Leaning over, I kissed her exposed shoulder. She stirred

and mumbled something unintelligible that probably made sense in whatever dream she was having, then turned onto her stomach, out to the world. I nuzzled the back of her neck, but she was really van-Winkled, not another movement in her. Resting back on my elbows, I stared across the room at the window, the sky there a kind of shiny blue; miserably, I recalled the love-making that had preceded our sleep. The physical act that should have been sweetened by lovers' reconciliation hadn't been good. Oh no, it hadn't been good at all. I think the effort of at least achieving a result had contributed considerably to our mutual weariness, because I know I flaked out immediately afterwards. Now I mentally apologised to Midge, more for falling asleep so fast than for my poor performance (we were both old and wise enough to know these things happened occasionally even in the best and most sensual relationships).

I tossed back the sheet, half hoping the movement would wake her, but it didn't. Slipping on my robe, I crept over to the door, deciding it really would be unfair to disturb such a deep sleep. My hand touched the wall for guidance as I neared the door and I was surprised when my palm came away wet. I stroked the plaster and my fingers slid through a sheen of moisture. A leak? No, couldn't be – this dampness wasn't running. Condensation, then? In summer? Had to be, though, and it *had* been raining for most of the day. It made me wonder what winter was going to bring! Obviously there was more work to be done on this place, but we wouldn't know what until the weather changed for the worse.

I went through to the hallway at the top of the stairs. I flicked on the light-switch, but the stairs still looked shadowy where they curved round the bend. To be honest, I didn't much fancy going down into the kitchen and I guess you know why, but I convinced myself I was grown-up and an unbeliever at that. I began the descent and stopped halfway, the black hole at the bottom that was the kitchen itself looking particularly uninviting. The 'hallucination' with the picture had obviously unnerved me a lot more than I'd thought.

Gritting my teeth in the best hero tradition, I continued down, my hand scrabbling ahead of me for the light-switch that was just inside the open doorway. The image – *the feeling* – of unseen, cold and bony fingers curling around my wrist was unbearably strong in my mind, almost strong enough to send me scurrying back upstairs, in fact, but I stalwartly (well, *stubbornly* might be more apt) resisted the impulse.

The light came on and it was a relief to find the room unoccupied. I padded past the table into the kitchen proper, going straight to the fridge (the same switch operated the lights in both sections of the kitchen) and taking out a milk carton. A tall glass had been left to dry on the drainer and I filled it to the brim with milk, drinking half standing there at the sink, then filling it again. Delving back into the fridge, I found some ham, and it was as I was spreading butter on a slice of bread that I got the curious prickling feeling of not being quite alone. I looked up and around: the window over the sink only showed me a pale reflection of myself. From where I stood at the working surface I couldn't see the table and chairs next door. But my mind could see someone sitting there.

I turned slowly so that I faced the opening. I didn't want to look, not really. As a matter of fact, I wanted to bang on the ceiling with the broom handle and get Midge down there fast, just for company, you understand. Naturally I couldn't do that, and naturally I had to poke my head through the doorway, unless I was prepared to wait there till morning. I moved cautiously and steadily towards the doorway, like a Hitchcock camera performing one of those famous tracking manoeuvres, the angle beyond the opening changing as I approached, revealing more and more the closer I got. The corner of the table, a shopping-list notepad lying there, a pepper-pot, the edge of a chair . . .

My own slow, deliberate movement was giving me the creeps, but the feeling that someone was sitting there waiting for me to peer around the corner of the doorway, waiting there and grinning, mouldy tea untouched, was just about overwhelming.

So I took the last couple of feet at a rush.

She wasn't there. Old Flora was lying up at the village cemetery, not sitting at the kitchen table in Gramarye. Thank God.

197

I leaned against the side of the doorway and steadied my breathing. She wasn't there, but oh, there was an atmosphere in that room. Maybe my imagination was running loose again, but I was sure I could sense a presence, something in the air that was almost tangible. There was an old person's smell about the room, you know the kind I mean? Sort of sweet and musty and ancient at the same time. I once read somewhere that certain parapsychologists claim ghosts are nothing more than the lingering dregs of a dead person's aura, and now I thought that theory could easily apply here inside the cottage, Flora Chaldean's psychic residue permeating the surroundings, her seeping vitality impregnating the furniture, the walls themselves. And that's what it felt like: she was gone, but a part of her personality remained locked inside Gramarye, perhaps in time to fade to nothing.

I shuddered at the idea, but at least it precluded any romantic notions of ghosts and hauntings.

I went back to the worktop and swiftly finished making the sandwich, then took it and the glass of milk through to the stairway, unable to stop myself from glancing at the table as I passed. I felt I could reach out and touch her, so strong was the eidetic image. It took some effort to switch off the light down there.

I went up the stairs faster than I'd come down, leaving on the hall light when I went into the round room. Despite my nervousness, though, I didn't turn on the light in there, and there was a simple reason for that: so as not to disturb my sleeping partner, I was going to eat my snack outside the bedroom, but I didn't want to look at that picture again, not in full light, just in case those vibrant colours worked their peculiar tricks again. Light from the hallway and moonlight flooding through the windows was good enough for me to see comfortably by, yet subdued enough not to make things *too* clear. I slumped onto the sofa and filled my mouth with ham and bread, my naked knees projecting whitely before me like the tops of two thin skulls, the milk glass held on one covered thigh.

Sitting there I contemplated Mycroft's assurance that he could help Midge contact her dead parents and the fact that she was falling for it, really believing this creep was some kind of mystic, able to converse with souls of the since-departed (while I might have gone along with the possibility of life after death, I just couldn't fall for the crazy notion of having a direct line to this other stratum – that was taking 'long distance' a bit too far). Yet my heart bled for Midge, because part of her still grieved so much for her parents. In a way, I think she was searching for her own peace of mind. Let's face it, for most of us the tragedy of death is its utter finality – 'now you see me, now you don't' – and that hardship, of course, is with those left to mourn. One moment Midge had a family, the next she was quite alone. Certainly there was a little time between losing both, but not enough to break up the trauma.

Her mother, then in her mid-fifties, had suffered from Parkinson's Disease for a number of years, Midge and her father having caringly nursed her through each degenerative stage. Drugs such as levodopa unfortunately had severe side effects for her, so much so that they could barely be tolerated; according to Midge, her mother's distress had been intense over long periods at a time. Yet the mother worried constantly about the well-being of her husband and daughter, deeply concerned that she was proving such a burden to them both, spoiling – or impeding – their lives, particularly that of her young daughter who was prevented from spending more time fully developing her own remarkable artistic talent. But Midge and her father were prepared to make any sacrifice to keep her as comfortable as possible, and between them they coped pretty well.

Until Midge's father was fatally injured in a car crash.

His skull had been cracked wide open, yet it took five torturous days for him to die. And in his very few coherent moments during that time, his concern had been only for Midge and her mother.

His death, it seemed, had broken down his wife's remaining reserves of strength, and with them the spirit that had helped her resist the worst of the disease. So rapid was her deterioration over the next couple of days that she was unable to attend the funeral. When Midge returned alone to the house after the ceremony, she had found her mother out of her sick-bed and slumped, fully clothed, in an armchair, a framed photograph of her late husband cradled in her lap. An empty pill-bottle lay at her feet together with a spilled glass of water. A transparent plastic bag, tightened around her neck by a thick rubber band, covered her head.

She'd left a note, begging her daughter's forgiveness and pleading for her to understand. Life had finally become too hard to suffer any longer, the loss of her dear husband, Midge's father, compounding the physical and mental torment; and by remaining alive she merely served to mar her daughter's young life, keeping her tied, stealing her freedom. Her regret was that neither parent would now witness the artistic success their beloved daughter was bound to find, but at least she, herself, would not hinder that talent.

It was easy to appreciate why Midge was so susceptible to Mycroft and his phony promises.

Her drawing board loomed in the semidarkness, surface angled, the painting held flat against it. Without looking, I knew the moonlight was illuminating the picture in its own eerie fashion, creating a different texture, maybe yet another spooky dimension. I wasn't curious enough to take a peek.

Black shapes skittered across the floor to give me a start, but I quickly realised that several of our night friends upstairs were leaving the roost, their winged bodies caught in the moon's glare, their shadows cast into the room. The sandwich consumed, I rose from the sofa, taking the drink with me, and wandered over to one of the tall windows, skirting the drawing board and studiously avoiding looking down at the painting.

The landscape outside was washed in that special brightness that had nothing to do with warmth, but a lot to do with ice and bleakness. So colourless was the grass that the expanse appeared frosty, and so deep were the shadows beneath individual bushes and trees that they were like black voids. The forest top wore an undulating silver-grey cover, an impenetrable layer over catacombed darkness.

I sipped milk, and liquid cold soaked into me. My eyes reluctantly scanned the dark boundary of woodland, looking for something I didn't want to find. Discerning a lurking figure would have been impossible anyway, so concealing were the shadows, but that didn't stop me searching, and the knowledge didn't even prevent a sigh of relief when I found nothing.

That relief was premature, though. Because my attention was drawn to something standing midway between the forest and the cottage. Something I didn't remember having been there before.

It was so still it could have been nothing more than a tall bush. But a pallid blob at the top of the motionless shape that could only have been a face said otherwise.

And another smaller whitish shape that now slowly rose up could only have been a hand.

And that hand beckoned me.

NOBODY THERE

I was scared. No, I was bloody terrified. But I'd also had enough aggravation for one day. I was hurt that I'd been accused of doping, confused by the afternoon's hallucination, and sick of being intimidated by this mystery onlooker who didn't have the nerve to knock on the door and properly introduce him- or herself. All that combined into anger inside me, which rapidly began to boil over.

I think dropping the glass of milk on my toes precipitated the final eruption.

With a shout of rage, I ran for the door, hopping the first few steps because of the pain. Shooting back the bolts with as much noise as I could make (Midge managed to sleep through all this), I yanked open the door, and then I was out there in the night, racing back around the cottage to the side where the figure waited, slipping on grass still wet and mushy from the day's rain, robe flying open so that air rushed in at my exposed body.

I didn't care, though; enough was enough. I was going to sort out this bloody watcher in the woods once and for all. Forget about discarnate beings and women in black and shrouded apparitions and something wicked this way comes and psycho and omen and exorcist and the evil fucking dead – I was going to confront the beast that wasn't a beast at all but somebody playing silly bloody games at my expense. Whatever fear may have been in me was easily overwhelmed by a furious indignation.

I pounded across the open stretch, ignoring sharp stones or twigs that painfully stuck to the soles of my feet, enraged sufficiently to leave caution well behind.

But I was running out to nobody.

I made for the precise spot where the figure had loitered, judging the position by the line of the window I'd gazed from and a low clump of bushes to the left. I swivelled my head around without breaking pace, not slowing until I reached the place where I was certain the figure had beckoned from.

He, she – or whatever – couldn't possibly have darted back into the woods, nor raced to the other side of the cottage. There wouldn't have been time. But where the hell was it? It couldn't have disappeared into thin air.

I kept running, perhaps more in an effort to keep up my flagging bravado than anything else, scooting round nearby trees, swiping at bushes to flush out anything hiding there. Something did run out from beneath one clump of foliage, in fact, scaring me half to death, but it was small and scurrying, an animal more frightened than me.

That little shock cooled me down a bit, and I stood there looking left and right, in front and behind, chest heaving as I wheezed in breaths, shoulders slumped and perspiration already becoming cold on my near-naked body.

I drew the robe around me as I sank to the ground. And there, squatting back on my heels, I howled in anguish at the moon.

COMPANY

We were sitting side by side on the bench around the back of the cottage, Bob and I, six-pack between us, the sun beginning to glow red. The evening was warm and bumble bees still droned, not yet ready for bed. Our girls were downstairs, tossing salad, slicing ham and probably making a lot of fuss over what was supposed to be a simple meal.

Bob poured himself another beer, surveying the darkening forest opposite. He shook his head. 'It's so fucking rural.'

I grinned at his discomfort. 'I'll take you for a walk in the woods tomorrow morning.'

'Not without a long string, you won't.' He drank and settled back, squinting up at the sun, then quickly averting his eyes. 'Don'tcha find it aggravating, all this peace and quiet? I mean, it's great an' all that, but doesn't it piss you off after a while?'

'You get used to it,' I told him.

'Yeah, but dontcha miss . . .' he searched for the appropriate word '. . . *life*?'

'There's plenty of that around here if you care to look.'

'No, not that kinda life, not nature. I mean – *life*. Something to do.'

'Funny enough, that hasn't been a problem. Sure, I get restless now and again – that's why I enjoyed our session so much this week – but we're close enough to Big Smoke to jump in the car and drive up for the evening.'

'And how often have you done that since you've been here?'

'We've only just settled in, Bob. We haven't had time to start yearning for bright lights again.'

He wiped a beer dribble from his chin. 'Yeah, well, you could be right. This could be the ideal way to spend out your days, listening to the grass grow, watching the birdies build their nests. You could start weaving baskets for a bit of extra cash.'

I chuckled at the wind-up. 'If you think I'm gonna stand a whole weekend of this . . .'

He slapped my thigh, enjoying himself. 'Only kidding, Mike, honest. I think you've made a good move, to tell you the truth. Might even do the same myself one day; I'll wait for a few grey hairs to come through first, though. Hey look, there's that bloody squirrel again. He don't care, do 'e?'

Rumbo had hopped into view from the embankment side of the cottage, obviously still curious about our company for the weekend. He'd been on the doorstep when Bob and his girlfriend had arrived an hour or so earlier, and had scuttled away, keeping his distance but not disappearing altogether. I was pleased that he seemed to have overcome his shock earlier in the week. However, I hadn't quite got over mine yet.

I'd toyed with the idea of confiding in Bob about what had happened on Thursday last, but somehow I couldn't imagine my old drinking buddy taking me too seriously. In fact, I knew bloody well he'd hoot his head off. Why hadn't I told Midge of my night excursion to confront that sinisterly beckoning figure? Because she was too full of a new expectancy (connected with Mycroft, of course), the episode with the 'moving' painting already pushed to the back of her mind, and things between us were still a tiny bit strained. Press me harder and I'll tell you I had a few doubts about myself by now. I was no longer certain that I wasn't suffering from some form of mental aberration (call it new-environment neurosis if you like); it all seemed so unreal and *fanciful* in the cold light of day. To tell the truth, I'd decided to bide my time, see what developed. There was really little option to do otherwise, anyway.

Rumbo came closer, one eye on the stranger in our midst. Bob clucked his tongue as if encouraging a dog or a baby, and the squirrel's head jerked up; he regarded Bob with some curiosity for a short time, then boldly leapt onto the garden table where two empty beer cans had been left. He peered into the triangular hole of one, almost toppling the can over. Steadying it with his paws, he licked beer residue from the rim, much to Bob's delight.

'Love it, love it!' Bob shrieked. 'An alcoholic squirrel. I can see you've done your best for pest control, Mike – turn 'em into alkies and let 'em drink themselves to death.'

'Rumbo's no pest; he's one of the family.'

Bob gave me an old-fashioned look, then grinned. He made no further comment.

I'd been looking forward to their visit, had, in fact, been slightly on edge with anticipation all day – a *good* feeling, I might add. Bob and Kiwi, and Big Val who should be arriving at any moment, were our first invited guests to Gramarye, and Midge and I (despite her earlier reservations about Bob) were taking great pleasure from that. Now I was beginning to relax, the second beer and my friend's amiable company helping me settle. Rabbits had turned out for their before-bed frolics, although this evening they kept well clear of the cottage itself as if sensing there were strangers about, and a few birds flitted around like late-night shoppers. The breeze was minimal, and even that carried warmth with it.

I sipped beer and soaked up the atmosphere.

We had more drinks in the round room before dinner, all of us together this time, Midge sticking to lemonade and soda while the rest of us indulged in the stronger stuff. Her agent had arrived twenty minutes earlier, desperately in need of a stiff gin and tonic to help her get over the journey down. Big Val and Bob had met on one or two previous occasions and the banter between them had always been on a basis of jovial hostility. Bob liked women to be most definitely feminine and non-aggressive – Kiwi appeared to be a paragon in this respect – so Val was something of a problem for him. He started off by complimenting her on her heavy country brogues – 'just right for yomping through pigshit', as he put it. She returned the compliment by admiring his pink leather tie – 'ideal for throttling', she suggested.

Opening pleasantries exchanged, Midge and I toasted the health of our first 'official' guests, and they in turn toasted our future happiness at Gramarye. We chatted generally for a while, but it was obvious that Val was impatient to inspect her client's latest work – her eyes had lit up when she'd walked in and spotted the drawing easel on the other side of the room – and she lost little time in sauntering over to it. The picture of the cottage was still taped there to the board, covered against dust by thin layout paper. I hadn't looked at it again since Thursday, but I watched the agent as she lifted the sheet, interested in her reaction. I don't know what I expected, but a frown wasn't it.

I caught the expression because I was watching closely; the frown quickly passed and Val smiled.

'Splendid,' she opined. 'Absolutely splendid.'

For her, as a hard-bitten twenty-per-center, well used to works of excellence, that judgement was pretty nigh over-the-top, and Midge beamed gratitude.

'It's not for sale or anything,' she said quickly. 'Just something for Mike and me, a sort of reminder of our first weeks here. Gramarye's initial impact on us before we got too used to everything. You know how easy it is to eventually become blunted to even the loveliest things around you.'

Val continued to study the painting as Bob and Kiwi crowded behind her.

'Oh yeah, that's something else!' Bob declared in his genuinely impassioned manner. 'Take a look at it, darlin'. Now that's what you call bloody art. Not crumpet with one boob and three legs and a nose where an earhole should be.'

'You obviously know what you like, Bob,' said Val drily.

Unsure of her, he nodded. 'I like to know what I'm looking at.' And he looked too meaningfully at Val.

'How're the posters Midge did for the agency coming along?' I asked, to change the subject.

Val disengaged herself from the other two around the drawing board. 'I've got first proofs in the car, actually – minis, of course, just for colour correction. I thought we could look at them tomorrow, Midge, and you can mark any comments on them.' She, too, was staying over, and working out sleeping arrangements hadn't been easy.

'Fine,' agreed Midge. 'Can't wait to see them.'

'Bear in mind they're only *first* proofs. We've plenty of time to put them right.'

'That sounds ominous.'

'I know how particular you are. The art director's pleased, by the way. As a matter of fact, he's got more work lined up for you, but we'll discuss that tomorrow, too. Oh, and Hamlyn want to discuss a new book.'

'Seems like the heavy season's coming on,' I remarked.

'That time of year, I'm afraid. Clients want to put work in progress before they go off on holiday.'

'I'm still not ready to take on too much,' warned Midge.

'We don't want you enjoying the leisures of country life for too long,' said Val, flopping down on the sofa. 'A lot of people would be very disappointed, especially your junior fans.'

'Not to mention your friendly bank manager, God bless him,' chimed in Bob, sitting deliberately close to Val so that she had to shuffle her broad bottom further along. 'I suppose we are going to eat tonight, aren't we, or has Band Aid got to do another record? And I see the booze is running like glue.' He waggled his almost empty glass at me.

With friends as obnoxious as Bob, any enemy could only be sweet. But I was used to him; he was an old habit with me, and they die hard, don't they? Besides, I knew part of his act was for the benefit of Val: he liked to rile anyone he couldn't get the hang of.

Kiwi tutted disgustedly at him, flicking her blonde hair back behind one ear. 'Sometimes your manners are just an embarrassment,' she scolded, nevertheless kneeling, then squatting on the floor beside him.

'It's my coarseness that makes me so lovable, am I right, Mike?'

I took the glass from him, replying, 'Yeah, adorable. Same in here again?'

'A little heavier on the vodka this time. I'm not driving tonight.'

'It makes a difference?'

He draped an arm around his girlfriend and smiled that close-lipped smug smile of his, the cat who'd not only had the cream, but knew there was more to come.

I sent out the mental message to him: *Behave yourself tonight, pal, and don't let me down.*

He didn't really. What happened later was only partly his fault.

Dinner was a great success.

The more wine we consumed, the more the conversation flowed. Bob and Val soon began to get the measure of one another, each jibe and riposte becoming more humorous and less antagonistic as the evening wore on. Salads were never my favourite fodder, but as Midge's agent was strictly vegetarian the menu had to suit all parties; besides, there was plenty of cold meat for us carnivores. The warm weather – we were seated around the kitchen table (spruced up somewhat by a lace tablecloth and red candles and things) with the outside door open wide to catch any breeze drifting our way – made such a meal even more appropriate. Kiwi proved to be a lot brighter than she looked (she refused to disclose how she had acquired that nickname, incidentally, but Bob hinted heavily and somewhat lasciviously that it had something to do with boot polish), and had no inhibitions whatsoever about telling us of her earlier years as a rock-band groupie (there's a great sociological study to be made some day by some learned professor on this particular species, because their motives are not *entirely* what you might expect).

More than once during the dinner I found myself watching Midge, her small-boned face transformed by candlelight from pixie to princess, almond eyes sparkling yet still soft with a beauty that came from somewhere inside. The steady flow of wine may have influenced my judgement to a degree, but the feeling was nothing new; I'd melted over the same indefinable quality many times before and in my most sober moments. So maybe I did put her on some kind of pedestal (and I was not alone in that), but I'd known her long enough for any cracks to appear in that column by now. None had, not ever. Don't take me for a besotted idiot, though: I was aware of her faults and weaknesses, and they only made her more vulnerable, more human. Let's say they brought realism to the dream, made her more accessible to me. And one of the things that tied me so closely to her was that she saw some goodness in me; and that somehow made me freer, allowed me to expose my feelings more easily than ever before. Call me a romantic fool.

I was a fool on another count that evening also, for Bob, he of the cast-iron bladder, had popped upstairs to the bathroom a couple of times during the course of dinner and it was only on the second occasion that I noticed he was chewing on something when he returned. It didn't occur to me until later, when he was giggling over the silliest remarks, that he was disappearing so that he could cut off tiny segments of cannabis resin, wary of lighting a joint in the presence of his hostess whose antipathy towards drugs was well known within our circles. He obviously felt the need for a stimulant other than booze, and no wonder he was in such hearty mood.

I let it go, although I was anxious that Midge shouldn't discover what he was up to: I'd taken enough stick over the matter of drugs that week, and wrongfully so. Fortunately, she appeared oblivious, presumably putting Bob's affable manner down to good wine, food and company.

It was pretty late when we finally closed the kitchen door against the cooler night air and took ourselves upstairs, Midge remaining behind to make coffee. I'd bought a good brandy from the village off-licence that day and poured for Val, Bob and myself; I was unable to produce a Malibu for Kiwi, so she settled for vodka with 'lots and lots of lemonade'.

I resisted bringing down the guitars, knowing that once

210

Bob and I got started, we'd play all night until everyone around us was slumped in unconscious heaps; instead, I put on a tape, keeping the volume low so that our own voices wouldn't have to compete with the music.

Even Val seemed mellowed and more charming than I'd ever known her to be, and we had a good-natured debate along the lines of: Agent – parasite or provider? I think she came out ahead, and I didn't begrudge her that.

The first yawns started around one-ish – clean country air took the blame – although Bob was ready to talk the night away, and Midge, clear-headed as usual, informed our guests of the bedding arrangements, suggesting a sensible rota for the use of the bathroom. Bob and Kiwi would be sleeping in the round room on the sofa, which was the kind that could be pulled out into a bed, while Val would be in the spare room next to ours on a small fold-away cot we'd always kept for such occasions in our previous place.

Midge and I went back downstairs to clear the dinner things, while they all made themselves ready for bed. I chuckled when I heard Bob's voice through the ceiling doing his impression of Michael Jackson singing butch.

Midge and I also took time to stand on the doorstep and watch the stars, which looked more unreal and numerous seen through unpolluted air than in any space movie. We took time, too, to kiss and fondle, like teenagers home from a date. I was glad I didn't have a last train to catch.

When we gazed upwards again, most of the stars had disappeared behind seeping black clouds. It looked as if there'd been a power-cut in the sky.

I've no idea what time it was when the screams woke us.

We both shot upright in bed as though activated by the same spring. There was just enough light to make out Midge's outline and I felt her hands clutching fearfully at me.

'Oh God, Mike, what was that?'

'I'm not sure –'

The screams came again, high-pitched and terrible, impossible to tell whether they came from man or woman. I scrabbled for the bedside lamp, nearly knocking it over before finding the switch to flick it on. We were both naked and Midge lost no time in pulling on her nightshirt while I reached for my robe. We made it to the door together.

I'll admit it, though: I hesitated just a fraction before opening that door. The screams sent an iciness through me that seemed to reach down and frost my testicles. I turned my shudder into action by twisting the handle.

With no barrier between us, the sounds were even more intense and scary.

A lamp was on in the round room, Kiwi kneeling on the floor beside it: she was staring horror-struck at a crouching figure on the far side of the room. That crouching figure was Bob, his face even more horror-struck, ugly and disfigured, like one of those stone gargoyles you find jutting from cathedral ramparts. What made his appearance all the more shocking was that he was white. I mean it – totally white. From his face down to his chest and stomach. Down to the waistband of his pyjama legs. Even his arms. Not just pale, or ashen, but *white*.

He was looking towards the open doorway leading to the stairs, and his eyes were wider than seemed possible. His jaw was dropped almost to his throat, his mouth a huge gaping hole, now his screams no more than dry scratchy sounds.

I ran to him, calling his name as if that might drag him back from the madness that was evident in his stare, skidding to my knees before him. His hands, like stiffened claws, were held up to his face as though to block out a nightmare vision; but still his eyes stared insanely from behind bent fingers. He was trembling, the movement jerky stiff, his body somehow brittle.

'Bob, what is it? Calm down and tell me what's wrong!'

He didn't seem to hear; he tried to push himself further into the curved wall, bare feet scuffing at the carpet. I pulled at his wrists and they were like juddering steel rods, impossible to move. Somewhere in the background I could hear loud sobbing, and I hoped Midge was tending to Bob's girlfriend – I had enough to cope with without offering any comfort there.

'Bob, for Chrissake take it easy!'

I shook his shoulders, although I was almost afraid to touch their milky whiteness, and he flinched violently. I persisted though, matching his strength with a roughness of my own. This time I grasped his hands and wrenched them down, moving my head close so that he was forced to look at my face.

Maybe I should have realised there and then what part of the problem was, because despite the room's soft light his pupils were small, contracted, as though affected by bright sunshine. And there was a glassiness to his stare that overlaid the horror expressed there; I'd observed that same faraway look over the years on the faces of several acquaintances who'd gone beyond cannabis.

But the atmosphere was too charged, too frighteningly potent, for me to take cognizance of that right away. I kept my voice soothing and controlled as I reasoned with him.

'There's nothing happening to you, Bob, everything's okay. You've had a bad dream, that's all. Or maybe you heard something that scared you. Was it the bats? We didn't tell you we had bats in our belfry, did we? They scare the hell out of me sometimes and I'm used to 'em. C'mon now, Bob, we're all here and nothing's gonna hurt you.'

I felt slightly foolish coaxing him like this, but it really was as though I had a terrified child on my hands.

For a brief moment, his eyes managed to focus on mine, and that seemed to help a little. He stopped struggling against me and tried to speak, but still that rasping sound emerged. He was having difficulty in closing his mouth to form words.

I looked away for a second to see how the others were and wished I hadn't. The round room somehow wasn't the same. Oh, everything was in place, the furniture hadn't changed, the carpet wasn't a different colour, nor were the drapes: but I was somewhere else. Everything was cold – without touching I *knew* that everything was tomb-cold – and everywhere there were shadows where they shouldn't have been. And the musty, damp smell was back. I thought I saw bubbling fungi on the curved walls, but the shadows were too deep, too obscuring, to be sure. And the room was growing smaller, the walls closing in so slowly that I couldn't be certain, even when I blinked my eyes and looked again, I couldn't be sure, couldn't measure it. The shrinkage *had* to be imaginary, had to be! The mustiness clogged my throat, making it difficult to breathe.

Kiwi was wailing, Midge kneeling beside her with an arm around the blonde's shoulders, doing her best to calm her and having about as much success as I was with Bob. Kiwi was trying to tell us something, but I could only understand a few choked phrases here and there:

'. . . thirsty . . . he . . . went downstairs . . . oh my God, I heard him scream . . . he saw someone down . . . there . . .'

More than enough for me to catch the drift, and centipedes fresh from the freezer crawled up my spine. Somehow I guessed what had confronted Bob in the kitchen.

Fingernails raking my chest returned my attention to my buddy lying propped against the wall, and I grasped his wrist to stop the painful scratching. His head was shaking like a palsied man's and his other hand was pointing generally towards the open doorway – I say generally because his arm was moving wildly, barely able to maintain any sure direction.

But I followed his gaze rather than his pointing arm, mesmerised by the stark insanity in his eyes: it was like following the dotted line in a cartoon, from eyeball to object.

There was no light on in the hallway, but a pale glow came from the bend in the stairs; from the kitchen itself, in fact. Bob must have switched on the light down there.

The room, seen only in the periphery of my vision, was growing smaller and the shadows darker, as if both conspired to crush those within. My subconscious sent the message that it was only imagination, my own fear, that was creating the effect; that fleeting realisation afforded little comfort. I still gripped Bob's wrist, and now I was shaking as much as he. My jaw locked open as I watched through the open doorway.

A shadow was rising from the stairway. A bulky shape, ill-defined, inky dark. Coming up from the kitchen.

Rising. Lit only dimly from the back. Now in almost complete darkness as it rose higher, came round the bend in the stairs.

Slowly emerging into the soft light of the round room.

BAD TRIP

I almost collapsed with relief when Midge's agent walked through the door.

'Jesus fucking Christ, Val, you nearly scared us shitless!' I thumped my fist on the floor in exasperation.

She was genuinely surprised. 'Good Lord, why? I went down to investigate the cause of all the fuss our gibbering friend was making.'

She reached for the switch by the door and turned on the overhead light. Walls immediately sprang back into place, shadows instantly evaporated. Val strode purposefully into the room, voluminous flannelette nightgown, worn with total disregard to the season, billowing out behind her. Never had she looked so formidable. Nor so reassuring.

'There's nothing downstairs, Bob, nothing at all,' she said, bearing down on us. 'Now just what is all this nonsense about?'

I drew my robe around me, feeling somewhat under-dressed, and hauled myself to my feet. We looked at Bob together and I was happy to notice a glimmer of colour returning to his flesh. He didn't look healthy, though, he didn't look healthy at all.

'Help me with him,' I said to Val and we both grasped his arms and pulled him up. There was no resistance left in

216

Bob, and little life either, and we all but carried him over to the sofa-bed.

'He was crawling across the room when I got out here,' Val explained as we gently lowered his body, 'screaming blue murder and pointing at the stairs. I thought perhaps you'd had burglars, so I rushed down there immediately.'

I always knew she had balls, but I never suspected how much.

'Empty, of course, no sign of anyone in the kitchen. I checked the door and windows, but there were no signs of their being forced. I think dear Bob must have woken from an extremely bad nightmare.'

Kiwi was still sobbing, but she managed to say, 'No, no. He was awake. He needed a drink of water. He went downstairs.'

I was still shaken enough not to take too much notice of her long thighs exposed beneath her short and flimsy nightie.

'Did you turn on the light in the kitchen?' I asked Val.

'No, it was already on. All right, so he did find his way down there, but I can't imagine what sparked off all this hoo-ha.'

Midge and I helped Kiwi sit on the edge of the sofa-bed; Bob lay on his back staring at the ceiling and murmuring to himself.

I lifted Kiwi's chin with a crooked finger so that I could look at her face. 'What did Bob take tonight? I know he was on cannabis most of the evening, but he took something stronger when we all turned in, didn't he?'

I felt Midge's eyes on me and risked a glance at her. I shook my head slightly, an apology as much as anything else.

'Come on, Kiwi, we need to know,' I persisted.

'He . . . he took some Chinese.'

I closed my eyes and silently swore. Smack. Heroin. Cheap brown powder that was mixed with all kinds of impurities, often strychnine and other toxics. The stupid bloody idiot!

'Not . . . not much,' she added quickly. 'He only sniffed a little bit. He wanted me to join him, but the stuff makes me sick. It's not good for my sinuses.'

217

Bob began to moan aloud and writhe on the bed. Then he sat bolt upright and slowly looked around the room. Still pallid, but his skin no longer having that eerie albescence, he shook less spasmodically than before, the movement becoming a steady tremble.

'This . . . pl – place . . .' he stammered.

It was Midge who came forward and put a gentle hand by the side of his neck.

'Bob, there's nothing here to harm you,' she told him, her voice low and as gentle as her touch.

It took a while for his eyes to focus solely on her, and when they did his chest slumped as though he were suddenly exhausted. When he spoke, his words were tearful: 'This fucking place . . . I've got to get out of here!'

'Hush, now,' she said, and I saw her hand become reassuringly firmer against him. 'There's nothing here to be afraid of.'

For myself, I was angry at him, almost mad enough to pop him. He'd had no right to bring that stuff into our home, no right at all, especially when he knew Midge's feelings against all drugs, hard or soft. It took a lot of restraint not to choke him.

'Snap out of it, Bob,' I told him severely. 'You've snorted some bad shit, that's the strength of it.' But I remembered the menace that I, myself, had experienced.

He seemed more in control of himself, and I think Midge's soothings had much to do with that. She continued talking to him, her tones moderated, her hand always working softly on the stiffened muscles of his neck and shoulder.

When he spoke again, the hysteria was held in check – only just, though. 'There was something down there in the kitchen –'

'There's no one else in the cottage,' I said.

'Not someone, *something*! Waiting for me in the dark, sitting there . . . ! Jesus, the stink! I can smell it now. Can't you? There's something terrible here!' His voice was rising in pitch once more.

'No, Bob,' Midge replied calmly. 'Gramarye is a good place, there's nothing bad here.'

218

'You're wrong. Something's . . . something's . . .' His mouth flapped open; he couldn't find the words.

Kiwi was sobbing aloud again and Bob turned to her, then to me, almost desperately. 'Mike, I'm not staying, I'm not staying here –'

'Take it easy,' I said. 'You're on a bad trip. It'll pass, just calm down.'

'No, no way . . . this room . . . the walls . . .'

I knew what he meant. Hadn't I been sure the walls were moving closer, that mould was forming on them in the shadows? Or had *his* hallucination, his hysteria, insinuated itself into my own mind? Not much was certain to me any more inside the cottage.

'You can't leave in the middle of the night,' I told him with a mildness I hardly felt. 'For one thing, you can't drive in your present state, and for another, you need to calm down and sleep this off.'

'Sleep? You're fucking crazy if you think I'm gonna sleep in this place!' He started looking around again, this time wildly.

'It's nearly three in the morning,' put in Val, who hovered over us all, 'much too late for travelling. We'll sit with you until it's light, then if you still want to, you can leave.'

Every one of us jumped back when Bob screamed.

'Now! I've gotta get out now!'

He threshed around on the bed like a spoilt kid who couldn't get his own way. I grabbed him and pulled him back as he tried to leave the bed, pinning him there by his shoulders and needing all my strength to do so. I was alarmed to see spittle glistening the sides of his mouth.

'Leave him be!' Kiwi shouted, and began tugging at my arm. 'I'll drive, I'll take him home!'

'He's in no condition –'

'I think it would be for the best, Mike.'

I looked over my shoulder at Midge in surprise. 'It could be dangerous for both of them with Bob in this state.'

'He'll be better once he's away from here,' she answered.

'We can't be sure of that.'

'It's more dangerous for him to stay.'

Bewildered, I turned my attention back to Bob; now

tears were running from his face onto the pillow beneath him.

'She might be right,' said Val. 'I should let him go, Mike.'

Uncertain, I relaxed my grip, but I didn't release him. 'Bob, listen to me now.' I held his jaw to make him look at me. 'You can get dressed and we'll take you down to your car. Kiwi will drive, okay? Can you understand me?'

''Course I can fucking understand you. Just let me up. Oh Christ, I've . . .' Again he couldn't finish the sentence.

I let go of him and rose from the sofa-bed. He sat and Kiwi pushed by me to throw her arms around his shoulders.

'Help him get dressed,' I told her. 'We'll wait downstairs.'

The three of us stayed long enough to see that Bob was more in control of himself, and although his movements were erratic and he shivered as if chilled, he gave the appearance of having come to his senses a little more. But we could tell he was still very frightened.

'I'll make some coffee,' said Midge quietly, and she and Val went to the stairs. I took time out to return to our bedroom and don jeans and sneakers, keeping the robe wrapped around me. I looked in on Bob again before going downstairs and found Kiwi already dressed, throwing spare clothes and bathroom things into their overnight bag, while Bob slowly did up the buttons of his shirt, his gaze fearfully roaming the room, checking that the walls weren't on the move again.

I was sorry for him and I was angry at him. And, of course, I was worried for him. But also, I was becoming very afraid for Midge and myself.

Kiwi helped Bob on with his jacket while I watched, ready to leap in and restrain him should his panic bubble over again: I could tell the hysteria was just below the surface, barely held in check.

'Bob,' I said, 'I'd feel better if you didn't leave . . .'

He looked at me as if I were the one in need of treatment, the wildness of his expression contrary to the usual appearance of someone on heroin: there was a kind of dreaminess there sure enough, but it was of the nightmare variety.

He suddenly gripped both my arms, his words forced and slurred. 'What is . . . this place?'

And that was all he said.

He let go of me just as abruptly and grabbed Kiwi, pulling her towards the door. He stopped before the hallway, though, and his girlfriend had to support his weight as he swayed there. He kept shaking his head, and for a moment I thought he was going to faint.

'He doesn't want to go down there again,' Kiwi called back to me. 'Let us out this way, Mike, please *hurry*.'

I pushed past them and unbolted the door in the hallway above the stairs. They were through before I could stop them.

'Hey, it's dark out there. Let me go first – those steps are dangerous.' The only reply I got was from an owl somewhere off in the woods.

They were already on the top step, Kiwi struggling with one of Bob's arms around her shoulders, using her free hand on the wall to guide herself, the other carrying the overnight bag. They tottered dangerously and I hurried after them before they could tumble.

Taking Bob from her, I slipped his arm around my neck, gripping his wrist tightly and sliding my other arm about his waist. We began an awkward descent and I was glad I'd cleared most of the moss from the steps. Even so, the stone felt slippery beneath me.

When my fingers brushed against the brickwork of the cottage itself, it too felt silky damp.

Twice my feet slid on the smooth steps, but both times I managed to keep upright, pushing Bob against the wall to steady ourselves. I breathed a sigh of relief when we made it into the garden.

The front door opened as we passed, throwing out some useful light, and Val appeared on the other side of Bob; she helped me guide him along the path, Kiwi running ahead to open the car. At the gate, I turned briefly and looked back at the cottage.

The black silhouette of Midge was in the doorway, so perfectly still that she could have been part of Gramarye's structure. It was a strange, fleeting moment.

We bundled our burden into the car, Kiwi quickly climbing into the driver's seat, and now Bob had his eyes closed. I tucked in his legs and before I straightened, my head close to his, he opened his eyes again and stared directly into mine. I still shudder when I remember that look (even though worse and more memorable events were to follow), because I saw not just his fear, but an intense and wretched despair within him. Looking into those eyes was like peering into a deep, shadowed well, at the bottom of which something indefinable in the darkness moved, writhed, reached upwards in a gesture of pleading. The drugs he had taken that night had closed certain doors in his mind – which is their true effectiveness – but that had left exposed a direct passage towards other, more inward senses. Whatever he had faced, whatever he had *imagined* he'd seen downstairs in Gramarye's kitchen, had been drawn from his own darker thoughts.

I pushed myself away and quickly closed the passenger door, the interior light automatically switching off to hide his gaze.

I heard Val advising Kiwi to 'drive very carefully', and then the car pulled off the grass verge and quickly gathered speed.

I wasn't sorry to see those red tail-lights disappear around the bend in the road.

CRACK

I don't suppose any of us slept well that night. We'd sat for a while and drunk coffee, but I guess we were too shocked to discuss Bob's hysteria, and maybe somewhat embarrassed by it. Midge had remained very quiet when Val discoursed upon the evils and the unpredictable results of drug-taking. Not that I added much to the conversation – my head was buzzing with other thoughts.

We turned in for a second time that night, and when Midge and I were in bed I held on to her, keeping her close against me; but she was unresponsive, as though Bob's behaviour was partly my fault (and privately I felt a fool for not having found a discreet way of warning him off as soon as it sank in that he was turning on, even if it was only cannabis at that time). At least Midge wasn't scared, unlike me.

I needed to get my own head straight before I told her what I thought he'd seen down there in the kitchen, and I wanted her to be in a more receptive state: I was well aware by now that Midge had a peculiar kind of blind spot where Gramarye was concerned. Keeping my eyes closed for long was difficult lying there in the darkness, but I must have finally drifted off some time before dawn, although I awoke once or twice during the hours that followed, but not fully until I felt

223

movement beside me. Midge was rising and I was grateful for the morning light. We went downstairs together.

Val arrived soon after, dressed and looking ready for business, events of the previous night dismissed for the moment. It was she who got breakfast organised and I discovered I was surprisingly hungry, although Midge hardly touched a thing. The meal was a dismal affair, even though Val, God bless her, did her best to spark up conversation on a variety of topics, none of them to do with the episode that was on all our minds.

Midge only brightened up when Rumbo appeared in the open doorway, birds already having begun to assemble behind him, trilling their impatient demand for food. Their arrival was somehow reassuring to her.

Val watched with a bemused smile as Midge broke bread and scattered the pieces outside, but Rumbo's sheer cheek evoked rumbling chortles from somewhere low in her ample chest. The squirrel jumped onto the table and scooped up bacon rind from my plate. He gnawed away, stopping only occasionally to chatter at us, presumably explaining his plans for the day.

I gave him a gentle poke with my finger. 'You didn't meet our guest last night,' I said. 'Rumbo, this is Val – Val, this is Rumbo. He likes to eat.'

'I can't believe it's so tame,' exclaimed Val.

'Shhh,' I warned. 'Don't refer to Rumbo as an "it" – he gets offended easily.' His presence was beginning to revive my own flagging spirits.

'How on earth did you manage to get so friendly with him?' Val was standing with hands on hips, shaking her head.

'We didn't need to,' explained Midge from the doorway. 'He trusted us right from the start. All the animals around here are friendly. Flora Chaldean, the woman who owned Gramarye before us, gained their trust.'

'She must have been quite a lady.'

'She was.'

Midge said that with such conviction that I turned towards her.

'Tell me about Flora Chaldean,' said Val, collecting up

used cups and plates. Rumbo hopped to the other end of the table, clutching the half-gnawed bacon rind protectively to his chest.

'We don't know a lot,' I said, draining the last of my coffee. 'Only that she was very old when she died, had lived most of her life at Gramarye, and that she had a reputation as a healer. We were told she had ways of curing animals *and* people.'

'Curing them?'

'Well, minor ailments, I guess. Apparently she used potions and faith – I don't think major surgery was ever involved.'

'And she lived here alone?'

I nodded. 'Her husband died soon after they were married, killed in the last world war.'

Val carried crockery into the adjoining room and dumped it in the sink. I followed with my empty coffee cup.

'I'll wash up,' said Midge, hurrying in behind us and turning on the hot-water tap.

'Okay, I'll dry.' Val made way for her. Then she said to me: 'Shouldn't you ring Bob and see how he is?'

I glanced at my watch. 'It's only a little after nine – he'll still be dead to the world.' I smiled grimly. 'But it'll give me great pleasure to wake him.'

Only as I climbed the stairs to the phone in the hallway did it occur to me that Val might have wanted to be alone with Midge for a short time. Midge hadn't offered much in our conversation about old Flora, so maybe Val thought she might be more forthcoming in private. Despite the agent's rise-and-shine briskness (or rise-and-growl in Val's case), I had caught her casting one or two ruminative frowns at Midge. One thing that this woman didn't lack was perception.

I dialled Bob's number, fairly anxious about him, to be honest: I really wanted to know if he was all right.

The phone rang for a long time before Kiwi's voice came on. 'Who is it?' she said, irritation undisguised.

'It's Mike. You got back okay.'

'Eventually. My navigator slept most of the way, so I took a few wrong turns.'

'How is he?'

'Speak to him.'

Bob was on the other end almost immediately. 'Sorry, mate,' he said humbly.

'You prat.'

'Yeah, I know. I can't understand it, though, Mike. I didn't take much.'

'You'd been drinking as well. How come you sound so bloody normal now?'

'Was I that bad last night?'

'Jes– hasn't Kiwi told you?' I almost thumped the wall.

'She said I was a bit hysterical.'

'I don't believe it. You were out of your skull!'

'Some nightmare.'

'You didn't have a fucking nightmare! Don't you remember any of it?'

'Not much. Pretty scared, was I?'

'You saw something downstairs in the kitchen, Bob. Surely you recall that?'

There was a pause. Then, 'Look, Mike, I freaked out – I don't know what I imagined I saw, or even if I went down there.'

'Kiwi said you did.'

'Okay, okay, maybe I did. Everything's a bit . . . you know, hazy. I'm really sorry I upset everybody. How did, uh, how did Midge take it?'

'Oh, she thought it was bloody hilarious.'

'Apologise for me, willya?'

'That's not gonna work.' I shook my head despairingly. 'Just think back, will you, Bob? When you were lying on the floor against the wall, when I came over to you – d'you remember anything happening with the walls? Anything that was . . . weird?'

'Are you nuts? Nothing happened to the fucking walls. I took a lousy hit, that was all, so don't blow things up out of all proportion, Mike. I feel bad enough already.'

'There's more to it than just a bad trip. You saw something in the kitchen that terrified you, and when you were upstairs you felt the walls closing in.'

'There's nothing unusual in that, is there? I mean, things coming out of the brickwork, monsters lurking in the dark – that's pretty standard stuff on spoilt smack.'

'You said yourself you didn't take much.'

'Enough to pick up bad vibes.'

'What?'

Again a pause, a long one this time.

'I gotta get back to bed,' he said finally. 'I'm not feeling as good as I might sound. Let me give you a call in the week, Mike, maybe say sorry to Midge personally. Take care of yourself.'

'Wait a minute –'

The receiver went dead. I toyed with the idea of ringing him back, but somehow it didn't appeal. Perhaps I was reluctant to press him further. I went back to the kitchen.

They were sitting side by side on the doorstep, Midge with her chin resting on her raised knees, arms tucking in the nightshirt she wore behind her legs. Val was leaning back against a porch post, stout legs stretched out onto the path before her. Birds pecked breadcrumbs, unperturbed by her brogues. The two women stopped talking when they heard my approach and looked over their shoulders at me.

'How is he?' asked Midge, and she really did look anxious.

'Would you believe he doesn't remember a thing?'

'Oh yes, I'd believe that,' Val commented drily. 'He was so far gone last night, anything's possible.'

'Could be he doesn't want to remember,' I said.

She regarded me quizzically, but I said no more.

Midge stood. 'I ought to get dressed and tidy up.'

'I'll give you a hand to straighten things upstairs,' I volunteered.

'No, you chat with Val for a while. I won't take long.'

I caught her arm before she could pass by. 'Bob says he's sorry.'

She managed a thin smile. 'I'm glad he's okay, Mike, but I don't want him here again. You know why.'

I drew her into my arms, not the least embarrassed by her agent's presence.

'I'm sorry too,' I whispered.

She hugged me back only briefly, and there was something feeble about the effort. 'You weren't to know,' she said. 'I don't blame you, Mike.' Even so, her eyes didn't shine for me as much as usual. She turned and disappeared up the stairs, leaving me standing there watching empty space.

'You've got a problem.'

Val was in the doorway, blocking daylight and slapping dust off the back of her skirt.

I raised my eyebrows, wondering how much Midge had told her.

She stepped inside, walking-shoes clomping over the tiles. 'Next door.' She indicated with her head.

'Huh?'

'Hadn't you noticed? I spotted it when your squirrel friend hopped onto the range. It's only a hairline now, but it could get very dangerous later.'

'What are you talking –'

'The crack in the lintel above the range. It's not that easy to see at first, I know.'

I went through, ignoring Rumbo, who was into the pots and pans cupboard beneath the working-top, unwisely left open by someone, and made straight for the iron range.

The crack was there all right, running from top to bottom of the stone. I gingerly touched the lintel and it seemed solid enough. I was shaking my head in disbelief when a shadow loomed up from behind.

'You should get that seen to as soon as possible,' Val advised. 'In fact, I'm surprised you didn't do so before you moved in; that could kill someone if they were bending over the range and it collapsed. I dread to think what will happen when the stone's heated by fire in the winter. Goodness, are you feeling ill? You look quite pale. That lintel's not going to fall in right away, you know; after all, it's lasted for some time by the looks of it.'

I straightened and faced this largish woman, someone whom I'd always felt had held me in mild disdain, who didn't actually dislike me – there had never been any true animosity between us – but who wasn't madly in love with me either; and something in my demeanour must have alarmed her, because there was genuine concern in her voice when she said, 'I think you need to tell me about things, Mike.'

And I did. We sat at the table and I went through everything with her, from the first visit to Gramarye, to the bizarre events of the previous night.

Then I went back, adding details, offering my own theories, feeling foolish in parts, but carrying on, getting it all off my chest.

Only the reappearance of Midge, standing at the foot of the stairs, brought my ramblings to a halt. Her face was screwed up in utter wretchedness and was blotchy-wet with tears; one hand buried itself in her hair, fingers working against the scalp.

I thought she'd overheard everything I'd said. But her other hand was pointing to the stairway behind her.

SPOILED ART

I could get no sense from her. I held Midge's arms and tried to calm her, but she could only shake her head, a few incoherent words emerging between sobs.

So I pulled her aside, as gently as possible, and took the stairs two at a time, stopping only when I was in the middle of the round room, looking left and right, turning my whole body round, then round again, searching for whatever had upset her so much. The room was now tidy, bed re-converted to sofa, and little evidence of last night's soirée remaining; the sun's rays blazed through the windows, glorifying walls and furniture. I could see the forest outside, presented as framed mosaics through the glass, green and lush, with no hint of threat.

I searched and found nothing out of place, nothing that could have caused Midge's distress.

I ran into our bedroom.

Empty.

The bathroom.

Empty.

The spare room.

Empty.

And back into the round room.

Where Midge, supported by her agent, now stood.

She was gesturing towards a window. No, towards the drawing board standing before the window. She seemed reluctant to go near it.

Val left her and strode across the room, and I quickly followed, catching up so that we reached the drawing board together.

And together we looked down at the picture of Gramarye, its overlay paper already turned back. I heard Val gasp, and perhaps I gasped too.

The painting was nothing more than a chaos of smeared colours, all shapes distorted and blurred, the picture's original vibrancy reduced to an ugly mess, made dull by the random mixture of pigments, a deranged artist's creation.

Even sunlight, reflected from its surface, failed to infuse any warmth.

ENTICEMENT

Just to add to our problems, Kinsella came knocking on the door a few days later.

I don't recall the time exactly, but I know dusk was vignetting into night and Midge and I had finished yet another melancholic meal only minutes earlier – I say another because there had been a marked lack of joy at Gramarye since the weekend, and you can guess why.

God only knows the impression Val Harradine had of us when she left for home later that Sunday, with Bob's strait-jacket antics, my Twilight Zone account of life in the country, and Midge's eventual melodramatic collapse into a weeping heap on the floor of the round room. Real Loony Times stuff. She must have thought – and who could blame her? – that there was something in the breeze down there that induced brainstorms and paranoia.

I'll skip over the recriminations and further tearful scenes that Midge and I went through over the next few days, because they'd bore you (and thoroughly depress me); it's enough to say we barely came through it all with our relationship still intact. I tried desperately to make her face up to the fact that there were inexplicable mysteries about Gramarye and I think she inwardly agreed; but strangely, she would never admit to it openly, as if to do so would mean accepting that the cottage wasn't quite the dream she had so fervently sought and imagined she'd found.

She accused Bob, of course, of destroying her painting, and when I rang him he naturally denied such (denied it pretty strongly, actually). I believed him. Midge didn't.

I went over everything that had happened since arriving at the cottage – especially the rapid healing of my scalded hand (which she persisted in attributing to the wonderful powers of Mycroft) – time and time again, but she . . . well, like I said, you'd get bored. The outcome was that we'd arrived at an uneasy truce for the moment, neither one of us inclined to argue (or reason) any further.

So there we were, facing each other across the kitchen table, in the lull before nightfall, when came the knock on the door (by then we'd taken to keeping the door closed as soon as it began to get dark outside).

We looked at one another in surprise and I rose to answer it.

Kinsella stood on the step, hands tucked into the back pockets of his faded jeans, an easy grin on his too-bloody-handsome face.

'Hi, good to see you two again.' He peered past me at Midge. 'Hope I'm not disturbing supper.'

Midge seemed glad to see him. 'Not at all – we finished a few minutes ago.' She joined us at the door.

'How's your arm, Mike?'

I begrudgingly held it up for inspection.

'Hey, looks good! Not a goddam mark.' His grin was well on the way to touching his earlobes. 'No pain?'

I shook my head.

'Boy, that's somethin'.' He glanced towards the gate, then turned back to us again. 'Look, we don't wanna intrude, but there's someone out here who'd like to meet you guys again. You know who I mean?'

I said 'Shit!' to myself and Midge said 'Mycroft?' aloud.

She stood on tiptoe to look over Kinsella's shoulder. 'He's come here?' she asked.

'Yup. He was kinda taken with you two. We were passing by and he thought it'd be nice to pay his respects, see how you were. Guess he'd like to see how your arm is, Mike.'

'Um . . .' I began to say.

'Oh, we'd love to say hello,' said Midge. 'Please go and fetch him.'

Kinsella looked awkward for a moment. 'Thing of it is, Mycroft's sorta old-fashioned, y'know? He's got great respect for other people's privacy and doesn't like to poke his nose in. It'd be nice if you invited him in personally, if you wouldn't mind that.'

'Of course we don't mind,' replied Midge, brighter than she'd been all week. 'Is he in the car?'

'That's right, sittin' in the back. He'll be glad to see you.'

Kinsella stood aside so that Midge could hurry down the path. We both watched her open the gate.

'That's some lady you've got there,' the American said, and I'm not sure whether the admiration in his eyes was for me or her. Then he leaned back against the door-jamb, hands still tucked behind in his pockets. 'So how've things been at Gramarye?' he asked, and I had to wonder at the casualness of the question.

'Wonderful,' I responded. 'Couldn't be better.'

'That's great.'

Was he mocking me? Or was paranoia really creeping in?

He pointed a finger. 'Don't mind me mentioning it, but you're gonna have to watch those weeds in the garden. Let 'em get a hold and they'll overrun.'

I followed his pointing finger and swore under my breath. I hadn't noticed them before, but now I realised there were thin green tendrils spreading through the flowerbeds, a disorganised network of infiltrators, and the more I looked, the more I found.

'Nature has a way of sneakin' up on you,' Kinsella confided and I nodded at his home-spun philosophy. 'I could get on over anytime, bring a coupla helpers, and give you a hand there, Mike. We'd clear the mothers in no time.'

'That's okay. I'll make a start tomorrow. It'll give me something to do.'

'You not writing?'

'Uh, I've had other things on my mind lately.'

'Well, the offer stands; just call on us any ol' time.'

Midge was coming back through the gate, Mycroft following, two others behind. It was beginning to look more like a deputation than a friendly visit. Mycroft waved a hand in my direction as he approached and I realised the two figures accompanying him were Gillie and Neil Joby.

As he drew nearer, the Synergist leader examined the cottage – somewhat intently, I thought, like a surveyor searching for faults. And when he was only a few feet away I had the feeling his composure was not quite as placid as his demeanour indicated. It was in his eyes, you see – they were too active, never settling on any one thing for long. Even when we shook hands he couldn't stop himself looking past me into the cottage. Then, not yet having said a word, he lifted my left hand and examined the fingers and lower arm, turning it over to study the other side. The rest of this amiable bunch gathered round and all but *oohed* and *aahed*.

They were making me so aware of my supposed debt to Mycroft, I wondered if I should offer a fee.

Mycroft fixed his gaze on me. 'The human will with the Divine Spirit, Mike,' he said quietly by way of an explanation for my unmarked arm.

'And a little help from that stuff you soaked it in?' I suggested.

'A sterilising fluid only. I hope our intrusion isn't inconvenient?'

I shook my head out of politeness.

'Won't you come in?' piped up Midge. 'We've been on our own since the weekend and some new conversation might be refreshing.'

I was dismayed by the barely-concealed barb; that wasn't like her at all.

'That would be very nice,' replied Mycroft, needing scant persuasion. 'This is rather impromptu, otherwise we would have bought some wine.'

'We still have a bottle unopened that Hub gave us on his last visit,' said Midge. 'We'll drink that, unless you don't enjoy your own brew.'

Her small joke was appreciated by the group, Midge

laughing with them. I suppose my grin was rather sickly.

She pushed between Kinsella and me, inviting Mycroft to follow, and he prepared to do so. But he faltered. He stood on the step and abruptly stopped. I'm sure, although the light wasn't too good by now, that he paled, just momentarily.

'It would be of great interest to me if I could see around the outside of this wonderful place before entering,' he said quickly – almost too quickly. 'These steps look fascinating.'

Fascinating? Worn stone steps?

'Perhaps we could then use the other door,' he added, and gazed up appreciatively at the white walls. He clanged the bell hanging outside for fun, and his brood dutifully chuckled.

Midge came back out and if her smile was anything to go by, the troubles of that week had evaporated. I began to wish I had some of Mycroft's charisma.

'I'm glad you like Gramarye so much,' she said, flushed.

He touched her shoulder for a moment. 'It's a house of great joy.'

Midge glanced uncertainly at me and I kept my mouth shut.

'The steps might be a little bit slippery, so please be careful,' she warned them.

Mycroft promptly linked his arm in hers. 'Then we'll rely on each other.' He said it lightly, but his eyes were unblinking and serious.

'I'll, er, take the less scenic route,' I said as they mounted the steps. 'I'll bring the wine and some glasses up, okay?' They ignored me, Midge engrossed in pointing out Gramarye's charms. 'Carry on, Jeeves,' I muttered to myself.

'Hello, Mike.' Gillie hadn't followed the others. Instead she stood on the path, long, patterned skirt and matching gypsy shawl blending in with the garden behind. She wore open-toed sandals, thin leather thongs tying around her ankles. As she came closer, I noticed she was wearing the tiniest amount of make-up, just enough to enhance her already pretty face. 'Can I help you with the wine?' she asked.

'Sure, if you don't want the Cook's Tour of the grounds.'

'I feel I know Gramarye well enough by now. It's the most peaceful place I've ever visited.'

'Not lately it isn't.' The words came out before I could stop them.

She frowned and I smiled back at her.

'Domestic problems,' I explained lamely.

'Oh. Then we've come at a bad time.'

I sighed, still smiling. 'No, maybe we needed some extra company about now.' I didn't add that even so, Mycroft and his clan wouldn't have been my first choice. Still, Gillie was a little different from the rest of them; I liked her simple gentleness. She'd have been very fashionable in the flower-power era.

'Let's hustle wine, shall we?' I said, turning away and going inside.

Gillie followed and stood on the threshold, the darkness in the kitchen now that nightfall was so close making her hesitant.

'I'll get the light,' I said, and crossed the room to flick the switch. I shivered; a chill was settling with the darkness.

Pointing to the dresser, I told her that glasses were kept in the cupboard beneath. I went to the larder next-door and took out a bottle of wine. Gillie was putting the glasses on the table when I returned.

'I'll open this down here,' I said, pulling out a dresser drawer and reaching for the corkscrew. 'The wine's not properly chilled, but I don't suppose anybody's gonna mind. D'you brew much of this stuff at the Temple?'

'Enough for ourselves, but not to sell in bulk. We don't have a licence for that.'

I got to work on the cork. 'Don't mind me asking, but how *do* you make money for your organisation? Those baskets and things can't bring in much.'

Her answer came easily, like the cork I was pulling. 'Mycroft is a very wealthy man in his own right. He once owned a huge manufacturing company in the United States that had subsidiaries in many other countries.'

'Yeah? What did he make?'

'Toys.'

'You're kidding me.'

She shook her head, enjoying my surprise. 'His company

produced dolls, puzzles, building blocks – all kinds of things for the very young.'

'Ah, so that's why he's so interested in Midge.'

She stared at me blankly.

'As an illustrator of children's books,' I went on. 'In a way, they're in the same business.'

She gave a small laugh. 'Oh, I see what you mean. But Mycroft renounced all commercial attitudes towards life once he founded the Synergist Temple. He's fond of telling us how the world's children helped him reach his Chosen Children, his Fosterlings, by providing the financial bedrock.'

'But the Temple still has to make money to survive, doesn't it? You still make trinkets to sell.'

That amused her. 'Not enough for us to live off, Mike. They provide a small amount of revenue, but we really use selling as a way of meeting people, of letting them know of the movement.'

'Then how . . .?'

'I told you: Mycroft is a wealthy man, the sale of his business and its subsidiaries ensured that. And of course, just as Mycroft himself donated everything he had to the Temple, so have his followers. Anything is welcomed and rejoiced over, even if it's only a few pounds. Fosterlings will give up any material possessions to cleanse themselves before our Temple.'

That sounds like a good deal for Mycroft, I thought, sniffing at the open bottle to disguise any expression of cynicism. Still, it appeared that he'd ploughed his own wealth into the sect. I was curious, though. 'What did you give up, Gillie?'

'Oh, a few pounds, hardly anything at all. And I was welcomed as much as anybody else.'

'No, I meant, *what* did you give up? Your home, your family?'

'Outside influences have to be rejected if an Adoptive is to fully embrace the doctrine.'

A nice bit of jargon, that. 'An Adoptive?'

'That's what we're called at our initiation.'

Her finger circled the brim of one of the wine glasses on

the table. I could hear footsteps and muffled voices over our heads, the others obviously having entered Gramarye through the door on the next level.

'You don't see your family any more?' I persisted.

'There's no need to. I quit college to join the Synergists, and I don't believe they've ever forgiven me for that. They did their best to prevent me, Mike, and all they succeeded in doing was to sever family ties completely.'

'How can you say that about your own parents? Christ, they must have been worried sick, probably still are.'

She looked uncomfortable, as if the conversation wasn't going the way she'd planned. That didn't deter me.

'How about someone like Kinsella?' I asked, changing tack. 'How did he become a Synergist and what did he throw away?'

'It isn't like that. We don't throw away anything – we give in order that we receive.'

Even better jargon.

'So what did he give?'

'We don't know what others bring to the Temple. Only Mycroft and his advisers are aware of that.'

'His financial advisers? So he employs accountants.'

'Yes, just as other Churches do. As any large or moderate-sized organisation has to.'

If the counter was meant as a rebuke, it was put very mildly.

She moved closer and her fingers touched my wrist. 'Are you interested in our Temple, Mike? Is that why you're asking questions?' She sounded hopeful and her fingers felt warm.

'Not interested enough to join,' I replied.

Her hand slipped away, but her eyes peered intently into mine. 'You'd find a great deal of happiness with us,' she said. 'You'd gradually become aware of many things that others aren't privileged to understand.'

'What kind of things?'

Now she averted her gaze. 'I'm only a Fosterling. Only the Selected have the authority, and the right, to instruct.'

'Kinsella?'

'And others. I could help you, though, Mike. Each Adoptive is allowed a spiritual companion.' Her fingers found my wrist again, but this time there was pressure, a firmness in her grip. 'We could talk at any time about matters that needn't relate to the essential doctrine. I could meet you . . .'

Don't think I wasn't tempted. She was an attractive girl, and lately I'd been feeling something of an outcast as far as Midge was concerned. And the steady but soft firmness of her grip implied there was more than just talk involved, that being a 'spiritual companion' meant other aspects were included in this special relationship. Or was it all in my own imagination?

'You're nice, Gillie,' I said after a pause, 'but I can only take one spiritual companion at a time, and she's upstairs at the moment. Grab a coupla glasses, will you?' I lifted the bottle and gripped the stems of three wine glasses between my fingers.

If she felt rejected she didn't show it, and again I wondered if I hadn't imagined the come-on.

'I understand what you're saying,' she said, holding a glass in each hand, 'but if you ever do feel a need . . .'

She deliberately left the rest unsaid and naturally my imagination continued to indulge itself. She turned away, but not before smiling at me with her eyes, not mockingly, not even seductively, but as if she understood a lot more than I did. Probably she was right.

'Tell me one other thing,' I said, bringing her to a halt. 'Why here?'

She looked puzzled.

'Why did Mycroft base his Synergist Temple here? He's American, and from what I gathered when I was at the Temple, so are quite a few of his followers, so why bring his organisation all the way over to England?'

'Because this is the –'

'Gillie.'

The voice was calm enough, yet the girl's head spun around as though she'd been lashed.

Kinsella stood on the bottom stair, hands inevitably tucked into back pockets. He was smiling amiably, but I thought I detected just a hint of irritation filtering through his expression.

'We were wondering what had happened to you both,' he said agreeably.

'On our way,' I responded, holding the wine and glasses aloft. 'Gillie was just filling in on some of the Synergist background, although I've gotta own up, I'm not much wiser.'

'Well, the man himself is under your roof, Mike. Mycroft can explain better than any of us. But you know we've never wanted to thrust any of this down your throat before, that's not our style.'

'I'm not that curious. Just making conversation.'

'Sure. Lemme give you a hand with those glasses.'

'I can manage. You lead the way.'

Kinsella glanced around the room as if looking for something before retreating up the stairs.

Again I asked myself what it was about Gramarye that made him so nervous.

'The limits of the human mind are those imposed by ourselves.'

Mycroft looked from face to face, examining the effects of his statement on both the initiated and the uninitiated – the latter being Midge and myself. He was seated in the round room's only armchair, while Midge and Gillie sat on the sofa, with me on the sofa's arm; Kinsella and Joby lounged on the floor, sipping wine and watching their leader intently. A single lamp lit the room and outside the windows there seemed to be nothing but blackness.

'Civilisation itself has served to dull our minds' intrinsic faculties,' he went on, 'the new material and scientific knowledge increasingly diminishing our self-knowledge. It's not by chance that the child without so-called matured wisdom has a greater psychic capability than the adult.'

'I understand what you mean,' I said, 'and it's hardly an original theory.' (I didn't mind being rude – we'd already sat through nearly twenty minutes of Mycroft's proselytising and

241

I was steadily becoming bored.) 'But look, knowledge tells me I can't fly: not believing that, or being unaware of it, doesn't alter the fact.'

'No, Mike,' he replied patiently. '*Self*-knowledge informs you that you can't fly. But in even that, you've learned to think merely in terms of your physical body, and not of your consciousness. Ultimately there is nothing that can restrict your own psyche. The force that's within us all – the psychic energy, if you wish – cannot be bound by the physical aspects of our lives. Unless we, ourselves, dictate otherwise.'

Somehow he no longer looked so bland. Maybe the shadows cast by the lamp gave depth to his features where none had been apparent before; or maybe it was the intensity in his eyes.

Midge spoke up, and I noticed she was hugging herself as though cold. 'If this energy is there inside every one of us, why can't we reach it? Why can't we use it?'

'First we have to discover the ability within ourselves. We must become fully aware of the source, must realise and accept its presence. And we have to learn to control and keep fettered all knowledge that isn't relevant to our true selves. For that we need guidance.' He smiled indulgently at Midge, but to me it was like the grin a spider saves for a fly. Why was it that the more I saw of these people, the less I liked them? Could be, I mused, that I had a natural antagonism against anything that smacked of fanaticism. And for all their quiet, amicable ways, the Synergists had that fanatical air about them.

'The Synergist Temple,' Mycroft continued, his language becoming less matter-of-fact and more high-flown by the moment, 'is no more than a foundation in which we seek our truth, where both the conscious and subconscious minds learn to combine with the omni-spirit that governs us all, the spirit that exists within yet is apart, is individual yet is greater than the individual.'

My eyes were beginning to glaze over. This was worse than Sunday sermon (as far as I could remember).

I stole a glance at Midge, and her face was serious, her eyes fixed on Mycroft's.

'How is it achieved?' she asked, and I shifted awkwardly on the arm of the sofa; she was spoon-feeding him all the right questions. 'How does a person learn to combine with this spirit?'

Mycroft let his smile wander among his followers, and they smiled back as if they shared the secret. 'It takes time,' he said, returning his gaze to Midge, 'and it requires a great deal of humility. Adoptives must surrender their thoughts, their wills. They must let the Founder have responsibility for all they do.'

Even Midge, in her present state of blind fascination, blanched at that.

'That's asking a lot of someone, isn't it?' I remarked.

'The rewards are impressive,' he countered smoothly.

'What would they be?'

'One-ness in spirit.'

'Sounds terrific.'

His flicker of annoyance was barely discernible.

'A regeneration of the mind's powers.'

I nodded as though checking off a list.

'A harnessing of earthly thaumaturgic potency.'

Now that did sound impressive, whatever the hell it meant. I felt it only right that I should ask.

'Unless you subjected yourself to each stage of the Synergist development,' he said by way of an answer, 'you could not hope to understand. Would you acknowledge now, for instance, that vast sources of power lie beneath our feet?'

I caught some anxious expressions directed at him from the others in the room, but Mycroft remained impassive.

'Of course,' I replied. 'Everybody accepts there's huge energy resources in the earth. There's nothing astounding about that proposition.'

'I'm referring to a power much more intangible, Mike, but equally real. Something incorporeal, yet vast in its reserves. And we, mankind, have almost – *almost* – forgotten how to avail ourselves of that force.'

Self-knowledge, oneness, regeneration, potency, thaumaturgic (*thaumaturgic?*), intangible, incorporeal (always a good one), and now of course, mankind – all those profound (and cliché) words you find in books on religion or the occult which sound great but leave you scratching your head wondering what it's all about.

'You've lost me completely,' I said flatly.

He smiled maddeningly again and I think my dumb incomprehension came almost as a relief to him, as though my provocation had led him into giving away too much, and now he was able to draw back. His philosophy obviously had to be administered in much smaller doses.

But Midge was more persistent. 'Is that how you healed Mike's hand so quickly, somehow combining your will with this special force? Is this power the spirit, the *Divine* Spirit, that you've mentioned before?'

I took a large swallow of wine.

'Ah, so young and so perceptive,' Mycroft patronised. 'But not entirely correct. The human will can be extremely potent by itself.'

She looked confused and I wanted to draw her close. I wondered how she'd react if I invited our guests to take a hike.

Something struck a window from outside – probably a bird, or maybe even a disorientated bat – and Kinsella spilt his drink. He and his friends turned towards the window, but Midge's attention remained on the Synergist leader.

'When we . . . when we spoke before, last week at the Temple, you told me that our individual spirit never loses its potential even if the body dies and even if the spirit has been neglected during the body's life.'

He nodded slowly.

'And you said that we, ourselves, could reach those spirits of the dead.'

'With guidance,' said Mycroft. 'But why so cautious? Why are you so afraid to voice your hopes? We spoke of your parents and I assured you then that the souls which existed within them can be touched, and heard, once more. That part of us will never expire.'

'Then will you help me . . .?'

'Midge!' I didn't want her to go on with this.

'No, Mike. If it can happen, then that's what I want. More than anything!' She turned back to Mycroft.

'What good will it do?' I demanded. 'You're only opening yourself up for more heartache, don't you see that?'

'I understand your concern for Midge,' Mycroft interrupted. 'And it's precisely because of your love for her that you should support her in this matter. I know you're aware that she feels a deep need to be reconciled with her parents.'

'Reconciled?' I stared at her and she lowered her face.

Mycroft was watching her too. He opened his mouth in an unvoiced 'ah' of comprehension, then settled back in the armchair.

'What's he talking about?' I leaned over and cupped her chin, forcing her to look at me.

'Mike, I . . .'

She pulled her head away.

'Would it be easier if I answered for you?' said Mycroft. 'I had no idea that you hadn't confided your feelings to Mike, but now I understand. Sometimes it's easier to reveal oneself to a sympathetic stranger than a loved one.'

'Midge, if there's something I should know, I'd rather it came from you,' I insisted. 'And I'd rather we were alone when you told me.'

Gillie put her hand on Midge's, and it was Kinsella who spoke up: 'This is sounding more dramatic than it really is, Mike. In our view, Midge's guilt is unfounded, but it needs to be dug out and tossed away before real damage is done. We can help her do that.'

'Guilt? What the fuck are you talking about?' I looked around at them all, bewildered, exasperated, and pretty angry, too.

Midge abruptly shifted round to me, her hands clutching my leg. 'On the day of my father's funeral, when I left Mother in the house – I knew, Mike, I *knew* she would take her own life! She'd spoken of it so many times, before his death even, hating the burden she'd become to both of us. When he died, suicide was on her mind more and more, something she mentioned every day and every night! But calmly, never hysterically, never emotionally. She was so sad, Mike, but she never indulged in self-pity. All she cared about was that her misery shouldn't ruin my life! And when I left her in the house that morning – alone in that cold, empty house – I felt it so strongly, so overpoweringly, but I never went back. I never tried to stop her!'

I shook my head despairingly.

'Midge, you couldn't know she would kill herself. Okay, you might have had the notion because she was so desperately unhappy and suffering physical pain, but you didn't hand her those pills, you didn't tie that plastic bag around her head! I can't believe you've been blaming yourself all these years.'

'I realised if the opportunity arose Mother might –'

'*Might!* That isn't the same as knowing for sure. It was her choice, don't you understand that! And what was so bad about that, for Chrissake? Don't you think your mother suffered enough? All she did was show herself a little mercy.'

'It's not that simple.'

'Nothing ever is. But even if you did feel so guilty, why go to these people, why tell them? Jesus, Midge, what was wrong in telling me?'

'I'd kept . . . I'd kept it hidden for so long.' Her grip tightened on my leg. 'That knowledge has never weighed so heavily on me until recently, Mike. It was only when I talked with Mycroft that I realised the guilt had been with me for so long.'

Friend Mycroft. I eyed him coolly.

And received some satisfaction from observing that he actually looked unsettled. Mistakenly, I assumed he was becoming wary of my anger.

Nevertheless, he wasn't short of words. 'I merely sought to understand the nature of Midge's deep-rooted grief, possibly to expose her self-doubts. Can't you see that she needs our guidance?'

'I can see that you've made her believe that. Any help she needs, she can get from me.'

'Not in the way that we can help.'

He'd become distracted, peering around the room.

'What can you do?' I retorted. 'Hold a seance, is that how you'll help her?'

'She has a unique gift . . .'

His voice trailed off when someone moaned. On the floor, Neil Joby was tugging at his shirt collar as if he found the atmosphere stifling. It did feel close in the room, but not uncomfortably so.

'Mike, you've got them wrong.' Midge was looking up at me with earnest eyes. 'Synergism is an answer if it's used correctly. If –'

'Jesus, you're really falling for this shit.'

She sprang away as though I'd struck her.

I quickly modified my tone. 'Listen to me: if there was any guilt over your mother's death locked up inside you, then it was minimal. Christ, I know you better than anyone, and that's something you could never have concealed from me. All this guy's done . . .' I stabbed a finger in Mycroft's direction '. . . is made you exaggerate the guilt in your own mind. Can't you see how he operates? It's nothing new – most religious nuts work on people's own self-imposed shame.'

She kept shaking her head, refusing to hear the words.

'You're wrong,' she said, 'you're so wrong . . .'

Something made me glance at Mycroft then, and I just caught the hint of triumph in his smile. The smile instantly turned into one of well-practised friendliness, forgiving me for my folly.

'Fuck you,' I said quietly.

A glass tipped over and wine spread on the carpet. Kinsella watched the liquid soak in before turning towards his leader and mentor.

And now Mycroft himself didn't look so bright.

The windows rattled in their frames and attention was diverted towards them. I noticed that Joby was deathly pale and still appeared to be having trouble catching his breath.

Rafters overhead creaked.

The sharpness of the sound startled Gillie so much that she stood and peered up at the ceiling.

'There's a wind blowing up outside,' I said, feeling no particular antagonism towards her. 'Don't worry, the roof'll stay on.'

She seemed uncertain.

I pointed at Joby and addressed my next remark to Mycroft. 'I hope he's not going to puke on the carpet.'

Now the front door across the hallway shook in its frame.

Mycroft rose and walked over to the younger man, placing a hand on his forehead. He mumbled a few words and I strained to hear, but the words were spoken too softly.

Joby noisily cleared his throat and recovered enough to push himself to his knees. Kinsella, looking shaky himself, grabbed his friend from behind and helped him the rest of the way up.

Even Gillie swayed uneasily on her feet.

Mycroft positioned himself before Midge, studying her with eyes that were now hooded. Had I really once thought his face was bland? It wasn't only shadows making his countenance creepy now, but his expression also. Mr Hyde was showing through.

His words were slow and penetrating, said in a low voice. 'Remember, we can help you. Believe in the regeneration of the spirit, understand that there are few barriers to the human will.'

I wouldn't have been surprised if he'd handed her his business card.

He took his eyes from her and surveyed the room once more, lingering on the windows, resuming the scan, taking in everything.

A different noise came to us, and it was from above our heads, a muffled pattering, almost a soft vibration, rising and swaying in volume and rhythm.

A frantic beating of small wings.

I knew where the noise was coming from and who was making it, and I began to get as nervous as our guests.

'Mycroft,' said Kinsella, a hint of pleading in his tone. 'It's time to go.'

Joby, sagging visibly, seemed in agreement. In fact, the three young Synergists looked as if strength was gradually draining from them. They were all very pale.

The windowpanes shook so hard I thought they might shatter. This time I was the one who jumped to his feet. Only Midge remained sitting.

'I'll see you out,' I told the Synergists.

Mycroft turned to me, no hostility in his gaze, only a cool appraisal.

'You mustn't stand in her way,' he said to me.

'What I can't figure,' I replied, starting to feel a bit trembly, 'is why you're so interested in Midge. D'you always take this kind of trouble to convert a new face?'

On the surface, his manner was easy, almost casual; but the giveaway was his eyes which were constantly moving, flicking this way and that, like those of a jungle explorer waiting for the first poison dart.

Midge, hunched forward on the sofa, hands clasped together on knees, spoke up: 'Would you *please* stop talking about me as though I'm not in the room? Mike, there are certain things that you obviously have no interest in, nor comprehension of, so please don't interfere. These people are my friends – *our* friends – and all they care about is my peace of mind.'

'Don't you think I care too?'

'Then show me! Help me!'

'We'll talk about it when they're gone,' I said more calmly than I felt.

'Yes, you should,' said Mycroft, the condescending bastard. 'Mike has a right to his opinions. It isn't difficult to appreciate his scepticism given the usually poor and biased publicity that sects such as ours attract. Misguided though they are, these prejudices are accepted and tolerated by our members. We've learned to have patience.'

Mine had just run out. I strode across to the open door and stood by it, my meaning fairly evident.

Mycroft smiled, but I could see the grimness there. He reached down and touched Midge's forehead in the same manner he'd touched Joby's earlier.

The frantic, if dulled, drumming from overhead was becoming hard to ignore, and the air in the room seemed too warm, too thick, despite the wind outside rattling the windows.

My head shot round when the door across the hallway rampaged against its lock and hinges.

Alarmed, I backed away, but at least the Synergists were galvanised into action. The three younger members grouped together and Mycroft indicated that they were to follow him. They came towards me like a worried Scout pack looking for the way home, Kinsella and Gillie supporting their companion between them. I observed, not without pleasure, that even the Synergist leader was wilting slightly under the heavy atmosphere.

The bats in the attic were working themselves up into a frenzy by now and I wondered if the cause of their upset was the freak gale was skimming through the roof's eaves, creating some kind of maelstrom in the loft. I thought I could hear their faint *peeping* shrieks, but put it down to over-stretched imagination.

Mycroft paused at the door to the hallway, and for a moment I thought he might take the downstairs route out; instead he turned back to Midge and said, 'I'm ready to be your ally whenever you need me, whenever you find your courage. You'll find only by seeking.'

She stared at him, a small, lost figure, her hands still clutched together on her knees; but she didn't say anything in return.

Then Mycroft marched into the hall and yanked at the outside door, pulling it open without hesitation.

I expected the wind to come howling in and steadied myself for the blast. But there was nothing. Not even a breeze to ruffle our hair.

He stepped into the night, the others crowding behind him as though anxious to keep close, and I hurried across the hallway to shut the door again. Before I did so, I watched them make an unsteady descent of the stone steps, the gloom out there making progress slow. If it wouldn't have proved inconvenient for me, I'd have cheerfully hoped that at least one of them would break a leg.

They disappeared around the curve and I relaxed a little, more than relieved to see them gone. But I blinked at the night, mystified as to how it had calmed so suddenly. As far as I could tell, not a blade of grass stirred, not a leaf was tossed. The air was mild and fresh and pleasant to breathe.

And when I went back inside, closing and locking the door behind me, even the bats had settled, not a sound coming down from above.

Only the strong musty odour was left to unsettle me.

GHOSTS

And that's not all. That wasn't the end of it that night.

I awoke later and it was very dark in the bedroom, shadows blending into deeper shadows, odd bits of furniture becoming more than they really were, transformed into sinister shapes that lurked rather than just stood.

Midge was sitting up beside me, and it was either her movement or the tension she gave out that roused me, because she hadn't reached for me, nor called my name.

Alertness sprang at me, not bothering with creeping up, and I pushed myself onto my elbows. Midge's arm was stiff and unyielding when I touched her, the skin roughened by goose-bumps.

'What is it?' I whispered urgently, not knowing why I'd whispered.

She didn't answer right away.

I was grabbing for the lamp switch when her voice stopped me.

'They were here,' she said breathlessly. 'Oh, Mike, they were here.'

I turned back to her and held her in the darkness.

'Who were here? What are you talking about?'

She shivered in my arms.

'I sensed them both.' There was a shaky kind of awe in

252

her whisper. 'I felt I could almost reach out and touch them. They were here in this room.'

'Midge, who the hell are you talking about?'

I heard her weeping, but there was no sadness in her voice when she spoke again.

'My mother . . . my father. They tried to speak to me. They need to, don't you see?'

I held on to her and my flesh prickled as much as hers.

BIRTH DAY

Waking up next morning was more gradual.

Still blurry-headed, I turned over in the bed to snuggle up to Midge. She wasn't there, though.

Cranking open eyelids that felt as heavy as garage doors, I squinted at her side of the bed to confirm what touch (or lack of it) had already told me. Further thoughts trailed along at a more leisurely pace, taking a little while to come together, but memories of the night before, post-Mycroft included, eventually shifted the last threads of drowsiness.

I rolled onto my back and stared up at the ceiling. Cold light of day and all that: last night's traumatic episodes, both of them, now seemed unreal. The Synergists' menace just stopped short of being farcical on reflection – I mean, neither of us was naïve enough to fall under their influence, we weren't kids, receptive to being drawn into such a ridiculous cult. We were non-consenting adults. Yet Midge had been more than a mite spellbound by Mycroft, there was no doubt of that, and I realised there was more to the man than I had assumed on our first meeting, when his charisma had been understated to say the least. Maybe that was part of his allure, his very ordinariness negating any suggestion of charlatanism.

After his fairly ignominious departure last night, Midge and I had been too wound up for a sensible discussion on what

254

had happened and where it was leading to. When I pointed out yet again that something was going on inside Gramarye itself, all she did was announce she was too tired for further arguments and was going to bed.

I followed her in, trying to make her see sense (sense? What I was trying to make her see was crazy even to me!), but she'd have none of it. Called me blinkered. Now that really sent me into a rage, considering that it was she who was turning a blind eye on all the weirdness that was going on around us! That night alone, with a howling wind battering the cottage, bats living up a storm in the attic, all quietening down as soon as Mycroft opened the door to leave. The question begged: Had there really been a gale outside? Was it possible for the night to have become so instantly calm? And look at the effect the place had on the Synergists! Christ, Joby had looked about ready to pass out in front of us, and twice now Kinsella had had to leave Gramarye in a rush. I went on. And on. On a bit more, exhausting *myself* in the end. I brought everything into it, the ruined painting, Bob's hallucinations – *my* hallucinations, for Chrissake! – the healing of the bird at the beginning, the trust of the animals and birds, the apparent regeneration of the garden. Even our glorious love-making (up until recently), even her beautiful artwork (before ruined), and even my inspirational guitar playing. I dredged up everything I could think of.

But it was like talking to a goddamn zombie. She didn't want to know.

Yet she did get interested when I ventured the theory that maybe it was *she* who'd healed my scalded arm, not Mycroft with his magic potion and phony mental projection, she and whatever enchantment was contained within Gramarye itself, within its walls, its grounds, its atmosphere – *in its bloody heritage!* – working through her, *HER*, Midge Gudgeon, innocent catalyst or intermediary or even instigator. Just as Flora Chaldean had been! And whoever lived in the cottage before her!

I was rambling, inventing, plucking notions out of the air. Or so I imagined. It could have been my tiredness and the emotional condition I'd worked myself up into, driving me towards one of those rare states when the subconscious mind takes over and throws out thoughts that are normally vague or even inconceivable.

And maybe, just maybe, my subconscious was being prompted by something deeper and even more mysterious, something completely outside of me.

And when I'd finished, said it all, it was me who became uninterested. I was the one who could hardly keep his eyes open any longer, who had to drag off his clothes and crawl into bed, totally and utterly exhausted, drained of any more considerations.

Like I said, she was interested, but she didn't try to rouse me. My last glimpse of Midge before slipping into sleep was of her sitting on the corner of the bed studying me with a peculiar glimmer in her eyes. After that I zonked out, and was glad to.

But later woke to find Midge bolt upright and staring towards the foot of the bed.

Now I wondered about that. Obviously everything that had gone before that evening had caused her nightmare, and I'd pulled her back down beneath the sheets and endeavoured to convince her of that. Although she hadn't verbally rebuffed my contentions, I sure as hell knew she hadn't accepted them. She lay there still and quiet, and when I touched her cheek I found it wet with tears.

I tried my best to comfort her but unfortunately it wasn't long before I did a three-apostles on her – you know, mind willing, flesh weak – and fell asleep again. I just hoped tiredness had soon overcome her own vigil and she'd done the same as me; the thought of her lying there in the dark, believing she'd seen the ghosts of her dead parents, possibly thinking they might return that night, made me shudder. And feel guilty.

I pulled back the covers and swung my legs off the bed, checking the clock on the move. Nearly ten. I tongue-tutted, wishing she'd woken me earlier.

First I noticed, sitting there naked on the edge of the bed and scratching my ribs, that the musty smell from last night still lingered, an odour of damp and old plaster; then I realised I was gaping at something across the room, my addled brain not quite able to comprehend what I was looking at. The long crack in the wall, running from floor to ceiling, somehow didn't register.

'Shit,' I said when finally it did.

I rose quickly and my stride across the room was broken when something small and soft squelched beneath my bare foot. I hopped and swore more loudly when the sting hit me half a second later, collapsing back onto the bed and grabbing for my foot. I found the tiny, thorn-like projection and, using my fingernails (fortunately finger-picking guitar length on my right hand) as tweezers, plucked out the barb. The area around the minute puncture was already swelling a bright red and I searched the floor for the culprit. The squashed bee lay a couple of feet away and I imagined its death rattle had been more of a vengeful chuckle.

Leaning forward, I peeled up the flattened furry mound and took it, together with its last-resort weapon, through to the bathroom, limping all the way, to flush them down the loo (not before peeing on the floating carcase first, though, my own petty revenge). Back in the bedroom, I examined the crack in the wall, the new plaster that had been used to seal and cement split into two jagged, serrated edges. It was a minuscule divide, but a crack is a crack.

So much for O'Malley's craftsmanship.

I found my robe and left the bedroom in search of Midge. She was downstairs, sitting on the kitchen doorstep, chin on her knees as she looked out at the flowers in the garden. Again I didn't notice at first what was out of place – or in this case, what wasn't in place at all.

I bent over and kissed her neck. There was little response. She moved over slightly as I shuffled down next to her.

Although we were on the shaded side of the cottage I could tell the sun was out in full force by the way it played on the brilliant colours of the garden. And above, the sky was the colour of faded denim, a washed-out blue, the vaguest wisps of clouds a long way off in the distance. But the air was cool in that shadowed part where we sat.

'How are you feeling today, Pixie?' I asked, deliberately keeping my voice light, testing. I laid a hand on her upper arm.

Her response was minimal. 'Very confused,' was all she said.

'Yeah, me too. But not so confused I can't see Mycroft and his creepy little sect for what they are.'

Her tone was flat. 'Let's drop it, Mike.'

Mine was reasonable. 'I don't think we can do that. You've become too enamoured with them and it scares me.'

She shrugged, a small movement, almost a flinch.

'Midge, have you thought about what I said last night?'

Still not looking at me, she replied, 'You said so many things. Do you even remember?' Now she did turn her head my way.

Right then, I couldn't. I'd said such a lot it had become something of a jumble in my own head, not so much scrambled as mashed. Only later were those notions (perceptions?) to become clear again. My head ached and you could have done a litmus test on my tongue; I wondered how I could be hungover from one glass of wine last night. Then I realised what was missing from the garden.

'What's happened to our friends today? There's usually one or two still hanging around for food at this time of the morning.'

'There were no birds outside earlier,' Midge replied without expression.

I frowned. 'Maybe they've found a better menu else-where,' I said lamely, refusing to believe there was any significance in the sudden lack of custom, but having a hard time of it. 'I guess Rumbo's been around, though, huh?' I said hopefully.

She shook her head. 'Not yet he hasn't.'

That bothered me. There had to be something wrong if that greedy tyke hadn't shown. Bob's words over the phone came to me: 'Bad vibes.'

Midge stood, my hand dropping away from her arm like a discarded accessory. 'I have to get dressed and go into the village for some shopping,' she said stiffly, and was already turning before I could scramble to my feet.

'Hey, hold on a minute.' I grabbed her arm again, pulling her to me. 'We're buddies, remember? Not just lovers, but good friends, the best either one of us will ever have. Don't keep your feelings locked away, Midge, no matter how badly you think of me. Okay, I upset you with my views on a coupla things last night, but that shouldn't prevent us talking, should it? Whatever I do concerning you, I mean it for the best. Christ, I love you more than I can say . . .'

At another time she might have added, 'Love you every single day . . .' and I'd come in with, 'Love you twice as much tomorrow . . .' and we'd have sung the rest as a duet. Not that morning, though. Not even a smile. All I got was a troubled silence.

Then the tenseness seemed to leave her body for a moment. She looked down at the ground, avoiding my eyes. 'I love you just as much, Mike, nothing can ever change that. But I have to find out –'

I gripped her hard. 'You've done nothing to be ashamed of.'

'You won't listen, will you?'

I controlled myself. 'I'm only trying to make you see sense, don't you understand? You know what I think? I think you feel guilty about your own happiness. You've got it so good now – *we've* got it so good now – you figure in some crazy way that your mother had to die so you could achieve it. That's what's bugging you, Midge.'

She shook her head vehemently. 'That's stupid.'

'Is it? You got your freedom when she died –'

'Committed suicide,' she insisted.

'Okay, committed suicide. You were young, you had a great talent, so maybe you did wonder how things would be with no ties, no liabilities. Who the hell wouldn't in your position? But I said *wondered*, Midge. You never *wished* it. Ever. That's something you're just not sure of right now; it's been so long you can't be sure of how strong that *wondering* was. And I wouldn't be surprised if it wasn't this creep Mycroft who instilled that little doubt in your mind.'

'He's not –'

'What d'you wanna do? Beg their forgiveness? When we first arrived here, you told me you wished there was some way of letting your parents know how happy you were. Remember that? Somehow that notion's become warped so that you want their forgiveness for being so goddamn happy! How did your feelings suddenly go off in that direction? Did it happen the day you went to the Temple on your own? When I was up in London?'

She tried to twist away from me, but I held her firm.

'He made me understand!' she shouted at me. 'You don't know him –'

'I don't bloody need to. What I do want to know is why he's doing this to you.'

This time she managed to tear herself free. She blazed at me, her body slightly bent at the waist like a recalcitrant child's.

'You said last night that there was something extraordinary about Gramarye.' It was almost an accusation. 'Those weren't your words, but it's what you implied. You also suggested that I was involved, I was a part of it.'

I vaguely remembered saying something to that effect, but right then I couldn't focus on the exact proposition.

'Do you imagine I'm a complete fool, Mike? Do you think I haven't *noticed* everything that's been happening around us?'

'Then why haven't –'

'Because it's too fragile to question! All right, I admit I've put up a barrier against it to some extent, but that was because I was frightened to lose . . . to lose . . .'

She shook her head in frustration, unable to find the words. Unable, I suspected, to clarify her own thoughts. I took a step towards her, but she backed away.

Her hands were clenched into small fists. 'Mycroft is the only one who can help.'

'No!' It was my turn to shout.

'He understands.' Her hands unclenched and dropped to her sides. As was becoming her habit, she didn't want to argue any more.

She slipped past me and I heard her bare feet mounting

the stairs inside the cottage, a stairboard cracking noisily as she went. I thought of going after her, but the truth is, I didn't want to argue either. My head was too sore for that.

'Mr O'Malley?'

'Speaking.'

'Mike Stringer here.'

'Mr, er, Stringer?'

'You worked on our cottage. Gramarye.'

'Ah, Mr Stringer.' Then more slowly. 'Yes . . . Gramarye. By the forest. What can I do for you, now?'

'I'm afraid a few problems have come back.'

The lilt of his accent hardened slightly. 'I can't imagine what they could be, Mr Stringer. We did a thorough job there.'

'Yeah, well, the wall in the main bedroom is cracked again. And some of the doors aren't shutting properly . . .'

'Hold on a sec, Mr Stringer. Let me find the worksheet on your property.'

A *clunk* as the receiver was put down at the other end. I stood in the small hallway at the top of the stairs, free hand tucked into my jeans pocket, and wished the three Paracetamols I'd taken twenty minutes earlier would get to work on my headache. The mustiness in the atmosphere wasn't helping to clear my head, either.

'Right then, let's have a looksee . . .' came the Irishman's voice again. Static on the line made me hold the phone away from my ear for a moment or two. 'Ah well now, we did a splendid job on that bedroom wall. I'm surprised to hear it's opened again. I take it y'haven't had any other structural work done on the place since, Mr Stringer?'

'Not a thing.'

'I see. Well, that's queer. What was the other item you mentioned?'

'The doors. They must have warped again.'

'There's no mention of doors on my list.'

'You had to plane them before painting.'

'No, no, it's not down here at all. We'd have smoothed them, of course, rubbed them down as needs be, just for the painting. I remember now, yes, I remember you mentioned them when we quoted for the job. Wasn't there a few cupboard doors and all?'

'That's right.'

'Ah well, my foreman told me the doors were fine. Nothing needed doing to them apart from smoothing the surfaces. Some of your window casements were terrible rotted, and we replaced them. It was all on my invoice to yourself, Mr Stringer.'

There was a noise from over my head.

'Uh, can doors warp with warm weather, Mr O'Malley?'

'Now that depends. In direct sunlight maybe, or sometimes in very damp weather. Sure that's a very old house you're living in, and the timber's not so young any more.'

'I've noticed some of the pointing on the outside doesn't look too good. It seems to be crumbling away.'

I heard him draw in a long breath, an indication of weariness rather than surprise. 'Now that's a different matter entirely. I can send someone over to take a look at that for you, but I'm afraid I can't spare anybody for at least a week or so. It's a busy time of year for us, with the weather so good.'

'There's something else that needs urgent attention, I'm afraid.'

'And what would that be?'

'The stone lintel over the range in the kitchen. There's a crack in that, too, and I've noticed the stone is beginning to sag in the middle. Only a fraction, but the whole thing looks pretty dangerous to me.'

'So it's a new bit of work you'll be wanting. As I say, we're very busy right at the moment . . .'

'The lintel was on my original list for repair. We noticed the break before we moved in.'

'I don't recall . . . ah, wait a moment. That's right, I remember more details now. You had a whole list of repair jobs, Mr Stringer, that required no attention at all. That's why our price was below the quotation figure; my men couldn't locate half the faults you mentioned.'

'That doesn't make sense.'

'Neither to me does it. My foreman remarked at the time that mebbe you'd confused your list with another property you had on your mind to buy. Any other firm that was a bit Tom Mix –'

'What?'

' – cowboy – would have charged you for the lot and not said a word about it. Still and well, I can send someone to take a look, but not in a hurry, I'm afraid. How about Tuesday week? Does that suit you?'

'That lintel's dangerous . . .'

'D'you use that range at all? I thought not. Prop up the stone and keep away from it, that's all y'have to do, Mr Stringer. Now I'll send my man over first thing Tuesday week and we'll see what we can do. There, I've written it in the book. He'll have a look at anything else that needs doing and we'll soon have you right as rain again. Good day to you, Mr Stringer, hope you're enjoying y'self down in that lovely part of the forest.'

The phone clicked and that was that. Problems solved as far as O'Malley was concerned.

And again that funny noise from upstairs.

Two steps and I craned my head around the stairway. I knew what that sound was.

But now there were other noises. From below.

I listened intently, undecided as to which I should investigate first and feeling disinclined to investigate either.

More from downstairs. Scraping sounds, then rustling paper.

'Midge?' Maybe she was already back from the village. No reply, but then she could still be annoyed at me.

'Midge, you there?'

Someone certainly was, but they weren't saying who. I stood at the top of the stairway and leaned precariously around the bend, looking down towards the kitchen. My favourite place.

A teacup rattled on the dresser (I hadn't left any on the table).

I refused to allow myself time to ponder, sick of my own

funk by now, and marched down there bold as brass (limped down really; my bee sting was still throbbing).

I stood at the kitchen door and sagged with relief.

'Rumbo, you silly beggar.'

From his perch on a dresser shelf he scolded me for giving him a scare too. A biscuit packet lay torn on the table, contents scattered, most of the biscuits gnawed into.

'At least you haven't deserted us,' I said. I picked up a broken biscuit and held it up to him and he snatched it from my hand, still complaining noisily.

'So where is everyone today?' I interrupted. 'Can they sense bad vibes in Gramarye too? Is that why the birds have missed out on breakfast?'

He was probably as puzzled as me.

'Takes more than that to frighten you off, though, right? But I oughta warn you – things aren't the same around here any more, and I'm a little scared myself. It's in the atmosphere – d'you feel it? Like something's creeping up, but ducks outa sight every time you turn around to see. Know what I mean?'

I don't think he did. He just nibbled away, cocking his head at me every so often in that dog-like way of his, but paying no particular mind to what I was saying. What did I expect from a squirrel anyway?

The door to the attic rooms was stiff in its frame (although the thought that someone was leaning against the other side crossed my mind).

I was on the step below, twisting the handle and pushing with my other hand at the same time. Rumbo had kept me company on my cautious journey up the winding stairway, as curious about the odd sounds drifting down as was I. Each time the noise came – there were long, long, pauses in between – his head had shot up as if on a pole, and he'd looked this way and that in fast, jerky movements. The sounds had a musical *thrum* to them, and that's why they were familiar to me.

They were sounds of a thumb playing across open guitar strings.

Yet softer even than that, a resonance only, the vibrations dying slowly, leaving what seemed a deep and brooding silence before the strings were disturbed once more.

Fortunately – having used up my bravado when I'd marched boldly down to the kitchen – an explanation had already occurred to me. A bird, or possibly even an insomniac bat, had somehow found its way into my music room and the creature's wings were brushing against the guitar every time it did a fly-past. Other than that, a mouse family could have nested inside one of the acoustics, members scraping past strings when they left or entered the soundhole. Both explanations felt reasonable to me, and I was still prepared to believe in reason (even after all that had happened).

I pushed harder and the door gave a fraction. There'd been silence inside for well over a minute now.

Next attempt I butted the door with my shoulder and, wood scraping against wood, it opened; my grip on the handle preventing it from flying wide. I gently shoved the door the rest of the way.

At first glance the low-ceilinged room appeared empty. At second glance there was no change. But I moaned aloud when I saw the condition my two acoustic guitars were in. I ran into the room and dropped to my knees before them, my moan turning into a wail of anguish.

The neck of the Martin, the instrument on its stand and set close to a shaded wall, bent towards me as if bowing at my entrance. The Spanish concert lay nearby on the floor, obviously having toppled at a time when the crash couldn't have been heard; its neck curved upwards like a thin man trying to rise. First and second strings had snapped on both, the rest stretched taut from head to bridge, pulling in the neck, the incredible tension in them almost palpable. I didn't understand how it could have happened: neither one had been left in direct sunlight, which might have caused the wood to warp – and that would have slackened the strings, not tightened them – and neither had been tuned to a high pitch – I kept the strings at normal tension, unless I knew I wouldn't be using the guitars for a time, in which case I always loosened them. Nylon strings could shrink if subjected to extremes in temperature and providing they didn't break first; but the steel strings of the Martin? Not likely.

I shook my head, bewildered and upset, the grief I felt not unlike, I'd imagine, having your pet dog run over.

A soft breeze blew in from the window I'd left open a few inches days before to freshen the room (maybe a stronger breeze had nudged over the classical) and played across the over-tightened strings, the vibrations picked up by the soundboards of each and amplified. The echo was more like a sighing groan than a musical shimmer.

I banged my thigh with a clenched fist and swore, then swore again. Although the guitars were irrevocably ruined (the necks might be replaced, but that would prove expensive and no guarantee that the tone would be as good), I nevertheless counter-turned the nuts on both instruments, loosening the remaining strings. It was with some nervousness that I opened my Fender case and examined the electric guitar lying inside (the feeling of opening a casket to take a peek at the corpse therein was strong). Thankfully, my jobbing machine was in good order.

After that, I could only squat on the floor and stare at my invalided – no, mortally diseased – instruments, while Rumbo had a fine time skipping around the room, oblivious to my misery. I let him romp, glad at least one of us wasn't concerned about anything.

I sat there gloomily for some time and wasn't exactly sure what had finally roused me – it might have been the squirrel's shrieking chatter, or the sensing of movement over my head. It had been a morning of distant noises, so I was neither disturbed nor surprised to hear further sounds. And of course, on this occasion the source was fairly obvious; the bats were fidgety.

But it wasn't curiosity about them that caused me to drag a chair over to the centre of the room so that I could reach the hatch. I'd dumped Midge's painting of Gramarye up there on the same day we'd discovered the grotesque change – just lifted the hatch and tossed it in, out of sight, out of mind. Burning the picture would have been too much like a ritual. Still mystified about that transformation, now I wanted to take another look. Maybe I thought it might have returned to normal, optimistic fool that I am; anything seemed possible in that place. Whatever, I wanted to study the painting in more detail than last time.

I balanced on the chair, one hand flat against the hatch cover, the other holding the flashlight I now kept in the attic room specifically for loft visits (usually made by Midge to check on our protected species up there). Straightening my knees, I heaved at the cover, nervous of our night friends but believing, as I'd been informed so often, that they really were harmless.

The hatch opened with an eerie 'Old Dark House' creak, causing Rumbo to shriek and disappear down the stairs. I promised myself I'd oil those hinges at the earliest opportunity. Flashlight on, I used the back of the chair for wobbly support and hauled myself up with my usual lack of dignity. Sitting on the edge, I cursed myself for having slung the painting with such force: I could just make out the rectangular shape before beaming the light on it, and realised I'd have to crawl across joists to reach it.

Before doing so, I swung the light around the loft and shuddered at the black hanging shapes, certain that they'd become denser than last time I'd looked. They filled every inch of space on the beams and rafters. Just like that first time.

But at least they were still and quiet, as though my intrusion had brought their previous activity to a halt. I wondered how they regarded my presence. With fear? Hostility? Or did they sense by now that Midge and I meant them no harm?

A single tiny squeak drew my attention to a crossbeam to the left of where I was sitting. I spotlighted a particularly thick cluster of bats; one, near the centre, was making small juddering movements, its head arched upwards towards its stomach. Jagged teeth were picked out by the light as the bat opened its ugly little mouth and emitted another barely audible squeak.

A few more squeaks answered from the darker regions of the loft, all single and somehow pathetic.

Drawing my legs up, I started making my way towards the painting, not wanting to stay in that inky cavern for a moment longer than necessary. The joists were hard against my knees as I crawled, and the smell of bats' excrement was stronger and more unpleasant than the last time I'd been up there; I comforted myself with the thought that the droppings might at least provide a natural form of loft insulation. I tried to keep my free hand out of it as I went, using the flashlight for guidance, but the stuff was everywhere and I was soon wiping my palm against my jeans to get rid of the sludge. I decided walking across the joists, bending low and keeping a steady balance, would be less of an ordeal, so I rose, swaying awkwardly for a couple of seconds with feet spread on separate sections.

I immediately brushed against one of the creatures.

That bat squealed and flapped thin wings at me, and I recoiled, wobbling on unsteady legs, hand flailing air. Half bent and still a little rocky, I stabilised and shone the torch at the offended bat, making sure it wasn't readying itself to attack.

What I saw created a clogging in my chest, a thick ball of softness inside there threatening to erupt up my throat and splatter the loft. I swallowed hard.

Only inches away from my head, the bat I'd bumped into was jerking in small spasmodic movements, wings flexed inwards, membraned tail curling downwards. Something flushed and shiny and repugnant was emerging from between its legs.

I watched mesmerised, repulsed yet horribly fascinated.

The pink, hunched thing grew in size, frail shape glistening in the light from the torch. The tiny body oozed out, smoothly and wetly, taking form – an unsightly form – discharged from the womb like an oval blob of pink topping squeezed from an icing bag, to plop onto the mother bat's stomach, caught there and suspended by its life-cord. The mother immediately wrapped wings and pouched tail around the newborn, its head striving upwards and tongue flickering out to cleanse the sticky fresh body.

The birth might have been wondrous to a nature-lover,

268

but to me, in those dark confines, among a mass of suspended gargoyles, it was an abhorrence.

I tried desperately to shuffle away, careful not to slip between the joists, and only succeeded in disturbing those behind me. And as I turned, the light sweeping around the loft, I saw others giving birth, more and more pink blobs surging forth to dangle at their mothers' breasts. Not just one or two more, but *dozens*. I swear I saw *dozens* oozing out. Everywhere I swung the flashlight I caught the same nauseating movement, the shiny gooeyness on the minute bodies reflecting the beam. They looked like transparent bags of pus squeezed from open wounds.

I scrambled towards the square patch of daylight, slipping off the timbers and cracking my knees against them, but not stopping, collecting wood splinters in my hands as I crawled, the flashlight bobbing wildly, agitating the bats so that they squealed in protest or alarm, probably both.

One fluttered by my face and I felt dank air waft against my cheek. Something thumped softly against my back, lodging there for a moment before dropping away.

I almost screamed.

Then I was at the opening, swinging my legs over, falling through, my hands and elbows saving me from plummeting to the floor. My feet found the chair below and I snatched at the hatch cover, ducking my head as a small body flew out of the darkness to skim against my arm.

I pulled at the cover and only just withdrew my fingers before it slammed shut.

I stood on the chair, hands on knees, flashlight rolling in an arc on the floor where I'd dropped it, and gasped in a huge lungful of air, hoping it would bypass my breakfast which was on the way up.

I drove away from Bunbury feeling angry, mixed-up, and I don't know what else. Mystified, I suppose. Oh yeah, and somehow *used*.

The late Flora Chaldean's solicitor had agreed to see me with considerable reluctance, and really he didn't have much choice. He had some responsibility regarding the sale of Gramarye and I was insistent on a meeting between us. Could be he felt some pangs of guilt, too.

I wanted to see him because there were certain matters concerning the old lady and the cottage that needed explaining, and Ogborn was probably the most important link (if not the only link). I wanted information. I wanted to learn more about Flora Chaldean. I wanted to know more about Gramarye. I wanted to find out what the Synergist connection was.

Well, I'd been given answers, but I can't say they were explanations. Now I was confused in a different way.

Bickleshift, the estate agent who'd sold us the property, was the first one I'd tried to contact after my sickening (literally) experience with the bats in the loft, but he'd been away on a two-week vacation. You might think, incidentally, that I'd over-reacted to that particular incident – after all, they were only small winged mammals with pointed ears having babies – but you had to be there to understand there was more going on, that there was nothing Bambi about those tiny, pulpy offspring, nothing cute about them, *that this new-life emergence was more akin to an excretion than a spawning.* You see, it was like witnessing the propagation of disharmony, the assertion of malign influences, rather than just a natural delight of nature, because it had become very plain to me by then that there were two sides to Gramarye, two climes, or latitudes, whichever way you'd choose to describe these opposing atmospheres. Different zones, maybe. Positive and Negative. We'd experienced the good, the Positive, when we'd first moved in. Now something was elbowing that aside. In the words of Dylan (Bob), times they were 'a changin''. And thinking back, the changes had started at the first appearance of the Synergists.

And these newborn bats somehow represented the unwholesome metamorphosis Gramarye was going through, a change that couldn't be sudden, that was a creeping thing, slow like a monster crawling from the ocean to slime its way up the shore, learning to breathe, gathering strength to rise. Urged on by those who could have use of its power.

Absurd? That's only the half of it.

But I'm getting ahead of myself, and I only mention these things because that's how insights were coming at me, like random droplets of awareness falling from some high place, spattering my head in tiny shocks before soaking through to my brain. Driving back to the cottage that day, I remembered exactly what I'd told Midge a couple of nights before, how I'd suggested she was some kind of catalyst or intermediary. I wondered if the Synergists, and more specifically Mycroft, were a different form of catalyst.

Anyhow, Bickleshift was away, so I'd rung the solicitor, who'd ummed and aahed and finally agreed an appointment for late afternoon the following day.

I hadn't said anything to Midge when she'd returned from the village, hadn't even mentioned how my guitars had warped, their strings, steel ones and all, shrinking inexplicably. I wanted some facts before presenting my case. She seemed too preoccupied with her own thoughts anyway and today she thought I'd gone into Bunbury to buy sheet music.

I'd spent an uneasy night and Midge had been restless too, but in her sleep. She'd murmured and tossed, her hands clutching at the bedcovers as though she were afraid of plunging into some dream-abyss.

My half-hearted attempts to break through her continued reserve next morning came to nothing, as much my fault as hers: we were like two punch-drunk protagonists, a little too dazed to see one another clearly, let alone throw a punch. Only when I was driving away from the cottage later that afternoon did my thoughts (and my energy) shape up again. Yeah, it was a relief to be away from the place.

Cantrip appeared almost deserted on the way back and I checked my watch. Nearly six – I hadn't realised it was so late. The shops were closed and the villagers were probably settling down for evening meals. The sun had decided to head for the hills.

Through the village, moving into the forest lanes. Soon to be home. And the question begged: What kind of home was it? Mycroft might know better than anyone.

I kept a steady speed, keen to be with Midge again, hoping this time she'd listen to what I had to say, to what Ogborn had told me. No, I'd *make* her listen. Whatever attitude she had, she would be forced to listen. Then we'd explore Mycroft's sinister motives together.

I was strangely nervous of the forest's louring deepness on either side of the road.

Gramarye came into view, walls still beacon-white in the slowly cooling rays of the sun. The garden was beautifully coloured. Only when I drew close did the flowers begin to appear faded, did the building's brickwork reveal its sneaking blemishes. I parked the car in its grassy space and vaulted over the fence.

I could hear the phone ringing inside the cottage.

The door was closed, and I was surprised at that; Midge loved the fresh air to waft through the rooms, up the stairways, and she adored the framed view of the garden from the kitchen. The phone was still ringing.

Quickly unlocking the door, I pushed against it, meeting with some resistance at first. Firmer pressure sent the door inwards and I stopped momentarily on the threshold, eyes adjusting to the gloom inside. That gloom seemed unreasonably slow to give way to the brightness surging past my shoulders.

I called out Midge's name, even though I was fairly sure she wasn't there: front door shut, phone left unanswered, and something else – the almost tangible coldness of her absence. Only the persistent ringing occupied the dank air.

I went to the stairs, thinking it could be Midge at the other end of the phone, that maybe she was calling to let me know where she was. But where could she have gone without the car?

I climbed in a rush, certain the ringing would stop before I got there, grabbing the receiver mid-shrill.

Static hawked in my ear and I jerked my head away.

'Hello . . . hello . . .?'

I could just hear the faint voice behind the interference: the call sounded as though it came from a remote battlefield with artillery fire all around. I thumped the earpiece hard into the palm of my hand, unclogging carbon granules with the impact, and for a while the distant gunfire quietened.

'Can you hear me?' asked the familiar voice.

'Yeah. Is that you, Val?'

The agent's voice remained a long way off.

'Mike? Mike, is Midge there with you?'

'Uh, no. I just got in myself, and she doesn't appear to be around.'

'Perhaps it's as well – it's you I wanted to talk to.'

The chill huff of apprehension tensed my neck.

'What's the problem?' I asked, my casualness forced.

'I'm not sure. It's all rather peculiar, actually.'

The ceasefire was suddenly over and she was almost lost in the barrage.

'Can you hear me, Mike?'

I could, but only faintly.

'This line is bloody awful.'

'Hang on, Val,' I shouted into the mouthpiece. I banged the receiver again, this time with more force. The crackle remained, but was at least less obtrusive.

273

'Okay,' I said, 'what did you have to tell me?'

'You might find this very odd.'

Oh really? I smiled thinly.

'It's to do with Midge's painting,' she explained. 'The painting of Gramarye.'

'Go on,' I told her warily.

'When I first saw the picture, before . . . before it was ruined . . . something struck me. I felt somehow I'd seen that picture . . .' static over-rode her words for a second or two '. . . remember where. I convinced myself that my brain was playing games after the tiring journey down. I'd seen the same view in the flesh, as it were, when I'd arrived at the cottage that evening. I assumed that what I thought had been déjà vu, was in fact the association of reality with the painting's fantasy.'

'Val, this line's gonna break up completely . . .'

'All right, I'm coming to the point. Mike, find a copy of a book Midge illustrated several years ago . . .'

I lost her again as the crackling crescendoed. The agitation settled after another hefty thump from me. The palm of my hand was becoming red with the bashing it was taking.

'Sorry, I missed that. What book are you talking about?'

'It's called *Sorcerer's Kingdom*, you know the one?'

'Yeah, I remember.'

'Well, look at page twenty-seven.'

'What?'

'Look *hard* and you'll see what I mean . . .'

I yanked the phone away as static all but exploded in my ear. It sounded like a direct hit at the other end.

'Mike . . . can you hear me?'

'Only just.'

'Can you hear . . .'

'Look, Val,' I shouted, 'I'll call you back later!'

'. . . at the illustration . . .'

'Okay, okay!' I don't know if she caught my hurried goodbye, but clunking the receiver down was a relief.

I didn't stay a moment longer in the hallway musing over what Val had asked me to do. I went straight into the round room and headed for the bookcase there. I searched the titles and couldn't find the one I was looking for. But then we had many books and Midge made no special display of those illustrated by her. The spare room, where we kept the major part of our collection, was the next place I tried. I scanned the loaded shelves and soon came across *Sorcerer's Kingdom*.

It was a modest-sized edition, a tale of fairies and witches and sorcerers and dragons, aimed at five-to-eight-year-olds but, as we understood from the publisher, bought by many adults for the cult pleasure of its illustrations. This particular children's story did a lot for coffee-tables.

I tugged at the top binding with one finger, then pulled the book free. Although it wasn't dark in the room, I carried my find over to the window.

Outside, the forest looked very still and very dense.

I flicked through the pages, looking for twenty-seven, the rich colours of the illustrations no more than kaleidoscopic patterns as they skimmed by.

Twenty-seven.

My hand pressed the leaf flat.

The focal point of the picture was a white, multi-turreted castle. I vaguely remembered how the storyline ran: this was an enchanted castle inhabited by a magician, the top gun in all the land, but who was aged and failing, and seeking a worthy successor before the darker forces which prowled the woodlands and underworld subjugated his territories.

I frowned, unable to make the connection with Midge's recent painting. Not until I looked closer, that is.

There was a pixie village in the foreground of the illustration, red-capped toadstools for houses, packed bright-coloured stones for a road. The pixies themselves were a jolly enough bunch. Further on, the forest began, lush and gouache green. But like the real forest outside the window, very still and very dense.

Beyond were lighter shades of the hills, the road re-emerging from the woodland, and rising up from one hill was the enchanted castle itself, the ancient sorcerer diminutive but clearly seen on the highest turret.

In the forest was a small glade, and in that glade stood a tiny yet finely detailed cottage. Part of it was rounded.

There was no mistake. That cottage was Gramarye.

VOICES

There's no closing-up time for a forest – the activity goes on all night as well as all day. But most of the action is unseen whatever the hour. In the evening, though, or night-time, there seem to be more noises, more scurryings, leaves rustling, and sometimes twigs snapping. The later the hour, the more unfriendly and secretive the forest feels. To an outsider, that is.

I did my best to follow the path Midge and I had used on other occasions, knowing where it would roughly take me and hoping that the sun wouldn't have sunk too low before I got there. I'd grabbed a jacket as I'd left the cottage, aware of how cool it could become beneath the trees at that time of evening.

Soft mulched leaf-mould shifted beneath my feet, my footsteps sounding like short gasps as I trudged through the thick layers. A springy branch taunted rather than challenged my progress along the path, and it swished back noisily into foliage behind as I pushed by, as if venting its spite.

I'd phoned the Synergist Temple to find out if Midge was there, but the line interference had become so bad I could barely hear the answering voice, let alone conduct a sensible conversation. Yet every instinct told me that's where she was and I was angry that she'd waited for me to be out of the way

276

before sneaking off there. I'd replaced the receiver without speaking.

Unless they'd picked her up in one of their own cars, Midge would have taken the forest route to reach the Temple and that's why I trekked along that path, too; I didn't want to miss her if she was already on the way back. This was quicker than by car, anyway, the journey by road circuitous as well as meandering.

If only she'd waited, if only I'd had the chance to tell her what I'd learned. Would she have trusted the Synergists so implicitly then? I speeded up my pace.

The book illustration was another ingredient in the brew I felt was fast coming to the boil. I now understood, at least, why Gramarye had seemed vaguely familiar to me the moment I'd stepped from the car on that very first visit. And again, why there had been a pale recognition when I'd looked upon Midge's painting weeks later. Val Harradine had made the connection, although not right away; she'd had to check through Midge's past work to be sure. The detail in the book illustration was small, but then the artist's style was meticulous and sharp, loving attention paid to every part of the composition. The cottage in the picture even had a sparkling garden leading up to its door.

And there had been a figure just inside that open doorway, a dark shape, no more than a shadow.

This is crazy, I kept telling myself. *Stark-staring bloody crazy!* The book was a fairy-tale, nothing more. A kid's bedtime story. Yet here I was, chasing through the forest to rescue my damsel in distress, desperate to save her from the evil clutches of the wicked old wizard or warlock or mystic or whatever the fuck they called these Brothers Grimm characters whose magic was murkish, not to say Black. All I needed was a white charger.

Yeah, hilarious.

I never slackened my pace for one moment.

Because I was learning to suspend my own natural beliefs. As one day we all have to.

Once or twice I thought I'd lost my way in the woods, but then I'd spot something I recognised – a fallen, rotting

277

tree trunk, a particularly odd-shaped oak, a rain-formed pond – and I'd know I was headed more or less in the right direction. It wasn't too long before I emerged from the forest to look down at the grey house at the bottom of the wide gradient.

The house, the Temple, visibly decayed as I approached, flaws sharpened by nearness. The reddening sun behind, becoming low in the sky, failed to tint the building with any warmth. My step was steady, resolute I suppose, yet there was an element of caution about me as I wondered if I were being observed from any of those dark windows.

Soon I'd left the grass of the meadow and was on firmer, though still uneven, ground. There were four cars parked in the turning area, one of them the familiar Citroën. I crossed the space, watching the house just as I felt it was watching me, and mounted the steps to the big double-door. I'd intended to march straight in but, of course, the entrance was locked.

I pushed the heel of my fist against the large brass bell set in concrete by the side and kept it there. For good measure, I thumped the bottom of my other fist against the panelling of the door itself, working up a good head of anger as I did so.

Presently I heard footsteps drawing near behind the barrier. A lock turned, one side of the door opened fractionally. The Bone Man stared out through the gap.

He pretended not to recognise me, but we both knew otherwise.

'Midge is here.' It wasn't a question from me, so it didn't require an answer.

'Midge?' he queried, his voice as skeletal as his features.

'Don't play silly fucking games,' I said, and pushed hard at the door, knocking him back.

I swiftly stepped through.

'Just a moment, you can't come in here,' he informed me, bony fingers against my chest.

I took his hand away. 'Where is she?'

'I've no idea who you mean.'

'Midge Gudgeon. She's here somewhere.'

'I think you'd –'

'Let me see Mycroft.'

278

'I'm afraid he can't be disturbed.'

I sighed for his benefit. 'Look, you're not getting rid of me until I've seen either her or Mycroft himself.'

'I've already told –'

A door had opened further down the hallway and Gillie Slade appeared, looking at us curiously, no doubt wondering what the fuss was about.

I strode purposefully towards her, Bone Man following close behind, his weedy protests like gnats in the air.

'Gillie, tell me where I can find Midge,' I demanded before I even reached the girl.

'Mike, you can't –'

'Yeah, I know all that. She's here, isn't she?'

I stared hard at her and she lowered her gaze.

'Isn't she?' I repeated.

'Yes, Mike. But she's with Mycroft and they really mustn't be interrupted.' Her eyes were looking up at me again, and they were blue and earnest.

'Interrupted? What the hell's going on?'

Other doors were opening, other heads emerging.

'For Chrissake, tell me!'

Her eyes avoided mine and I wanted to shake her. Instead I brushed past and peered into the room she'd just left. Blank faces goggled back at me. The only furniture in the room was stiff-backed chairs, spread randomly around, the Syngerists sitting on them with no books in their laps, nothing at all in their hands. I assumed it was their version of the Happy Hour. Meditation time.

Midge wasn't among them.

I backed out and crossed the hallway, two people in the door there parting without a murmur, allowing me to see inside. More Synergists and scarcely any furniture apart from more of those very uncomfortable-looking chairs. Several of the members were squatting on the floor, with nothing visible occupying their minds either.

She wasn't in there.

Nor the next room.

Nor the next.

Now the library. I felt lucky.

And was unlucky. The room we'd been ushered into on our first (and my one and only) visit, where my scalded arm had been dipped in the greenish liquid that could have been used for washing dishes or cleaning metal for all I knew, where Mycroft had endeavoured to impress us with his special powers, was empty. Not a bloody soul.

My frustration was growing. I by-passed the broad stairway and all but burst through the double-doors of a room opposite. Empty of people, but more interesting than the others. Leather armchairs, small and delicately shaped tables, a magnificent oak fire-surround that virtually ran the length of one wall. Above the jutting mantel hung a long tapestry depicting a patterned cross, an emblematic rose at its centre, the arms and upright post decorated with repeated symbols of some kind. On other walls, between the tall windows, were shapes I recognised as zodiac signs, and at the far end was a large mosaic mandala, within the circle a square, another small mandala within that. A wooden mask lay on a nearby table: high pointed ears and sloping, slit-like eyes above a long protruding snout – the carved face of a jackal. Even though the window drapes were half-drawn so that the room was cast into befitting dimness, the contents were incisively impressed into my mind, as though I'd taken time to study the interior. In fact, I'd stood in the doorway for no more than a few seconds. I think the impact was somehow due to expectancy, not surprise.

I turned away, unhappy with the view. The Synergists had left the other rooms to crowd the hallway, some of them muttering among themselves, while most continued to watch me silently, a kind of dumb resentment on their faces. I felt like a visitor to an asylum whose inmates thought I was the lunatic.

Gillie was near the front, and at least her expression conveyed something more than cold hostility. I went to her and rested a hand on her elbow, my touch gentle, not wanting her to react against me.

'Please help me, Gillie,' I said. 'I only want to talk with Midge.'

Her eyes were the giveaway, even if she didn't speak. I

wondered whether the glance upwards was inadvertent or intentional.

I looked in the same direction, towards the top of the stairway, then let go of her, striding to the stairs and starting to climb two at a time. Halfway up Kinsella appeared, the Bone Man not far behind. The latter pointed at me unnecessarily and Kinsella's smile had a hint of reluctance to it.

'Hi, Mike, is there a problem?' he called down to me.

I didn't answer until I was on the top step. 'I'm looking for Midge,' I told him, 'and I know she's here.'

'Sure. Let's go down and I'll getcha a cup of coffee and we'll talk awhile.'

He laid a friendly hand on my shoulder and I shrugged it off.

'I'd like to see her now,' I said.

'Uh, well, that's just not possible right now, Mike.' Jesus, I hated his mild tone. 'Y'see, she's in with Mycroft and they really can't be disturbed.'

'Why not?'

'You know what she wanted.'

I suppose I must have registered a fair amount of alarm.

He nodded, still smiling. Only there was the tiniest hint of malicious pleasure in the All-American blueness of his eyes.

'You got it, Mike. Mycroft's helpin' Midge reach her folks.'

'Oh shi . . .' I pushed by, intending to search every room along that corridor until I found her. But his arm sprang up across my chest like a steel barrier. I shoved him away and carried on.

He grabbed my arm and whirled me around and, for a brief instant, it looked as though the cream had curdled on his apple-pie face. The grin quickly came back, but a piranha's greeting might have had the same warmth.

'Sorry,' he began to say, 'but you —'

This time I pushed harder and he took a step or two backwards. I hadn't even half turned before he grabbed me again, one hand around my neck, the other beneath my armpit, and sent me crashing noisily against the wall, my legs giving way so that I slid to the floor. The hero doesn't always win the physical tussles, you know.

Gillie, who'd followed me up the stairs, knelt beside me as I tried to regain some of the puff I'd lost. Kinsella wasn't grinning any more, and that was okay by me. I started hauling myself to my feet.

'No, Mike,' advised Gillie.

Kinsella seemed almost eager.

I wasn't looking forward to the next few minutes, but I sure as hell wasn't going home on my own.

I was on my feet and squaring up when we all became aware of a presence further along the corridor. Kinsella and Bone Man turned as though they had been called (I hadn't heard a word spoken). Mycroft was standing down there, a thin cane in one hand. In the doorway behind him was Midge.

She saw me and I felt her gasp. While their attention was diverted, I ducked past the two men blocking my way and hurried along the corridor towards her.

'What are you doing here?' was her welcome.

That kind of stopped me, because there was a lot of irritation in the question.

'I could ask you the same,' I returned. Then, still catching my breath, I said, 'I want you to leave with me right now.'

She was indignant, the negative response trailing off: 'No . . .'

'I think this is an inopportune moment for you to ask that.'

I glanced at Mycroft, who'd spoken. He seemed about a hundred and fifty years older, all that blandness suddenly gone. There was nothing dried or cracked about his voice, though; it was as smoothly mild as ever.

'There are several matters Midge and I wish to discuss, Mike, and I've invited her to stay with us this evening. No need for you to worry – someone will drive her back to Gramarye later tonight.'

I shook my head. 'She's coming home with me.'

Midge stepped in front of me, eyes alight, but not with affection. 'Who are you to say what I can or can't do? What gives you the right?'

I kept my voice low. 'He wants the cottage.'

She stared wide-eyed at me, then she stared wide-eyed at him.

'Are you out of your mind?'

That was to me.

'They tried to get the cottage from Flora Chaldean,' I persisted steadily. 'They tried to buy the place legitimately from her, but she'd have none of it. D'you know she went to the trouble of having a clause put into her will specifically forbidding the sale of Gramarye to the Synergists or anyone connected with them? That's why we were vetted. That's why the solicitor wanted to know about our private lives. I went to see Ogborn this afternoon and he told me everything – after some persuasion, that is. She wanted them *never* to have Gramarye, Midge, and there had to be a good reason for that.'

'It can't be true.'

'Ask Ogborn yourself. Or why not get Mycroft to tell you? I doubt he'll give you an honest answer, though. She wouldn't sell and so I think they tried other methods. I think they tried to frighten her out.'

Mycroft's response was a sad shake of his head.

'We were led to believe you'd never been to the cottage before,' I said in his direction, 'but a coupla nights ago you knew there was another entrance around the back.'

'A reasonable assumption, I'd have thought, considering there were steps leading around the side. And don't most homes have a back door?'

'True enough. But it was the way you acted that set me thinking. You were so bloody uneasy, like you didn't want to go through the kitchen. Even Kinsella got the shakes sitting there once. I couldn't help wonder if you got the jitters because old Flora died in there.'

Midge gave a small gasp. 'Mike, you don't know what you're saying.'

'You saw for yourself what happened when they came visiting. Christ, Midge, they couldn't get out fast enough in the end.' I could sense Kinsella and the other man sidling up behind me. I grasped Midge's arms. 'Okay, it all sounds crazy,

I admit that; but there was enough going on to start me worrying. Christ, there's been enough going on since we moved in to scare the hell out of both of us! Yet you've turned a blind eye to most of it, and I can't help wondering about that, too. That's why I finally went to Ogborn for some answers.'

'If Flora was under some kind of threat, why didn't she inform the police?' Midge demanded.

'And tell them what? You've seen how they work, how they've wormed their way into our lives. Nothing too forward or obvious – they're much too subtle for that. And certainly no apparent physical violence as far as the old lady was concerned. A weird cult organisation can't afford to step out of line; that would give the law too good a chance to come down on them. Yeah, the people around here would have loved that, if Sixsmythe is anything to go by. But there's nothing stupid about Mycroft and his crew, they don't take any risks. What I can't figure is why Gramarye is so important to them.'

Kinsella and Bone Man were breathing down my neck.

'You have a remarkable imagination, Mike,' said Mycroft without a trace of irritation. 'Of course I can appreciate your curiosity about our sect, although not why you've jumped to such painfully wrong conclusions about us.'

'You can't deny you harassed Flora Chaldean.'

'That's an incorrect term to use. Yes, we persisted, but our intentions were misunderstood. Flora was a lonely and somewhat helpless old lady, living a very uncomfortable existence. We merely offered our care and attention.'

'You wanted the cottage!'

He smiled benignly. 'A legal way of making a proud woman accept our charity. She would have continued to live there under our administrations, while having a considerable financial gain that would have allowed her to feel independent.'

I smacked my forehead in a cartoon gesture. 'Oh God, you're good. You're so bloody devious.'

'I wish for nothing more than to help Midge come to terms with a personal grief that's been with her for far too long.'

284

'And maybe she'll become one of your so-called Adoptives along the way?'

'She has that choice. But I'd also like to help you, Mike, and perhaps convince you of our sincerity. You're a troubled young man, full of misconceptions, filled with cynicism. I could help you find your way.'

'I hadn't realised I'd lost it.'

'But you've never known the right path. Do you believe in Magic?'

The sudden shift startled me. 'Magic?' I asked stupidly.

'The discovery and application of the unknown forces of Nature through the human will. An alliance between both powers. You might describe it as a synergism.'

'What's that got –?'

'The most important objective of Magic is the discovery of one's true and ultimate self. With my guidance and my will, I can help you attain just that.'

'Midge, we're leaving.' I tugged at her arm.

'A short while to explain,' said Mycroft, 'that's all I ask.'

'Please, Mike.' Midge was resisting my pull.

'He's a crank, can't you see that?'

'Mike, I've just spoken with my parents.'

First startled, now stunned.

'He helped me reach them.' She was almost weeping, but she was smiling too. 'I spoke with them only moments ago, but the noise out here disturbed us, upset the thought-patterns Mycroft had created.'

'You saw your mother and father?'

'No, but I heard them, I heard their voices.' The first tear began to slide, soon trickling into the crease of her smile. 'They've forgiven me, Mike.'

'There's nothing to forgive, for Chrissake!'

'Listen to me. They're happy for me, but they told me there was a path to follow –'

'Let me guess –'

'*Listen*, damn you!' she screamed.

Mycroft touched her shoulder. 'Calm yourself. Anger has no purpose inside this Temple.'

I rolled my eyes.

'Perhaps only by showing him will he be convinced. Would you be prepared to open your mind and heart to us, Mike, to lay aside that shield of distrust?'

'Will it improve the dialogue?'

Midge slapped at my chest, stinging me. 'For once will you hear somebody else? Can't you . . . can't you accept there's more around us than we can just see and hear?'

'If my answer's no, would you leave with me now?' Something heavy was dredging across my very core and I knew I was losing her.

She knew it too. 'I can't go with you,' Midge replied, and she was so small and defenceless. 'I need this, Mike, don't you understand?'

Idiot that I was I turned to Mycroft and said, 'So let's talk.'

The satisfaction was somewhere at the back of his eyes, only room for affable benevolence at the front. I could almost feel the sighs of relief from Kinsella and his buddy warming my neck: they figured he had me now.

Mycroft stood aside and with a short gesture of his cane indicated the room he and Midge had left a few minutes ago. (This new affectation with the thin stick puzzled me, and it was only later that I discovered its significance.) 'I think it's best that we talk in here,' he said as an invitation.

Midge didn't hesitate. She seemed eager to be back inside.

I followed less keenly.

To step into the weirdest room I'd ever seen.

THE PYRAMID ROOM

It was in the shape of a pyramid, the tapering walls steep and high, apexed so that there was no ceiling.

And black.

Even the floor was black.

Above us – ten feet above, at least – shone small recessed lights, one on each angled wall, their thin beams picked out by dust motes, striking downwards like straight translucent bars, creating four soft-edged moons on the smooth floor. Their glow became substantial only when the door was closed behind us.

When that happened, the darkness beyond the pale neons became infinite.

I realised that the room above had to be part of the pyramid, the sloping walls cutting through the ceiling, maybe even piercing the ceiling above that one.

Only a single chair stood in the centre of the floor, the light beams like four slender posts spaced around it.

'What d'you do in here – sharpen razor blades?'

Despite the lack of adequate light, I could tell my remark hadn't amused Mycroft. 'Just as a church spire is constructed to draw spiritual grace towards the congregation below, so the pyramid seeks to direct psychic energy,' he said. 'The shape is repeated beneath us, inverted, of course, so that the tip grazes the earth.'

He lowered himself into the chair, resting his hands on the short blunted handle of the cane. 'Midge, would you like to sit as before, and perhaps you'll do the same.' (He hadn't bothered to use my name.)

I wasn't keen on squatting at the Synergist's feet but it had, after all, been a long run through the forest. I followed Midge's example, though I declined the lotus position, preferring to lounge on one elbow, ankles crossed, and giving the impression of being quite relaxed about all this. Midge and I were between two light beams, and I twisted my neck to glimpse her profile, which was intense as she gazed up at Mycroft. There was the smell of incense about the place.

The Synergist leaned towards me. 'You failed to answer my question,' he said.

'Question?'

'Do you believe in Magic?'

'There's a coupla card tricks I know –'

He interrupted, although still not riled. (That can be irritating when you're being deliberately crass.) 'Can you comprehend Man as an identical counterpart to the universe and every force it holds, that the universe itself is no more and certainly no less than an infinitesimal human organism? That the energy driving and governing the universe is the same energy contained within ourselves? Can you understand that Man, with this inner knowledge, could learn to transcend all material limits, and eventually time and space itself?'

I wasn't sure if he was expecting an answer, but I gave him one anyway, maintaining the crassness for my own pleasure and maybe in the hope of piercing his smooth veneer.

'I can't even understand the question,' I replied.

'No, of course not. Perhaps I've overestimated your intelligence.'

There it was, the first chink. I nodded grimly to myself, appreciating the insult.

'None the less,' he went on, his eyes lost in shadow, 'I'm sure it's not beyond you to realise that human knowledge purposely confines itself to a limited reality, one that it doesn't have to fear, and one that scientists and material philosophers show us to be true. Sadly, we choose to see only the least important actuality. The other realities around us – and *within* us – have tended to be ignored for the last few hundred years.'

'No kidding.'

His hands grasped the metal cane-top just a fraction more tightly. 'Except that now, recently, the reality of precognition, extrasensory perception and psychokinesis has become accepted by even the most ardent of sceptics. Those hidden powers that have been rejected for so long by scientists are now the subject of scientific study.'

I was becoming impatient. 'I don't get what this has to do with so-called Magic.'

'Surely you can see where I'm leading? Those powers that are inevitably being recognised by the most pragmatic sectors of our society were once considered Magical or supernatural. The view used to be that such powers set aside the natural order of nature, but that was a huge misconception: Magicians merely strive to discover those hidden forces and to work through them and *with* them, whether they are part of us or part of the whole.'

Much as I tried to remain aloof from all this, I have to admit Mycroft was getting through to me. No, I don't mean I followed what he was saying, but his voice had become soothingly persuasive, almost mesmeric (have you ever been hypnotised? You know what's going on, but you don't realise what's happening), the oddness of the room, with its smell of incense and the soft downcast lights, providing helpful special effects. It all had to be consciously resisted.

I pretended a yawn.

He pretended he hadn't noticed.

'We must learn in stages, first casting off restraints imposed upon us since birth, becoming refreshed again. Convention, rationalism, materialism, our principles and ethics: these are nothing more than psychological screens. We must become children again, innocent of such influences. The very young believe in Magic until they are influenced otherwise. The beliefs of unenlightened maturity must be overturned, and the shackling doctrines of religion thwarted because religion reserves divine power for God alone, whereas the way of Magic offers divine power for all.'

289

I cringed inwardly, waiting for a thunderbolt to strike. Disappointingly, it didn't.

'Each step the initiate takes must be experienced and mastered, every new mystery revealed must be contemplated, each developing phase considered. And perhaps the first and most important secret is that which lies within ourselves.'

He leaned forward so that his chin very nearly rested on his hands clutched over the cane, and his voice lowered.

'That is,' he said gravely and confidentially, 'the mystery of our own energy, our own astral forces in the earth itself, and so, too, the infinite forces of the universe. A Magician, my friend, is always in search of those hidden links.'

He straightened once again, his face gone to stone. My throat was dry.

'And when those links are discovered,' he added in the same low voice, 'they may be employed for the Magician's purposes.'

He gave me time for it to sink in.

'All that to pull a rabbit out of a hat?' I said.

He allowed a cold smile.

'All that to discover our true self and the veiled power we hold. There is nothing more basic, nor more transcendent. With that knowledge, a man has access to the limitless forces of his own will. He can evoke an imagination so concentrated and so vivid that it can create a reality in the astral light.'

He pointed the tip of his cane at the floor, close to my leg.

'That reality may be reflected in this physical world, if we so wish.'

My rabbit appeared on the spot he was pointing at.

I jumped back and Midge gasped.

The rabbit twitched its nose.

Tentatively, I reached towards the white furry bundle, not believing it was real.

And snatched my hand back when it turned into a black, wicked-toothed rat. I hate bloody rats.

Then it was gone and Mycroft was wearing a *'so what d'you think of that, Smartarse?'* smile.

I blinked my eyes at the faded illusion, but refrained from asking him how he'd performed the trick. Nobody likes a show-off. Besides, I wanted my jarred thoughts to settle.

'Magic of a sort,' Mycroft intoned depreciatingly. 'A trivial example of the will's power.'

He pointed his stick at a space between two down-beams of light to my left and a narrow table appeared, on it a bottle of wine and an empty glass. As we watched, the bottle lifted, tilted and poured red liquid into the glass.

In my astonishment I turned to Midge and her face was full of awed delight, like that kid's in *Close Encounters*. The sheer gullible innocence of her expression made me want to grab her and run fast from that dark, pointed room where the aroma of incense was now tainted with a faint corruption. My mind was concentrated on flight, and when I returned my gaze to the table and the wine its image was wavery, its lines softened. But the sight steadied, became solid once more.

'You may drink,' Mycroft offered very casually. 'You'll enjoy the taste, I promise.'

'No thanks,' I said, and he lowered the cane, the image quickly dissolving to nothing.

I knew what he was doing, but not how: I'd always assumed that hypnotists had to tell you verbally what they wanted you to see or do, or how you should react. Nevertheless, I was certain that what we'd witnessed hadn't existed outside our own imaginations.

I was searching for my next quip when Mycroft made the light beams bend.

The puddled circles of brightness started moving inwards quite slowly, the two in front touching the Synergist's feet while the two behind crept up the chair legs. He'd inverted the cane so that the tip was aimed at his own face, and that's what the dust-filled rays were travelling towards, bent like jointed drainpipes about four feet from the floor, their slopes gradually becoming more acute until right-angled to the down-beam. Mycroft's head was spotlighted from the front and behind, and his skin glowed with the attention.

I sensed more in Mycroft at that moment than I ever had before.

Energy, vibrancy – whatever that invisible vigour can be called – seemed to dance across his cheeks as tiny sparks of static, and his eyes, fixed on mine, were crystalline and dazzling, multi-faceted pupils sparkling back light. The deep fissures on his face I'd observed outside in the corridor were gone, bathed away by the sunny glare, each plane of his skull reflecting a different light, some shiny brilliant, others more subdued but never dull. No shadows there, his features merged, nothing prominent, nose levelled with lips, forehead levelled with eye sockets; a simple mask whose form depended on degrees of reflected light. Even his hair effulged silver.

It was a sight to make you gulp.

For a briefest instant, his whole head flared – or appeared to – a spectrum aura radiating outwards, expanding until the triangular room was filled with its variegation, driving away the blackness and forcing me and Midge to shield our eyes.

But not before we'd both perceived other worlds inside those subtle and lifting rainbow colours, floating planets that resembled body cells, stars and suns that shone green, blue, the deepest mauve, shapes that were sometimes human and sometimes vast expanses of protoplasmic masses, a coagulation of life-forces. We experienced the lonely darkness of infinite space, which was the pitch umbra of time itself, both casts of the same non-entity; we felt huge tides of shifting emotions sweeping through those gossamer galaxies, shaping destinies and creating forces that would become rock and flesh and more emotion, emotion being the creative energy that bred with itself, the source of everything, the progenitor of all we knew and all we didn't know.

And at the centre of this revelation we saw a whiteness that would have seared our eyes had it been real; and it was this, not the brightness inside the room, that caused us to cover our faces.

But all this was only a glimpse, no more than that. A glimpse allowed by Mycroft.

We cowered, and the vision was gone.

Darkness came back with the smell of foul incense.

I shook my head dazedly, more wearied than alarmed;

there was a peculiar sensation in my stomach, as if there were a shining down there, something alight and warming my veins. The heat surged into my limbs, to my fingertips and toes, then vanished, dissipated through them.

I shifted over to Midge, not sure I wanted to stand just yet. Mycroft, returned to normal self, the light beams rigid posts once more, watched impassively, an entomologist studying a specimen beetle who struggled with a pin stuck in the shell of its back.

'Midge? Midge, are you okay?'

Her hands were still held to her face, and I gently pulled them away. She blinked, seemed not to recognise me, and I caught sight of the white light still twinkling in her pupils, but distant, diminishing, finally snuffing out. She looked past me, at Mycroft, and her smile was tentative, unsure.

I turned and his visage remained impassive.

'What was it?' Midge asked in a small breathless voice.

I expected a profound answer from the Synergist, but he only smiled enigmatically.

'Yeah, I'd like to know too,' I said.

'You were spectators to the mysteries.'

Pretty profound.

'That doesn't tell us much.'

'What do you feel you saw?'

It was Midge who replied. 'I felt I was witnessing the source of all things, but it was incomplete, only a fragment.'

He nodded slowly (and a little too sagely, I thought, like it was part of the show). 'A *vision* only of a glimmer. Nothing more than that. Your imagination rendered the truth into a vision your mind could perceive – but only just. At such moments sight can be as useless as words, imagination as inadequate as reason. Even dreams can barely sense the Unity.'

Whatever, it had given me a headache. 'A nice display, Mycroft, but what was it for? To impress us?'

'Perhaps.'

'We're impressed. Now can we leave?'

'You let us see your power,' said Midge, leaning forward eagerly.

'I revealed a channel to power, one that courses through my own body and mind,' Mycroft replied. 'There are other . . . stronger channels around us that can be sought and found. Access points, conduits – call them what you will. They can be used . . .'

He suddenly clammed up and avoided our eyes. I think he'd been getting carried away by his own genius.

'I don't understand what you want from us,' I persisted. 'We're not interested in becoming Synergists, or anything like this . . .'

'I think your partner is,' he came back, mysterious as ever.

'Find them for me again,' Midge said to him. 'Let them speak to me. Let Mike hear for himself.'

We both knew whom she meant.

I touched her hand. 'This is madness. Can't you see what he's doing? Thought projection, mind manipulation, plain old-fashioned hypnotism – it's all part of the same thing. Nothing really happened. Mycroft is *making* us see all these things, they're not real –'

'Their presence is in the room,' interrupted Mycroft. 'I can sense them, and so can you.' He was addressing Midge.

'Yes,' she said simply.

'They've more to tell you.'

She nodded.

'They want you to listen.'

She nodded again, and her eyes closed.

And now I could feel something else inside that room. But I wasn't sure if it was because Mycroft wanted me to.

'They're speaking,' said Midge in a hushed voice.

'I can't hear anything.' My own voice was a whisper.

A breeze stirred around us.

'They're faint, but they're here.' Midge opened her eyes again.

I noticed Mycroft's were boring into hers. Then he turned his attention to me and his pupils were like tiny black holes, bottomless but not empty.

There was a shadow behind him. Grey and wispy, and moving forward. Another behind that one, appearing just beyond his left shoulder. Both taking on shimmering form.

Voices, an eternity away. So faint. From another dimension. Yet not voices at all. Thoughts that pressed into ours.

'Father?' said Midge.

One of the flimsy clouds at Mycroft's shoulder shifted as if stirred by an air current. And the thought in my mind answered her.

The breeze became a gust.

'Show Mike that you're really here.' It was a plea from Midge.

The nebula took on more form: a vaporous head, a line of a shoulder. It became almost liquid, rippling as features shaped themselves. Those features slowly grew familiar to me, although they remained wavery and indistinct.

A word insinuated itself into my mind:

'. . . *Trust* . . .'

But I didn't want to trust, because it was telling me to put my faith in Mycroft, this hazy spirit of Midge's dead father was telling me to believe in the Synergist, and I didn't want to because I *knew* he was a charlatan, that he had a purpose for Midge, but I didn't know what that purpose was, and I was going to resist, *resist*, I was going . . .

My incredulous gaze was drawn to the second fluid shape hovering there by Mycroft's other shoulder and it, too, was familiar, a face from photographs shown to me by Midge many times in the past, and she, this ghost of a woman, told me the same:

'. . . trust . . . in . . . him . . .'

Midge was on her knees, reaching towards them, her upturned face fresh with its own glow despite the surrounding dimness, and I held her back, one arm around her shoulder, my other hand clenching her wrist; but still she shuffled forward, and it was towards Mycroft that she moved, on her knees, a cripple towards a faith healer, a follower towards her high priest.

For one fleeting moment his concealing mask fell away, his resolve failing as he indulged in the pleasure of triumph.

I caught that jubilant glint and something clicked inside my head, like a fingernail tapping on the window of my brain, warning me to accept none of this. These ghosts were just vapours, with no form and no thoughts.

'It's a trick!' I yelled at Midge, dragging her down so that we both sprawled at Mycroft's feet. 'That isn't your parents! He's making us see them!'

She cried aloud, refuting my words, struggling against me.

The gust had steadily risen to a gale, ruffling our clothes, dispersing the mists so that they were spread thinly, eventually to be whipped into nothing.

Mycroft looked around as if startled, and that puzzled me. I wondered what new game he was playing. He suddenly seemed as confused as me. The Synergist half rose, but the wind tore at him so that he stumbled back. He raised the cane to beat at the storm, but then his eyes caught mine.

On another occasion I might have laughed, seeing his mouth drop open the way it did. Right then, though, the situation wasn't conducive to humour. He was staring disbelievingly at me and I didn't understand why.

Until I became conscious of the cloud dribbling from my mouth like cigarette smoke.

It came from my fingers too, snaking out in tendrils, curling into the air to be torn away by the wind that now howled, drawn from me into the room. It was as if my innards were burning and my mouth and fingertips were the points through which the smoke could escape; yet there was no pain, only a feathery lightness inside me.

The mist billowed into the room, more and more extracted from me so that it gathered force, revolved in the air like a miniature whirlwind, with us at its centre.

And in it, there were other voices.

They may have been as those before, sounds in our minds alone, but they *seemed* to come from around us. These had nothing to do with Mycroft, because he was cowering behind his cane as if it were a shield.

When the voices became coherent their message was different:

'. . . *Leave this place . . . leave this house . . .*'

Two voices, two mental sounds; and they howled together with the wind.

Midge watched the storming mists and her face was sodden with tears.

Her voice was like a child's, a five-year-old's: 'Mummy . . . Daddy . . .'

I was scared shitless.

'Mum*eeee* . . . Dadd*eeee* . . .!'

Now she looked like a child.

I clambered to my feet, relieved at least that the cloudy flow had stopped trailing from me. Midge's eyes were wide and imploring. Mycroft was still crouching on the floor, his eyes wide too, but with fear. That suited me fine.

'Come on, Midge.' I reached for her.

She focused on me instantly. 'Yes,' she cried. 'Yes!'

As she rose, so the winds quickly died, and the vapours were soon drifting, then hanging, in the air. They began to dissolve.

I didn't wait any longer. I dragged Midge to the door, scraping my back as we entered the squared section of the sloping wall. I yanked the door open and there were Kinsella and Bone Man waiting, a couple of other Synergists with them. They looked anxious enough.

I bunched my fist. 'Keep away from us! Just fucking keep *away*!'

Kinsella looked uncertain, but he had the muscle. He began crowding me.

'No!' came Mycroft's voice from within the pyramid room. 'Not here! Let them go.' Then weaker: 'Let them go . . .'

We went. We went like bats out of hell

FLIGHT

That sloping field to the woods might not have seemed so steep on the descent, but going up was different: I had the feeling we were climbing a down-escalator. My thigh muscles were soon aching, the weight of Midge clinging to me making the ascent even more awkward. The first line of trees seemed a long way off.

But we'd been frightened, and there's nothing like a good scare to get the adrenalin pumping. Our flight may have lacked style, but it wasn't short of effort.

Midge stumbled once, about halfway up the incline, and as I hauled her to her feet again I glanced back at the house. It stood as a huge monolith, brooding grey and tomb-cold; it looked about ready to uproot and lumber after us. Although I couldn't see into those dark window eyes, I knew the Synergists were watching from them.

Midge was already breathing hard and there was a fragility about her that was worrying.

'What . . . what happened in there, Mike?' she managed to gasp.

'Mycroft,' was all I said.

Gripping her elbow, I pulled her onwards, keeping her upright and moving, keen to be under cover, away from those eyes. Progress seemed bad-dream slow, as though mud was sucking our feet; yet the soil beneath the grass was summer-dry and firm. Eventually I had to slip an arm around Midge's waist and support her against my hip to keep her going.

The light was poor, the sun no more than a florid dome on the horizon. Night was sinking in. And the forest would soon be a dark place.

Without stopping, I twisted my head to look behind us again, and maybe I was expecting Synergists (the initiates – that's what they really were) to be pouring from their Temple, giving chase; no figures were loping up the hill after us, though, and the house was still and grave as before. So why the hell did I feel *someone* breathing down our necks?

We made it to the trees, running as if to a Vangelis soundtrack, motion dreary slow, exertion exaggerated. But we were finally there and the relief was immediate, a burden lifted, a rubber band snapped. I told myself the reviving coolness of the forest was responsible, but I sensed there was more to it than that. We were out of sight of the house.

Midge leaned against me, arms limply going around my neck, her chest heaving as she struggled to regain her breath. I kissed the top of her head, welcoming her back, sinking a hand into her hair and keeping her close. I gave her time to recover, letting her calm herself, reassuring her with whispers. But I didn't want to wait there too long.

The dusk was fast becoming threatening, the shadows between trees concealing. Branches above us were like contorted arms, agitated by our intrusion, some reaching down as if ready to snag us should we pass within reach; nearby foliage rippled as something slithered beneath its sprawl. There were other eyes inside this forest, and these were wary, uneasy at our presence.

'We'd better keep moving,' I said to Midge, stroking her cheek with the back of my finger, 'before it gets too dark to find our way home.'

'I need to understand, Mike. I need to know what's happened to us, what happened there inside the Temple.'

'We'll talk as we go.'

She held on to me.

'Forgive me for the way I've acted over the last few days,' she said quietly. 'I can't explain why, or what I was thinking – why I blamed you for so much.'

'It isn't your fault. I think . . . I think other influences have been involved. Look, I don't know, this is all so weird, everything that's happened since we came to Gramarye has been crazy, and somehow we've accepted it – or let's say, not questioned the craziness too much. It's not your fault, Midge, but it is something to do with you. You and the cottage.'

I led her away, taking her by the hand as if she were an infant, and I talked as we went, telling her about the picture she'd painted for the storybook years before – *the one her own mind had not let her remember* – how Gramarye had been part of that illustration long before she'd ever set eyes on the place, that it had obviously already existed somewhere inside her, locked away in her subconscious, a precognition of something or somewhere that would eventually *be*. I reminded her that it was she who had spotted the ad for Gramarye in the newspaper – had ringed that one alone, ignoring any others. And the association, the *union*, was sealed as soon as she arrived there. It was meant to be! Flora Chaldean's solicitor had told me of the instructions the old lady had left with him before she'd died, details of the type of person who should be allowed to buy and live in Gramarye. Someone young, someone sensitive, someone whose decency was plainly evident. Someone '*special*'. Those were the requirements and no wonder the aged solicitor had shown such keen interest in her.

'The cottage was meant for someone like you, Midge.' I pushed away branches blocking our path. 'Don't ask me why, I can't give you any sensible answers. All I can guess is that there's something inside you that's attuned to whatever magic there is in Gramarye.'

She pulled me to a halt.

'Magic?'

I shrugged. 'Yeah, I'm embarrassed. But what else can I call it? Remember the bird with the broken wing? We kidded ourselves that it couldn't have been as badly hurt as we'd thought when we found it flying around the kitchen the next day. And all those other little things. The flowers that sprang up, the animals and birds that flocked around the door. That isn't *normal* – we just adjusted ourselves to make it seem that way. Maybe some kind of relationship with the wildlife could have been built up after a few years – but right away?'

I started walking again and she hurried to keep up.

'The cottage itself. Look at all those things that were wrong with it – the warped doors, rotted wood, the cracked lintel! O'Malley didn't fix those things. They fixed themselves, for Chrissake! Because of you!'

My voice reverberated around the forest. I stopped again to look at her.

'And, yeah, my arm. We thought Mycroft had healed the burns, but now I don't think it was him at all. Sure, he's got some kind of power – we've just had a demonstration of that. But that's from his head, it's what he makes people believe! He convinced me my arm didn't hurt any more – maybe that liquid he used helped somehow – and something got the better of my scepticism. Shit, who wants to hurt if they don't have to? But my guess is that you were the one who really *healed* it. No – you *and* Gramarye. You're a goddam team! Jesus, no wonder Mycroft was interested in you! What a great little catch for his Synergist movement. Human will and Divine Power – you're a living example.'

She was watching me and shaking her head, but I could tell by her eyes that she believed what I was saying. A bird fluttered from a tree ahead of us and we turned to watch nervously. A section of leaves had been left swaying and we stood there until they'd steadied themselves. The forest became still once more and we noticed the gloom was weighing heavier.

'Are we on the right path?' I asked Midge, looking every-which-way.

For a moment she was uncertain; then she nodded. 'There should be a branch-off soon. We take the right-hand fork.'

'If you say so,' I said grimly.

We moved on, keeping to a fast walk, ears and eyes

open. Sometimes there's a hush in a forest when the light's on dimmer that's almost church-like, where a cough or even a whisper seems irreverently loud; I kept my voice low, not wishing to disturb anyone.

'I can't help wondering what went on between old Flora and Mycroft, why she went to the trouble of putting that clause in her will barring him from ever taking possession of Gramarye. What difference would it have made to her once she was gone? And why the hell did he lie to us about never having been there unless he had something to do with her death?'

'You really think they tried to frighten her into selling?'

'I think they succeeded in frightening her so much it killed her. We've seen for ourselves what Mycroft's mental powers are capable of. Making rabbits and rats appear out of thin air is nothing to him. Wine? I bet I could've drunk the stuff without realising it was an illusion. And making us believe he could bend light beams. He's ace, Midge, a *numero uno* illusionist. I hate to consider what he might have made that poor old lady imagine. A tiger on the doorstep? The kitchen on fire around her? Her own heart crumbling to dust inside her chest? He wouldn't have had to lay a finger on her.'

'I don't believe she was that helpless, Mike.'

'Matter of fact, neither do I. She'd have put up quite a struggle, but then her age was against her. Maybe her old heart just gave up of its own accord.'

We'd reached the fork in the track and I stepped aside to let Midge take the lead. 'It's up to you, Chingachgook. You've got the nose for direction. You sure it's right?'

'If we don't come across a fallen cedar on the path within two minutes then you'll know I got it wrong.'

'I remember. It's lying head-down in a gulley.'

'That's the one.'

She went ahead of me and I followed her slim form through the forest, our footsteps never slackening for a moment, both of us eager to be out in the open as soon as possible. I didn't like the feel of the woods and the way Midge constantly looked around her instead of straight at the path in front; neither did she. And although we'd left the Synergists far behind, the prickly sensation of being followed was still with me.

Midge pointed and I saw the dead tree about a hundred yards further along. We broke into a trot as though the barrier were a goal to be reached, and our footfalls were mushy-loud in the stillness. I caught sight of a tawny owl, perched high on a branch and watching us with aloof interest, lids occasionally descending like camera shutters over the big round eyes as if recording the event.

Midge collapsed against the rough bark of the tree and I collapsed against her.

'Best we keep going,' I advised, breathing heavy and slumping onto the trunk.

She ran her hands down her face, continuing down her neck. 'Was it them, Mike? Or was that just Mycroft's trickery too? Their voices . . . they sounded so much like . . .'

I hesitated before answering. 'I'm pretty sure it began as a fake. But later on . . . hell, I don't know what happened later on.'

'At the end it *was* my parents. I *know* it was them! Their warning brought me to my senses. Everything I'd believed about Mycroft just fell away . . .'

I slid over the tree trunk and extended an arm back for her. 'There's too much to think about for now, Midge. Let's just get back to the cottage while we can still see our way.'

She scrambled over and took time to kiss my neck before we hurried on. I don't think I'd have found my way back without her, the trail was becoming so dim; but she kept on, only occasionally stopping to examine a choice of direction or a particular landmark (a cluster of red toadstools beneath another, virtually hollowed, fallen tree was the only one I recognised). My back was damp with sweat and a stiffness was developing in my thighs; ahead of me, Midge was beginning to falter, her steps losing rhythm.

Our nervousness hadn't abated either, and when a huge white-streaked shape blundered across the path we both nearly jumped out of our skins. The badger was equally alarmed and quickly scooted into the bushes on the other side of the track; we watched and heard the animal's progress as he bludgeoned his way through the undergrowth, foliage shaking violently as he went.

Further along I tripped over a creeper or root that I hadn't noticed Midge hop over, going down heavily and sprawling on the earth. I gasped in air as she knelt beside me, her hand gripping me beneath an arm in an effort to lift. I rose unsteadily and stood there, bent like an old man, one hand on my knee, the other on Midge's shoulder.

'How much further?' I asked in between laboured intakes of breath.

Her features weren't clear, so shaded had they become, and she sounded almost as breathless as me. 'It can't be too far – we've come a long way.'

'Yeah, about a hundred miles. You ok –?'

The shadow I saw as I straightened was nothing more than a tall bush shaped like a cowled figure, lurking behind a tree. The sighing I heard was nothing more than a newly born breeze passing through the leaves. The thumping in my chest was nothing more than my own heartbeat.

'Christ, I've got the jitters,' I admitted.

Her voice was soft. 'Are we dreaming all this?'

'My bruised knees say no. My head's not so sure.'

Now arm in arm, squeezed together by the narrow track, we carried on the journey, not caring that movement was awkward in this manner, needing the closeness for mutual encouragement and to keep the wood spooks away. Darkness had settled into the forest like smoke in a lung.

We hobbled, we held each other steady, we moved as fast as we could, and soon, thank God, we saw gaps in the trees ahead of us, the lighter greys of open space. Relief gave strength to wearying limbs and we broke into a jog once more, hurrying, running, hand in hand, with me shouting my elation and Midge laughing at my shouting.

We burst from the wood like popped peas.

Dusk had practically thickened into night, but at least the air was several shades lighter than under the cover of trees. We sprinted towards Gramarye, eager to be behind locked windows and bolted doors, and it was only when we drew closer that we began to realise something was wrong, that what we saw in the dimness wasn't making any sense. We slowed. We walked. We looked at Gramarye in dismay.

My foot kicked something soft lying in the grass and I stopped when I saw the dead rabbit, small, no more than a baby, a rictal smile of terror fixed to its tiny face. A choker of blood stained its neck. Midge's fingers stiffened in mine and I saw the other slumped form that she'd discovered. This rabbit was larger than the one at our feet, maybe the mother, and its body was raked from head to tail, the fur stiffened with drying blood.

We didn't speak. We guessed a fox might have killed them, but we didn't put the thought into words. Around us there were other slumped bodies. We walked on, our steps cautious.

And couldn't comprehend Gramarye's transformation.

The walls, reduced to grey in the ailing light, showed only in odd patches.

Black was the dominant colour now.

And still we couldn't understand.

Until we saw the walls were swollen with life.

Black, furry life.

Wings stretching and retracting.

Bodies, grossly bigger than before, pulsating as the creatures breathed.

We could only stare numbly at the clinging bats engulfing Gramarye.

HOME AGAIN

For a while we stood and gawked, our flesh creeping and our senses not quite together. How could there be so many? They couldn't *all* have been from our loft, many of them had to have come from other places. Maybe it was a bat convention. And how could they have grown to monster size? Most serious of all: what was their intent? These were questions we asked ourselves, not each other – we didn't want our voices to disturb their rest period.

The inclination, you'll understand, was to make for the road, jump in the car, and get away from that bat-coated place as fast as possible. The only problem was that the car keys were inside the cottage where I'd left them earlier, and when I mentioned that to Midge (in a very low voice) her body kind of sagged.

'You go sit in the car,' I told her in a whisper.

Even as I spoke, though, two bats detached themselves from the wall and fluttered around to the other side of the building. The moon was up, unclouded but showing only a profile, and in that clean, eerie light the size of the bats' wingspans froze me. We found ourselves crouching, ready to head back into the forest.

'Get going, Midge,' I urged again.

'No, Mike,' she whispered. 'I'm staying with you; we'll get the keys together.'

'That's stupid.'

'I won't let you go in alone!'

Her voice was so forceful, although hushed, that my shoulders jerked upwards and my neck sank in.

I drew in a breath and squeezed her hand. 'Okay, okay. But if they get busy I want you to head straight for the car without waiting for me.'

'What will you do?'

'I'll be ahead of you.'

She returned the squeeze, but couldn't manage a smile.

'Let's skirt around and try the kitchen door,' I suggested. 'Maybe there won't be so many down there.'

Her breathing was fast and shallow as she summoned the nerve to follow me and it wasn't just the moonlight that gave her face such an unnatural pallor. My own skin tones probably matched hers pretty well at that moment.

We slunk away slowly, bodies bent, not wanting to draw the slightest attention to ourselves. It seemed to me that a whole section of wall rippled, the movement black, a wave in an oil slick. We kept going, retreating, then moving towards the embankment. Everything was still and somehow unearthly around us, the dark mass of brooding forest behind, while in front was the bizarre spectacle of the smothered cottage, wearing bats like a tattered hood. Half-moonlight revealed more bodies prone in the grass, the sickening aftermath of the rabbits' before-bed gambol.

We reached the short but steep slope and I quietly slid down, reaching back to help Midge once I was on the flat again. She fell into my arms and stayed there for a few moments, reluctant to leave them. The grey strip that was the garden path leading to the gate beckoned invitingly, the road beyond representing manmade normalcy, a concrete reality, and the temptation to hoof it was strong; but the village was a long way off and the road ran through miles of woodland. Better to take the car.

I'd been right about the bats on this side: they clung mostly to the upper reaches, a dark thatch that twitched and bristled with life. Cautiously, eyes ever upwards, I led Midge towards the kitchen door.

A bat fluttered away from the wall above us. Then another followed. Another.

The urge to rush for the door was almost overwhelming, but the thought of alarming them *all* into flight held us in check.

Take it easy, I kept telling myself. They're only flying mammals, not a vampire among them.

Tell that to the bunnies, came my own wicked reply.

The door was on the latch and my hand was trembling when I stretched to press the catch. I thumbed it down as smoothly as I could, but the click still made me grit my teeth; I expected fangs to puncture my neck at any second.

I pushed the door and the smell of must and rot wafted out as a forewarning that things weren't quite so well inside Gramarye, either; as I widened the gap, the waiting blackness was as welcoming as the stench. If shadows could grin, then they'd have been beaming their darkest right then.

The interior was menacing, and yet . . . and yet it was somehow *alluring*. I felt as I had as a kid, standing there at the first door of the funfair ghost house; scared, but I'd paid my money and I was sure as shit going *in*.

I almost tripped over something on the doorstep. Committed to stepping in, I didn't stop to investigate. I went through, pulling Midge with me, and immediately turned to scrabble for the light switch. I brushed it down and, momentarily blinded, reached back to slam the door shut. Midge caught my arm before I did so.

I blinked questioningly at her, anxious to set the barricade between *them* and *us*; she was staring at the doorstep.

Rumbo was lying there, his furry little body discoloured with blood, his jaws locked open in shock. His eyes were corpse's slits.

BREAK IN

We laid him on the kitchen table, Midge weeping openly, me choking back tears. I hadn't realised 'til then how fond of Rumbo I'd become.

The marks on his back were vicious; deep, bloodied grooves running the length of his back where the bats – more than one had done this to him – had raked him. The wounds around his throat were even deeper, but I wondered if fear alone hadn't been the ultimate assassin. He was bald of fur in parts and one tufty ear had been completely shredded; I think he'd put up one hell of a fight.

Without hope I checked for the slightest beat of a heart, and there was none. His body had not yet turned cold and I stroked him, talking softly all the time, as if encouraging his animal spirit to get back inside and loosen up those congealing arteries again.

Rumbo was gone, though, and surprisingly (or maybe not – when it really comes down to it, women are always more realistic than men) it was Midge who first accepted the fact. She took my hands in hers.

'Poor little chump,' I said, unable to shift my gaze from the still bundle.

'What *are* those creatures outside, Mike? They can't be

the same bats that were in the loft. Their size . . . Why did they attack the animals?'

I shrugged, maybe the only answer to insanity. My eyes had blurred over and I didn't want to speak right away in case my voice broke up. So instead I looked around the kitchen, turning my head away from Midge before blinking. It wasn't grief that I was hiding from her – we'd shared enough of that in our time together and tears had never been an embarrassment: what I didn't want her to see was my fear.

Gramarye's personality had altered. The disease that had been gnawing at its innards since Flora's death had been halted by our arrival, like a cancer checked by a new drug. Decay had stopped, regeneration had begun. Its magic had been renewed.

I was aware of that now, even though a side of me said, *Listen, you're crazy, you're talking about stone and timber, not a living person, not even a mindless organism. An inanimate, insensible pile of bricks, for Chrissake!* But I knew different. Something on the sidelines of all this had my ear, was whispering to me like it had before, instilling the notions, maybe chuckling while it did so. Or maybe this something was in dead earnest, afraid I wouldn't hear. Or understand.

And in truth, the thoughts were so insubstantial, so tenuous, I didn't know myself whether I heard or I imagined. Who was I to judge my own state of mind?

But the idea persisted. It wasn't the structure of Gramarye that was alive, but the *anima* of those who had existed within its fold, absorbed by walls, ceilings, floors, locked in like energy into a battery, so that with time the building took on the semblance of a living thing. Until that life had been corrupted, had been cancered, by other less pure influences. I believed that the degeneration had begun when the Synergists had first visited the cottage.

With Flora's death, so had the power inside Gramarye withered, started to rot. Only our – or, more accurately, Midge's – presence had held the rot, even initiated a rejuvenation. That's what the silent voice told me, that's what I believed. And in part, I was right.

I cleared my throat, then said in a rush: 'Where the hell

did I leave the keys?' 'Keys' came out somewhat strangulated and Midge clasped my hands more tightly.

'Perhaps upstairs. God, it's so cold in here.'

As if for effect, she gave a small shiver. Yet I was clammy hot. The thought occurred that we were experiencing Gramarye's fever.

A rending crash from next door brought Midge into my arms and I barely heard her cry above the follow-up tumble of masonry. A dust cloud drifted through into our part of the kitchen. We guessed what had happened but, in the way you sniff milk you know has gone off, we edged towards the opening to see for ourselves. We loitered in the doorway, swiping away unsettled dust before us.

The lintel had finally thrown in its hand and crashed down onto the range, a serious section of brickwork falling after the halved stone. The reverberations hung in the air with the powdery dirt, and the sooty wound in the chimney breast, gaping and jagged, gave a glimpse of Gramarye's dark core, a rent in stone flesh that revealed its black inner substance.

'*No, it isn't true, it isn't like that!*' wailed Midge, and I understood the image had been the same for her. The misery and rejection on her face was the same as if she'd discovered her favourite uncle was a child-molester.

I pulled her away, anxious to be out of there, as far away from the cottage as possible and in the fastest time. We'd fled the Synergist Temple only to find there was no refuge for us here; the cottage had become allied to the grey house, a collaborator in whatever ill-cause was possessing that maleficent place. Confused or crazed, I didn't know which I was at that point; all I *was* sure of was that it was the open road for me.

We could hear the boards creaking beneath the carpet as we hurried upstairs, one cracking clear and loud so that I thought my foot would sink right through; the carpet itself prevented that and we kept going, with Midge careful to avoid the particular step. I flicked on switches as we went and the lights seemed to stutter before gaining their full glow. Into the round room, where the malodour was almost gangrenous and the walls were dribbling wet. I didn't even bother to stop and think about it.

The car keys were lying on the coffee table and I made a grab for them. 'Get anything you need from the bedroom, Midge, and be quick about it. I don't want to stay a minute longer than necessary.'

She didn't reply, just took to her heels and disappeared into the bedroom, leaving me a moment to look around. I wasn't too happy about the black mould that had formed between the top of the walls and the ceiling, the fungus spreading downwards in thick spotty patches as if Midge had splattered the walls with her thickest paint brush. Even more peculiar was the bumpiness of the carpet: the floorboards underneath had warped, the ends risen in places, giving the effect of moles trying to break through but thwarted by the thick surface layer.

'*Mike!*'

It took me no time at all to reach the bedroom.

'Oh no –'

Where there had once been a hairline split in the wall, there was now a one-inch furrow running from floor to ceiling. I imagined I could see the night peering through from the other side.

'Forget about packing,' I told Midge. 'We're getting out right now before this place falls apart.'

She was hesitant. There was a turmoil going on inside her that was almost visible. I could appreciate her dismay, her bewilderment; my only wonder was that she wasn't totally traumatised. Midge's dream had become a nightmare, everything that had happened here illogical and disconcerting (to say the least). An idyll had been corrupted by forces that neither of us understood – and frankly, as far as I was concerned, didn't want to understand. It was worse for her, because she was aware that she had a role in this disorder of things, but she had no idea what that role was. I'd had a glimmer, and I'd tried to convey that to her, but when it came down to it, what did I know about anything? The only thing that *was* obvious was that Gramarye was no longer a safe place to hang around in.

I was about to go to Midge and drag her out of the bedroom – drag her from her own introspection – when her eyes widened and she pointed towards the window.

Headlight beams were gliding to a stop on the other side of the garden fence. More headlights from behind lit up the yellow Citroën.

'Bastards,' I muttered.

Grabbing Midge by the wrist, I stomped out into the hallway.

'What are you going to do?' She clung to me as I snatched up the telephone receiver, and her trembling ran through me as though I were touching a tuning fork.

'It's about time the police got involved in all this. I don't know what the fuck I'm gonna tell 'em, but I'll think of something. Holding you against your will might do for a starter.'

'But that's not true.'

'So I'll lie a little. We just need the police here.'

Static leapt out of the earpiece like a gremlin up to mischief.

I cursed and held the receiver away as I dialled. More terrible static, and then a whining screech, the kind of sound we might all hear one day when the Bomb has dropped and line meltdown has started as we ring to check on loved ones.

'Shit!' I said again (times of pressure, my language gets pretty poor). I jiggled the cradle contacts until the less strident interference returned, then re-dialled. Same sound, ear-piercing sharp.

We both winced and I slammed down the receiver. 'Out through this way,' I shouted, already reaching for the door. 'We'll hide in the forest – they'll never find us there.'

'No, Mike. We're safer inside Gramarye.'

I stared at her incredulously. 'Are you kidding? Can't you see what's happening to this place? This is condemned property we're standing in.'

'I don't think we'll be harmed here.'

'Flora Chaldean probably felt the same. Look, I don't know what Mycroft and his loonies have in mind, but I think club membership is now out as far as we're concerned. And Mycroft let us come here because that's where he wants us. God knows why, but I'm sure he's got his reasons. So let's get, come on!'

I opened the door, and dislodged bats beat against my head and raised arms before skittering off into the gloom. In the chill of the moment I'd forgotten about them. I waited for a mass launch. None came, but my relief was only momentary.

Lights were emerging from the woods.

I was back inside and locking the door in a flash. 'They followed us through the forest too.'

Midge was wearing a stupefied expression.

'He split his forces, sent some by road, the others through the forest after us. Seems I was right – he wants us trapped inside the cottage.'

Understanding appeared to sink in slowly; then she nodded her head and was suddenly very calm, no longer trembling.

'Christ, the front door! We didn't lock it!' I lost my footing at the bend of the stairs in my haste to get down to the kitchen and only managed to control my tumble by sticking my flattened hands against either wall. I slid some of the way, but was up and running by the time I reached the bottom. I shot both door bolts, top and bottom, and rested my forehead against the wood, catching my breath.

It was several moments before I plucked up the nerve to peek out of the window. The car lights had been doused and I could just make out moonlight bouncing off the metal tops beyond the fence. No people out there, no Synergists. As far as I could tell.

'Midge!' I called back up the stairs. 'Find Sixsmythe's number and call him – we might get lucky this time.'

I drew the kitchen curtains, not wanting *them* to see in if they were out there. As I passed the table on my way to the stairs, I couldn't help touching the furry heap lying there. It wasn't a conscious gesture, and certainly not dwelt upon; a passing contact, no more than that. Could be it was a token of affection, a regret that Rumbo was gone. Maybe a private 'so long, buddy'.

Then I was pounding stairs, expecting to find Midge dialling or at least leafing through the local directory. The hallway was empty.

She was in the round room, silhouetted by the half-moon

314

brightness, and she was watching the gathering outside.

'Midge, why didn't you call –'

'He can't help us, Mike.'

'Sixsmythe? He's the only contact we've got around here.'

'He wouldn't know how to help. It's too late anyway.'

I followed her gaze and didn't like what I saw. No, I didn't like it at all.

Mycroft and his motley mob were in the open, their shapes distinct and black against the moon-drenched grass. They stood apart, separate entities, spread like stone menhirs and just as still. Those who had arrived from the forest had switched off their flashlights and although each was isolated, occupying his or her own space, they were a pack, united with their Synergist leader in some mysterious cause that terrified me.

They watched the cottage as we watched them.

I stood closer to Midge and she said quietly, 'They want us to die.'

That's how she put it. Not 'They want to kill us,' but 'They want us to die,' as if they'd have no part in the act, they wouldn't bloody their own hands.

'That's a bit drastic.' If my scorn was reassuring to her it didn't ease my own concern. 'They can't go around murdering people just because they like the look of a house. There's laws against that kind of gazumping.'

'They wanted Flora to die and she did.'

So much for humour.

'She had a heart attack. Okay, so maybe they frightened her enough to cause it, but she was an old lady; how they gonna scare us that much?'

'Weren't you frightened inside their Temple, inside that terrible room? Weren't you scared in the forest?'

'Sure. But we're on home base now – let's see what Mycroft can do here.'

You know, sometimes bravado is the worst thing for tempting fate. What could he do? Plenty, and we were about to find out.

It didn't happen immediately. Seconds ticked by and

nobody and nothing seemed to be moving – there wasn't even a drifting cloud in the sky. And it was quiet, so graveyard quiet. Even the floorboards had stopped groaning. The loudest thing was the stench in the air.

I wanted to step away from the window – we weren't too close, not near enough for the Synergists to see us – but somehow I was rooted to the spot. Fascinated, you see, morbidly curious as to what (or was *not*) going on outside. Even breathing was a bit of a chore, my skin feeling too tightly wrapped around my chest. We stared out and they stared in.

Then the nearest figure raised an arm, in his hand a long cane.

That's when hell let loose.

The first sound was a muffled roar like an underwater explosion, a sort of deep *whoosh* which disintegrated into an agitated irregular drumming. For a moment the moon was lost and I assumed a cloud had passed over; but light patterns returned quickly when the blackness above broke up.

The bats had risen as a whole and were swarming over the cottage, a mass of dark, erratic motion.

They flew higher, over the moon, as if heading for the stars, the frantic beat of their wings growing distant. We moved closer to the windows, craning our heads upwards, because the spectacle was incredible, subjugating even dread.

We lost sight of them. We lost sound of them. But for no more than a few seconds.

The drumming returned, a devil's tattoo, increasing in volume, becoming so loud that the building seemed to judder with its approach. We turned from the windows and looked towards the ceiling, neither of us breathing, neither of us capable of speaking.

The rushing noise centralised, descended to a low rumbling, and our gaze shifted across the room towards the chimney breast.

They swooped out of the fireplace like Hitchcock's birds, storming into the room, filling the air with their screeches and terrible fluttering wings. Midge's scream (God knows, it could have been *mine*) was cut short as glass exploded inwards from behind.

316

We went down in sheer reaction, and it was just as well: bats irrupted through with the glass, bursting in to join the others cycloning around the curved walls.

I felt something land on my back, tiny claws digging in for purchase. As I reached to dislodge the bat, another settled against my neck and stung me with its teeth.

I rolled, grabbing the one at my neck and squashing the other. The feel of small bones crunching beneath me was repugnant, but holding on to the wriggling thing that was opening an account at the blood bank of my throat was even worse. Above me was a turmoil of flapping wings, its draught ruffling my hair; movement in the darkened room was so fast that everything had become a crazy blur. Through it all I could hear Midge screaming.

Two more bats landed on my chest and I beat at them furiously with one hand while the other clenched to crush the bat still nibbling at my neck. Because it was close to my ears I heard the squeals as my grip tightened. I tore the bloodsucker away without experiencing any pain as my own flesh broke, then tossed the feebly struggling body into the mass of others. With both hands I wrenched off the two bats at my chest, their claws and teeth making a mess of my shirt. Even as I threw these into the air, still more landed on my arms and legs.

In the glow from the hallway I caught sight of Midge's writhing body, although so covered in the creatures was she that she resembled a multi-winged horror rising like some hideous beast from the pages of one of those splatter comic-books. She was shrieking and beating at herself in terror, and I crawled towards her, ignoring the bats clinging to my own body.

She fell to her knees again and I beat at those hugging monsters in blind fury, snapping wings and breaking bones with a wildness even these tenacious bastards couldn't withstand.

They fell away. I ripped out two that had become entangled in her hair. I beat them from her shoulders, pulled them from her back. We had to get away from there, but to where? All the rooms had windows. And all the while I struggled, more bats were settling on me, while others were returning to her. I swiped them from the air, but for every one stunned, three more took its space. My own frustrated exertions were wearying me, and the bats' combined weight, insubstantial though it may have been, was gradually bringing me down. Midge and I sank together, bodies enveloped by the black-winged vermin.

We lay close on the floor and the pain wasn't that bad – nips and scratches were all we felt. It was sheer terror that kept us there.

I slumped over Midge in an effort to shield her, although knowing it was no use, the fuckers were going to get us. Just like they got the rabbits. Just like they got Rumbo.

I closed my eyes and waited.

Until the bats were suddenly gone.

THE POWER

The air was empty of them. Their weight had been lifted from our bodies.

We listened to the retreating sound of their wings and we stayed there, faces buried into the bumpy carpet, waiting for the mass *flip-flap* to become distant, waiting for it to disappear completely.

Only when that happened did I raise my head to make sure we were really alone. A weak fluttering nearby caused me to search alarmedly for the source: one of the bats, a wing broken and useless, was rotating on the floor, pushed round and round by the tip of its good wing. Another dark shape across the room flinched feebly. Others, those I'd managed to kill, lay in silent mounds. The smell of them all, those dead, those flown, lingered in the room, combining with the musty dampness and rot; even the breeze cooling in from the broken windows couldn't dispel the corruption.

'Midge.' I eased my weight from her, but she remained inert, face downwards. 'It's over, Midge, they've gone.'

Her back shuddered and I realised she was weeping. I knelt back on my haunches and, with bloodied hands, I drew her up against my chest. By now we were both beyond questions and I could only hold and gently rock her in the way you'd calm a baby.

319

Our clothes were torn, shredded in places; yet although we were patchy with blood neither of us was seriously hurt. Even the wound in my neck only bled a little. As I stroked her hair, Midge's tears seeped into the material of my ragged shirt.

A soft click struck me motionless once more.

The noise had come from the hallway where the light still shone brightly. The click was from the door. The outside door. Impossibly, the key on this side was turning in the lock.

Midge, alerted by my sudden stillness, raised her head. She, too, watched the key.

Which turned completely round, clicking finally into its new position.

The bolt at the foot of the door began to slide, slowly, evenly, drawn back by an invisible hand. The metal bar stopped only when it had reached the end of its run.

Nothing happened immediately.

Then, almost leisurely, the door swung open.

Mycroft stood in the shadows outside.

I moaned and Midge collapsed into me.

He stepped into the light and his smile couldn't have been bettered by Boris Karloff himself. It made me cringe just to see it.

Mycroft strolled into the cottage, thin cane poised before him like a blind man's stick, and although he wore that plain grey suit he was no longer unimpressive. In fact, knowing what I did about him, his very blandness was all the more sinister: it'd assumed a strikingly direful quality. He stopped at the threshold of the round room, countenance in shadow again, light from behind outlining his figure. I heard him draw in a long, deep breath as though he were sucking in all of the room's foul air, filling his chest with the stench.

He'd used the bats to soften us up and now here he was, in person.

A big hand for Mycroft the Magician, illusionist *extraordinaire*. Only the bats had been no illusion – a breeze flowing in from the broken windows and blood staining my ripped clothes told me that. And the door really had unlocked itself – his presence in the room asserted that. I wondered if part of his act was making water boil in car radiators; and if he had such mental powers, then luring us close to his lair that Sunday couldn't have been much of a problem.

Mycroft reached out and flicked on the light before stepping all the way into the room. His smile was no more pleasant.

Others filed in behind him, going to his right and left alternately, keeping near to the curved walls to form a human claw that closed around us. I suppose there must have been a dozen or so of them, the others presumably keeping watch outside, sentinels in the moonlight.

I looked from face to face and they impassively returned my gaze. Even Gillie, who was among them, displayed no feelings, and I expected at least a leer from my old chum Kinsella but he, too, was stony cold.

'Some–' My voice cracked and I had to start again. 'Something we can do for you, Mycroft?'

I didn't think that was bad under the circumstances, but it didn't seem to cheer up anyone, least of all myself.

'Not any more,' he replied, and the idea that we were no longer of any use to him chilled me further. He pointed his cane at Midge. 'She could have helped me, but chose not to. For that, I blame you.' The cane singled me out.

I shook my head in protest. 'We still don't know what's going on. We don't want to fight you, Mycroft, we don't mean to get in the way of your Grand Plan, whatever the hell it is. So how about just leaving us out of this?'

'Unfortunately it's too late for that. You've become an integral part of Gramarye.'

'That's crazy. You want the place? So take it. Make me a reasonable offer. I don't give a shit.' And I meant it; I really didn't.

'*No!*'

That was Midge crying out as she sprang away from me.

'Don't you know why he wants Gramarye, why Flora fought so hard to keep it from him?' she said to me. 'He told us back there in the Temple, don't you remember?'

Again I shook my head, this time blankly.

'Gramarye, or at least the ground it stands on, is a

channel for the power he uses, a supply source of some kind. Don't you see that? Whoever occupies this cottage is the guardian of that power. Like Flora, like the person who lived here before her, and before even *her*. The line is probably endless.'

A month before – no, a *week* before – I'd have laughed at such a suggestion; now I wasn't so sure. It was hard to swallow, but then so was everything else that had happened there. And hadn't I had my own 'insights' about the place recently?

Mycroft seemed amused. 'Finally you're beginning to understand. You can feel the magic that gives life to this earth, makes air so that we may breathe, creates springs that become rivers so that we may drink, provides food to sustain us. Could you really imagine that all we live amongst is one vast accident, that Nature has no design, no driving force? Don't you see there are sources contained within this planet that can never be understood? Sources sought after only by the enlightened through the centuries? Are you foolish enough to think all those legends of old, stories of wizards, of witches, of magic kingdoms, are no more than children's fairy-tales?' He laughed aloud, Karloff at his finest, and there was appreciative murmuring from his henchmen around the room.

'That foolish hag,' Mycroft went on, really getting his teeth into the part, 'prevented me from striding the chasm, from absorbing its potency into my being, stopped me from using the ethereal vitality that leaks from this point in the earth's crust. But she was old and feeble, and soon cast aside.'

I started to giggle then. I couldn't help it. Maybe it was the onset of hysteria, a combination of exhaustion and fear, but I couldn't help thinking that the situation had got out of hand. God knows why, but I kept wondering what good old down-to-earth Bob's reaction to Mycroft's diatribe would have been. Christ, he'd have been high for a week! The more I thought of that, the more I laughed. I fell back, one arm resting against the sofa for support.

But Mycroft didn't like me laughing. He didn't like it one bit. He pointed the cane in my direction again and I suddenly realised he was using it as a wand. *Mycroft the Wizard and his Magic fucking Wand!* Tears rolled from the corners of my eyes I was laughing so much.

Midge stared at me as though I'd finally flipped (I probably had at that point). I wanted her to see the joke but I was guffawing so much I couldn't speak. *Bob's face, listening to the bullshit Mycroft had just come out with.* Too much, too much!

The Synergists gathered around the room were glaring at me. Christ, *they'd* never see the joke!

I buried my face into the soft material of the sofa, my shoulders jerking with the effort of laughing, wanting to ask Mycroft where he kept his long pointed hat and black kaftan, but too choked up to manage the words. I felt the sofa begin to undulate beneath me. Still giggling, I raised my hand in surprise. My outstretched arm was waving up and down with the material's motion.

A pinpoint in the surface frayed, became a hole. Something black wriggled through. Another multi-legged creature followed, popping through and scurrying off. Another and another, becoming a stream of black-shelled bugs.

More holes appeared. More bugs crawled out. More holes. More bugs.

I leapt away and watched in horror as hundreds more – *thousands* more – gnawed their way through the material, the sofa soon turning into a seething mass of shiny black fermentation. They broke off in well-ordered lines, hurrying down the side of the sofa to drop onto the floor and advance towards my outstretched leg.

Then I remembered that ultimately Bob hadn't been so cheerful in this room (his wit had been scared out of him) and my own manic humour drained away. I pulled in my foot as the first bug climbed aboard.

'*Stop it, stop it!*'

Midge was on her feet screaming at Mycroft. He merely smiled back at her.

'You can't use Gramarye this way! It's meant for good, not for your perversions!' Her eyes were blazing, her face screwed up in anger.

'The power contained within this place can be controlled in any way its receiver chooses,' Mycroft replied. 'The old woman could no longer direct its force, she was too weak, made too infirm by her years.'

'You killed her!'

Now he grinned, apparently keen on the idea. 'Yes, yes, I believe I did. I tempted her with the other side, you see, what you and your like might call the dark side of Magic. Her ending was very sudden –' he seemed surprised, then snapped his fingers '– like *that*! One moment alive, the next, dead. She couldn't cope with the revelation, you see, she couldn't accept the blackness inside her own soul. How else could I have revealed such darkness to her if it didn't lurk within herself. Strange how her body corrupted so fast, as if that badness inside swept through her physical being, shrivelled her up like an old prune.' He chuckled at that, unconcerned at the disgust on Midge's face.

The light faded and rose as though somebody had just been electrocuted next door, and Mycroft's poise momentarily wavered. He peered around at the walls, the ceiling, the floor. Then his grin returned.

'Can you feel the surge of kinetic force?' he asked his followers. 'Be receptive, blend your thoughts and absorb its strength. *Fill yourself with its vitality!*'

Most of them closed their eyes, faces strained in concentration. I saw Gillie, standing close to the wall, sway and almost fall backwards. Another woman on the other side of the room moaned aloud. Kinsella continued to watch Midge and me.

Strangely, such was the power of suggestion as Mycroft encouraged the Synergists further, that I also felt a tingling starting in my own spread fingers. The sensation emanated from the floor itself, passing up into my arms and across my shoulders and chest. I suddenly remembered the bugs that had been set to crawl up my leg, yet when I checked, they'd gone, disappeared completely. The sofa contained nothing more than a couple of cushions. The bugs had been another of Mycroft's illusory games.

'I can stop this!' shouted Midge. *'That's why I'm here, why I was chosen!'*

'Ah yes, *you*,' said the Magician slyly. He pointed the cane and Midge toppled backwards. She didn't go down

324

though. She regained her balance and glowered at Mycroft, shoulders bunched forward and fists clenched.

'*I can!*' she yelled, and I loved her for her defiance. I scrambled to my feet.

She stood with her legs apart, rooting herself to the carpet, and slowly raised her hands to her face, unwinding her fingers and bringing them together almost in a praying gesture. Then she twisted her wrists so that her fingers were levelled at Mycroft, and his expression turned anxious. That, at least, was heartening.

Midge was shivering and it looked as if every muscle in her body was tensed, every ounce of strength she possessed directed at Mycroft. I wanted to cry out, to goad her on. She could do it, I knew she could do it! But my cry was only a whisper.

'Zap the fucker, Midge.'

Her teeth were gritted so tight that her face had become a grimacing mask, and her figure was taut, her body like a divining rod into which energy coursed.

'You can do it, Midge!' I called out, still in a strained whisper.

And I was certain she could. She *was* Flora Chaldean's successor, the natural heir to those weird powers whose source was Gramarye and the ground the cottage stood upon. Everything that had happened over these last few months had been directing her towards this critical point. Whatever governs these mystical laws of sorcery and all that entailed had decided she was the one to carry on old Flora's good work, she was the guardian, the keeper of the power, the one who would prevent it from being perverted. In a funny way, I felt proud (although I could have done without the trauma).

'Get the bastard, Midge!'

Her arms were fully extended, palms and fingers flat together. It was as if she were aiming an invisible gun at Mycroft's head and I revelled in his growing discomfort. The tension constricted my throat and I could cheer her on no more. Instead my fists trembled in the air before me. Now she had him, now she'd put an end to his lousy bloody tricks! Her arms were ramrod straight and I could almost see the energy pouring through.

Mycroft's eyes had widened so that the pupils were surrounded by white.

Kinsella was trying to move in and I got ready to tackle him. But he'd stopped dead, unable to move.

Mounting pressure was drumming in my ears.

Midge's fingers opened.

She exhaled squealing air.

And nothing happened.

'Shit!' I shouted, and stamped the floor.

Mycroft was perplexed. Then very happy. He raised his cane and suddenly Midge's feet left the carpet. She floated upwards.

Her body tilted and she screamed my name. She rose, four feet, five feet, rigid as a board and becoming horizontal. She put her arms over her face as the ceiling came closer, and I could only look on in shock, unable to do a thing.

Her body was only inches from the ceiling when he laughed and let her go. She plummeted down and I moved fast to get underneath her, catching her in my arms, both of us crashing to the floor.

We lay there battered and gasping and all I could hear was Mycroft's laughter – his *cackle*. Kinsella and the others were also amused. Except for Gillie: she'd fainted.

We were finished. He'd kill us and probably make it look like a lover's tiff gone wrong. Or maybe the conclusion would be that someone had broken in, burglars on the make, and had launched a frenzied attack on us when they'd been discovered (just look at the state of the place). He'd find a reasonably rational way, of that I was sure, but why should I worry what that would be? That was his problem.

I raised myself on one elbow, ready for the worst, but determined to make a match of it.

When the doorbell downstairs clanged.

FLORA

It was a ludicrous situation: Midge and me sprawled on the floor, the Synergists spread around the room, edging in for the kill – and now the Avon Lady was calling.

Only it wasn't someone selling perfume out there. And we hadn't heard door chimes: the 'bring out your dead' sound had come from the old bell hanging outside the kitchen door. The urgency in its tone told us the caller wasn't going to go away (and all the cars out front indicated that somebody had to be home).

Mycroft gave a barely perceptible nod of his head towards Kinsella, and before I could move the American had dashed forward to slip an arm beneath Midge's throat. Her feet kicked air as he lifted.

Mycroft came closer to me. 'You'll get rid of whoever's out there. I'm not concerned with how, but you'll do it. Your sweet little loved one will suffer if you fail. A sharp pull of his arm and her windpipe will be crushed instantly. He can do it, believe me he can easily do that . . .'

I looked up at Kinsella and didn't doubt for a moment that he could and would. Taking in that wide, handsome face I wondered whatever had happened to Mom's Apple Pie and the American Way.

I rose unsteadily and considered rushing him, grabbing

his arm or knocking him flat before he could do any damage, but I soon dismissed the idea: the bastard was too strong and too quick and I'd be too slow and not strong enough.

'If you hurt her . . .' I said unconvincingly, and he loved the threat. He squeezed one of her breasts with his free hand just to show me how scared he was, and the craziness in his smile made me shudder.

Midge squirmed against him, unable to cry out because of the bar against her throat.

I took a step towards them and he increased the pressure on her neck so that Midge's eyes rolled upwards with the pain.

'I'll finish her and then you'll be next,' he warned amiably.

I backed off, hands raised. There was nothing I could do. The bell downstairs rang more insistently.

'Don't be foolish in any way,' Mycroft advised.

I shrugged and brushed by him, going into the hallway. Madness, I kept telling myself as I stomped down the stairs. The whole bloody thing is total, unbelievable madness. And if these lunatics were going to get us anyway, why not make a break for it when I opened the door? At least I'd get to the police. But the car keys were still upstairs, dropped in the mêlée. The caller would have come by car, though. Grab whoever it was and run for it, drive into the village and bring back help; that was the thing to do. But leave Midge alone in the hands of these freaks? That question didn't even need a conscious answer.

A stairboard gave beneath me and I abruptly found myself sitting down, one foot sunk deep into the carpet. Movement from behind and I knew one, or maybe two, of the Synergists lurked at the bend of the stairs, waiting to pass the word back should I misbehave when I answered the door.

The bell stopped clanging.

I felt a terrible despair.

Then the door was being pounded.

I picked myself up and hurried down the last few steps, crossing the kitchen and reaching the door without further deliberation. The wood was straining against the frame as though the person outside was angry and impatient, and *desperate* to be let in. My fingers touched the top bolt and froze on the cold metal; I was suddenly aware of who it was out there. I don't know how I knew, I just knew. My arm slowly lowered as if of its own accord and I stared at the door.

She'd been trying to reach us for a long time now.

My fear had reached a new zenith, rising from the slushy morass of dread like a dripping creature from a swamp.

Did I really want to face that figure who'd watched us from a distance? Did I want to come face to face with that ravaged countenance, to stand within feet of her? Did I want to smell her putridness so close, the stink of corrupting death that had already fouled the air inside the cottage? Did I finally want to meet my own nightmare?

Did I have a choice?

The banging had stopped as if she knew I was on the other side and that it was only a matter of time before the door opened. I reached up for the bolt once more and slammed it back, compelled by a will other than my own.

My fingers slid down the painted wood, sinking to the metal bar at the foot of the door. I snapped the lever horizontal, then began to slide the bar open.

'*No!*'

Still crouched, I turned to find Mycroft at the bottom of the stairs; something had made him follow me down. The hint of panic in his command told me he knew who was out there, too.

'Don't open that door!'

My grin may have been nervous, but it *was* a grin. I shot the bolt all the way back, stood and twisted the key in the lock. Then I opened the door.

I stared at the figure on the step, stunned speechless.

Because, of course, I was wrong again.

She marched by me, grousey as ever. 'I thought you'd never open up,' Val complained, well into the kitchen before turning to face me. 'I saw the cars parked outside and assumed you were entertaining, but I've been ringing that bell and thumping on that door for ages. I was just about to come around to the other side.'

Big, bristling Val; tweed two-piece suit, heavy brogues and thick stockings. Gorgeous, mustachioed Val.

'Val,' I croaked. I wasn't angry like last time.

The breeze from the open doorway cooled the back of my clammy neck.

'Good Lord, you'd think I was a ghost the way you're standing there. Are you all right, Mike? I drove down because I was anxious over what we discussed earlier today. You know there's something very odd –'

'*Get rid of her!*' shrieked Mycroft.

Val had obviously noticed him immediately she'd stepped into the cottage, but now she gave the Synergist her full attention. 'I beg your pardon?' she said, and I'd withered under that tone and that glare myself a few times in the past.

'*Make her leave.*'

Mycroft spoke in a low, even voice, but I could tell his rag was going. Me, I was glad to see her, although I realised her presence didn't help the situation any; formidable though Val was, we were up against something more than mere numbers.

'Mike, I'm sorry if I've interrupted anything, but will you kindly inform this ill-mannered cretin . . .'

She'd spun towards me again and indignation trailed off with the sentence as she looked beyond me at the doorway.

The breeze wafting in was even more chilly, bringing with it a faint and peculiarly sour-sweet fragrance.

A hand touched my shoulder from behind.

Afraid to look all at once, I twisted my head and saw the shadow. Her breath touched my cheek.

I turned all the way.

She was small, much smaller than I'd expected. Tiny. And frail. And she had the oldest and sweetest face I'd ever seen.

Her eyes were pale, paler even than Midge's, and it seemed as though clouds drifted in them. Her lips were ancient-thin, the edges curled under; but all the same, it was a kind mouth, the lines at each end not spoiling her expression. And although her nose was sharp, it portrayed no arrogance, only a determination of will. Wrinkles splayed around her features in whorls and ridges, yet it was a clear, unsullied face, full of vibrancy and compassion, a Mother Teresa vision that had seen so much and felt so much, the experience etched in with those age-lines as explicitly as words in a book. Around her head she wore a shawl, many colours woven into its coarse material with no distinctive pattern formed; white hair, strands seeping over her shoulders, peeked from beneath the shawl. Her dress was long, high-necked, and dark grey in colour, of a vogue in favour with Whistler's Mother.

Flora Chaldean stretched up her other hand, so that both rested on my shoulders.

I suddenly understood with that touch the extraordinary gathering of spiritual energy it had taken for her to reach this point. Her past peripherality, her gradual drawing closer to the cottage, had been no more than a visual (or visionary) representation of her struggle for materialisation, the accumulating of psychic forces, the moulding of her spirit existence into tangible form. Yet somehow I felt that only what was happening inside Gramarye that night had allowed the final barrier between the spiritual and the physical world to be breached.

I saw all this in her cloudy eyes, as though those vapours were her very thoughts. And I was aware that her presence was a warning, as it had been throughout our time at Gramarye, when her form had been observed only as a spectral shadow in the distance.

She drew close and her mouth opened, but again, I've no idea whether I heard the word or sensed the thought.

But what she said with her mouth or with her thoughts, was.

'You . . .'

And then she began to decay before my eyes. It was as though she had burnt up all the psychic energy it had taken to bring her to this moment, the final thrust of entering Gramarye using the last of her strength; now the process was going into reverse, into decline, the advancement towards the physical sense backtracking like a video rewind. Soon I was glad I hadn't got close during those early stages, those times I had seen her out there near the forest watching Gramarye.

The wrinkles in her face and hands deepened then dropped away leaving only faint lines, as her flesh became . . . loose. Passion went from her eyes as if the clouds had joined in a blanketing fog. Her hands shook on my shoulders, tapping a soft, irregular drumbeat, and her skin became waxen, almost shiny like glazed meat. It began to stretch, become paper-thin; it began to tear.

Her decomposition was rapid, taking no more than a minute or two, yet each second was timeless in itself.

The festering of her body started.

Where flies had settled on her as she had lain slumped at the table in Gramarye's kitchen all those months ago, so their spawn reappeared, white rippling maggots that feasted and grew, forming a correlation of restlessness, a superbly drilled regiment of minute carnivores. They disappeared into holes that they, themselves, created.

The deep stench poured over me and I held my breath, afraid to take in the fumes.

Her meat began to sag, to drop away, exposing muscle and bone, uncovering those crawling things busy inside. Her eyelids were no longer firm enough to contain her eyes, which drifted out onto her ravaged face. One hand that had rested on my shoulder slowly slid down my chest, the bones of the fingers – there was little flesh left on the hand – snagging against the tattered material of my shirt.

She shrank before me, a figure that had been small in life becoming smaller as bones and muscle relaxed into each other. Her other hand – the skeleton of her other hand – fell away.

Other things wriggled in those dark, bone-ridged eye cavities, black things that scuttled over each other, things like pieces of string that curled and slimed, all glorying in their treasure house of sustenance. Her jaw gaped open, nothing left to control its movement, and it seemed that even her blackened, withered tongue had joined the ranks of the crawling beasts, had become one of them.

The shawl slipped from her head and her white hair hung in sparse, limp clusters, and skin was only islands of tissue layers on the grey skull.

Her body slowly collapsed and mercifully started dissolving before reaching the floor. Clothes, bone, and liquefying flesh lay in a heap on the tiles, but within moments, those too were gone. There was nothing left of Flora Chaldean save for the smell.

I staggered backwards, jolting hard against the door frame. Val was staring at the kitchen floor in disbelief. Mycroft had all but collapsed against the stairs. I saw that his eyes were half closed as though he had been wearied, drained of strength.

Yet strangely, I felt charged, a kind of chemical energy sparking within me, sending blood pounding round my body, causing nerve-endings to tingle and throb. She had touched my shoulders and her eyes and thoughts had filled me. *But still I didn't understand!*

Until I found Mycroft watching me warily and I sensed his fear and respect. Then I began to know . . .

THINGS UNLEASHED

Mycroft vanished back up those stairs – and there were other footsteps too, obviously of those followers who had remained out of sight – as I held up my hands and studied them, wondering why they palpitated so and why my scalp (and other hairy parts of me) prickled and felt so itchy-dry. I touched my head and my hair was brittle (I'd almost expected it to be standing erect, punk-like). So was this the physical sensation that came with the possession of Magic?

The possession of Magic. Now that just couldn't be! Not me, not Mike Stringer, sceptic and part-time infidel. But I was being carried along by something that had little regard for my own self-doubt and confusion.

'Mike . . .'

Val was resting against the table, hands on either side clutching the edge. She looked shocked, and that was hardly surprising with all that had happened since she'd stepped inside the cottage. Now, though, she was growing curious about me, sensing the change that was taking place.

I don't suppose that change was visible in any real way, but she knew it was happening all right. Of course, there might have been blue sparks shooting from my ears for all I knew, but I didn't think so. The shift in my mind was slight, however, otherwise I think I'd have been totally overwhelmed by this metamorphosis.

The funny thing was, I was afraid, but the fear didn't frighten me. Does that make sense? The fear *excited* me, because this was something new, and with the acquisition – or I should say, the *releasing* – there came a feeling of well-being, an essential element that helped balance the power. Imagine being born blind and then, one day, a knock on the head enables you to see (the ability having been there all along). Think of the excitement, the awe for everything around you. The fear of it.

Yet still I wasn't a hundred per cent certain. Flora's touch and thoughts had instilled the knowledge, flicked the switch of awareness, but what the hell? – I could have been hallucinating. There was only one way to find out, and a nervous thrill flushed through me as I headed for the stairs.

Val attempted to grab my arm as I passed, but something made her withdraw her hand before she made contact.

I ran up the stairs, ready (and eager?) for combat.

The Synergists were waiting, but were in some disarray; it wasn't just Mycroft's evident panic, nor my approach, that had caused their disorder.

A blue-violet sheen emanated from every object in the round room – the sofa, the chairs, the units, books, pictures, the mantelshelf, the windowframes, curtains: everything – bathing the room in its eerie light, the ceiling light itself tainted by the electric colour. Spielberg himself couldn't have produced a more startling effect. To a lesser degree, but equally mind-boggling, the same glow outlined the living bodies in the room. If someone had snapped their fingers, static would have thundered in the air; if someone had sneezed, air currents would have created a storm.

The round room was alive.

It throbbed and hummed with its own power, but there was no sound and there was no movement: its existence could only be sensed and wondered at.

I stood in the doorway and felt the room breathe on me. Off to one side, Gillie was being helped to her feet by the girl called Sandy. Others were peering anxiously around at the walls, the furniture. Neil Joby looked about ready to throw up again. I watched as one of the men touched the drawing-board easel beneath the broken window and quickly drew back as the glow spread along his arm, strengthening his own light for a moment. The Bone Man was there and I could tell he wanted out, only I was blocking the doorway; he stood frozen in a loping attitude. Kinsella still had hold of Midge, and he seemed calmest of all.

Even calmer than Mycroft, who was near the centre, his eyes for me alone.

Now was the testing time. I gulped.

First, Kinsella.

I was hesitant — and who wouldn't have been in my position? — so maybe that was why it didn't work immediately. I needed time and experience to build confidence, and had neither.

Kinsella suddenly found himself with an armful of goat. I've no idea why I chose a goat — it just flashed into my mind and I transferred the thought into his arms. Unfortunately, the image was only fleeting: Midge was back there under his grasp before he had time to register surprise and let go. His astonishment followed a second later, but he still held on to her, his jaw dropped and eyebrows arched. He blinked, thinking there'd been some mistake, and Midge struggled to free herself.

None the less, *something* had happened and that at least lent a grain of credibility to what I was asking myself to believe. I could do it! I only had to concentrate hard and it could happen! I'd been wrong all along about Midge: she was certainly an important element in all this, a catalyst of some kind, but she wasn't the successor to Gramarye. Oh no, it was *me*, for Chrissake! *Me!* But now wasn't the time to ponder.

My thought struck again, and I tried to sustain it, already learning the tricks, or the art, or the craft, of Magic. Kinsella discovered he had an arm-lock on a grinning python. The image was more than momentary and, with a girlish shriek, he let go.

Midge collapsed to the floor.

'Get over here, Midge!' I yelled and she began crawling, not understanding why the American had dropped her and probably not caring – she just wanted to get to me.

But Mycroft's cane prodded her back and froze her there.

'Do you think you're a match for me?' Mycroft shouted in my direction.

And, honest-to-God, I chuckled. I think hysteria had returned and was sweeping me along at that point.

He became undeniably enraged – I suppose he felt I was mocking him (and maybe he'd got it right). He aimed his cane/wand and the doorframe around me burst into flame. I stumbled back into the hallway, singed and frightened, as the opening became a door of fire.

I had time to notice Val watching me bug-eyed from the stairway, her horrified face lit up by flames. I'd never known her lost for words before, but to give her credit she did her best to speak. All she managed was to flap her mouth.

'Don't ask,' I said to her.

Then I plunged back through the fire-filled doorway without giving myself time for further consideration, because at this stage of the game either I believed or I didn't – there were no halfway measures.

I heard Val's raspy scream, but other noises inside the room quickly drowned that. The fire behind me instantly snuffed out and I found I wasn't even scorched.

Mycroft and I faced each other across the room, while around us his Synergists moaned and groaned, not particularly concerned with me, more interested in what was going on around *them*. Everything in the room – the supposedly inanimate objects, I mean – was not only weirdly glowing, but was now pulsing: chairs, units, even the walls, were now all beating like odd-shaped hearts. The carpet was moving as though strong hands underneath were pushing upwards. And the glass fragments that had been scattered from the windows were oscillating inches from the floor like jumping-bean crystals. Bone Man was reaching for a window-catch, several followers jostling him from behind, eager to be off and away from the cottage; but when he clasped the metal catch his body vibrated and what hair he had crackled as if he'd been shocked. He leapt away, taking the others with him in a tumble of thrashing arms and legs. There were screams from women in the room (and no doubt from several of the men) and I saw that Joby had finally given up the contents of his stomach, except his vomit refused to leave his body completely – it flowed down his neck and chest and over his shoulders in a lumpy coating. Bricks and soot crashed down into the fireplace, a cloud of dust spreading outwards to curl and linger in the air; the fungus on the walls seemed to be bubbling putrescence.

The round room had lost a lot of its charm.

Mycroft was mouthing something I couldn't quite catch over the hubbub; I guess it was an incantation rather than a grumbled complaint, and I wondered what he had in mind. I soon found out.

A web began ravelling itself around me, pinning first my arms and then my legs, spinning round and round, taut like fine steel, covering my chest and lower body, taking no time at all to join the weave that rose from my thighs. The silver web crossed over my shoulders and I saw there were scores of tiny spiders among the strands, busy at work, darting hairy-legged to and fro. The cocoon grew rapidly, taking less than a minute, soon reaching my throat, where it tightened. In fact the whole mess became tight, so that I had difficulty in breathing.

Midge was on her knees, held there by Kinsella, whose hand dug into her hair. She shrieked out my name.

And me, scared? Yeah, more than I can say.

But I forced a calmness on myself because this was only trickery, only as real as my own mind allowed it to be. I drew an invisible blade down the strands.

They popped apart and before the cut had extended to my stomach, the whole web disappeared.

'That your best shot?' I taunted Mycroft, displaying a cockiness I didn't altogether feel.

The unseen sledge-hammer that punched me out into the hallway again told me he'd only just started. I lay against the back door, winded and vowing to watch my lip in future. The pain came from my shoulders, though, where they'd

338

struck the door, and not from my chest where I imagined I'd been hit.

Pushing myself up, I ran back into the round room, colliding with Synergists who were making a break for it, fear finally overcoming loyalty to their leader. They flinched away from me as though I were a plague carrier, hurrying back into the room. I had to admit I couldn't blame them for trying to escape, because it was a decidedly unhealthy place to be. If Midge hadn't been in there, I'd have cut and run myself.

The floorboards were ripping through the carpet, curling upwards as though sucked by a whirlwind; even the ceiling was becoming bowed, dome-shaped. Long, jagged cracks were striping the walls.

Lightning streaked from Mycroft's cane towards my heart and reflexively I blocked it with a thought. And then sent it back.

His cane exploded, burning shards flying into the air. He staggered backwards and almost fell. But recovered and stared at me with a mixture of astonishment and terrible hatred. The apprentice had shaken the master, I mused grimly.

Then he showed me things I don't want to see – or *imagine* – ever again.

He unzipped a nightmare and shoved me through. I was no longer inside Gramarye but was somewhere else, in another dimension that was gloomy and limitless, where rot and decay were fragrance, where pain and suffering were succour. A dark plain where loathing replaced loving, where obscenity substituted for purity. I don't know if he'd slipped me through the side door of hell, or had led me down a lost corridor inside my own mind. Maybe they were both the same thing.

All I knew was that unless I retreated from this underworld where horror shuffled in the darkness around me, unless I found my way back within moments, then here I'd stay for ever. It had something to do with the relinquishment of my own will.

I saw a mass lumbering towards me from the shadows, a mass that I thought was an advancing mob, saw their legs hobbling forward, outlines of waving arms, a bobbing head here and there; but when they drew close I realised they were just one burned mass of people, fused together by a fire that had melted their flesh into each other's. I saw a river that flowed through the air over my head, creatures inside its putrid waters that were neither fish nor man, but partly both; they fed upon each other, choosing one in a pack to ostracise then devour. I saw reptilian things that slithered over the black-ash earth, and when they drew near they were merely membrane sacks filled with a multitude of wriggling forms, different species of worms, grubs and insects all sharing the same transparent shell, their own restlessness causing the movement of the whole. I saw shapes of monsters that defied description, I absorbed thoughts too despicable to relate. I existed in a sullen and tenebrous nether region whose very hideousness had its own allure.

Something slimy cold coiled around my ankle and I screamed.

And before the scream had died on my lips, Midge's voice brought me back to my proper world, bizarre and chaotic though it had become.

I didn't know how she'd got away from Kinsella, but there she was, shaking me, pounding my chest, jolting me from that other dimension, bringing me back from somewhere deep inside myself, a dark and secret place that lies within us all.

She stopped bullying me only when recognition dawned in my eyes; she buried her head against me.

'Oh, Mike, Mike, I was so scared! It wasn't you standing here – for a moment it was just an empty shell, there was no life!'

I hugged her, relief turning into elation – the feeling you might get after surviving a horrendous accident; the haunting dread of what might have been would come later.

Although I'd been mistaken about Midge's role in events leading to this moment, I realised again that she'd had a major part to play: she was certainly a catalyst, but not the kind I'd thought; she had always been the motivator for me, the link between myself and Flora Chaldean – the intermediary who had brought me to Gramarye. She had her own special goodness. I moved her aside.

Mycroft had backed away against the mantelshelf, and dust was still billowing from the fireplace below, sweeping upwards to form a sooty mist around him. How could I ever have described his appearance as bland? With his baleful eyes and his shoulders hunched, hands held in front of him like claws, his mouth a downward grimace and face, now etched with lines where there had been none before, smeared by the dust – Jesus, he looked like a resident of the nightmare I'd just left.

He was failing, though, his bag of tricks had so far come to nothing; and he obviously found that hard to take. Yeah, it's true to say he looked not only dishevelled, but deranged too. I liked that: I was sick of his smugness. But there was life in the bastard yet.

He waved his hands and created a wall of vermin between us, their bristling, filth-haired bodies literally forming the brickwork (did I mention before? – I *hate* bloody rats!), piled five feet high, so that I could see only Mycroft's head beyond, as though perched on top of the twitching fur like a manic Humpty Dumpty.

More panic among the Synergists – they didn't care for the image either.

The wall toppled when I pictured a demolition ball hurtling into it, and the rats scurried in all directions, fading before they reached cover.

I smiled at him, ignoring the turmoil around me.

He split the air in front of me so that a widening rent of absolute nothingness appeared; a fierce wind endeavoured to suck me into the void.

I sealed the opening with imaginary stitches.

'I'm younger than her, Mycroft!' I shouted across at him, and he knew I meant Flora. 'I can take all the stress and strain you put my way. Young and fresh to all this, you see! It doesn't hurt a bit!'

Would I never learn? I stepped back when some of those things I thought I'd left behind in the nether region began crawling from the holes created in the floor. Carpet was ripping explosively all around me, and slug-like monsters oozed over the edges in shiny slimes. Hands that were scabbed and dripping pus clawed at the frayed carpet in an effort to drag the rest of their forms out into the open. Those membranes, full of wriggling life, quivered their snouts in the air before curling over the edge. Wispy black smoke tendrils drifted up in lazy spirals, and these were full of diseased micro-organisms, the corrupting evil that roamed the depths, subversives that searched for ways to surface, intent on finding exposure, definition – *actuality*. These were the infiltrating substances of evil.

I sagged, went down onto my knees, because their existence depended on me also; I was their source, and they sapped my strength.

Kinsella was on his knees too, close to one of the growing holes, hands clasped between his thighs (now I understood how Midge had got away from him) and the thing that had coiled around my ankle when I'd been lost in that brief but eternal nightmare of my lower mind was reaching from the opening and circling his.

He shrieked and beat hard at the glistening cord with his fists. It shrank away, retreating into its pit, and Kinsella pushed himself on hands and knees across the room, blubbering as he went.

Shapes were emerging that even Mycroft seemed afraid and in awe of; they were muddied and grimed, as if squeezed from the earth that was beneath the round room.

Wind rushed by me, catching my hair and clothes; others around the room were falling, wailing, clutching those near them for mutual support. The electric glows were more intense, as though radiation hot. Furniture was rising, books flew across the room. Midge's drawing easel smashed itself and a Synergist – I think it was Bone Man, I'm sure it was the Bone Man – against a wall.

And now the walls were cracking apart.

A body thudded down next to me, and suddenly Midge was pulling my face around to look at hers.

'*You can stop them, Mike!*' she shouted over the noise. '*You can make them go back! You can stop Mycroft!*'

'*No, I don't know how! It's all a mistake, Midge, I'm the wrong person! I don't know how to use Magic!*'

'You just think it, that's all you do! Gramarye will help! The forces are here – you only have to direct them!'

Could it be that simple, that easy? Voices – thoughts – told me it was, and the assertion whether spoken or insinuated was from those who had lived here before me, others who had been guardians, who had kept the power of this place, these grounds, for the Good. Not Flora alone, but those before her, others before them, going back to a time when this site was no more than a circular clearing in a dense forest, when maybe it was the era of dragons and wizards and white castles, the time of legends we think we invented. Maybe an age before even that.

I imagined those times and the imaginings expanded from my mind.

I yelled at those rising obscenities and they hesitated, began to slide away, back down to the slimy depths they'd climbed from. Back to the deepest realms of my own thoughts.

Gradually, another sound grew beneath the tumult, a drumming-fluttering, an underlying rhythm to the howling of the wind.

The chimney breast throbbed with their flight and once again the bats swept from the fireplace opening, screeching and swarming over Mycroft, beating him with their wings. In seconds, he was engulfed and they drove him against the mantel.

They covered almost every inch of him so that his image was akin to the creatures who were slinking back into their underworld.

A brilliance was in my mind, subduing the darkness that had threatened to overwhelm, a dawn defeating the night.

I struggled to my feet, Midge helping me, and Mycroft and I gazed into each other's eyes one last time before his face was enveloped by those feasting monsters. I've no idea what he'd felt for me: I'd only observed a vast emptiness in his eyes.

Blood flowed between the frantic bodies of the smothering bats, soaking them and trickling down to puddle the floor. They drained him while he stood there.

Through the hallway, the back door crashed open and

shut, an enticing trap for those people trying to escape. Some made it outside, others were crushed against the frame, their broken bodies spat back into the hall like pips from a chomping mouth.

Cracks in the curved walls were widening and more bats were squeezing through, others entering by the smashed windows. They wheeled around the room, carried by the wind, swooping to attack exposed faces and hands. Bricks began to dislodge themselves, hurtling across the room like missiles.

Midge clutched my arm and pointed upwards.

The ceiling was rising in the middle, becoming more warped, more bowed, than before. Floorboards ripped free of the carpet and lifted, blasting up to the ceiling's apex to collect there along with books, cushions and ornaments. The sofa began to rise, spinning in the air, only one corner remaining in contact with the floor. Several of the Synergists had become flattened against the crumbling walls as if Wall-of-Death riders. I felt gravitational pressure on myself, outwards and upwards, and had to stand firm and resist. Gramarye was shuddering down to its very roots (and God only knew where *they* were).

'*We must get out!*' Midge shouted, her hair whipped around her face. '*Something even more terrible is going to happen here, I can feel it!*'

Me too. I knew she was right. Forces had been revived, set free, were pounding through like an oil gusher, and I didn't have the know-how to cap the flow. Gripping each other tightly we staggered towards the stairway, leaving behind the carnage, the awful sight of Mycroft being emptied of blood, the pulped faces of those who'd been struck by stone or raked by bats, the gale that tore around the curved and breaking walls. All bathed in that eerie, electric gleam.

We were almost through the doorway when rough hands seized my throat from behind.

I was hauled backwards, thrown to the roaring, erupting floor. Then a hefty weight on my chest was pinning me there, the hands at my neck now attacking from the front. Stunned at first, I opened my eyes to find our American Hero snarling at me and he didn't look so clean-cut any more. His nose and cheeks were smeared red, and there was a deep gash in his forehead, right across from corner to corner, blood soaking through in spurts. His blond hair was tangled and dusty; God knows how, but clumps of it had been torn out so that his scalp, pinky-blue in the unnatural light, showed through. The madness in his gaze confirmed he was a true disciple of Mycroft's.

I grabbed his wrists and tried to pull his hands away, but he only enjoyed my struggle, leering down at me and steadily increasing his own pressure.

Then Midge was on him, scoring his face with her fingers, catching the edge of the cut in his forehead and lifting the skin like a flap. The bone beneath was bloodied, hardly any white showing.

Kinsella smacked her aside easily with the back of his hand, ignoring his own pain and the blood flooding down to blind him. But the next bulky shape that lumbered forward wasn't so easy to dismiss.

A thick hand grasped him beneath the chin and jerked his head backwards, continuing to pull as another hand chopped hard at his stretched windpipe. Spittle showered my face, but I didn't mind that in the least.

She tossed him away and, before he could raise himself from the floor, one of her heavy brogues crunched into his ring-of-confidence teeth. Val was playing for keeps.

She reached down for Midge and hauled her up, ducking as objects and bats flew over her head, then turned to help me; but I was already lurching to my feet.

The room was exploding around us, the middle section of floor completely gone, many of the remaining floorboards angled upwards and waving like stiffened streamers; earth and mud was spewing from the opening, spraying the domed ceiling with their dirt. Brickwork was dropping from the walls in huge chunks too massive to be borne by the wind. Those Synergists who hadn't escaped – those not sprawled on the heaving floor – were clinging to the walls, unable to tear themselves free.

Val propelled Midge and me towards the doorway, as

resolute and indomitable as ever, even though she was plainly scared out of her wits.

The back door still flapped wildly, inviting us to chance our luck, to beat the devil – you'd better be nimble, you'd better be quick.

'*Through the kitchen!*' commanded Val without even contemplating the challenge.

We rushed for the stairs as one, slipping on loose boards and carpet at the bend, the three of us tumbling down in a rolling avalanche of arms and legs. We came to an untidy halt near the bottom, and the walls were throbbing on either side of us.

We unravelled ourselves with much grunting and groaning and got going again, the noise from behind becoming even louder. We ran across the kitchen, Midge in the lead, the ceiling light dimming and brightening in quick succession. The floor tiles were all loose, rattling against each other like broken crockery, and it wasn't easy to keep our feet. Something caught my eye but I kept moving, pushed on from behind by Val. Midge threw open the front door and all three of us cleared the step with a jump, literally bursting from the cottage. We kept moving, racing down the path, flowers and weeds waving in the air on either side as if we were runners in the hundred metres, and we knew something catastrophic was about to happen back there, that the place was going to explode, or collapse, or be swallowed into the earth.

But I skidded to a halt halfway down the path.

Midge and Val were at the gate before they noticed I was missing.

'*Mike!*' Midge screamed back at me.

'*Keep going!*' I shouted, then turned and ran back to Gramarye.

I could still hear her screaming my name as I plunged inside.

ENDING?

So there you have it, that's the story.

I warned you at the start that you'd have to suspend disbelief, and if you found that difficult, imagine how I felt at the time. Even today I sometimes wonder . . .

I wish I could explain more and neatly tie up any loose ends like the psychiatrist at the end of the *Psycho* movie, when he gave us lot sitting out there in the dark (as well as his fellow actors, who were probably equally puzzled) reasons for Norman Bates' odd behaviour; but he was only dealing with human complexities: this is something else. This is Magic. Explanations can't be so pat.

What I have learned, by the way, is that there's no such thing as Good Magic or Bad Magic, White or Black. There's only Magic. It's how it's used, or by whom, that matters. It comes under our direction – *if* we have the power.

All along I'd assumed Midge was the one, and it turned out to be me. That was something of a shock – although once discovered, it was fairly easily and rapidly accepted, as you'll have noticed. Like riding a bike – once you *knew* you could do it, you *did* it. But it just goes to show how little we really know about ourselves, what lies hidden away, probably never to be used. It shows, too, how little we know of the rules that govern such things – like there are no rules anyway.

Midge had been important in all this: she'd been used to bring me to Gramarye; at least, some spark in her own subconscious had guided her to guide me there. She was special – but then I'd always known that – a chosen one in the Grand Design of things. Whose Grand Design? The Grand Designer's, of course, whoever He, She or It, might be.

Mycroft was in the tradition of those old-fashioned villains who want to rule the world: he desired Gramarye's power for his own ends – and I've no idea what those ends ultimately were. He vanished inside the cottage along with those followers who hadn't managed to escape before the walls came tumbling down, and that included Hub Kinsella (hard to shed a tear for *him*). Gramarye didn't explode or merely collapse, incidentally. Oh no. It *imploded*, went back into itself. Became nothing but smouldering rubble, the channel beneath it sealed, I hope for ever.

That was kind of difficult to explain to the police and fire services when they were later sent out to investigate. *We* owned up, told them we had no idea what had hit the place. *They*, eventually, figured a pocket of natural gas had been trapped beneath the cottage, expanding for some time and finally blasting off the way a pressure cooker with a faulty lid might. That didn't make a lot of sense to me – and probably didn't to them either – but you know how the authorities like to pigeon-hole things, keep them nice and tidy, neat and reasonable. Fortunately for us, Gillie Slade came forward (yeah, she was one of the lucky who'd been both nimble *and* quick) while enquiries were going on and dispelled any notions that something funny might have been happening between us and the Synergists. What was left of the Synergists, in fact, disbanded soon after, and scattered for parts unknown – and I hoped they'd stay there.

So why didn't we tell the truth about what had happened? Would you have? D'you think anyone in their right mind would have believed us? Damn right they wouldn't.

We three stuck to a story of complete ignorance. The Synergists had paid us a social visit and while they were there, disaster had struck. What more could we say?

Midge and I are back in the city once again, with Val

keeping a motherly eye on us both. I have to admit, I've grown pretty fond of Big Val. After some wrangling with the insurance company – just what *does* constitute an Act of God? – we received a handsome cheque to compensate for loss of the cottage, which enabled us to set up house (or in our case, apartment) again. Things are going pretty well for us now: I finished my rock musical – the final version included lots of wizards, pixies and Magic – and Midge designed some quite breathtakingly beautiful sets (I think they had a lot to do with the show's overall success). It's playing up in Manchester at the moment, and Bob's looking for a suitable venue in London so that we can bring it down. I've written a couple of chart-reaching numbers (mainly thanks to the big names who recorded them) and am about to embark on my second kiddies' storybook which Midge will illustrate. And her? She just goes from strength to strength, with more work than she can handle (although she's reached the stage where she can really pick and choose), and Val's even arranged a couple of one-woman art exhibitions for her. She's had Sunday Colour Supp features on herself and her work, and even appeared on Breakfast TV. She's as pretty as ever and modest with it, too. And I love her more than ever (the good thing is, it's mutual).

So far, I guess you could say, we're living happy ever after.

Me and Magic? Well, whatever power I derived from Gramarye isn't with me now. Occasionally I'll do something that will amaze both of us, but the ability comes in rare flashes. Very rare. I'm still struggling with the three-card trick.

I suppose I need to be somewhere near the power supply, the source itself, wherever it channels up into the atmosphere, but I'm not too bothered. Out of curiosity, Midge and I took a trip back to the New Forest recently, and all that was left of Gramarye was a perfectly round patch of black earth on top of the embankment where the round room once stood. It's weird and it made us smile. We drove on to the local pub where the landlord told us that the council has to keep a close watch on the site: apparently those so-called magic mushrooms, the kind that induce hallucinations, used to grow there in abundance, making the area a great focal point for travelling hippies. The council had the ground sprayed, churned over, impregnated with all sorts of poisons, but it took a long time for those mushrooms to stop growing.

Oh yeah. You might be wondering why I dashed back inside the cottage just before it fell apart that night. Remember I said something had caught my eye when we ran like hell through the kitchen? Well, I'd glimpsed that little furry bundle we'd left for dead on the kitchen table stirring, Rumbo poking his head in the air and looking around wondering what all the racket was about.

What I'd seen hadn't registered until I was halfway down that path, and that's why I turned and ran back inside.

I managed to scoop him up and get out moments before Gramarye disintegrated.

I think he appreciated the gesture, or maybe he was happy to be alive again, because he licked my face and hands like a puppy dog. He'd never again be the handsome squirrel he once was – those scars on his neck and throat might eventually fade, but fur would never grow over them – but I don't think he gave a hoot about that.

I let him go once we were on the other side of the gate and, after Midge had made a huge fuss of him, he scampered off into the darkness, jaunty as ever, heading for the forest and whatever secret sweetheart he kept in there. That was the last we saw of Rumbo.

So, it's all behind us now, and life's pretty good for Midge and me.

And yet . . . and yet we both get kind of restless now and then. Midge ringed an ad in the newspaper today and left it on the breakfast table for me to see. The ad was in the Properties for Sale section. A small but pretty house, situated in a secluded spot. Somewhere up in the Cotswolds.

Maybe I'll give the agent a call tomorrow.

Maybe.

'*Magic has power to experience and fathom things which are inaccessible to human reason. For magic is a great secret wisdom, just as reason is a great public folly.*'

PARACELSUS

'*The question of magick is a question of discovering and employing hitherto unknown forces in Nature.*'

CROWLEY

'*Magic is believing what you shouldn't – and enjoying the believing.*'

STRINGER

JAMES HERBERT

☐	04970 1	The Dark	£2.95
☐	05822 0	Domain	£2.95
☐	03828 9	Fluke	£1.95
☐	03045 8	The Fog	£2.50
☐	05316 4	The Jonah	£2.50
☐	04546 3	Lair	£2.50
☐	38999 5	Moon	£2.95
☐	02127 0	The Rats	£1.95
☐	05659 7	Shrine	£2.95
☐	04300 2	The Spear	£2.50
☐	05326 1	The Survivor	£2.25

All these books are available at your local bookshop or newsagent, or can be ordered direct from the publisher.
Just tick the titles you want and fill in the form below.

Prices and availability subject to change without notice.

Hodder and Stoughton Paperbacks, P.O. Box 11, Falmouth, Cornwall.

Please send cheque or postal order, and allow the following for postage and packing:

U.K. – 55p for one book, plus 22p for the second book, and 14p for each additional book ordered up to a £1.75 maximum.

B.F.P.O. and EIRE – 55p for the first book, plus 22p for the second book, and 14p per copy for the next 7 books, 8p per book thereafter.

OTHER OVERSEAS CUSTOMERS – £1.00 for the first book, plus 25p per copy for each additional book.

Name ....

Address ....

....